Captain Monty Takes the Plunge

To all me little ♥ ties Matt, Ben, Parris,
Melissa and Mandy — J.M-S.

For Avi, my favorite sea chantey singer — L.S.

Text © 2017 Jennifer Mook-Sang
Illustrations © 2017 Liz Starin

Kids Can Press gratefully acknowledges the financial support of the Government
of Ontario, through the Ontario Media Development Corporation; the Ontario Arts Council;
the Canada Council for the Arts; and the Government of Canada,
through the CBF, for our publishing activity.

Published in Canada and the U.S. by Kids Can Press Ltd.
25 Dockside Drive, Toronto, ON M5A 0B5

Kids Can Press is a Corus Entertainment Inc. company

www.kidscanpress.com

The artwork in this book was rendered in ink, watercolor,
crayon and colored pencil on cold press watercolor paper.

The text is set in Happy.

Edited by Yvette Ghione and Jennifer Stokes
Designed by Julia Naimska

Printed and bound in Shenzhen, China, in 3/2017 by C & C Offset

CM 17 0 9 8 7 6 5 4 3 2 1

Library and Archives Canada Cataloguing in Publication

Mook-Sang, Jennifer, author
Captain Monty takes the plunge / written by Jennifer
Mook-Sang ; illustrated by Liz Starin.

ISBN 978-1-77138-626-5 (hardback)

I. Starin, Liz, illustrator II. Title.

PS8626.O59264C37 2017   jC813'.6   C2016-906871-4

Captain Monty Takes the Plunge

Written by Jennifer Mook-Sang

Illustrated by Liz Starin

Kids Can Press

Monty the Malodorous was a fearsome pirate who sailed the six or seven seas. He was brave. He was bold. He was brilliant with his sword. When he raised the Jolly Roger, other ships turned and fled. And when he cruised into port, other pirates handed over their treasure.

But Monty had a secret: he could not swim.

While the other pirates jumped into the ocean for their Saturday scrub, Monty stood on a cannon and bellowed, "Real pirates don't bathe! Yar-har-har!"

This attitude earned him much respect (and a great deal of personal space).

Then one day, Monty spied Meg. She lounged in the shallows, her long hair streaming. When she lifted her ocarina to her lips and began to play, Monty's heart went *ka-thunk*. He tumbled head over boot heels in love.

Monty gave Meg a star-shaped pearl he'd found and lent her his favorite book, *Gulliver's Travels*. He made her laugh with his jokes and riddles.

"Why *did* the fish cross the ocean?" repeated Meg.

"To get to the other tide. Yar-har-har!"

"And what *do* sea monsters eat for dinner?"

"Fish and ships," chortled Monty. "Yar-har-har-har-har!"

In turn, Meg showed Monty how to scrape barnacles from his ship's hull and led him to the best fishing spots. She taught him to set his course by the constellations.

Monty was impressed. But more than anything,
he admired that Meg swam like a fish.

He asked her over for dinner.
"No, thanks," she said. "You're a real nice
pirate, Monty, but you smell like stinky boots."

Monty was the saddest pirate on the six or seven seas. He tired of treasure hunts and refused to go on raids. Instead, he huddled in the crow's nest and moped.

Not even the strains of his first mate's harmonica or the crew's rough songs of pillage could cheer him up.

One afternoon, as he gazed wistfully over the ship's rail, Monty saw Meg perched on a rock, combing her tresses.

"Ahoy!" he shouted.

But as she turned to smile at him, a huge tentacle snaked out of the water and closed around her. Meg's "eep!" of surprise was cut short as she vanished under the waves.

Then all was still, except for the *thump-thump-thump* of Monty's heart.

"All hands on deck!" he yelled, but there was no reply. The entire crew had gone cutlass shopping ashore. Monty gathered up every bit of his courage. He climbed up on the cannon and stared, trembling, into the shadowy water.

He took a deep breath, held his nose,
closed his eyes — and jumped!

Monty swam like a stone, plummeting through the cold water. He opened his eyes and kicked out his feet — right on top of the octopus's head.

The creature looked up and coiled a tentacle around Monty's waist. Monty reached for his sword. Another tentacle slithered over his shoulder and swiped the blade away. Monty's heart sank to the bottom of his stinky waterlogged boots. What kind of pirate couldn't defeat an octopus?

The creature tossed its head back in glee.

"Aha!" thought Monty. He gritted his teeth and curled his fingers. Then he reached out and planted his fingers right in the octopus's middle. He gave it a mighty tickle. The octopus doubled over, helplessly waving its tentacles. Meg joined in and they didn't stop tickling until the octopus let go and whooshed itself away in a cloud of ink.

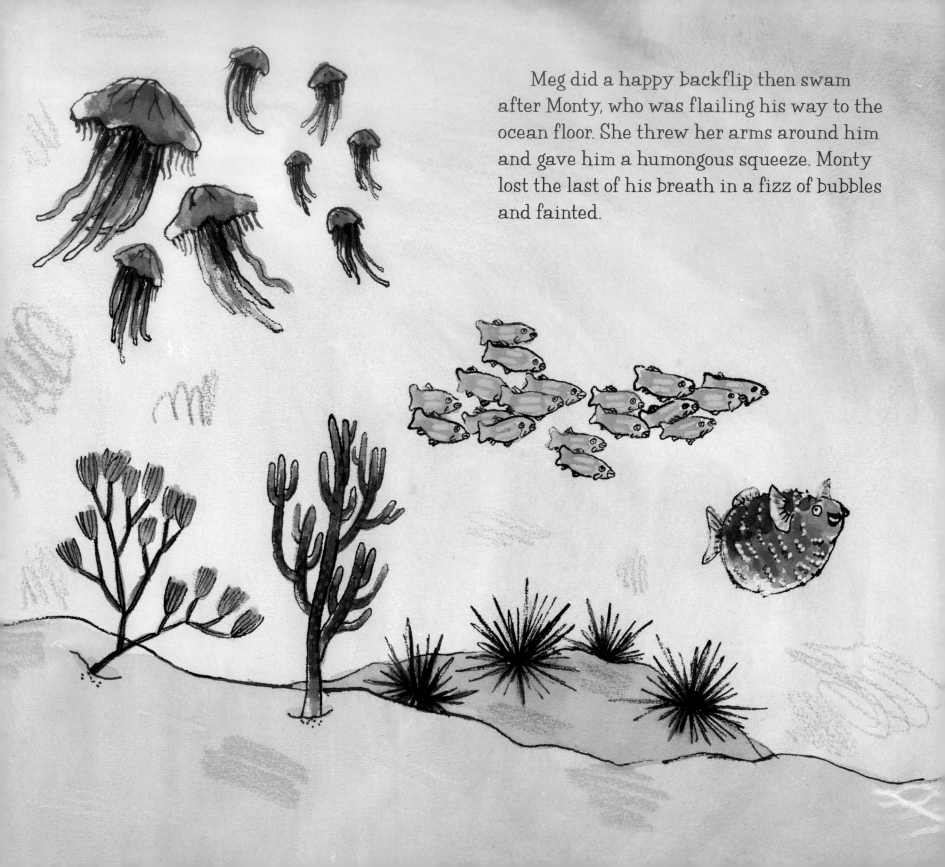

Meg did a happy backflip then swam after Monty, who was flailing his way to the ocean floor. She threw her arms around him and gave him a humongous squeeze. Monty lost the last of his breath in a fizz of bubbles and fainted.

He awoke on the shore with Meg by his side.

"My brave Monty," she said. "Now that you smell like fresh air and seaweed, would you like to have dinner with me?"

Monty gazed into Meg's sea-green eyes. For the second time that day, he gathered up every bit of his courage and said, "Aye, Meg, but only if you promise ..." he blushed and whispered, "to teach me how to swim."

"Is that all?" said Meg. "I'll have you doing the backstroke by Saturday."

Monty was the happiest pirate on the six or seven seas. Soon he could tread water, do the dead man's float and salty seadog paddle like nobody's business.

And every Saturday, before dinner with Meg, he leaped off the ship's rail into the ocean, shouting, "Yar-har-har! Real pirates don't just bathe. They *cannonball*!"

A TREACHEROUS COAST

1796. Pearce and his wife Emily are living in Bath, when Minister of War Henry Dundas turns up and suggests a second mission to the Vendée, this time as a liaison between the French émigres intending to land in Brittany and the British naval and military commanders who will accompany them. The proposed expedition looks promising and Pearce takes the bait. Once at sea, however, Pearce and his crew encounter a French fleet and an indecisive battle ensues off the Ile de Groix. Pearce, accompanied by his faithful Pelicans, must go ashore to check where the forces of the Republic are gathering to crush the rebels...

A TREACHEROUS COAST

A TREACHEROUS COAST

by

David Donachie

Magna Large Print Books
Long Preston, North Yorkshire,
BD23 4ND, England.

British Library Cataloguing in Publication Data.

A catalogue record of this book is
available from the British Library

ISBN   978-0-7505-4459-7

First published in Great Britain by Allison & Busby in 2016

Copyright © 2016 by David Donachie

Cover design © Christina Griffiths
Cover illustration © Fotolia/istockphoto by arrangement with
Allison & Busby Ltd.

The moral right of the author is hereby asserted in accordance with
the Copyright, Designs and Patents Act, 1988

Published in Large Print 2017 by arrangement with
Allison & Busby Ltd.

Magna Large Print is an imprint of Library Magna Books Ltd.

Printed and bound in Great Britain by
T.J. (International) Ltd., Cornwall, PL28 8RW

Dave and Jane Austin
who regularly tease my brain

CHAPTER ONE

The situation was playing on the nerves of everyone aboard HMS *Spark,* John Pearce included. Moving with barely steerage way, in inky darkness, under a heavily clouded sky, with nothing much of a wind, allowed the tension to mount. There were none of the usual artefacts of shipboard life to ease expectation by familiarity: no bells, jocular calls or lamps lit to guide a fellow on his way along the deck, while the lack of stars or moonlight, leading to near Stygian darkness, left all aboard with a feeling of being cut off from the entire world.

This was alluded to, albeit in a whisper, by Lieutenant Somers, the man in command of the two patrolling vessels, his own sloop as well as the brig HMS *Troubadour,* which was presumed to be within hailing distance, for she could not be seen.

'We could disappear and no one would be aware of how and why, not even our consort.'

This seemed to Pearce an indication of how much strain Somers was under, these being amongst the very few words he had addressed to the fellow, who, with his command of French, had been seconded by Admiral Sir Hyde Parker – a character whose reputation preceded him – to help undertake the present mission. If that spoke of a definite amount of gallantry, that was offset and coloured in the minds of naval folk by the way he had come about his rank. In King George's

Navy, John Pearce carried a name that ruffled feathers.

A glimmering layer of light was just visible along the imperceptible horizon, the combined candle and oil power of the port of Genoa not strong enough to reach out far into the Ligurian Sea. Yet it was hoped it would serve to silhouette what they were presently to intercept: vessels seeking to supply the so-called Army of Italy, now encamped before the town of Nice.

Between Genoa and the forces of Revolutionary France lay a combined Austrian/Piedmontese/Neapolitan army under the elderly German general, the Baron de Vins: a coalition force funded by Great Britain, the major player in the fight against what Europe saw as Jacobin madmen; creatures who lacked total control of their own polity; given the country to the rear of their southern arm was in utter turmoil.

Brittany and the Vendée were in open revolt while it was rumoured that Lyons, the second city of France, had risen against the rule of Paris, this as they presided over a treasury rumoured to be close to bankrupt. Thus supplies for the forces opposing the coalition were near impossible to come by, which rendered Genoa as their lifeline.

Supposedly neutral, profit took precedence over principle, as it ever had in a city state founded on trade and ruled by its merchants and bankers. Quite apart from old habits, the present situation required a pragmatic approach from the Doge and *Signoria,* the council of leading citizens who ruled the Ligurian Republic, given that the danger threatened their polity from both sides.

12

Austria was a historic enemy and one that had for a very long time controlled much of the land on Genoa's borders. The Habsburg Emperors had always had designs on subsuming the republic, as it had Venice and neighbouring Pisa. To be allied to them, or even to ease their situation, flew in the face of centuries of hostility.

The French, too, were too-frequent historical invaders of northern Italy, and if they were static now due to dearth and the approaching winter weather, they were a threat to be taken seriously for they had enjoyed outstanding military successes in the years since their revolution had swept away monarchical power.

At Valmy, three years previously, they had broken a mid-European coalition army seeking to march on Paris, led by the noted general of the age, the Duke of Brunswick. In the following year they had, merely by clever manoeuvre, obliged the Duke of York to abandon the Low Countries. Closer to Italy and more recently, by the employment of artillery, they had chased the combined British, Spanish and Neapolitan forces out of the main Mediterranean French fleet base at Toulon.

So there was a real possibility the French would break out into Piedmont. The route to the fertile Po Valley lay along the coastal littoral and the Alps precluded any serious alternative, for its passes were well defended. The land that lay immediately in their path was ruled from Genoa, a rich prize in itself for a revolution short of the means to feed its citizens. If Liguria was a republic, it was not one that Paris would see as comparable to its own, being an oligarchy run for and by the leading

13

citizens who made up the ruling *Signoria:* men of wealth and pride of position, not proponents, in any sense, of *Égalité.*

Somers, a short, rotund fellow with a vinous, bloated countenance, a man who struggled to do up the buttons on his waistcoat, lifted the canvas cover that masked the light on the binnacle to look at his watch, his voice reflecting his low mood.

'If they don't come soon we must get back out to sea.'

'I think they know we are here,' Pearce replied. 'They might be more cautious if they could see it also.'

It was as if Somers had been talking to himself and had only now realised anyone else was close enough to hear. He had to crane his neck to answer, the man he was addressing being so much taller. 'If I seek an opinion, Mr Pearce, I commonly ask for one. Be so good as to keep your thoughts to yourself.' The response was terse.

'If I'm minded to have them, sir, I am also inclined to state them openly.'

He heard the intake of breath from a man who was his superior by many years of service. Pearce was not willing to let that affect him; he had never been a respecter of rank and that extended to admirals, never mind long-serving and irascible lieutenants.

'Since I am as likely to suffer as anyone else aboard from any errors of judgement, and I am not part of the ship's company, I feel I have a right to air my apprehensions.'

'Your arrogance is astounding!' Somers spluttered in his response, but then he did that a lot,

14

Pearce being convinced the mere sight and sound of his person brought resentment to the fore, based on more than his dubious elevation to the rank of lieutenant. Envy for good fortune, given he had enjoyed much success, a handsome appearance as well as several added inches in height only compounded the bitterness.

'I cannot fathom what Admiral Parker was thinking for seconding someone like you to me.'

'Someone like me?' Pearce responded with a growl, one that implied a physical follow-up.

'I also think, on reflection,' Somers spluttered again, either out of frustration or caution, 'I require you to leave the quarterdeck.'

'Odd to see reflection in pitch-darkness. You must have extraordinary powers.'

The smoothly delivered pun went right over Somers' head, but he knew an insult when he heard one. He was audibly inhaling to issue a reprimand when a soft voice called from above.

'Two sail, your honour, they crossed the glim onshore as they cleared the mole.'

'No lights?'

'None, sir.'

Exiting the harbour would have been the only point of risk; any trading vessel seeking to get to sea in a clandestine fashion would hug the harbour wall until they were obliged to clear the entrance. This only underlined the objection John Pearce had raised: whoever was seeking to break their cordon knew that British warships were in the offing, just as they knew they would not be the kind of capital ships that could sink them with ease, not that such a thing was in any

15

case permissible.

In seeking to stop supplies getting to the French, the Royal Navy was engaged in a delicate task and one that required a nod to diplomacy. Interdiction had to be carried out while avoiding incensing the Genoese, this in case they abandoned their supposed and tenuous neutrality to go over wholly to the enemy, a move which would seriously impact on the role of the Mediterranean fleet.

Led by Sir William Hotham, its main task was to bottle up the French Navy in Toulon, and if they came out, to beat them. He had done so twice, but his triumphs had been partial rather than total; the enemy was still a fleet in being, so that task had not in any way been diminished. Ports like Genoa must be allowed to trade as normal with the wider world; indeed, much of the cargo came and went in English bottoms.

Ships came into and out of the harbour from any number of other ports on the Italian mainland as well as the entire middle sea. Merchant vessels from North Africa, the Levant, Spain and even the Americas were common. To embargo the entirety of that would be to create another active opponent.

Hotham had a concomitant problem. To simultaneously impose a full blockade on Genoa as well as Toulon was fraught with peril for a fleet seriously lacking strength, added to which, with winter approaching, the waters of the Mediterranean were dangerous per se, none more so than those off the coast of Liguria. It was a time for ships of the line to find a safe anchorage, not to be endlessly at sea when they lacked the facilities for repair or the numbers that would allow such an action to be truly and continuously effective.

Subterfuge was required in Hotham's opinion; no British warship could be openly seen to interfere with Genoese trade, hence the lack of lights and the need Somers saw to get out of sight of land by daylight. Pearce, not by nature bellicose, was of the opinion, and not alone in such, that the best way to contain Genoese chicanery – the oligarchy openly colluded and profited from these nefarious trades – was to threaten a devastating bombardment of the city and port if they did not cease their duplicity.

Quiet orders were now being passed for men to ready themselves, the ship itself having long been cleared for action. Those below, who would have been nursing their boarding weapons, crept onto the deck to crouch between the cannon, while others took station on those very same weapons ready to fire off a first salvo, it being axiomatic that any vessel seeking to come out at this time of night could not be engaged in any kind of legitimate dealings.

Pearce had moved forward to the place allotted to him in the forepeak, where he would command four of the twelve-pounder cannon as well as some of the men about to board against whoever they were set to face; that could be anyone, including their fellow countrymen. The Army of Italy would pay well for supplies of any kind and a Briton was as greedy as any. There was a very active French consul in Genoa and he was ever busy in his efforts to support his confrères, while he cared not from whom willingness came.

17

'Can't see bugger all,' came a voice out of the darkness, one of the gunners remarking on the obvious.

'Belay that,' Pearce hissed, 'and use your ears.'

'Got a bandana round them, your honour,' came the sniggering reply, followed after a short pause by, 'What was it you'se saying?'

This was the cause of suppressed laughter; in this light a man could speak and avoid identification, especially with a blue coat on board temporarily, a man who would struggle to recognise a voice. Pearce had to hold back a loud response and not only because it might carry. He reasoned a rebuke would mean nothing and he was disinclined that way in any case. Let them have their jest while he concentrated on listening out for their quarry.

He could hear the cordage straining on HMS *Spark* and he sought to force that to the background. Whoever was coming out, even in light airs, would create more noise as they tried to get what benefit they could from what was no more than a zephyr. At the same time, he was reflecting on how he had got here, on this deck, when he had been about to foreswear the navy in its entirety. So much for showing his mistress, Emily Barclay, a flash of independence.

'You could get yourself killed, John Pearce, just to satisfy a bit of stupid flummery.'

Whatever he thought of Lieutenant Somers, and that was not a great deal, Pearce had to admit he ran a tight ship; that bit of seaman's banter had been exceptional. The crew had been together for years so they knew each other well,

18

and such continuity could only have two out-comes: discontent enough to render the ship useless or mutual respect, the latter seemingly being the case here.

So it was the innate discipline of HMS *Spark* that gave them the advantage; they maintained a degree of silence, something their quarry failed to achieve. The call was faint but telling – a man used to daylight and easy communication forget-ting his present position and aim, though the words used were incomprehensible.

In a situation where Pearce had expected any-thing spoken would be in French, a language in which he could play the native and which had seen him seconded to this task, what he now heard was more guttural, perhaps German. That mattered less than the fact that it was audible enough to allow Somers to send aloft a pair of blue lights.

The rockets whizzed into the air leaving their trail of golden sparks, which alone would alert and hopefully alarm their enemies enough to have them put up their helm and head back to the safety of Genoa. Somers was not necessarily here to fight; he was here to dissuade, and if they turned tail, his task was done.

The overhead explosion bathed the seascape in the ethereal light, showing not only two trading ships, but also HMS *Troubadour*, half a cable distant, precisely where she should be. Pearce could see Somers on the quarterdeck with a speaking trumpet at his mouth, ready to shout out an order to reverse course. It did not remain there as the very visible blast of a cannon preceded the sound of firing, followed by the whistling of a ball as it swept at head height across the deck.

There was no need to command the response; the gunners were prepared with their cannon loaded, the gun captains already having had their men levering on the trunnions to adjust the aim as soon as the blue lights broke. They hauled on the flint lines as soon as the weapons began to bear, working on the assumption of superior force. The lanyards were pulled before Pearce even gave the order to fire, gratified to see evidence of damage just as the illumination provided by the rockets began to fade.

Replacements were sent up from both warships and it was plain their targets lacked the will to counter the weight of shot. All four vessels were trying to gain steerage way: the traders to get back to safety, the two warships now seeking to get close enough to board. They had fired on the Royal Navy, so if the vessels could be taken and their purpose could be proved, it would be Hotham complaining to Genoa for the laxity of their customs controls, not them to him for interference.

The fact that they were up against coastal trading vessels – small, with deep hulls and a couple of defensive cannon – had registered, so there was no contest when it came to the ability to get a modicum of way on or to maintain steady fire. More troubling was the lack of sea room in which to effect a capture with so little wind; if their opponents made the harbour entrance, they would be safe.

Somers had hauled men off the guns and any thought of boarding to get as much canvas aloft and drawing, *Troubadour* doing likewise, while their quarry had naturally come round to run for safety.

'Why in the name of God did they fire?' he yelled out.

Pearce thought it futile to speculate, with panic as likely to be the cause as any plan, but it was a measure of Somers' frustration at the lack of speed. At times like these a captain could do little, something Pearce had himself experienced in a similar circumstance. The crew were working flat out, any orders needing to be issued being made vocally by the yeomen who commanded in the tops and on deck by men with years of experience, who did not require creatures in blue coats to remind them of their duty.

Under such light as was sent aloft, it was impossible to see if they were closing, which took no account of the common difficulty at sea of discerning distance without a fixed point of reference. Sweeps appeared on the merchant vessels as they sought to use those to compensate for the lack of wind, this while Somers made a slight alteration of course, which he hoped would get his ship between them and safety.

Pearce wanted to point out that sweeps would serve *Spark* better than canvas – with a much bigger crew they should be able to overhaul – only to decide that any observation of his would be unwelcome. Thus it was with a feeling of growing pessimism he reckoned the gap to be increasing not closing. Unless something was done, they were going to get away and in thinking like that, the solution became clear. The ship's boats with boarders would catch those two lumbering coastal traders easily and that was too favourable a solution to be left unsaid.

Somers' face was thunderous even as he approached, it being obvious Pearce had something to say, and an abrupt command came that he should get back to his station. The bulbous eyes almost popped when the captain saw he was being ignored.

'I told you to return to your station, Mr Pearce.'

The temptation to shout at the man had to be suppressed; getting him to act was more important than displaying anger, so the view imparted was delivered in a voice too low to carry; wounding this man's delicate pride would achieve the exact opposite of that which he sought.

'Your opinion is not welcome, sir. I repeat: return to your post or face an order to go below and stay there.'

The need to be polite evaporated as Pearce's temper, never easily controlled, came to the fore, adding to a carrying voice that paid no heed to Somers' dignity.

'If I wondered why you have stayed a lieutenant for so many years, I do not do so now.'

That was like a slap and a well-aimed one. Somers had been a lieutenant for a very long time, indeed even before he had come out from England with Lord Hood to a station where the attrition of officers was high due to incompetence, illness, wounds or death in action. A man like him should surely have been promoted, but he was demonstrating now, by his lack of imagination and stubbornness, why he had not been elevated.

'I intend to close enough to sink them.'

'Why, when you can capture both the vessels and their cargo, which has to be of value?'

'Sinking could send the message Sir William wishes to impart.'

'I think I know Hotham better than you, Mr Somers. Line his pockets and he will be a happier man, which also goes for your crew.'

Somers was spluttering once more. 'I look forward to telling Admiral Parker you are affected more by greed than sound policy.'

'And while you are cogitating on that, your quarry could well make Genoa harbour, which will satisfy neither.'

'You forgot to mention your purse, sir, which I assume has great bearing.'

'It is a pity striking a superior officer is so frowned upon. I daresay the navy would be a sight more efficient if it were not.'

Somers chose to ignore him, instead moving to the bulwark to look at the two trading vessels, now using the long oars to make headway; there was no doubt the gap was increasing. It was only when Somers turned to give an order, perhaps one to break off the chase that, with fresh blue lights sent up, he saw *Troubadour* had her boats in the water and they were closing fast.

Pearce rushed back to his station, shouting to the cannon to fire off a salvo, then to load with grape. Those boats would take time to close and the best way to slow their quarry was to make the deck too deadly a place on which to be working. He had no fear that Somers would question his actions; what had happened with *Troubadour* had driven home the point. Somers would now be

23

wondering how to quickly get his own boats in the water as well as how to frame his despatch so, if the ploy was a success, he could claim the credit for the actions of his consort.

The people they were after were no fools. They saw what was coming and took men off the sweeps to line the side with muskets, in the hope of driving off the assault, thus presenting Pearce with the perfect target. Now it was a case of timing his grape salvo so that those muskets would be fired off in panic, while the closeness of the boats would deny them time to reload. The eyes of his four gun captains were on him, Pearce reckoning if Somers had ordered them to fire, they would have awaited his agreement.

He did not shout the order to do so; there was no need.

CHAPTER TWO

'That is hard to credit. Boots, by damn?'

This statement was posited by Horatio Nelson, the expression on his face showing the measure of his surprise. Having always been possessed of a lively countenance, youthful for his years, the damage to his right eye, sustained at the siege of Calvi, now gave it an odd, unbalanced cast. He was obliged to slightly swing his head to the left in order to fully fix an object or person, yet anyone looking at him full face would think his wounded eye seemed normal; plainly, it was far from the case.

Happy to get rid of John Pearce, Lieutenant Somers had put him in a pinnace with instructions to rendezvous with Commodore Nelson, his immediate superior, who was beating to and fro off Cape Noli, and inform him of what had happened. He had already related the tale of the boarding operation as well as praised the man commanding HMS *Troubadour* for the way he had read both the situation and produced a solution.

There was no point in him alluding to his own attempts to persuade Somers it was the right course of action; that would smack of boasting. Nor, except by omission, did he seek to ditch the man and his comparable incompetence, which probably flew counter to the despatch the commodore had just read, one written by the captain of HMS *Spark*.

This told Nelson the two captures were now on their way to Leghorn, where their cargo would be landed and handed over to a naval commissariat that had little use for it. No doubt the cargo of boots would be sold to the coalition forces to use as they saw fit, the price gained added to the total prize value, part of which would come Pearce's way.

'I do suppose,' Nelson said, with a jaunty air, one that indicated a coming jest, 'that contrary to the common old saw about stomachs, an army actually marches on its feet.'

'Droll, sir, very droll,' Pearce responded, knowing it would please one of the few naval seniors to whom he was willing to defer. He got a wide grin for his observation, one that made the commodore look like a mischievous child.

'I shall no doubt get a sharp letter from the *Signoria* condemning this action, copied of course to our C-in-C.'

'I would say, sir, that on this occasion they would be best to hold their tongue.'

'Not an Italian quality, Pearce. As a nation they think to shout and gesticulate is the way to win a dispute, though I think here we have the right to protest first. Not even those devious souls can claim that a cargo of military boots counts as a legitimate cargo and, as to their coming out in darkness, well, that fact alone pins it.'

'They could only have one destination in mind, sir.'

'Which we will tell them,' Nelson insisted, before calling to his servant, Frank Lepeé, more sober than was normal, to fetch a midshipman.

'"We", sir?'

'I think it wise that someone involved in the action is on hand to describe how it came about, albeit not the exact location. Best if it was seen to be further out to sea and a fortuitous meeting rather than a planned one; not that they will be fooled, but we must play the game. You are conversant in French and it will aid me to know what, if he interferes, the French consul is actually saying instead of what is passed on to me by an Italian interpreter.'

'You exchange matters with the French consul present, sir?'

'It is hard to see the oligarchs without him there. They are in terror of the Revolution and rightly so. The beasts are less than four days' march from the city and they no doubt anticipate their heads will roll off a damned guillotine if Genoa is taken.'

'The enemy have to fight to get there, sir.'

'Indeed, and let us hope our allies and the Baron de Vins have the stomach to stop them. For myself, I would be happier with a younger and more spirited fellow in command. Vins is long on two things, Pearce: verbal bellicosity and years. It is only in activity that he can be found wanting.'

After a rap on the door, Midshipman William Hoste entered the cabin of HMS *Agamemnon*, an eager expression on his face, while a smile was aimed at Pearce. This served to remind the recipient that of all the ships in which he had sailed, this was the happiest; such an attitude manifest most in the youngsters. It was also one on which he was genuinely welcome.

Such a state of harmony was entirely due to the man who commanded the vessel; all his officers took their cue from Horatio Nelson, who saw encouragement as the way to gain efficiency and, having sailed himself as a common seaman, albeit in a merchant vessel, had ways of connecting with the crew that few of his peers could match.

If there were many in the fleet who thought him lax in the article of discipline, Admiral Sir William Hotham being one, they had never been aboard when the ship engaged the enemy. HMS *Agamemnon* cleared her sixty-four guns for action faster than any of her consorts, then plied her cannon with such commendable speed she was well capable of engaging more powerfully armed opponents on equal terms.

'Mr Hoste, do I have to remind you of your manners? A grin will not do. Say good day to Lieutenant Pearce.'

'Delighted to renew your acquaintance, sir.'

'Reciprocated, Mr Hoste.'

The voice had broken since Pearce last saw the lad, while along with that had come a modicum of facial eruption in the article of spots. Hoste was one of the commodore's favourites, being of Norfolk stock, yet Nelson was even-handed in his pleasure in young company, easy when he only took on board spirited, skylarking types who appealed to his own slightly juvenile nature.

'Regards to Mr Hinton, we need to shape a course for Genoa.'

'Aye aye, sir.'

'And you and those of your berth not on duty will join Mr Pearce and I for dinner, where, I am sure, in order to further your education, he will recount to you every detail of the recent action.'

If such a prospect delighted the fifteen-year-old midshipman, and it plainly did, it made Pearce inwardly groan; if there was one naval habit he abhorred, and there were many, it was the constant reciting of past battles and exploits, in which valour naturally tended to grow through repetition. Being asked to recount his own adventures always made him feel like a fraud, made doubly so by the attitude of those listening.

If not aboard *Agamemnon,* many, in other wardrooms in which he had been obliged to relate some action, while paying lip service with their congratulations, were consumed with envy at what they saw as his good fortune. To say, truthfully, he had walked blindly into any action in which he had partaken and not sought either danger or glory, was ever brushed aside as sly modesty.

The sounds above, running feet on worn planking, were of a ship of war coming round onto another course. Pearce knew there would be few raised voices on the deck; everyone on HMS *Agamemnon* was a volunteer, many from Nelson's home county of Norfolk. They had sailed with him in previous commissions and were so well versed in avoidance of press gangs they could with seeming ease, at the outbreak of a new war, cross half of England to get to the ship in which they wished to serve.

He watched as the sunlight worked its way across the salt-streaked casement windows, until the ship was heading west, the wind causing the whole to heel. By the time the manoeuvre was complete, Pearce had excused himself and made his way to the wardroom, leaving Nelson, quill in hand, writing letters.

Genoa was an impressive city – how could it not be when for centuries it had been a premier trading port through which a great deal of the wealth of Italy flowed? In olden times that had included fine and colourful cloth from Florence, made from wool imported from England, also armour from Milan, which had the means to forge weapons and protective fighting equipment of the highest quality. Lying to west of the fertile Po Valley, the breadbasket of Piedmont and Lombardy, it had also been a major exporter of foodstuffs, and part of the task at hand for the

British fleet was to ensure none of the abundant surplus was available to the French army.

The republic had never quite matched the imperial pretentions of its great competitor, Venice, yet it did produce as one of its sons Christopher Columbus, as well as many of the ships and admirals who had beaten off the expansion of the Ottomans at Lepanto. From the sea the city was framed against the forested blue-grey mountains, the smell of pine wafting outwards on a foul wind, which, in forcing HMS *Agamemnon* to beat up tack upon tack, afforded plenty of time for examination.

The most obvious sign of long prosperity lay in the number of remarkable church spires and domed basilicas that formed the skyline as well as, once landed, the fine buildings that fronted the quays. The harbour itself was a great sweep of pallid stone, hooked to the south to keep at bay the tempests that plagued these waters every winter, for Genoa's climate was much affected by the proximity of the Maritime Alps. There was a twenty-eight-gun French frigate at anchor, *La Brune*, which Nelson eyed greedily and swore he would take one day.

'But not today, Mr Pearce. Their damned neutrality, which is false to my mind, prevents me acting as I would wish.'

'A cutting-out expedition in darkness, sir,' Pearce replied mischievously.

'Tempting,' Nelson replied, a wicked gleam in his good eye as they approached the quayside, 'very tempting.'

Traversing the streets, it seemed as if all the

buildings had the dimensions of a regal palace, being large, square and constructed from alternating black-and-white marble. The telling point was made by Pearce that if they were replete with windows, none existed on the lower floors, while the high gates were formidable, hinting at a fear of violence.

'They will get all the violence they can handle,' Nelson insisted with almost wishful thinking, 'if the *sans-culottes* ever get within the city walls to plunder the place.'

Mr Drake, the British consul to Turin and, for London, the man at the political heart of the coalition, was the first person to call upon, the British representative in the city being seen as more Italian in his attitudes than English. Drake was coming through Genoa on his way home on leave and would provide an appraisal for Nelson of the state of the allied defences as well as how he should proceed when presented to the men who ran the Genoese Republic.

Pearce was surprised at what was proposed as a solution to their secret supplying of the French, nothing less than a blockade to stop neutral vessels trading anywhere along the Ligurian littoral. The response from Nelson so worried him he felt it incumbent, in the coach ride back to the harbour, to take it upon himself to propose caution.

'If you implement this, sir, it would be wise to ensure you have written backing from the C-in-C–'

'Which I am highly unlikely to receive. Hotham issued a recent order demanding care when dealing with neutrals, I assume on instructions from London.' The knowing nod from his inferior was telling. 'Yet Mr Drake did point out that political courage is required in an officer as well as military courage.'

'An argument hard to counter, but I think that the courage you speak of belongs to flag officers of the highest rank and must be promulgated in a manner that avoids excuses.'

In the silence that followed, Pearce wondered if he should speak freely. In his dealings with Sir William Hotham he had found the admiral to be devious to the point of an utter want of trust. The way Hotham and his slippery clerk, Toomey, had exposed not only him but many others to danger still rankled; the fact that he was no longer in a position to easily exact retribution on the scoundrels was even more galling.

If he told Nelson of what had happened in the mission to the Gulf of Ambracia, he doubted, it seeming so outlandish, it would be believed. How do you tell such a fellow, who seemed to see good in most people, that his C-in-C was a practised liar as well as a conspirator enough to be absolutely at home in the land of Machiavelli?

Against that, he was well aware Nelson was not as happy as he had once been, serving under Hotham, having much preferred Lord Hood as the commanding admiral. Nothing exposed more the difference between the two flag officers than the twin actions in which Hotham had led his fleet: one in March off Cape Noli, another subsequent encounter with the French in July, at the Hyères Islands.

Given two chances to overwhelm them, Hotham had, to the thinking of many of his senior officers, flunked both, settling for partial success where near annihilation of the enemy had been possible. Admiral Samuel Goodall, the man commanding the van of the fleet and thus in the best position to press home an assault, had reputedly kicked his hat all over his quarterdeck in frustration when he was ordered to desist in his attack on an enemy he was sure he could destroy. Nelson had been just as upset, though he had been less open about his disquiet.

If open criticism of a commander was muted by service convention, Pearce suspected many letters home would contain subtle criticism of a man seen as too weak and fearful for the task he had been given. Yet there would be a residual fact of naval life included: everyone in command could be faced with difficult choices when they were so far from home and definite instructions, so it was never acceptable to be overly harsh.

'I asked Drake,' Nelson added after a long silence, 'if the forces ranged against the French could hold their positions in the face of an attack.'

'And his response?'

'Was not reassuring, Mr Pearce, not reassuring at all. He reckons morale to be poor. The Neapolitans wish for nothing more than to go home, while the Piedmontese show little willingness to defend even their own hearths.'

'So it falls to the Austrians.'

'Who are serving, as I said to you previously, under an old man and, I suspect, old habits. The Army of Italy is far from formidable and will remain so when denied that which they need, boots and foul-weather clothing being one with winter coming, which will impact on their morale. Thus it falls to the Royal Navy–'

'You mean to you, sir.'

'A telling interruption.'

'I apologise.'

'Please do not.'

'Would I be correct in pointing out that if you interdict neutral trade, then the owners of what cargoes you seize will have the ability to sue you personally for their losses in the British courts?'

'Of course,' was the impish reply, 'but that does not mean they will win.'

'And you are seriously considering taking upon yourself such a burden? Any suits could be for sums running into hundreds of thousands of pounds and I have never met a man of the law who entertained a certainty of winning even the most seemingly sound case.'

'If it is the only way to contain the French, then I must.'

'I wonder, sir, if I would be allowed to relate to you some of the actions of Admiral Hotham, which have impinged personally upon me and may give you pause?'

'I know him not to be the warrior, Mr Pearce, but I must abjure you from saying anything more. He is a flag officer; I am a very senior captain who must support him. Your rank does not allow you to question that.'

Drake was present when Nelson made his representations to the Doge, he flanked by the Genoese *Signoria:* men dressed in unrelieved black as if attending an interment. These were no gesticulators in the normal Italian mould; they were a stony-faced, arrogant-looking bunch, but silent, leaving their elected leader to listen and respond.

John Pearce stood several places to the rear of Nelson, his eye on the French consul. He was much given to whispering in any available ear, no doubt to counter what was being said about breaches of neutrality, it being galling that there could be no knowledge of what was being imparted, he being too far off to overhear.

If the words the commodore used, directed at His Serene Highness Signor Brignole, had any effect, it was far from obvious on the face of the man he was addressing. Richly garbed in his official robes – those bejewelled – he was a master of sophistry, too long in the tooth to react to accusations of collusion, and nor could he be anything other than compliant to the views of his black-clad fellow citizens. In Genoa, the Doge was elected biannually; if he wished to continue in office, the support of the *Signoria* was essential.

When the matter was summed up, it was with deep regret that such a lapse had occurred; not even he could term it properly as duplicitous. Brignole sonorously announced that customs controls would be tightened to ensure such an unfortunate incident never happened again; with the caveat of an inability to check every cargo departing the port, as well as its destination, ship's masters were not always truthful.

'A full blockade is what is needed,' was Nelson's conclusion, once they were back in his barge and making for *Agamemnon*. 'Only Sir William can authorise such a thing, so I will ask that he accede to it.'

The opinion of John Pearce, that he would not, remained unspoken.

'I fear I must condemn you to a pinnace once more, Mr Pearce. HMS *Spark* needs her boat back so you must take it to Leghorn, which I am sure will please you, while I make for the anchorage in Vado Bay, the flank of our armies, suggested by Mr Drake.' The reference to Leghorn got Nelson a sharp look as he added, 'And from there, unless our C-in-C has other duties he wishes you to perform, you will soon be sent back to the deck of your own ship.'

He wanted to say that any request to him from Hotham would be thrown back in the sod's face, not that such a chance was likely to occur given their mutual hatred and history. It had been Hyde Parker, captain of the fleet, who had engaged him for the mission on HMS *Spark*, and even he had done so with reservations, having seen as the executive officer of the fleet how Pearce had shown scant respect for Lord Hood.

Parker had been surprised at his ready acquiescence, unaware that Pearce had his own motives, wishing for two things: to be off his own ship and out of Leghorn. Had Nelson been indulging in any form of deceit regarding Leghorn and happiness? The conclusion was that he was not, or if he was, it was so expertly done as not to show. Emily Barclay was in Leghorn and, much as he longed to see her, Pearce knew their relationship to be far from as simple as it had once been, and that too had been larded with complications.

The next day found him sailing down the coast past endless bays of hemmed-in fishing villages, with only steep, rocky paths cut with steps providing a way out landwards; this allowed him many hours in which to think, while gnawing on several problems. He gave a decently wide berth to La Spezia and Pisa, where the mountains that lined the shore finally gave way to an open landscape and the wide delta of the River Arno. The sight of Leghorn harbour, Livorno to the locals, only served to heighten his mixed feelings at what he would face, not helped when he saw that not only was HMS *Spark* in harbour, but so too was HMS *Flirt*. He had supposed her to be in San Fiorenzo Bay.

Her beautiful lines did not lift his heart as they should, for he would be obliged to go aboard and not proceed ashore as he had intended. It proved worse when he did get his sea chest hoisted onto the deck, it being plain the fourteen-gun brig was preparing to get to sea. It was with mixed feelings that he was informed they were off to join with Commodore Nelson.

CHAPTER THREE

John Pearce had for some time been suffering from a whole portfolio of frustrations and being back on board HMS *Flirt* was only one; only this was now a daily affliction. Relations with her commanding officer, Henry Digby, were far from cordial, their association not having recovered from the latter's repudiation of his promise to help Pearce against Sir William Hotham.

A commitment given when Digby was far away from authority and recovering from a serious wound had, despite the fact that Pearce had probably saved both his life and his reputation, been retracted when he came back within the admiral's immediate orbit. Digby's attachment to the advancement of his career had come to take precedence over his principles and a bounden promise.

The fact that he had not acted to stop Pearce remaining aboard seemed surprising, given the heated exchange in which they had engaged, one in which his first lieutenant and supposed friend had used some very harsh words on both his character as well as his honour and they must still rankle. He had expected Digby to demand his removal, and when that did not happen he looked for motives, which were not too hard to fathom.

A request to dismiss his first lieutenant would have to go to the flagship while it could not be made without some form of explanation, and Digby would shy away from providing one. It was easier to tolerate Pearce than risk his demanding a court martial, which was his right, at which certain things would be aired, matters that would be more than detrimental to any number of people, not least Digby himself, for the defendant would have the right to question him under oath. On board he could be controlled; in front of a panel judging his case, even if they were appointed by Hotham, Pearce was a loose cannon.

The captain had another reason to disapprove of Pearce, this relating to his relationship with Emily Barclay, which had been no secret aboard the ship and it made no difference to Digby that the lady was now a widow. When last seen by anyone from the brig, she had shown unmistakable signs of being with child and no great calculation of dates and who was by her side at the probable time of conception was required to put the likely paternity at the door of John Pearce. It was doubly galling the man made not the least attempt to hide the fact that the supposition was correct.

Since, outside of the efficient running of the ship, they now barely spoke, Digby was utterly unaware of the other matter troubling his premier. Emily would probably have been relieved that he had not landed, which would risk for her embarrassment, something of which she was in terror. She did not share his desire that he should be openly acknowledged as the father of her child, insisting it would be too shameful to her reputation. This oddly mirrored Digby's concerns for his naval career; in his wilder flights of fancy, Pearce reckoned them more suited to each other than he to her.

Emily had declined to go home in her condition, fearing the risks of a sea voyage, with the very strong possibility that the birth would occur before she reached England. Safely ensconced in Leghorn, she was insisting that the child must be born there and under her married name of Barclay. The future possibility of adoption was mooted, that not possible for at least three years, the time polite society allotted to a respectable widowhood.

She had also talked of their future life together – a distant prospect to him, the right and proper gap to her – in a manner Pearce found unappealing, not least that she expected him to live off the wealth her late husband had acquired in prize money. The life she was mapping out for them both, based on what she would inherit, went against everything in which Pearce believed. In order to avoid disputes, and he had to admit it was at Emily's bidding, he had accepted an active naval role, one that had put him under the temporary command of Somers and now back aboard *Flirt*. If it had its discomforts, it provided peace of a sort.

The fact that Emily was free of a man they both despised had come as a shock; Pearce had witnessed Barclay's seventy-four-gun ship-of-the-line being captured after a desperate battle, to then subsequently find Emily had been aboard and not, as he had supposed, safe in Naples. In order to rescue her from an extended incarceration he had sacrificed a set of papers that could have seriously threatened not only her husband, assumed to be still alive, but also Sir William Hotham. His reward was not, he thought, commensurate with that which he had given away.

From the tiny quarterdeck he could see the poles and triced-up sails on the yards of the anchored vessels; these made up Nelson's squadron, HMS *Brilliant* being one of the five frigates, a sight that produced several conflicting emotions. She was the ship into which he had been press-ganged by the very same Ralph Barclay. It was also on board

Brilliant that he had first met Emily.

At a distance the squadron looked to be in good order, but he knew that would not survive proximity: nearly every vessel in the Mediterranean fleet was in need of refitting. They lacked even such a mundane article as paint, while in many cases a dry dock would be required to bring them back to a proper condition. On some, their scantlings had sprung, requiring frapping to keep the hull watertight, with rot an internal problem throughout the beams and futtocks. The deck planking was worn from two years of daily sanding and the same wear and tear applied to the weathered rigging.

There would be no gleaming cream sails when they were dropped from the yards; after such extended service in warm climes they were a dun-brown colour, while the dress of many of the less well-off officers was likewise faded. Was it a reason to be thankful that HMS *Flirt* was in better condition than most and thus likely to be employed? Pearce reckoned, being nimble, she would be used for inshore operations.

'Mr Conway, please be so good as to inform the captain that we are about to make our number to the commodore.'

HMS *Flirt* was flush-decked and nor was she large, and that applied especially to the space between the quarterdeck and the captain's cabin, below Pearce's feet and a short companionway distant. He could have shouted that piece of information and would have fully expected to be heard. But this was King George's Navy, which required messages be delivered in a way that

41

enhanced the dignity of the recipient.

He smiled at the alacrity with which Ivor Conway lifted his hat and ran to oblige. Fourteen years of age and not large for his years, from the island of Anglesey, the lad had been a midshipman aboard Barclay's ship, HMS *Semele,* when much battered she struck her flag to a trio of French frigates. Sent to a brig lacking officers, he had shown he could stand a watch as long as nothing untoward troubled the ship.

Conway also worshipped John Pearce and was not shy of saying so, though not to him personally; the mid rated Pearce as the man who had rescued him from life in a French dungeon. If the orders to exchange prisoners had come from Hotham, it was John Pearce who had seen them executed. Never stated to anyone was the fact that it was he who had initiated said transaction, for that would smack not only of boasting, it could also expose the fact that he had blackmailed Hotham into acting, which he was bound by his word not to do.

As Digby came on deck he was afforded a lifted hat, but not a verbal greeting, while Conway stood stiffly behind the captain, clearly in awe of his rank and position. Digby and Pearce were both lieutenants, the former longer serving by not much more than a year, but it was enough to make a difference; added to that Digby had been given command of this non-rated ship, so he was now ranked as a master and commander. That carried with it all the powers the navy afforded a captain, as well as being a sure route to being made post and elevated into a rated vessel like a frigate. This alone put a person on the captains' list, which if they stayed alive long enough, would see them one day promoted to admiral, with all the pay and perks that went with flag rank, even if they spent the rest of their life ashore.

'Is the signal gun ready, Mr Pearce?'

'It is, sir.'

'Carry on.'

Manned by a pair of experienced hands, the small brass signal gun was also within earshot; indeed, they could not have avoided hearing the order even if they so desired, but once more custom required it be relayed, the first blast of black smoke following immediately. Repeated nine times, this acknowledged Nelson's rank in what John Pearce considered to be a piece of excessive flummery, a waste of precious powder, which would be better employed in propelling balls at their enemies.

Flags broke out at the masthead of HMS *Agamemnon* to order Digby aboard and, as soon as the anchor bit into the seabed of the Bay of Vado, the cutter was hauled in from astern. Digby fetched his logs along with the despatches he had brought from the main fleet base of San Fiorenzo Bay; he had only stopped in Leghorn to revictual.

The logs would be examined by Nelson's clerk, before being copied into the ledgers of the ship-of-the-line. The information would later be passed to Hotham's flagship, HMS *Britannia,* for yet another perusal, in time to make its way back to London and the Admiralty. Once there it would be pored over by crab-fingered clerks looking for faults in the use of stores, the distribution of food and rum in the barrel, the wasting of powder and shot, as well as the improper use of cordage and canvas. For such people war was waged with their own naval service, not that of the enemy.

Whistles blew and hats were raised as the captain departed and, once all was secured, the sails on the yards and the decks prettied up to please Digby when he returned, John Pearce felt himself relax, something he found hard when his captain was aboard. Retiring to his screened-off cabin below decks, he was brought a welcome cup of coffee; he was also brought news of the less-than-content feelings of the crew now he was back aboard.

'The lads don't care for it, John-boy. It was easier when you was absent. You two being at loggerheads makes them worry.'

These softly spoken words came from the only person Pearce reckoned he could open up to about his problems. The concomitant of that was the reverse; he was talking to a man who had it within him to check his superior in a way no one within the service would normally dare.

In title his servant, Michael O'Hagan had neither the build, manner nor, indeed, a true inclination for the role. The Irishman was massive in both height and girth, while his broad face was scarred enough to show that he was not averse to the odd bout of fisticuffs. Indeed, he had bare-knuckled in any number of contests and always as the victor. Yet he played the role to perfection when they were not alone. When that happened, he became a friend and one who could not be ignored.

'There's not much I can do about it, Michael.'

'Sure, a bit of pretence wouldn't go amiss. The way the lads are gabbin' they fear that it will all go ahoo in action and they will pay in blood for your squabble. Mind it, they will attend to you, for they trust you.'

'More fools them,' was the astringent response.

Pearce knew that part of the problem was loyalty and he had more of that from the crew than Digby, a fact of which the man could not be unaware. These were the very same tars who had come out with him from England, manning the armed cutter HMS *Larcher*, the only vessel he had ever rightfully commanded. They had enjoyed both some success as well as near catastrophe under his hand, but in the end he had brought them to safety. The shared experience of what happened had melded them.

The feeling of fidelity was not, of course, universal; there were those who would never like a blue coat, especially given he had once tested their tolerance to the limit. In addition, no ship of war ever sailed without one or two natural malcontents, men for whom a feeling of satisfaction was alien to their nature. Yet, in the main, the crew tended to look to him when danger threatened, for he had shown himself as a man who could not only handle such situations but keep the majority of them whole in the process.

'The only fight I have at the moment is not on this ship.'

Michael pulled a wry face. 'They say being with child does strange things to a woman, changes the way they think, as it does to a man when he

45

first holds his bairn.'

The response was bitter. 'I doubt I will be granted the pleasure of any handling, Michael. I won't be allowed near the thing for fear of shaming its mother.'

To John Pearce, Emily was being foolish with her prating on about respectability. If, the likes of Michael excluded, no one spoke of their liaison in his presence, it had to be the subject of gossip, some of it malicious. It was he who had detached Emily from her marriage vows and brought her out to the Mediterranean, to lodge her in Leghorn on arrival, before shifting her to Naples to avoid the repercussions of an unfortunate contretemps.

As the main revictualling port for the fleet, Leghorn not only had standing officials – a consul and a Naval Board office overseeing fleet supplies, added to various functionaries to see to pay and the like, as well as merchants from home – it was constantly visited by the vessels of the fleet in rotation, so they could make up their water and stores. If the ship's commander was of a mind to allow it, there would be liberty to go ashore for the members of his crew trusted not to desert, not that there was much to fear in that quarter, being so far from home.

Officers were another problem altogether. They normally enjoyed the right to come and go as they pleased off watch and Leghorn was like any other port – not short on fleshpots and, for the less carnal, social entertainments, though they were held to be of a low calibre. As such, it was a hotbed of gossip and some of it had to be about the newly-widowed Mrs Barclay, her association with him, as well as her present condition.

The male of the naval species might be woefully ignorant of the ways of Mother Nature – Pearce reckoned some still ascribed to the Ancient Greek belief that pregnancy came from a northerly wind – yet there had to be enough women and wiser coves who, appraised of the time at which Ralph Barclay had appeared to join Hotham's fleet, set against a visibly swelling belly, could calculate that he was unlikely to be the father.

This left as the culprit the man too often seen in her company, which Pearce did not care one whit about. In a peripatetic life he had seen much, lived in a louche manner and formed an opinion that eschewed hypocrisy; he was Emily's lover and he wished to make little attempt to disguise the fact. This had been an attitude never shared by her, and pregnancy, allied to widowhood, had made matters worse.

She was set on pretence, making friends with the few naval wives who had elected to join their husbands on station as well as joining in the social life created by the small British community, set up for their own pleasure as well as to entertain visiting officers. She was playing bereavement and the weeping widow left with what would be a fatherless child to the hilt, a point made to O'Hagan.

'If you were to think on it like a tar, John-boy–'

The Irishman never got to finish the point before he was interrupted with 'God forbid', which was a strange epithet from a man who had little certainty that any such deity even existed. If John Pearce saw himself in any guise, it was not of a lieutenant in the King's Navy. It was a ser-

47

vice he had come into as no volunteer, a point he now made forcibly to his fellow victim of Ralph Barclays press gang.

'Were we not damned in numbers,' was O'Hagan's mordant response, for there had been many others taken.

'Do Charlie and Rufus still talk with you of it? That foul night?'

'The Pelican Tavern comes up from time to time, and they seem to remember it with fondness when it does.'

'A fondness for dearth? When I met them they lacked the means to buy a pot of ale, just as I recall you did have the means and were loud in your drunkenness. Do you too see it as past joy?'

'Jesus, is it not the way of us all to think back and see only the warmth?'

'Not for me, Michael. I curse the day Ralph Barclay and his brutes ever entered the Pelican, even with what it has brought me.'

The Welsh-accented voice, croaked by being in the process of breaking, came through the canvas screen. 'Captain's putting off from the flag, sir.'

'So soon?'

'He's already in the cutter.'

'Thank you, Mr Conway. Please alert Mr Grey. I take it Mr Bird knows.'

'By the gangway, sir.'

More tradition; a captain coming aboard had to be properly greeted. That meant the bosun piping on his whistle along with a quartet of the marines, half the ship's total, in uniform and spick and span, ready to be inspected by a man who had last set eyes on them only a few hours

48

past. And, of course, it was essential the premier be there to add his greeting.

Once on deck, Pearce was reminded of the fact of how few people he had to openly converse with. He wanted to allude to the short time Digby had spent aboard HMS *Agamemnon*, to suggest the possibility that his captain did not enjoy much respect in a cabin and wardroom that was always welcoming to him. There was no one to say it to.

A careful eye was cast over the deck to ensure all was shipshape. A warm greeting to the marine lieutenant, Mr Grey, went along with a glance at his men to ensure they were both properly attired and as smart as was demanded. He nodded to the master, Mr Dorling, to acknowledge his presence, for it mattered not that others had responsibilities. He was the first lieutenant: all ended at his door if there was anything amiss and he was determined never to give Digby the slightest excuse to criticise him.

The watch on duty knew too how to behave: if they were not required for ceremony it was wise to look busy. In their number Pearce could see Charlie Taverner and Rufus Dommet coiling falls that did not require such attention, and he smiled at them even if they would not see it, they having also been his companions in misfortune on the night he had been pressed. With Michael O'Hagan they made up what he termed the Pelicans and the thought promoted a memory of those now absent: Ben Walker and old Abel Scrivens, the latter dead for certain, Walker almost certainly so.

Looking out over the gangway, he saw Digby sat upright in the thwarts, staring straight ahead in

49

what was such a false but commonplace pose for naval officers. It was not enough to have the rank, one always had to behave like one and never let the men you led observe even a hint of weakness.

'Stuff and nonsense,' Pearce murmured to himself.

'Sir?' asked Edward Grey, his face showing unease. Was something amiss?

'Talking to myself, Mr Grey, and reflecting on follies, which is, I acknowledge, a questionable habit.'

'Common to us all,' the marine replied gaily, for he was by nature a cheerful soul.

The cutter, under the experienced hand of Tilley, the coxswain, swung in a wide arc to fetch the captain alongside the scantlings without so much as a bump, with Digby quick to grab the man ropes and haul himself aboard, greeted by the piercing whistle and the stamp of marine boots. He lifted his scraper to the quarterdeck. Pearce, hat raised also was afforded a cold look of acknowledgement as his captain passed him by.

'My cabin in ten minutes, Mr Pearce.'

This was delivered over his shoulder and with scant pretence at politeness, which got glares from any of the crew who heard it and were foolish enough to react with hard looks aimed at Digby's retreating back.

'Be about your duties,' Pearce barked.

This caused him to recall the words of Michael O'Hagan so recently imparted. If their regard was a thing to savour it was not something he could allow to interfere with his responsibilities. He took out his watch and examined it; when Digby said ten minutes he would mean it to the second, for if Pearce was late it would be his first remark.

To be so constantly on guard for openly stated disapproval was wearing and it was within his rights to ask to be transferred in order to avoid such slights. But he could not take his fellow Pelicans with him. He was sure Digby would block it if only for the sake of malice and he could not countenance such an outcome, they having been through so much together.

'Mr Conway, you have the deck,' he said when the time was up.

He had to stoop to enter the cabin and remain in that pose, so low were the overhead deck beams, which was annoying since it always gave the initiative to the man seated at the desk, as it had to him while, with Digby wounded, he had temporary command. He could see the pocket watch was on the table, the captain glancing at it in a meaningful way before speaking. Pearce was not asked to sit and when Digby spoke, his head was lowered to avoid eye contact.

'We have our orders, Mr Pearce: we are to raise anchor and sail west along the coast beyond Nice.'

'Are the French stirring, sir?'

'It is our task to find out.'

The reverberating sound of cannon fire penetrated the cabin, which had Digby raise his head for a moment and smile. Pearce knew it could not be the sound of battle, but clearly some event had occurred of which he was ignorant, one that would create the grounds for noisy recognition. The fact that Digby had come from San Fiorenzo Bay

51

carrying despatches and had only just returned from Nelson's flagship hinted he might be aware of the reason. It was galling to have to ask.

'They are saluting the new commander-in-chief. I was given the privilege of passing on to Commodore Nelson the news that Sir William has been replaced. We will very shortly, as soon as he arrives, be under the command of Sir John Jervis, Vice Admiral of the White.'

'Hotham?'

'Has decided to retire to Naples, I gather, and leave Hyde Parker in charge.' Pearce wanted to ask why not Sam Goodall, who held superior rank to Parker, but he feared a rebuff. 'So your attempts to bring Sir William down turn to dust. If you had a fox, Pearce, I would say it has been shot.'

'And you did not think to pass it on till now?'

'Your rank does not qualify that I tell you anything.'

'Rank,' Pearce said with some deliberation, for Digby had taken pleasure in that put-down. 'Now there's a word with more than one meaning.'

The inward taking of breath was audible; premiers did not slight captains.

'I believe your place is on deck.'

'Thank you, sir,' was the deeply sarcastic response. 'I will take comfort from the fresh air.'

CHAPTER FOUR

HMS *Flirt* could not come into Vado Bay without attracting attention and that was long before the firing of any signal gun. The sight of topsails in the offing, to a squadron of fighting vessels at anchor, guaranteed scrutiny, peace or war being irrelevant. Any number of people had used their spyglasses to identify her, few mystified regarding her name and class, least of all Passed Midshipman and Acting Lieutenant Toby Burns.

On the deck as the officer of the watch aboard HMS *Brilliant,* his only question was to wonder at who might be aboard. Indeed, he was so taken with his curiosity, it was some time before he realised he had failed in one of his standing duties, which had him growling at a midshipman ten years his senior.

'Please inform the captain that HMS *Flirt* is making her number.'

Several factors initiated the reprimand he later got for his laxity. First was the amount of time between the sighting and the message being passed to Captain Taberly, established by the gap between delivery and the banging of the signal guns. Next was the person sent to relay the information, who could not help – and this was brought on by malevolence – but apologise for being late in its provision.

Tobias Garforth was a fellow in his mid twenties,

53

who for years had failed to rise above the rank of midshipman. This showed in his attire: a badly worn and patched coat, down-at-heel shoes that had long lost both their buckles and their shine; a man who clung zealously to his position to avoid the alternative, which was to be cast ashore to fend for himself in the article of food and a place to lay his head.

Garforth had sat for lieutenant four times and failed to pass on every occasion, unknown to him by a serious margin and, Taberly apart, who knew his father, he lacked the interest to alter his situation, being singularly bereft in both high connections and the kind of flag rank patron who could ease his passage into paid service.

He was thus obliged to acknowledge an incompetent like Toby Burns as a superior, a fellow who had passed the examination, though he was yet to be confirmed by the Admiralty. Never once, his self-esteem being so high, could Garforth accept that he too was not in the first ranks of naval personnel when it came to ability.

He also heartily disliked Burns, a view shared by many members of a crew who knew him of old, so every time he was given an instruction it made his blood boil. Common gossip had it that Burns only got his step in rank through the personal attention given to him by Sir William Hotham and at an age that did not qualify, with many allusions being made to dubious motives.

Added to that, he had a reputation aboard the frigate that flew in the face of the heroic one in which he was shrouded and nothing he had done since coming back on board from HMS *Britannia* had altered that. The frigate HMS *Brilliant* had once been commanded by Ralph Barclay, his uncle by marriage. This was the ship in which he had first put to sea as an eager midshipman something over two years previously, a feeling of enthusiasm that had long since atrophied until a great deal of his being wished for nothing more than to be shot of the navy for good.

On deck, looking through his telescope at a sleek brig preparing to anchor, his heart sank at the sight of John Pearce on the quarterdeck. As he saw him lift his hat to Henry Digby, another old *Brilliant* hand, Burns felt a pang of envy as well. He was looking at a man who seemed to be in possession of all the things to which he aspired but lacked, not least his acknowledged and unquestioned bravery.

The last bell had been rung, which brought up from below the men coming on watch, those they were replacing glad to be off the deck for, at this time of year, the Mediterranean was no benign location wafting warm breezes. Autumn brought on rough seas and frequent gales, while if the wind was in any way northerly it also brought biting winds.

Burns handed over his duty to the next officer to have the deck and went below to the wardroom, with John Pearce at the very forefront of his mind. He had good cause to worry that the man could be his nemesis, all to do with a case for false impressment brought against his late uncle. Any hopes that such a problem would die with Ralph Barclay seemed misplaced, the worry for Burns being the pack of lies he had told at a gimcrack court martial to help get his uncle off the hook.

There were times when he reasoned that his having been coerced would save him, others when he imagined a black cloth on the head of a judge passing sentence on him for the capital crime of perjury. John Pearce had the means to bring that fate down upon him.

'Grim of face as usual,' cried the marine officer, as he entered the wardroom and made for the stove to remove his gloves and warm his hands. 'You're like a bad penny, Burns, to whom good cheer is alien.'

The remark had all those present look up from whatever they were about, to check the veracity of the statement. This had Toby altering his expression from the one caused by gloomy reflection to an insincere smile, but the result was as dispiriting as his mood; heads shook with dejection as they examined the latest addition to their assemblage.

'I should leave the young man alone, McArdle, don't you think? He is yet nervous in our company.'

That support came from the second lieutenant, Thomas Whitlow, who threw a look of sympathy in the direction of Burns, which began to lift his mood; the next words sent it down again for it was only an excuse for a reprimand.

'And I would remind you of the conventions of our naval profession, from which the possession of a red coat and a captain's commission does not excuse you.'

McArdle, who saw himself as jocose and spirited, was a constant offender against the rule that within the wardroom it was essential to be polite, it being an overfull space within which the same men could be cooped up as companions for months or even years. The habitués grew accustomed to each other's foibles, but that did not exclude them causing exasperation, which had to be contained and disguised lest it break into the kind of open disagreement that could create a poisonous atmosphere.

Captain Leyton McArdle was a soldier by trade, red of face and brusque of manner, needing to be constantly reminded of his manners. He hailed from the Irish province of Ulster, was a rabid Protestant supporter of the Plantation and never shy of saying so, not that he was in much danger of offending a papist in these quarters: no one of that denomination could be an officer in any of the services of the British Crown.

'What have I said but the plain truth, Mr Whitlow?'

'I refer again to the concord of the wardroom. Some truths are better kept unspoken.'

The increase in the number of servants indicated it was approaching time for dinner and that required that folk move to allow the tables to be set up. When the time came to be served, Mr Glaister, the premier, came from his quarter cabin and took his place at the head, which was set upon the cover of the tiller, with the light from the casements behind him partially hiding the bony face that had earned him the soubriquet of 'The Skeleton'.

As the most junior, Toby Burns took his seat at the opposite end and tried to partake of the conversation, difficult given his inner turmoil, which led to his being excluded, driving him even deeper into miserable reflection. He had seen John Pearce more than once in the last few months, but he had managed to avoid a meeting, something he dreaded because the last words he had said to him face-to-face were chilling.

This was none other than the promise of a duel as a reward for perceived chicanery, one Burns knew he could never win; indeed, he doubted he could even face the prospect, for death was sure to follow. Not for the first time in his life, as he fought to hold back shaming tears, he cursed a man who had brought him nothing but trouble.

At one time eating aboard HMS *Flirt* had been communal; including Grey there were only three officers, no surgeon, and she even lacked a purser at present, a duty that currently fell to Henry Digby. If never truly animated – the captain was not that way inclined – meals had been tranquil affairs, albeit certain subjects were skated round and it was not just Pearce's relationship with Emily Barclay.

The one topic never raised was how he had come about his rank, it being held that King George had suffered a recurrence of his madness when he insisted that Midshipman Pearce, in showing outstanding courage and resource should, in the face of scant precedence, be promoted to lieutenant without being examined. This was something only those long in years could ever recall happening and that had been once, during the Seven Years' War, to a midshipman of many years' experience who might have passed for lieutenant anyway.

The monarch was not to be dissuaded so it became an act that, when it rippled through the service, caused deep resentment from aspiring midshipmen who saw themselves as more entitled, all the way up through lieutenants and captains to a whole raft of flag officers, both active and those termed 'yellow', which basically meant retired. The navy treasured their professionalism even if it was occasionally flouted; not for them purchase of a commission as it was in the army. If some folk got a step through their connections that was tolerable. It was not that any man should get it on a royal whim!

There was no reason to dwell on that or any other of his manifest problems as Pearce ate in solitude. Digby had invited Edward Grey to join him in his quarters, that being his prerogative, which was very obviously another public snub. Much more important were the reflections on an uncertain future, for the one mapped out to him by Emily Barclay did not appeal in the slightest, while satisfactory alternatives seemed in short supply.

Why could she not see the lack of attraction, to him, of a respectable life in a country town? John Pearce had enjoyed what could be termed a colourful childhood. He had also lived long enough in post-Revolutionary Paris to be a man who appreciated metropolitan life, albeit he knew himself to be endemically restless, no doubt a result of his upbringing with a father who was peripatetic and a dangerous radical to the men who ran Britain.

Adam Pearce, a one-time alumni of the University of Edinburgh, had formed in his youth and had gone on as an adult to promulgate views that in many ways mirrored those espoused by the leading lights of the French Revolution: universal suffrage, equality of the sexes, an end to monarchy and the depredations of the rich visited upon the poor. Unwelcome at home it had turned out to be equally so with the hypocrites of Paris.

Obliged with his son to flee to France in order to avoid a writ for seditious libel, a typical piece of judicial trickery from the government of William Pitt, Adam had found the ideals that had prompted the Revolution were being abused by those who had taken power in a way that caused him to speak out against their lack of virtue.

Such open outbursts had not gone down well. From being feted on arrival as a fellow thinker, the likes of Robespierre and his cohorts on the Committee of Public Safety had hauled Adam before a Revolutionary Tribunal, a court in which only one verdict was ever passed: guilty. To get the writ in Britain lifted so his father could return home from his Parisian incarceration brought John Pearce to the banks of the River Thames and the Pelican Tavern, and so subsequently to where he now sat.

In whirling, unsettled thoughts, he was soon mentally having the argument with Emily he had never in fact engaged in, partly he knew from fear of driving her into a position from which she would not withdraw. If he could be stubborn he knew her to be cut from an equally uncompromising mould. If she had been otherwise, how could she have defied her husband in the first place?

60

Pearce had no doubt Ralph Barclay regretted the day he ever thought to take his young and beautiful wife to sea. Emily had explained it as a desire to reduce domestic outgoings – after five years on the beach, Barclay was beset by too many creditors to leave a bride half his age alone and tempted in their hometown of Frome. Who knew what she might get up to? What bills might she run up? He thought he had wed a mouse; instead he got a tartar.

Her first rebellion had been aboard HMS *Brilliant* against the article of flogging, of which she strongly disapproved, this made obvious to a husband who saw it as essential to the proper running of a ship of war. It was also the case that she did not understand her husband expected her to respect his position as a post captain without question, which prior to their nuptials had been to him the sole reason for his existence, he having worked for twenty-five years to get there.

The difference in age had counted as well, Barclay doubling hers, added to which he had come to manhood in the rough element of a midshipman's berth and up until his captaincy his experience of women had been bought and paid for. Emily knew only gentle if not overly well-endowed respectability in a parochial backwater. It was that to which she wished to return, taking John Pearce along, and the prospect made him recoil. He could imagine nothing worse than a sort of squire-like existence, mixing with folk who could barely see beyond their own town limits and, very often, hardly over the borders of the county in which they lived.

There would be local magnates, large and probably titled landowners, expecting deference if not outright subservience and he knew he could not abide such a life. There would too be a town full of petty prejudices, bigotry and gossip, hemmed in by endless provincial conventions. Whatever codes of behaviour existed, John Pearce would break them, for that was both in his nature and part of his inheritance.

Then there was his child, within a few months of being born and one he would be denied full access to until all the bonds of that kind of society had been met.

'I may love you,' he said quietly to himself, 'but sometimes I do feel the need to damn you.'

Emily Barclay felt the blow and smiled, it being the sign of a healthy confinement, a child with the spirit to kick out strongly in her womb. Free now from tight garments, she had risen, breakfasted and dressed in a gown of loose cotton, before going back to the chest of papers that had belonged to her husband in an effort to make sense of them. Never having had to oversee even domestic accounts, she was somewhat at a loss and aware of her ignorance, with no real way of seeing how to alter it.

'John would deal with this,' she said quietly to herself, words followed by a hand on her stomach and a whispered, 'Your dear Papa.'

It was said quietly even though, here in her small set of rented apartments, it would not be overheard and certainly not by anyone who spoke English. Caution ruled, for the true paternity must never be spoken of openly, regardless of how much she would have loved to acknowledge the man she had given her heart to as the father. For the sake of the coming child that could not be. How could she bring an infant into the world branded from birth with the taint of her adultery?

As she opened the folded pieces of parchment, listing investments, Emily sought to calculate how long it would be before she might receive a reply from London and Messrs Ommaney and Druce, her late husband's prize agents. It was they who had handled his money and fought any disputed claims regarding prizes. The account book which had come with these papers indicated she was rich by her standards, but it seemed to her opaque as to their true value and she wished for clarification.

There were funds in three per cent government consols and that was both sound and to the good, but there also seemed to be many investments in such things as canals. She had sought, on first realising this, to recall her father's conversations on such matters, sure he had named them as highly speculative, which could not be a proper use of funds, except in a limited manner.

That said, it seemed there was enough to provide that she, Pearce and their child, and in time children, could live in decent comfort, albeit the proprieties had to be observed. Certainly she was well set now; the same chest had yielded a large amount of coin, while the Leghorn pay office had provided more as that due to Captain Barclay up until the day he died.

The papers put away and the chest locked, Emily prepared to go out to take the air, donning a thick cloak to ward off the chill and carrying a parasol to ensure that not even a wintery sun should bring blemish to her delicate complexion. Her routine was a walk along one of the many canals that bisected the city, which avoided the busy harbour quay as well as any ribald comments from the labourers working there. They might speak in their own tongue, but gestures left no doubt as to their hopes, in sight of a comely woman yet to be burdened by a too obvious belly.

Her walk completed she would repair to the Naval Commissariat to see if any post had come in on the packet from Portsmouth, before going to the cemetery to lay some flowers at the bronze plaque raised in memory of Captain Ralph Barclay RN. If she had come to hate him in life, and had done everything in her power to avoid his company, her Christian duty required that she pray for him in death. It was also the case that it did no harm to be seen to be doing so.

There was a part of the environs of Livorno into which no one of respectable demeanour ever went: the section of the port occupied by privateers, many of them British. The men who manned these letters of marque were mainly ruffians, close to pirates in the minds of the Royal Navy, even if their captains often carried themselves with pretentions towards decency.

It was a close call that had her nearly bump into Cornelius Gherson, her late husband's clerk, a man she despised even more than her spouse. He was on his way to the privateer's harbour, which they shared with the local fishing fleet, and it was only the sight of her parasol that drew his eye enough for him to recognise her. He was swift to dart into a doorway in which she could pass without him being spotted, but he could watch her pass, albeit briefly, enough to stir in his breast the hankering he had always harboured when in her presence. Emily Barclay was a rare beauty and one he would have dearly loved to bed.

What also surfaced was the number of times he had been rebuffed in his overtures, a far less comfortable feeling and, to a man of his over-weening vanity, a recollection that seriously rankled. He had been unaware that she was in Leghorn, but he was quick to surmise if she was out alone then she would be living in that estate. Such a conclusion began to revive a thought long buried: at one time he had contrived to have enough time alone with the bitch to teach her a lesson, to show her that he was man enough to make her scream with pain, before he would turn that to pleading pleasure.

Where was she staying? Was that swine Pearce with her? Could he find out and perhaps...? Gherson had to stop himself then, he had more pressing fish to fry. Having failed to find another captain to take him on as a clerk – they were a breed that tended to outlive fighting sailors – he needed to contrive some way to make a living. Never having been a stranger to illicit methods, he was on his way to mix with the kind of people he saw as being more of his ilk.

Privateers had one purpose and that was to make money, often illegally taking neutral vessels and sinking them once they had transferred the cargo instead of doing what their letters of marque said, helping to spoil the French ability to trade. Sometimes they put the crew ashore at a place from which it would take the poor creatures years to get home. On other occasions it was seen as more pressing to just kill them and let their remains go down with their vessel.

Gherson had survived in life through a winning way, no scruples and good looks. Some said he possessed a near feminine beauty, to others he presented the soul of corruption, but he was clever, if low cunning could be termed that. Surely, added to a head for figures, there must be opportunities in such a band of ne'er-do-wells. The means to exist was what was needed now; Emily Barclay could wait.

CHAPTER FIVE

Vado Bay was not an anchorage secure from hazard; indeed, Horatio Nelson had named it as basically too shallow in its arc to be of any use at all, given it would provide scant protection against serious storms. Yet it was the closest to the French forward positions and as such, assuming they employed spies, would underline that the squadron would be acting as support for the coalition armies. This might just give the forces of the Revolution pause, given the route by which they must march into Liguria often ran right along an easily bombarded seashore.

The French still had a fleet in Toulon, which

also meant the squadron was under threat from warships, even if they were under blockade, for if the wind favoured them they could get to sea despite the presence of their enemies. Thus the routine of the morning was as it would have been at sea: everyone on deck, officers especially, guns loaded and run out, with Henry Digby looking to the western arm of the bay, the area from which the enemy would approach, a duty being enacted on every other deck, until each captain could see, 'A grey goose at a quarter-mile'.

The order to 'carry on Mr Pearce' was curt.

For HMS *Flirt* it was more than worming and housing the cannon, sanding, swabbing and flogging dry the decks and getting the men to breakfast. Prior to anything being done the brig had to be put to sea. John Pearce thought it a bit of Digby nonsense: they had been required to go through a rigmarole just so as to be seen doing so by the commodore. They could just as easily have plucked their anchor well before dawn.

Sails raised, they passed slowly along the line of frigates, with Pearce denied raised hats from his contemporaries, who knew who would have the deck at such a time, and disdain lasted until they came abreast of HMS *Agamemnon*. From there the reaction was different, with Lieutenant Dick Farmiloe raising a speaking trumpet to wish them 'Godspeed' as a body, with a special personal greeting and hearty wave for the premier himself.

'What in the name of all that is holy is going on, Mr Pearce?'

'Exchanging pleasantries, sir, with our old shipmate, Mr Farmiloe.'

He had answered over his shoulder, which was openly disrespectful and would be taken as such. If Pearce knew every eye was fixed on the tiny quarterdeck, he paid it no heed, keeping his gaze steady on the ship-of-the-line.

'Then I require you to desist, and if I had any authority over Farmiloe I would tell him the same.'

That did make Pearce turn, the expression on his face, a sort of knowing half-smile, one that could be construed as mockery. 'Then I daresay, Mr Digby, he is mightily relieved to have to answer only to a mere commodore.'

That left a man, hatless and coatless and with a napkin at his neck, searching for a response that would preserve his dignity; the turmoil of finding the means and the right words evident on his face. Pearce's reply had carried enough to be overheard by half the men on deck and it was telling that once more all movement had ceased. They were in anticipation of an explosion; all they got was a barely audible hiss.

'I have authority over you, sir, and by God I will see it exercised.'

As Digby disappeared, Pearce began to softly sing a low rendition of 'My Dear Peg' and that had the crew begin to laugh, to which he was required to put a stop. Digby's action in publicly checking him for something of which he should have no concern had been too much to bear. From now on he was determined to challenge the man, while at the same time wondering what had happened to the fellow he had known and had been on good terms with previously. A bit too upright certainly, but not as he was now.

On their first voyage together, Digby had noted his lack of knowledge in the article of seamanship and set out to correct it, teaching Pearce a great deal, including in his instruction the very same Dick Farmiloe, then a midshipman, which had helped make Pearce feel he was not in receipt of special treatment. There had been disputes on their second voyage, that was true, all centred on his relationship with Emily Barclay and the way he seemed prepared to bend every rule of the service to get his own way.

Such exasperation that Digby suffered had surely died before and during the action in the Gulf of Ambracia. The mood after that event was to bring to mind a completely different person – one grateful as well as seemingly humble – only to see that dramatically altered when he rejoined the fleet in San Fiorenzo Bay by the withdrawal of his promise to help bring to book Pearce's enemies.

Cruel words had been spoken certainly, regarding honesty and integrity; of a man putting his own perceived needs against those of his conscience. Was Digby, with his strong Christian faith, so suffused with guilt that he could alter so much and become like some form of martinet? Or was it, and this was more troubling, that he believed in the righteousness of his choice?

'Do I not have your breakfast set out, your honour, an' getting stone cold it is?'

Pearce smiled both at the form of address and the way. Michael made his non-attendance in his cabin sound like a rebuke. 'I shall be with you presently.'

'Soon would be better than presently, your honour. We are not basking in a supply of fresh food.'

'Mr Conway, you have had your breakfast?'

'I have, sir.'

'Then I give you the deck.'

'You lookin' to pick a fight, John-boy?'

These words came from O'Hagan as soon as Pearce was seated and his breakfast of eggs and bread, still fresh from the market of Leghorn, uncovered, which showed why Michael had come to fetch him, the yolks being close to congealed.

'I doubt I have a choice.'

'I can get you more cooked, we have it still.'

Pearce shook his head and cut into the near-cold egg. 'It's a fitting repast for someone so insubordinate.'

'Now you know I am no friend to bein' bossed about–'

That elicited a grin. 'As you remind me every day.'

'Our captain has it in for you, sure. I'm wondering in the name of Jesus why you put up with it.'

Jesus always got a sign of the cross on O'Hagan's breast and it did so now, along with a look in anticipation of a reply. Did Michael guess that he was part of the reason to decline, along with Charlie and Rufus? Would he believe the other partial truth, an avoidance of Leghorn and having to behave as though he and Emily were not lovers or even connected to each other in any way? Pearce was not certain himself, but one thing he did know: he would not succumb to Digby, regardless of what motivated his malice.

70

'There will be no more putting up with it, Michael.'

'Then I might as well pass it on, that what is bad now is about to get a mite worse.'

'Tell the crew not to take sides, Michael. Myself I can look to, but I would scarce now put it past Digby to resort to the cat if he saw mass dissent.'

'The man has changed that much?'

'Who knows? I'm damn sure I don't. Now oblige by seeing if you can get me some hot coffee.'

There was no sign of military activity once they passed the defence lines of both the coalition forces and the Army of Italy, not much more than the smoke from fires in those two entrenched locations. If it was war it had been put into abeyance, perhaps by the approach of winter, exhaustion or disinclination, and this had Pearce wondering at the nature of what they were about. Did Digby, unwilling to pass on information to him, have some mission to perform? He could not imagine Nelson, a man wedded to action, sending the brig on a cruise to no purpose.

The shore, under a heavy sky threatening rain, was far from alluring. Where the rocky shore did come down to the sea it was high hills with cultivated terraces, opening enough to show little sandy bays, each with ramshackle dwellings on the high-tide mark as well as fishing boats pulled up onto the strand. They passed many of the same kind out at sea: small craft never manned by more than three bodies, some of which made a point of avoidance, others coming close to shout and wave, eager to sell their catch to folk who would pay much more than their fellow countrymen.

Occasionally, Digby would come on deck to examine the shoreline and the hills, ordering more sea room when they passed the ancient coastal fort of Monte Carlo, tucked into and overlooking yet another mountain-backed bay. It flew a tricolour, evidence that the Grimaldi principality was now in French hands. A useless cannon boomed out from the ramparts to underline the possession, dropping a ball into the sea well short of the ship.

'I require our colours to be struck, Mr Conway,' Digby ordered. 'You will find a tricolour in the flag locker. Please be so good as to raise it, which will save these peasants from wasting powder and shot.'

The latter part of that sentence would normally have been taken as a jest, producing some kind of humoured reaction. Nothing came, which had Digby bark at his premier as he made his way back to his cabin.

'Call me when we weather Cape Ferrato, Mr Pearce.'

Which he did, not long after the crew had eaten their dinner, to be immediately ordered out to sea. This time Digby stayed on deck, relieving Pearce, who could go below to a broiled chicken shared with the marine officer. When he came back on deck he noticed Digby close by Mr Dorling, the young ship's master, with much concentration aimed at the slate on which their course and speed was recorded.

This held until daylight began to go, at which

point HMS *Flirt* was put once more on a course level with the shore, and Pearce and Edward Grey were called into the tiny cabin to join the captain. Digby, seated, ran a finger along a map of the shoreline, the digit followed by the two officers left to stand on opposite sides of the desk.

'I have orders to reconnoitre the shore between Monte Boroni and the Cape Ferrato peninsula.'

'To what purpose, sir?' asked Grey.

'The road to their forward lines runs along the coast at the head of the bay and the commodore thinks it might be vulnerable to attack at a point they would not expect us to even consider, it being so close to the main base of operations.'

Having been looking at the charts all day and knowing their destination, Pearce had a very good mental image of what Digby was talking about. He also knew that if it meant going ashore, this was not a duty that fell to a ship's commander but to his inferior officers. On HMS *Flirt*, Ivor Conway, being so young, that was him, with Grey and his marines as support to the chosen members of the crew.

'I take it you will stand off and we will be going in by boats, sir.'

'Why would we do that?' was the brusque reply.

'On the grounds that the French may have defences, if not on both sides of the bay, then certainly on the heights of Monte Boroni.'

'We have no knowledge of that.'

'If they have, sir, the entrance to the bay is no more than a quarter of a mile land to land. It does not require heavy ordnance to defend it – field guns have the range, and those I seem to recall as

73

an article that the French have in quantity as well as good men to ply them.'

'While we may catch them napping. What information we have points to a rabble, not an army in the proper sense.'

'How good is that intelligence, sir?'

'As good as our Austrian allies can make it,' came the terse reply.

'Monte Boroni is a perfect spot to mount defensive cannon.'

'Which is what we are here to find out. Of course, if the duty seems to you too arduous, or should I say dangerous, Mr Pearce, you are always at liberty to decline it.'

Digby had a smile on his face when he said that, but it was not one of affability; the smirk spoke instead of a test and it took Pearce a little time to fathom a reason. He was being challenged, he knew that, and in front of a witness. If he declined the task, Digby could have him removed, with an accusation of being shy providing the reason. Under that cloud, Pearce would struggle to get a court martial in which he could air the things he would want said.

'I see you have spent a fruitful afternoon in contemplation, sir.'

'It could be said I have been thinking of the good of the service.'

About to put out a rude reply, Pearce remembered Grey was present, not hard given his proximity. It would not serve to involve him in what was about to turn into a quarrel.

'So you intend to take HMS *Flirt* into the bay?'

'I do, and with those on board who will be

obliged to accept my authority. You spoke of boats, Mr Pearce, I am happy to provide you with one, if you so desire, in which you can stand off and observe from a place of safety.'

'I seem to recall, sir, that when last called into action you were the man in need of a place of safety and that was to protect you from your own folly.'

'Oblige me by departing the cabin, Mr Pearce. Lieutenant Grey and I have matters to discuss, but I will require that you put your disinclination to follow my orders in writing.'

'What I will put in writing, sir, is my suggestion that it would be safer to reconnoitre the shore using the ship's boats and add that it is an expedition I am willing to lead. I will also note that to expose the ship in a place of which we have no knowledge of the state of the defences is folly. I will now go and put quill to paper, while asking Mr Dorling to append his name as witness.'

Which was as good as saying, 'It will be you facing a court martial, matey, not me.' And Dorling, being the master and appointed by the Navy Board, was in a very strong sense outside the terms of Digby's authority, enough that he could not be intimidated.

'Mr Grey?'

Digby had fixed the marine with a determined look and the nature of the question did not need to be explained; he was being required to provide an opinion. Grey was young, brave and it could be said after the way he had behaved in the Gulf of Ambracia, capable of being foolhardy, he having stretched his orders somewhat. But Digby was putting him in an intolerable position, virtually demanding his support with the implied consequence of refusal. It was a look-to-your-career moment.

'Sir, I do not wish to question your judgement—'

'But you reckon boats a better way to carry out the task?'

'I do, sir. I cannot see the sense in risking the ship.'

Digby did a complete volte-face then, though he allowed himself a short period of contemplation before acceding to what Grey had said. This had Pearce marking him as a damn sight more devious than he had hitherto thought possible. Digby had never intended taking HMS *Flirt* into a bay where, if the enemy had placed a set of batteries, she could be reduced to matchwood. It had just been a ploy to pin his premier with the stain of cowardice and in his own written hand. He fully expected him now to abandon the whole enterprise. He was wrong.

'Very well, boats it will be,' Digby said. 'I take it, Mr Grey, you will not object to serving under Mr Pearce?'

The 'Of course not, sir' was too enthusiastic for Digby and made him frown. When he spoke to Pearce it was with his eyes firmly lowered to avoid contact.

'Then he will lead and choose which hands to take with him. That will be all, gentlemen, given you have only two bells, by my calculation, to prepare.'

Outside, Grey pulled at John Pearce's sleeve and spoke in an agitated whisper. 'What in the name of creation is going on with you and Digby? We have had too much of this.'

The marine was taken further along the deck to a place where Pearce could speak normally, having to avoid as they did so the men on deck putting the ship on a reverse course.

'That is a question you should pose to him, Edward, not me.'

'I reckon to have done myself enough damage for one day in the cabin by questioning his intentions.'

'I must ask you why you did not demur.'

'John, what he was proposing was folly and I knew that as well as you.'

'He knew it to be folly, also.'

'What are you saying?'

'Nothing that would make sense, Edward. But I thank you for your support.'

'I did not support you, John, but myself and my experience. When it comes to action, I can do no other than side with both common sense and proven ability. I recall the risk Digby took in the Adriatic. In his cabin, I wondered if he still carried his damned death wish.'

Pearce laughed softly. 'Be assured that it is gone or he would now be sharpening his sword. He wishes to live long enough to raise an admiral's flag and that dream is what animates him. Now, let us get together those we're taking ashore, for we have, as our captain said, little time.'

CHAPTER SIX

The town of Nice, recently taken from the Duchy of Savoy and known to be where the French commanders were quartered, was visible due to the number of cooking fires lining the beach, no doubt those of soldiers who had camped on the long strand of pebbles, which formed one of the major open indentations along this shore. A proper harbour had recently been constructed at its eastern end, but that being in darkness, these flickering flames formed just about the only point of reference by which they could enter the deep bight of Villafranca, which lay just to the east.

Pearce thought it somewhat like the action off Genoa: a cloudy sky, only occasionally clearing, cutting out much of the star or moonlight and, as soon as the boat passed beyond the western outcrop enclosing the eastern quay of Nice harbour, little to steer by, bar a few pinpoints of lit lamps. Some of those were night-fishing boats, which, raised on the stern and having the virtue of a constantly bobbing movement, could be identified and avoided.

The illuminations used as a guide were those on the ramparts of the fortress of Monte Albano, which overlooked the town of Villafranca – faint certainly, hung braziers elevated enough to act as a distant beacon, their purpose to light the glacis below the walls and protect against a surprise assault. There was the occasional breakout overhead as the cloud thinned enough to allow a modicum of penetration, but only very rarely did that extend to a full clearance.

The ship was out to sea and now invisible, lanterns extinguished – again a replica of Genoa – and the only thing by which the main body of sailors, ahead in the cutter, could normally fix the pinnace carrying Grey and his marines, was by the small flashes of white water created by the slowly dipping oars. Pearce had to assume the same applied in reverse but he could not see for himself, he having taken up station in the prow. Ivor Conway, having near begged on his knees to be permitted to come along, had the tiller and was set to respond to any whispered order sent back.

Despite Digby's instructions regarding the road to Italy, which did indeed run along the shore at the head of the bay, the man on the spot had a different aim than just landing and fixing whether it was possible to cut that route of supply, not easy given the presence of that formidable fortress, as well as other bastions in the hills to the north. Much was known about this bight; some fifty years previously a British fleet had fought an action in support of a Sardinian army contesting possession of Villafranca with the French, who had landed but been driven off.

The main defences might be nearer the head of the bight, but nothing could enter these waters if they faced fire from shore-based cannon at the narrows. Ships' boats could be splintered and sunk by small ordnance, while not even a ship-of-the-line would be safe from serious damage given the lack of room to manoeuvre. That said, once through into the wider bay, in generally calm and deep waters, capital ships could trade fire with fortress- and land-based cannon on relatively equal terms.

The bight had for centuries been a safe and much-used fleet anchorage and trade hub, the construction of Nice harbour reducing its importance. Yet no great intelligence was required to see that Villafranca and the surrounding land, held for even a brief period and blocking supply, would place the Army of Italy, already struggling for regular supplies, *in extremis*, the possibility of which was no doubt what Digby had been sent to establish.

'Two flashes on the lantern, Michael.'

O'Hagan obliged as the message, the shutter opening twice, was passed back to Conway, the previously issued command being to use both oars and tiller to turn, he hoped, due west, a call over the stern made to ensure Grey and his marines did not just row on. Quite apart from the uncertainty brought on by darkness, Pearce, who was acting from memory, seeking to make a landfall to the north of an outcrop, called on the maps of la Ponti di Madonna.

A slight break in the overhead cover allowed him to see the wavelets breaking on the shore, these having first been audible as a hiss running over soft sand. There would be people living on such a shore, the same as those dwellings he had seen as they had sailed along from Vado Bay: peasant folk who existed by fishing, but not, he thought, fighters and besides, many would be out seeking to fill their nets. If those who were not heard anything, he hoped they were of the kind to stay within their slender walls.

As the keel eased into the sand, the oars were raised then put aside as men eased themselves into the water to drag the cutter up the beach. It was not necessary to go far, for in the Mediterranean, with its lack of a serious surge, the difference between high and low tide was small, while the coast hereabouts shelved sharply.

It was all muted calls and hands on shoulders to get the thirty-strong party up the beach to a place where Pearce reckoned it safe to unshade the lantern and ensure everyone was present and accounted for. Other lanterns were produced to be ignited from the one Michael held, before they too were shaded, to only be used sparingly, when absolutely necessary, to make movement possible.

'Mr Grey, as already stated, I require you to hold the beach with your Lobsters. Should we be in trouble we will be forced to run, and those boats may well be our only hope of survival.'

'Sir.'

Pearce looked for displeasure in that response yet if it was there it was something he failed to detect. He had decided before setting out not to arm his sailors with muskets, first of all due to a lack of familiarity, added to the fact that they were useless in what he anticipated unless loaded and primed. With that, in darkness and stumbling, came the very strong risk of one going off in the hands of whoever was carrying them, so cutlasses, knives and clubs would serve. The marines would have their muskets but be static, ready to slow down anyone in pursuit should Pearce and his party be forced to flee. If it was not seen as glorious, it was nevertheless reckoned wise.

Then it was anxious eyes on the sky, waiting for either a break in the clouds or that thinning previously experienced, which would allow them to find the path that led off the beach – there had to be one for the locals to use – to hopefully then come across those that traversed the lower reaches of Monte Boroni. It happened eventually, not that progress was either easy or quick.

The side of the hill was covered in thick scrub on which it was too easy to become snagged, given the narrowness of the tracks. If unshading lanterns for short periods was a risk, it was one that had to be taken often as they progressed first up a steep slope, before finding another path heading towards the promontory. They were on that for half a glass of sand, Pearce reckoned, before anyone spoke.

'Smoke, John-boy, can you smell it?'

He had not, but by sniffing the slight onshore wind Pearce eventually picked it up, not that it told him much. This was a part of the world where the locals liked to be warm and they were most of the year. To such people what he and his men thought of as temperate might feel like chill, so it could be no more than the fire in a peasant hut, there being no sign of the source. Just then the cloud cover thickened, which forced them to halt and wait, the men told to rest where they could.

'We'll be in a fine pickle if John Crapaud discovers us stuck out here bare-arsed.'

This was whispered by Charlie Taverner, never one to hold back on an opinion, a voice John Pearce knew of old. The quiet reply was familiar too, being from Rufus Dommet.

'They'll run if they smell your stink, Charlie. Who needs muskets when a fart from you will serve?'

'Belay that talking,' croaked Conway.

'Beggin' your indulgence, sir.' That came from Rufus, and if it flew in the face of the instruction, it was enough to satisfy the midshipman.

John Pearce was looking across the narrows, to where a few twinkling spots of domestic light were visible, thinking the whole notion of coming ashore in such small numbers hare-brained. Come to that, a full assault by large forces was not much of an improvement, given who would be tasked to carry it out.

In any wardroom conversations in which he had participated, and there had not been that many in which he was ever a full participant, the general opinion was straightforward. The best way to deal with the Army of Italy was a full-out assault on their defences, albeit the King's Navy would have it carried out not by the forces presently engaged but by a few regiments of British Foot Guards.

The waters beneath him began to shimmer slightly, Pearce able to see the break in the coming cloud cover long before it reached his stationary party. He called out to be ready to move, wondering how much the noise of them getting to their feet, their hissed exchanges and jocose insults would carry. His heart came near to stopping when he heard a loud scream, that was until he realised it was not to his rear, but from up ahead.

'Still, everyone,' he shushed, before calling out to Conway, who came close, Pearce bending to talk in his ear, only to be faced first with a fearful question.

'What in the name of the devil was that, sir? It sounded like some fiend.'

Saying he had no idea was the simple bit; wondering whether to respond to the palpable tremble in the youngster's voice, even when he was speaking so softly, was more of a problem. Being out on a night such as this, engaged in something clandestine and dangerous, was affecting him, so how much more was it playing on the mid? He had been eager enough at the prospect of action. By the sound of it, the reality he was finding terrifying, which would not serve.

'Steady yourself, Mr Conway, it was not some banshee, but a human.'

'But–'

'And flesh and blood we can deal with!'

'Sir.'

If the tone was yet unsteady, it had to serve; there was no time to include Conway's nocturnal terrors in his calculations. One single call was all Pearce had to go on and the direction was far from fixed. There was something up ahead and it was yet to be established what and who that was.

'I require you to stay here and take command of those I leave with you.'

'Command, sir?'

The tone of Pearce's voice hardened; if he had sympathy he required composure. 'It is what you joined the service to do, Mr Conway. If you wish to be an officer, you must carry yourself as one.'

'I will do my duty, sir,' came a soft croak.

'Which is all that can be asked of you. I am going forward to see what I can find, though it could be damned little in what light we have even now. If I encounter trouble, it will be up to you to judge whether to come to my assistance or make an immediate return to the boats.'

A sharp intake of breath.

'Neither are either pleasant or easy choices, but you will find that most fighting is done in a fog of ignorance, wherever you are. To act as you think right will make those who love you proud and the men you lead safe.'

'I would very much wish to make you proud, sir.'

'Mr Conway, you did that by your eagerness to accompany me.'

Pearce moved away slightly, determined to call to his Pelicans to join with him. He knew the rest of the party well, men who had sailed with him all the way from Buckler's Hard the previous year, yet there were none as familiar to him as that trio. He reckoned what he might need was Michael's strength, Charlie's sharp wits and as for Rufus, well, he had grown from a freckled, diffident youth into a fiery ginger battler.

'Mr Conway, one last instruction. Whatever happens, the need for subterfuge will likely have gone. If retiring, make good use of the lanterns to speed your progress.' Pearce tried to convey humour as he added, 'There's not a demon born that takes to a lit candle. O'Hagan, Taverner, Dommet, to me.'

That he had a special relationship with the trio

was no secret aboard HMS *Flirt*, certainly not to those he had selected to accompany him, who were all good fighters. Would the others see it as favouritism? He reckoned not, on reflection; half of them would have jitters for the same reason as Conway, having not anticipated what they now faced.

The break in the cloud cover came over them and if it was not daylight, it was possible to move without difficulty. Pearce did so quickly, for already that sea shimmer was gone, returning the bay to its inky blackness, meaning the overhead light would soon go for him, also. That said, movement still had to be as silent.

The sparks shooting into the sky just ahead brought them to an abrupt halt, and within the spill there was billowing smoke. The effect did not last long, added to which the light above evaporated at the same time, leaving Pearce and his companions stood stock-still in a situation where the use of a lantern would be unwise. That brief spray of rising orange cinders had been close by.

'I would say,' whispered Michael, as the now strong smell of smoke wafted past them, 'that was some soul throwing a log on a fire.'

In retrospect, John Pearce wondered at the conclusions he drew and the speed at which he did so, yet they came to him naturally at this point. A fire indicated a piquet of some kind; one man or several? If the latter, what was being guarded? It could only be because there was something to defend. They had a fire but there was no reflection of it on the overhead canopy, which meant no trees, which suggested a clearing. Given the depth of woodland he had observed along the coast, such a clearing might be man-made. If so, for what purpose? A quiet explanation was necessary prior to instructions.

'Rufus, back down the track and ask Mr Conway to bring up the rest of the men. Charlie, you hold here till they come and tell him what we suspect. Michael, we must be on our bellies and going forward.'

'Sure, there are times I wish I was back in Ireland.'

'Whatever makes you say that now?' Pearce hissed.

'Blessed St Patrick got rid of the snakes, did he not, and I doubt this land has had his like.'

Pearce wanted to laugh, even if what Michael was saying had truth in it. The temptation had to be suppressed. He tapped the broad shoulder and got himself down on hands and knees and began to move. It needed fingers held out to feel their way, a touch on the bushes either side making progress painfully slow, sore on elbows and knees. The sound of a loud snore brought a halt, then a touch more progress showed the path ahead opening up, but only by the faintest light, and that unsteady coming from flames, which had Pearce drawing Michael to him.

'A fire, right enough.'

'Numbers, John-boy?'

'If they are many, we must rely on surprise.'

'Holy Mary, Mother of God, preserve us.'

That was not fear but a sure sign the Irishman was crossing himself again. This was no time for Pearce to make a comment, which he frequently did, on the excess of superstition. Instead, he whispered that Michael should stay still and crawled forward a few paces more, though being on an upslope this did not afford him much other than his assumption of a clearing was correct, judging by the distance to the treetops, the upper branches of which he could now see.

He tried to visualise how to attack while being determined he must do so. There seemed to be before him too good an opportunity to miss. Even if all he did was cause panicked flight, it would resound through the French forces that it was not safe to sleep at night. With command of the sea their enemies could strike where and when they pleased. There was another side to that, of course: what he had in mind could be reversed; perhaps it would be he and his men stumbling down a winding trail, trying to get back to those boats with Grey's marines aiming to shoot above their heads.

Time seemed to stand still, the only thing to break it another shower of sparks as what he assumed to be another log thrown onto a fire. The same one or another, for the more fires the more bodies and it would not be necessarily for heat, but more for the need to cook in the morning without having to ignite a fresh blaze.

The sound of scrabbling was faint but with every nerve stretched taut it was audible. Soon Michael was by his side to whisper that the men of the raiding party were close by and ready. Pearce thought it unwise to have them crawl up to him, it would be difficult to do that in utter silence. Better to pick a spot from which to rush into action, so he tapped O'Hagan and began to crawl back until he felt safe enough to get up and walk.

'Gather round, you all. Form a circle so we can use a lantern.'

There was much shuffling but eventually Pearce gave the instruction to illuminate the gathering, the light shining upwards making his party look more like ghouls than tars. Soft words were employed to tell them what he thought they faced and how they were going to go about it, pleasing that none, not even young Conway, hinted at hesitation.

'We will move forward as silently as we can but it must be swift, for our best weapon is shock. I have not been able to see, but I reckon the men ahead of us to be asleep, with perhaps one or two on guard and they are staying close to their embers. Also, I say this, we have no time or numbers for quarter. You have your weapons, use them well.'

'Ready when you are, sir,' croaked Conway, his breaking voice rendering the words unconvincing.

'We need a bit of light, Mr Conway. We move as soon as we have it.' Looking out to sea, there were patches where the moon had broken through to create a circle of silver but nothing seeming to come their way. 'We must wait, and those of you who have brought with you the means to drink, do so now.'

CHAPTER SEVEN

The amount of time it took for any kind of decent break in the cloud cover had Pearce wondering if the fates were against him. He required enough to both get back to the boats, as well as make a show of reconnoitring the head of the bay, in pursuit of Digby's orders. Was there a time when he would have to abandon his own plan in favour of what were clearly instructions from on high? Given the notion went against everything he held to be sound, it was not one that held for long.

His party was getting restless and beginning to talk too much, which, soft as it was, became a collective noise he was required to terminate. He could only imagine the feeling of the marines on the beach, who, through ignorance, must be chaffing even more at what might be happening ahead of them. He did contemplate sending Conway back with a message, then reasoned it would not be a good idea to send him off on his own; he might get lost, and to give him a couple of hands as escorts would diminish his own force in the coming assault.

The hand that shook his shoulder was followed by an insistent whisper. 'Wake up John-boy, my prayers have been answered.'

'I fell asleep?' was the blinking response.

'Sure you did, and would have snored had I not

pinched your nose. But look to the sky. We have a bit of light on the way.'

'Brought on by divine intervention, I suppose?'

O'Hagan paid no heed to the rasp of disbelief; his certainties were so strong he was ever able to ignore, or was it able to forgive, the doubts of his friend. Nor would he have cared that the man espousing them was more angry with himself for his inability to stay awake than bothered about celestial help. The excuse he could have used, of being overtired by the need to lead and think for all, would not wash.

If the break was visible, it did not come scudding towards them; throughout the night, the cloud canopy had moved even slower than the wind on their faces would indicate. But it did give Pearce time to re-examine what he was about, to check with himself that what he planned was sound, it being only sensible to entertain doubts. A quick question to Michael was enough to establish that nothing had come from up ahead to change the opinion that they would achieve surprise, so he called for another huddle.

'No waving of blades until we are upon them. That approaching light might be enough to flash off the metal and alert anyone set to guard.'

'Will there be one, sir?' asked Conway.

'Most assuredly, for there will be someone with rank in charge. For his own security, if not for that of his post, he will have detailed at least one sentinel, if not more. But it is to be hoped such people will struggle to keep their eyes open.'

'Hard it is too,' O'Hagan opined and there was enough lantern light to show a malicious grin.

Pearce wanted to time the actual assault to coincide with the arrival of better illumination. To try to close the distance in what was still near total darkness carried too great a risk, so his impatience was not in any way abated. As soon as he could make out the shape of the bushes closest to him he called for his men to move, unsheathing his sword, though keeping it low by his leg.

He could hear them behind him; for all their efforts men could not avoid scuffing their feet or brushing against vegetation, he being sure if it came to his ears it must run ahead to others. Moving at no great speed he felt his heart pounding in his chest, aware as well of a sensation he had experienced before, of his senses in a high state of alert, the prelude to combat.

Why was that so agreeable? What was it about him that he not only seemed to crave excitement, but to take positive pleasure in the kind he was about to engage in? Was he alone in this? Were those following him in a similar state of anticipation? Odd now to be thinking of Emily and her dreams of a bucolic country life. At this moment, even more than others to which he had been previously prone, he knew he could never abide such an existence.

Stopping at the point he had reached previously allowed his band to bunch up. They must burst on what lay ahead of them as a body and noisily, using screams and shouts to induce terror as well as panic. At that moment he felt himself to be like a dog straining on a leash, so it was disappointing that his first yell, as he began to run, came out as something of a loud croak, his throat being so dry.

Those following more than made up for his muteness as they burst into the circle of the low glow given off by a pair of fires, these several yards apart and no more than a red radiance. They must have appeared, to the men sat by those glowing ashes, like a vision of hell. One had a musket, promptly dropped in panic in the act of standing, which had him hold out his hands to plead uselessly for mercy. He was cut down by Pearce's sword.

The act of dealing with him slowed their leader enough to allow the rest to rush past him and he was vaguely aware of Conway, young and fleet of foot, seemingly at the head of the pack. All around, men who had been slumbering on the bare ground were struggling to get out from their coverings, not too many looking to fight, it seemed. Yet two were so inclined and Conway was heading right into the arc of their hastily grabbed bayonets.

'Michael, the boy!' Pearce yelled.

This shout came as he was himself running, having seen Conway stop before two men who towered over him, the youngster's cutlass waving uncertainly before he took up the kind of fencer's pose he rehearsed daily on the foredeck of the ship, one unlikely to serve him in what would be a melee. This was proven as a jabbed bayonet slipped past his guard to slice down on his arm.

In his heightened state of alert, even as Pearce noted the danger Conway was exposed to, he was also aware that Frenchmen were dying in numbers, cut down by swinging cutlasses or brained by clubs, enough to discourage many of their fellows from offering resistance. The lad had recoiled from what was clearly a wound and, in the act of falling backwards, half impeded Michael O'Hagan from closing with the men seeking to skewer the lad.

Never one to be shy of clouting a body, that was what Conway got, a swipe that sent him tumbling out of the arc of danger and those intent on harming him; they now faced a towering giant carrying a cutlass in one hand and a marlin spike in the other. They quickly lost a great deal of their enthusiasm for a contest, doubly so when Pearce took station on the Irishman's shoulder.

What followed was no fancy swordplay. The weapons were swung furiously to drive these two Frenchmen back until Michael's greater reach got the point of his sword slicing through a neck, to produce a fount of spurting blood, sign enough to have the dying man's confrère drop his weapon and fall to his knees, with Pearce, blood boiling, swinging his to sever neck and head, the blade stopped less than an inch from contact.

'*Où es votre commandant?*' he shouted.

The arms opened in futility, but the question was answered by another shout, this time from the edge of the clearing where, for the first time, Pearce observed a dun-coloured tent under a canopy of trees, outside it a fellow in night flannels furiously waving his arms and yelling, this just before he headed for the trees and disappeared, followed by those who were close enough to what had to be another track. For the rest they were either dead, seriously wounded or

94

begging for succour.

'What the hell was he saying?' Michael gasped, his chest heaving.

'"Save yourselves", Michael.'

'So we have beaten them.'

The truth of that was in the comparative silence, so different from the banshee yelling that had preceded it from both sides, French and British. Pearce turned to where Conway was on his knees, close to one of the dying fires, one arm holding onto the other, which was pressed to his body, his pained face reflecting the light. A strong hand was used to raise the boy up.

'You have taken a blow, Mr Conway.' The youngster tried not to sob but failed, his head nodding to the sound of snuffling. 'Then it is best examined, is it not?'

The arm came out as Pearce called for some light, Charlie Taverner crossing to him quickly with an open lantern, miraculously, given it had been tied to his belt, still alight. That showed the gash in the uniform coat and the wetness of blood but not the wound itself, and if Pearce knew it needed attention, he also knew that he had other more important things to do.

'Your coat, Mr Conway, you must ease it off, and Charlie, bind the wound and if the flow of blood is strong, tie a tourniquet.'

'Will do, John.'

Conway reacted to that lack of respect by up-lifted eyebrows, which reassured Pearce that he was not too badly hurt. 'Pay it no heed, young fellow. If you are lucky, when you are older, you too will have men fighting under your command

95

happy to use your given name.'

Those captured, some half-dozen, were in a huddle, the ones killed just heaps lying where they had been slain, with the odd fellow wounded and moaning. Pearce noted they had no uniforms to speak of; indeed, the men seemed to be clad in rags, while even the sentinel who had died first was barefoot, though one was bandaged and showed, when quickly examined, a seepage of blood. A few abrupt questions established the wound as very recent – he had stood on a piece of sharp flint – which had Pearce wonder if the cry that had alerted them to this outpost had been caused by this fellow.

'Somers should see this,' he said.

This got an enquiring look from several of his sailors, but no elucidation. There was no time to tell them about an interdicted cargo of boots. Since those sparks had flown into the air, Pearce had wondered why he had seen no evidence of them on entering the bay, not even a reflected glow. The answer was soon established. At the point where the ground sloped away to the shore there was a high rampart made of tree trunks, with openings cut through which the muzzles of the cannon could be pushed, masked with canvas to conceal their presence in darkness.

The cannon themselves, four in number, were the very heaviest of field pieces, still capable of being wheeled. They were pulled back from the rampart and around them stood stacks of balls as well as charcoal-filled braziers with powerful tongs. The way they would be employed was obvious and provided another good reason to keep alight the campfires at night. That charcoal could be quickly lit.

From this elevation, under a normal sky, any unfriendly vessel seeking to enter the bay would be seen long before it could make and clear the narrows, giving ample time to heat the shot, a weapon to be feared aboard a wooden warship. Contact with canvas would set that alight and the tarred cordage with it; if not immediately, if embedded it would eventually smoulder the start of a fire in the scantlings or the deck, which untended would ignite.

The narrows imposed difficulty for an attacker, the lack of sufficient sea meant less room to be able to respond, to be able to draw back enough to elevate their own guns in reply to a battery placed so high on the slopes of Monte Boroni.

'Do we have any spikes?' Pearce demanded.

This was a query to which he received no affirmative reply and nor was there any sign of shame. No one had thought to bring the nails needed to spike the touch holes of a battery not known to really exist and, in truth, it should have been an order from him to include them. Grey might have brought some, the marines more accustomed to the need. That being true, there was still no way he could just leave them be, yet the notion of sending for heavy nails was no more feasible. He had no idea of how long it would be before those fleeing Frenchmen met with more of their kind and in numbers he could not contest with.

'Mr Conway, are you bandaged and fit for duty?'

'I am, sir.'

'Then to you falls the task of guarding that path our enemies used to make their escape. I want to know well in advance if any of their fellows are coming to take back this battery. Do you feel able to carry that out?'

The affirmative had Pearce detail two men to go with him, with instructions to pass no forks for fear that if they went too far over the crest of Monte Boroni they would risk losing the route back. Another pair were despatched back down the way they had come, to carry to Mr Grey information of what to expect so he would not be alarmed.

He then set everyone searching for spikes. The French might have them, even if that was unlikely – what gunner keeps with him the means to disable his own weapons? As this was happening, he and his Pelicans sought out the powder store, something never placed too close to the guns for fear of an explosion.

They found it behind that dun-coloured tent, barrels covered in tarred canvas to keep out the rain and ample in quantity. Pearce ordered these to be taken to the rampart while he searched the tent of what had undoubtedly been an officer, the hung-up captain's uniform coat and good breeches, set above a pair of high-polished boots, turning supposition to fact.

The hurriedly vacated cot was naturally a mess, but the small travelling desk in polished brass-bound oak, set on a trestle, had upon it a quill, ink and papers in a tidy heap. These were folded and stuffed in Pearce's pocket along with a decent-looking watch. The desk drawer yielded a small purse that jingled with coin, while at the very rear there was a large basket-covered flagon of cognac.

He decided, uplifting as it might be, brandy was an artefact too risky to hand over to a company of tars, men who could never resist a free wet nor control their consumption. It would be unlikely to get back to the ship, and how would his men behave full of drink? He grabbed the uniform, holding the jacket to his own body to note that it was much of a size to his own. Those and the boots were taken out and given over to the care of Rufus Dommet, who jested he would be happy to wear them.

'Well, you can ply a gun, Rufus,' Pearce responded, 'for we have done it together, so happen you would suit being a captain of artillery.'

'Is that like bein' a ship's captain, John?' he asked, softly enough for the familiarity not to be overheard.

'Never fear, or I would rip it off you,' came the laughing response. 'What, have you giving me orders?'

'Now that, I will say, would be pleasing.'

'For you, happen.'

The conversation had got them back to the ramparts, where the powder barrels were now being stacked in a heap directly on top of it. Michael had found some slow match, so now it was a case of getting the barrels of the cannon set over the powder, then running a line of match back to the still-glowing embers of the nearest campfire.

Conway, holding his wounded arm as he ran, along with the men sent with him to watch the path over Monte Boroni, came scudding into the clearing to report the line of torches making their way over the crest and coming their way. To ask such a youngster for an appreciation of the time available was a lot, but it had to be put to him.

'Not half an hour, sir, and I would reckon that is enough to get us to the boats.'

'Do I have time to make an appreciation?'

'You do, sir.'

'Then come and show what you have observed.' Pearce turned to Michael O'Hagan. 'I want all ready to fire before I get back, Michael. Cluster the cannon and pack the barrels round, with one broached.'

'Sure, I know what to do.'

'Then I leave you in command.'

'Will you be wanting this jacket, Michael?' called Rufus, holding up the officer's bottle-green artilleryman's coat. 'You being elevated, an' all?'

'You'll get an elevation of my boot if you show less care, Rufus,' Michael replied, but with no real malice.

Pearce heard only the former part of the exchange; he was jogging down the path with shirt-sleeved and bandaged Conway on his heels, the occasional sound of pain from the lad something he had to ignore. It took little time at all to reach a point where the approaching line of torches became visible, nor was it difficult to note the length of the column, the last of them yet to cross the peak and thus formidable in numbers, while to stand still and calculate their pace took several deep breaths.

'Sir, I have lost all feeling in my right hand.'

'That is the tourniquet, Mr Conway, best left in place till we are back aboard ship, which I must tell you is becoming a pressing matter. I reckon we have less time than you estimated to make our escape. I will be running, young sir, and you must keep up with me. Pain cannot be allowed to intrude.'

'I will not fail you, sir.'

'Never thought you would,' Pearce replied, already moving, words he hoped would lift Conway's spirits.

The work he had asked for was not quite complete, with Pearce quick to reckon that half a loaf was the best he could hope for, so he sent everyone but Michael away with orders to move fast for the boats, with the midshipmen to lead.

'I want them in the water too, Mr Conway. Tell Mr Grey of the numbers coming and that there will likely be no time for musketry.'

As soon as they were gone, Pearce cut the line of slow match in half, which got him a query from Michael O'Hagan, who had a strong belief in his maker, but no desire to meet with him.

'When that goes up, John-boy, there's going to be a rate of metal and wood in the air.'

Pearce had used the tongs for heated shot to fetch a smoking log from the fire and was standing over the newly cut end. 'If we leave the whole length, those coming at a run will get here before it blows.'

Michael crossed himself again. 'Then best set that burning wood to it and get on our way.'

Pearce dropped the wood, and the slow match, highly flammable, began to fizz immediately. He and O'Hagan were by that time running as fast as their legs would carry them. It helped they were heading downhill and, since they were out of sight, they did not see the first of the pursuit gingerly making their way into the clearing. Nor did they see the fellow to the fore spotting the hissing slow match and making a move to extinguish it, one that did not last the distance. He realised he was going to fail and turned, ran and yelled for those who had been to his rear to do likewise.

Pearce and Michael O'Hagan were some two hundred yards distant when those twenty barrels of powder went up, sending a huge orange ball into the night sky, with it a mass of splinters from the rampart, the wheels of the guns, as well as all the metal parts that held everything in place, the cannon being thrown forward by the blast to roll downwards towards the seashore, the wooden rampart to restrain them no longer whole.

The blast hit both running men in the back to send them tumbling onto their faces, sliding along the dry ground until they came to halt with heads covered, this as debris rained all around. There they stayed until it stopped.

'Are you whole, Michael?' Pearce called, hauling himself to his feet and feeling pain in various places.

'Damn the Devil, I will not know that until I can stop and check.'

'Blasphemy,' Pearce panted, 'you must be in one piece.'

They recommenced their flight, unaware of the lack of need. Being either close to the explosion or on a higher elevation, surrounded by trees smashed into splinters, those in pursuit had been more a victim of the blast and the subsequent debris than the men who had set it to blow.

When they got to the beach they found the boats afloat but Grey and his marines still on the sand, for which Pearce could be nothing but grateful. It was not long before all were aboard and they could haul off. Sat in the thwarts, he realised the sky to the east, above the low-lying eastern arm of the bay, was beginning to show a glim of daylight. Digby's orders could go hang; there was no time left to carry them out.

'Steer for HMS *Flirt,* if you please, Mr Conway, where I daresay after our exploits we may well be justified in demanding an extra tot of rum.'

CHAPTER EIGHT

What had occurred on the slopes of Monte Boroni was no mystery aboard HMS *Flirt.* It had been visible out at sea; initially only those on deck but soon the whole crew, many woken by the sound of the huge blast, were there to observe. If they had failed to see the actual explosion, there was enough evidence in the burning wood of the rampart and the surrounding forest creating an orange glow that stood as testimony – to what?

Speculation was, of course, rife, but few of the men who had sailed for so long with John Pearce doubted his hand was in it up to the elbow, talk that ceased when Henry Digby appeared on deck.

He stood looking towards the shore for a whole minute before he spoke in a voice utterly lacking in passion.

'Mr Dorling, I require the ship's lanterns to be uncovered. Once we have set a course to close with the Bay of Villafranca the deck is to be cleared of this gawping. The men not now on watch are to be sent below to their hammocks.'

'Sir,' Dorling replied, noting that while everyone else was still looking towards the shore, Henry Digby had ceased to.

'Once the shore party is back on board, shape a course for Vado Bay.'

The order rang out to trim the sails as the man on the wheel spun the rudder, bringing the brig round till the prow seemed to be aimed at the heart of the blaze. That complete, Digby returned to his cabin, well aware that his injunction that those off watch should sleep had little chance of being complied with. After all, his order to his premier had obviously not been obeyed, so why should anyone else bother?

To sit and stare at his desk solved nothing, but he had little inclination to do otherwise as he ruminated, and not for the first time, on his relationship with John Pearce. The words the man had used to castigate him as HMS *Flirt* lay anchored in San Fiorenzo Bay, to condemn him as both an ingrate and a hypocrite, were all too easy to recall, and since Pearce had elected to come back aboard, despite his declaration he would not, his presence had been a constant reminder of the nature of the dispute.

Digby had been in a weakened state when he

promised to support Pearce against Sir William Hotham and Ralph Barclay. Recovery and reflection on the consequences had altered his thinking. Why could Pearce not see that any attempt to bring down a vice admiral and a serving fleet commander was doomed to failure? The Admiralty would move heaven and earth to protect Hotham in order to keep pure the reputation of the navy. And who were they but a pair of lowly lieutenants.

It was just another example of the lack of understanding Pearce had about the arm in which he served, all, no doubt, due to the way he had entered the service and the unwarranted and far too early elevation in rank he had enjoyed. Added to that, of course, was his background as the son of a radical orator and pamphleteer. If he was not quite as rabid as his sire, some of the old man's views must have rubbed off to make him contentious by nature.

How different his own life had been. Digby had entered as a midshipman aged twelve and had risen to his present position through dint of hard work, application and, he was forced to admit, a bit of luck to be serving in a theatre where the shortage of everything, officers included, was acute. It had taken him sixteen years to get to his present position and in that time he had become steeped in the traditions of the service and that extended to how you dealt with superiors.

He had experienced the usual victimisation meted out to new arrivals in a midshipman's berth, had his possessions stolen from his sea chest, been the butt of practical jokes, some humorous, many not, and had survived bullying until he rose high enough in the gunroom hierarchy to be the one who could mete it out, not that he was that way inclined.

Passed for lieutenant, he found himself serving on HMS *Brilliant* under Ralph Barclay, a far from pleasant captain, and if John Pearce had been a rather distant figure on the frigate, a mere pressed and common seaman who was struggling to learn the ropes of life in the navy, it seemed to Digby his life had intertwined with the man ever since. The Bay of Biscay, the Gulf of Ambracia had both been successes, yet what might have been a blessing had turned into a curse.

Pearce was as much taken by the exploits of his raiding party as anyone on the ship to which he was seeking to return. Increasing daylight slowly muted the orange glow on the slopes behind them; now it was billowing black clouds of smoke that poured skywards with the redness of the fires barely visible at the base. At this time of year, before the autumn rains, which were now overdue, the forest timbers were bone dry so the explosion had started a conflagration that would be hard to extinguish and one that might well consume a great deal of the forest covering the mountain. On an east wind, if one were to spring up strongly enough, it might threaten Nice.

He wondered then about all those Frenchmen who had been on their way to reverse his capture of the battery; were they caught up in it or had they managed to run away to escape the flames? The lack of wind might save them, a true forest fire requiring a robust blow to be really deadly. He found himself, somewhat hypocritically, hoping for their safety.

'HMS *Flirt* closing fast, your honour.'

Pearce spun round to look out to sea and the dun-coloured canvas of the brig's sails, wondering how Digby would take what had been achieved. Would he be fool enough to insist that his orders should have been obeyed to the letter in the face of what was before his eyes? However he reacted, Pearce was ready to dispute with him, for it would be a poltroon indeed who observed such a result and quibbled.

The men in the boat had filthy faces and dust-covered clothing, while Conway – still in only a shirt, with the bloodied sleeve and his hair awry, his midshipman's short coat, with the cut-open sleeve across his lap – looked as if he had been dragged through a hedge backwards. This had Pearce examine his own coat, an old working garment, seeing it was streaked enough to make him wonder at his whole appearance, while the breeches were black at the knees. Would the captain allow him to wash and change prior to making his report? Could he have a dip in the sea, something he had not been able to enjoy for many a week, given Digby disapproved?

'Damn him!' Pearce exclaimed, and seeing they were close to the brig, he began to strip, kicking off his shoes and throwing his clothing to Michael O'Hagan until he was down to the buff.

'Not much there to trouble his lady,' was the comment of one sailor, but not until John Pearce had dived over the side.

'His lady is the trouble,' commented another,

proof that his affairs were common knowledge. 'Too damn pretty, that's what, an' the size of his tackle matters not when she is so sweet on 'im.'

'It does not please me to hear you talk of her or Mr Pearce in that fashion.'

No one chose to catch Michael O'Hagan's eye then; the Irishman was no bully, but they knew how he would act in the face of anything he saw as an insult to the man he served, that multiplied by ten if Emily Barclay was slighted.

'Belay that talking,' Conway croaked, which was obeyed, more as a way to ease the atmosphere than any acknowledgement of authority.

Pearce was swimming alongside, just out of the arc of the dipping oars – those plied easy as he had ordered, there being no rush to get back aboard – feeling refreshed by the immersion and the chill of the offshore waters. He lay back, arms outstretched as the boats came alongside the brig, his men greeted with so many questions about their exploits it was doubtful if anyone got a satisfactory answer.

Michael, carrying the discarded garments, got aboard quickly and went below to fetch a towel, this flapped over the side to indicate that Pearce could come aboard. The man he was waiting to dry was taken by the fact that Digby was not on deck, which was a clear affront about which he could do nothing. He swam to the side and, grabbing the man ropes, hauled himself aboard, dripping seawater, until Michael covered his nakedness.

'Mr Conway, to Mr Bellam immediately and get that arm looked at. It requires to be bathed in hot water and the cook will have that in his coppers. He is also a dab hand with needle and thread if it requires to be stitched. On reflection, you may wish to take a swim, for seawater is said to be efficacious for wounds.'

The midshipman looked at him with horror; he, like many of his ilk, saw water of any kind, fresh or salty, as mortal to his health.

'Mr Grey,' he said, as the marine came aboard, his uniform and appearance pristine. 'You have suffered from grime less than I. My compliments to the captain and please tell him I will attend upon him as soon as I am dressed, if it is convenient.'

That too engendered a look tinged with dismay; Grey was equally aware that Digby should have welcomed them aboard, while it had ever been obvious he was as reluctant to interfere in their dispute. There was, however, no choice, unless he required John Pearce to issue a direct order, one that would be embarrassing before the whole crew.

'Sir,' came the reply, emphasised by a frown to let Pearce know of his disinclination.

'Mr Dorling, do you have anything requiring to be reported?'

'No, sir.'

'Then I ask you to continue on deck until I have seen the captain. Do you have instructions?'

'I do, sir, to set a course for Vado Bay.'

'Then carry on, but I would wish the men I took ashore with me to be fed, provided with a tot of rum, and then stood down for a full watch.'

Michael O'Hagan had disappeared while these

exchanges were taking place, to reappear with another towel and a bucket of fresh water, plentiful given the ship was acting off a river-fed coast. He tipped this over Pearce's head to wash the salt off his hair and body, leaving a huge puddle around his feet.

'Forgive me for adding to your work, lads,' was the hearty shout as he went below.

Behind him mops were produced – they had been fetched in anticipation, this being no strange ritual with the premier – and the deck was swabbed before being flogged dry with cloths. Throughout, many a glance was thrown at the now distant shore and the still-swelling clouds of smoke, now high in the morning sky.

'I am thinking red rags and bulls, John-boy,' was the comment made as soon as the canvas screen was pulled shut.

'Ask yourself who is waving it, Michael, for it is not I.'

'First you dip, when you know Mr Digby thinks it unseemly in an officer, then you shout all that jolly nonsense on the deck so he is bound to hear.'

'I did it to bait him,' Pearce replied, slipping on his best breeches over his smalls, this as Michael fetched a clean shirt from the sea chest. 'And before you talk about the concerns of the crew, recall what we have just been about.'

A black stock was handed over to be tied round the neck, the hair combed in the small mirror, until Michael added, 'A success that will wound him.'

'Damn me, I hope so.' Pearce said, as his blue coat was handed over. 'Now, I suggest you look

110

to your own needs, not mine, while I go and check on the progress of Mr Conway. To think a mid comes aboard with a wound and I doubt his captain is even aware of it.'

'Food, John-boy.'

Pearce picked up a pear, fresh from Leghorn, and bit into it. 'Mr Bellam will have something for me, and you.'

He found the midshipman, stripped now of his shirt to show his pale pubescent body, with the one-legged cook bent over his arm, the men who had come with the mess pails to fetch food being attended to by Bellam's assistant. The boy's face was a picture as the needle entered then emerged from his skin, while he was using the chicken leg he was eating as a way of suppressing any cries of pain. Pearce too bent over to look at the long gash, now an angry red colour, as the two edges were being pulled together.

'We are on course for Vado Bay, Mr Conway, where I suggest you request permission to go aboard HMS *Agamemnon* as soon as we arrive. It would be wise to have Mr Roxburgh look at your wound.'

'Then let's hope he appreciates my handiwork, your honour,' Bellam said, slightly aggrieved. 'Wound is clean and soused in vinegar.'

'I'm sure he will, Mr Bellam, but he is a surgeon and you are not. We cannot have Mr Conway risking an arm for want of attention.'

'Will I lose an arm, sir?' the boy asked fearfully.

'Not if your shirt was clean. Did you obey my instruction to don a clean one before we left the ship?'

111

'I think so, sir.'

'Which means no, Mr Conway. Always keep one garment clean and change into it whenever you go into action. The wearing of soiled clothes is to risk contamination.'

'Mr Pearce, captain is asking after you.'

Pearce turned to acknowledge the bosun's message. 'Thank you, Mr Bird.'

Pearce was once more obliged to stand, head bent, to observe nothing more than the top of his captain's head; the man would not catch his eye.

'I asked Mr Grey for an outline of what happened, but he seemed either particularly ill-informed or reluctant to tell me. What I do know is this, sir. I lack any information on the route by which the French must be supplied, which is what I sent you to discover.'

'You would have observed the fire, sir, perhaps even heard the explosion.'

'I did both, and I also noted it did not emanate from the location to which I despatched you.'

'I admit to stretching my orders, sir.'

Digby finally looked up, his tone sceptical. 'Stretching, you call it?'

'My appreciation of the situation differed, I think, from yours and being on the spot I acted as I thought best. We destroyed a battery that would have closed the entrance to the bay for even a fleet.'

The head was down again. 'A singular success, then. Oblige me by producing a written account.' Having prepared himself for an attempt at chastisement, Pearce was thrown by that calm request. All he could do was acknowledge it. 'That will be all, Mr Pearce. You will, of course, be excused any other duties until your account is completed.'

There was a method of writing such a report, one in which any form of personal praise was anathema. By all means allude to the sterling actions of those he had led but any hint of glory hunting would be frowned upon. The way he had 'stretched' his orders had to be handled delicately too; that had to be reported as a wise precaution leading to a need for a response, one that made it impossible to carry out his verbal instructions from Henry Digby.

Any hint they had been deliberately circumvented had to be avoided, while allusions as to their wisdom, or in this case to both John Pearce and Edward Grey and their lack of same, needed to be sidestepped. Conway got a mention for his bravery and his wound, while the steadiness of the crew of HMS *Flirt* was heavily remarked upon, without the inclusion of any names; conspicuous individual gallantry was recognised on the lower deck, but only rarely.

Passed to Digby, Pearce wondered if he would be summoned to add anything. He was not, and the journey back to Vado Bay proceeded without another word passing between them. On opening the anchorage Pearce noticed two of the frigates were absent, cruising no doubt, this while all the rigmarole that attended ships joining was repeated, with Digby immediately once more setting off for *Agamemnon* as soon as *Flirt* was at anchor, though this time there was no flag requiring his attendance.

'Happen he'll steal John's thunder,' suggested

Charlie Taverner, for no one doubted he would be delivering the despatch about the successful raid. 'Odd how the man has gone sour.'

'Too much time sat in his cabin brooding on things,' Michael O'Hagan replied, this accompanied by much nodding from Rufus. 'For me, sure, I wish they would make it up.'

'One'd have to make a move, Michael, and John is not that way inclined.'

'And nor,' Rufus insisted, 'is Digby.'

'Be best if he shifted – John, I mean.'

'You know why he won't as well as we do, Rufus,' Charlie responded. 'It's the Pelicans all together, or none.'

'Which is never said openly.'

'Nor will it be,' Michael said. 'He thinks we don't know.'

'We could ease it for him. *Flirt* would be as good a berth as any with one of them gone.'

'Happen you would go back aboard *Brilliant,* Charlie,' Michael posited, half in jest.

'No fear. It were bad enough with Barclay but I reckon that Taberly to be worse.'

'He is,' Michael said in sour tone, having been the one to serve under the man. 'The word "bastard" scarce covers it.'

'Now there's another one who hates John,' Rufus added.

'He has a gift for making enemies,' Charlie responded, with a definite trace of pride.

The person mentioned they could see from where they had gathered on the forepeak. Pearce had a telescope trained on the flagship, observing a somewhat crowded deck and strange uniforms,

114

many of them white, which indicated high-ranking Austrians being aboard. That took his eyes to the boats in the water and the pennant on the stern of the largest, a substantial barge bearing the twin eagles of the Habsburgs, so Pearce assumed they were aboard to discuss what actions they were planning to take, something that would break the present deadlock.

Again, Digby was not on *Agamemnon* for long, though that was likely to be more to do with the commodore being busy. He was received back aboard with due ceremony and went straight to his cabin without a word spoken. There he remained while whatever was happening on the ship-of-the-line was concluded, the high-ranking visitors departing. They had not been gone long before Nelson's barge was in the water and it took very little time after it set off to realise where it was headed.

Digby was on deck in double-quick time, his eyes ranging over the planking to ensure all was shipshape and tidy, many an order barked out that something perfectly proper and in no need of attention should be seen to, his concern obvious. It was not at all common for the likes of a commodore to visit a mere brig; normally the commanders of such a vessel were brusquely summoned, but here it was. The barge swung smartly to the side and Nelson came aboard in sprightly fashion, his smile wide as he lifted his hat to the quarterdeck.

'Mr Digby, I hope you will accept my apologies. I was heavily engaged with our allies when you came aboard and could do no more than acknowledge you with a wave, which is a great pity, for had I read your report on your recent exploits, I could have used it to impress on the Baron de Vins the advantages of action over his present sloth.'

'May I invite you into my cabin, sir, where my servant has laid out some wine?'

There was a bit of the actor in Nelson and he indulged in that now, his face becoming mock serious, his tone an attempt at being gruff, which singularly failed given the high pitch of his voice.

'What I should do, of course, is excoriate you for your blatant breach of the orders I gave you. Damn near worth a flogging round the fleet.'

'My cabin, sir,' Digby repeated, in a slightly strangled tone, one that intrigued John Pearce, an invitation ignored for a second time.

'I order you to do nothing but observe and how do you behave? You blatantly disobey.'

'Sir I–'

Nelson's face lit up again. 'Never fear to do so, sir, if opportunity presents itself, as it has on this occasion. Action I will always support and it is to your credit that you saw an opening to smite our foes and took it with both hands. That, sir, is what the service needs more of.'

Digby could not look at John Pearce; indeed, he could not look at anyone as Nelson added, 'Might I suggest your wine would be better taken on the quarterdeck, where I can toast not only you, but your officers and men?'

Nelson turned to Pearce and gave him a fulsome greeting, he taking the good arm of the wounded midshipman, to haul him forward. 'Might I bring

116

to your attention this young man, sir, Mr Conway, who behaved with outstanding *élan?* I would also point out he might be in need of your surgeon.'

'Then, Mr Pearce, he will return to *Agamemnon* with me and I will give him dinner where he can relate his exploits. Now, Mr Digby, that wine?'

CHAPTER NINE

It was hard to be sure what sunk so low the mood on board HMS *Flirt*. The fact that the captain seemed to have claimed credit for something not of his doing and had been found out shamed the ship, for it was bound in time to be spread by gossip. Then there was the duty upon which they were engaged and the weather within which it had to be carried out. Beating to and fro off the port of Genoa in generally rough winter seas was bad enough; to be required to continually launch boats into such conditions, in order to inspect cargoes and scrutinise paperwork, was wearing in the extreme.

Little was seen of Henry Digby outside those duties he could not avoid: being on deck at sunrise – not that there was much of that commodity – witnessing punishments, which had become more prevalent despite the attempts by John Pearce to avoid bringing transgressions to his attention. Then there was the one he clearly enjoyed: the Sunday service following on from his inspection of the lower deck, a time at which he, deeply religious, could allude to what he saw as the evident sins of those over whom he had command.

That apart, Digby took much advantage of the ability of a ship's captain to obtain privacy. He was, of course, punctilious in the carrying out of his duties, but it was done by verbal delegation, not hands-on control, which placed added burdens onto his first lieutenant.

Called upon to board a neutral trading ship, it was John Pearce who had to close in the cutter, through freezing, choppy waters, often slopping over the gunwales, to then clamber aboard and seek to discern if he was being fed truth or lies. Was the vessel truly headed for Genoa, or trying to slip through the screen set up by *Flirt* and a distant HMS *Troubadour* to interdict those seeking to supply the French?

Despite all the attention he had received, young Mr Conway's arm was slow to heal, requiring to be regularly cleaned. It was also causing him pain, which meant that he could only very rarely share the duty of inspection. Calm seas he could manage, but Pearce feared to put him in jeopardy when the wind was blowing and the waves were high, for he risked being ducked as he tried to board a trader one-handed.

Edward Grey was not expected to undertake the duty as it fell outside the marine officer's remit, a stricture that did not apply to his men, a pair of whom had to man the boats with their muskets to ensure compliance. As of this moment, John Pearce was obliged to call upon his captain to relay some vital information.

'It is the opinion of Mr Dorling that the

118

weather is set to worsen considerably.'

Digby examined Pearce for several seconds before he turned to look out of his casement windows at the troubled sea, hard to visualise through the small panes of salt-caked glass, ignoring the fact that, while he was safely seated, his premier was required to keep a hand on the deck beams to compensate for the telling pitch and roll of the ship.

'And he would wish to take precautions?'

'He would, sir. If I am allowed an opinion—'

The interruption was sharp. 'You rarely decline the opportunity.'

'I was about to say that in all the time I have served with Mr Dorling, I have never had cause to doubt his appreciation of what may be in the offing as far as weather is concerned. For all his lack of years he has a feel for the matter.'

'Even if I have been at sea for longer than he?'

If that statement was true, it masked certain obvious facts. Dorling was a ship's master and thus had studied the needs of his profession in a way those wishing to be officers rarely did. Charts to him were like books: a source of enlightenment. His sail plans were generally exemplary and if the likes of Digby understood them too – John Pearce reckoned he was now not bad himself – it was telling how few times Dorling's decisions were questioned.

In addition, the young man had been in receipt of the combined wisdom of his peers. Masters, like everyone else in the King's Navy, kept copious logs and produced drawings, and these, stretching back over many decades, were studied by the men

119

who succeeded them, providing a collective knowledge that any commander ignored at his peril. As a group they were fond of relating the tale of Sir Cloudesley Shovell, who had ignored his master's opinion on a safe course to pursue, only to run his entire fleet aground on the Isles of Scilly, the abrasive Admiral of the Fleet forfeiting his own life in the process.

'I am sure he would welcome your opinion, sir,' Pearce said in a mollifying tone; better to get a result than win a row.

'He can have my opinion whether he wants it or not, Mr Pearce, or does he require to be reminded who commands?'

That was not worthy of an answer, so Pearce returned to the wind- and rain-swept deck, pulling tight the oilskins he was wearing to keep out both elements. The wind was a robust north-easterly, while above their heads it was hard to see how fast the clouds were moving given they were an unrelieved dark grey. In this corner of the Mediterranean, the armpit of Italy, the currents tended to swirl, procuring the same kind of choppy waters that plagued the English Channel. Big and regular waves with long troughs were rare, yet that could change in a blink if the wind suddenly shifted.

Rain notwithstanding, hats were raised as Digby, well wrapped against the elements, came on deck, scanning the horizon as if he required to check there was no other vessel in sight, not even HMS *Troubadour*, patrolling further to the south. Tempted to remind him that he would have been informed of anything seen, Pearce held his tongue; it was all for show.

'Mr Dorling, what is it that you anticipate?'

There was no overhearing the exchange that followed, it was carried out with heads bent over the binnacle – not that what was being imparted was a mystery; Pearce had already been informed. The Ligurian littoral lay close to the Maritime Alps; indeed, on a clear day they were easily visible as they rose beyond the shoreline towards the high, snow-capped peaks. If the 'armpit' was capable of being stormy, the high mountains and the unique conditions they could create added to the risks of sailing in these waters. There was a reason no other vessel was in sight: anyone with sense had run for the nearest harbour.

That was what Pearce would have done if he had been in command; staying out at sea in conditions expected to worsen was futile when those they were there to interdict were either safely tucked up in Genoa or any of the harbours further south. Digby was adamant that their orders did not allow for that, of course, but to a man given to endemic disobedience such things meant nothing against the risk of losing both the brig and many lives, not least his own.

'Very well, Mr Dorling, take what precautions you must, but I abjure you to keep us on our station if you can.'

The master looked at Pearce when Digby staggered away to his cabin; the response was a shrug. That said, there was work to do: rigging storm canvas and extra backstays, getting anything loose off the deck that could do harm, putting extra lashings on the cannon trunnions, while matters had to be as secure below decks as they were up above. Throughout those tasks the wind increased, in addition beginning to gust dangerously.

The cant of the deck was acute, for staying on station meant beating to and fro with the gale on their beam, exerting heavy pressure on one side, and when they, with some difficulty, came about, immediately reversing it with an increasingly buffeting wind made it recognisably more difficult each time. Dorling's mouth was by Pearce's ear now, the foul-weather hat lifted so he could hear.

'This is not sense. We should let the wind take us where it will. Run before it as we have previously.'

The message was plain: you took my advice before and happen that saved us. Dorling went on to state his worry that with the increasingly unpredictable gusts, fed by the wind howling down the Alpine valleys, one was bound eventually to catch *Flirt* as she was wearing to come about, and in that lay great danger.

'You need to speak to him, Mr Pearce.'

'It could be better coming from you.'

'If I was to say it, it might come to overruling him, what then?'

It was as if all around him died away, with Pearce contemplating what Dorling was suggesting. Digby was being so intransigent as to endanger the ship and in that case he should be superseded. A loathing of hierarchy was one thing, what was being advocated could be construed as mutiny and it would be down to the vagaries of a court martial as to how such an action was perceived. Precedents were both very rare and not promising, palpable madness historically the only sound reason to remove a captain.

And Dorling had the right of it; he was the only one, as second in command, who could replace Digby, but he would require the backing of everyone aboard imbued with authority. Would Grey support him? Could he ask Conway? Dorling might say he would do so now – would he hold to that when faced with a line of belligerent accusers? For that was what it would come to; the navy took as sacrosanct the power of a captain.

At that point the marine lieutenant appeared, indicating he had come from Digby's cabin, his expression grave. He waited for a moment to assess the heaving deck before the dropping hull had him scurrying towards Pearce to grasp at the binnacle, and now it was his ear pressed close. Even then his voice needed to be loud.

'I have been ordered to put a pair of my men outside the spirit room.'

'Which will inflame those already alarmed,' Pearce shouted.

'It will,' Grey acknowledged.

Outside the need to alter course there had been few hands on deck, yet anyone by the wheel would have needed to be blind not to observe the looks thrown in that direction. This was mainly a crew of volunteers, people who made their living at sea in both war and peace, tars who left the merchant service as soon as a conflict was in the offing for the better pay and conditions – flogging notwithstanding – of the King's Navy.

With all those years of experience came knowledge, which if it did not match that of Dorling was yet acute. Those looks were asking what those in command and steering the vessel were about, holding this position in such conditions. The cook had doused his coppers, the fire being too dangerous on a ship behaving like a bucking horse. So it was cold provender and strong hands needed to keep a place at a mess table, while movement, when down below and blind to what was coming from wave and wind, could be fraught with the risk of injury.

Hardly surprising the men were disgruntled and worried. It mattered not how Digby, stuck in his cabin, had assessed the mood as dangerous, he had clearly done so. Sailors, if they faced drowning, were wont to wish to do so in a blind stupor and the way to that lay in the barrels of rum in the spirit room; hence the marine guard.

'Hold on that, Mr Grey.' The master was called to huddle with them, Grey's eyes widening when he heard what Pearce said. 'Mr Dorling, I will speak with the captain but I want you prepared to alter our course to one that will ease matters and if necessary the command will be issued by me. Should you feel it essential to act when I am off the deck, do so and I will back you.'

'John–'

'It could be that or drown, Edward.'

'That's the truth, Mr Grey,' Dorling insisted.

'Precedent says you should include Conway.'

'He's too young and besides, Edward, I am not even going to include you. This is a decision I will make and live by.'

'No, I will stand with you.'

'Thank you.'

Digby had one of Grey's marines guarding his door, if hanging on for dear life half the time could be termed that. Even instructed he would not have impeded the first lieutenant so; after a perfunctory knock, Pearce ducked his head and entered, with Digby making a good fist at surprise to see him present.

'Sir, I wish you to order a change of course.'

'You may wish, Mr Pearce, it is my job to decide.'

'Which would make sense if you were in command of the deck instead of skulking in your cabin.'

The word 'skulking' struck home. 'How dare you–!'

Digby got no further than that expression of protest, because Pearce shouted over him. 'I dare and I will do more than that. I cannot sense what it is that is animating you: hatred of me or a shame so deep at your own reprehensible actions that it has rendered you spineless.'

'I have orders to stay on this station and my right to command will see those orders obeyed.'

'Nelson would tell you to throw them overboard if he were present.'

'He is not, Mr Pearce, and I am. Leave my cabin this minute and I will forget the words you have used. Continue and I will have you replaced.'

'By whom, Henry?' came the reply, utterly lacking in passion. 'No one will obey you.'

That forced him back in his chair, his face flushed. 'Has it not been ever thus, you snake? Ever since I took command you have undermined me.'

'I reckon you to have done a better job in such a thing than I, Henry.'

125

'I am not Henry to you, I am Captain Digby!'

'Shame is a terrible curse, but I will not allow you to take everyone aboard to perdition to assuage your guilt. I give you the choice, sir, either give the order to change course or I will have you confined to this cabin and take command.'

'Which will see you damned.'

'To be damned I will have to be alive. Choose.'

At that point *Flirt* yawed and the deck dipped alarmingly, forcing Digby to grab his desk to stay in his chair – his hat shot off the desk – while Pearce was thrown onto the bulkhead of the captain's sleeping cabin, hands held out to prevent injury. Very slowly, groaning like a wounded animal, she righted again, with Pearce wondering at how much water had been shipped to either get below or hopefully spill out through the scuppers.

Running feet came as the first sign, but it was not long before it was obvious that Dorling was coming round to get the wind on the stern; all the while this was happening the two men stared at each other with locked eyes until finally Digby blinked, which allowed John Pearce to speak.

'You have two choices, Henry. Either write in your log that you ordered the change of course or take the consequences. For myself, I will keep what has been said in this cabin private. I suggest you do the same.'

'I will take the deck, Mr Pearce,' Digby growled, standing and bending to grab his hat.

Pearce followed him out, both requiring man ropes, and as he came onto the deck it was not just Dorling who looked at him; those men who

126

had so recently manned the falls and were still looping the excess onto the bitts did so likewise. The gap before Digby spoke seemed to last a lifetime until he said, 'Carry on, Mr Dorling. Mr Pearce you may go below and rest.'

'Sir.'

'Mr Grey, my previous instruction. Please put it in abeyance.'

'Damn me, Mr Digby, I was sure I had lost you. Babbage and *Troubadour* came into Leghorn days ago and in a poor state.'

'We are not much better, sir. Had we not altered course I am not sure I would have been reporting to you, though I regret it overturned your orders.'

'I never do other than trust the man on the spot, Digby. It would be an asset if London did likewise, but they don't.'

That got a sympathetic murmur but neither agreement nor demurral; if it was not wise to traduce senior officers, that applied tenfold with the Admiralty. Sir John Jervis might be on his way to take command but there was no news of the very necessary reinforcements of both ships and men that the Mediterranean fleet required to be truly effective. In addition, their so-called Spanish allies seemed ever more disinclined to move from their base at Minorca to undertake any of the heavy work of containing the forces of the Revolution.

'Trouble is,' Nelson continued, his unnaturally young-looking countenance closed up and bellicose, 'the French have been making hay while the weather has moderated. As soon as it was observed

127

you were blown off your station and the storm had abated, half the vessels in Genoa harbour sailed for Toulon and Marseilles. If the so-called Army of Italy was on short commons before, they are unlikely to be so now.'

'Then I need to get back on station, sir, though you will see from my logs there are repairs required and we did lose a rate of canvas and cordage. Mr Pearce is at the Navy Board office now, seeing what he can garner as replacements.'

'Good fellow,' was the hearty response to the name. 'Though it is a fairly barren locker.'

Had John Pearce been present he too would have wondered at the fulsome nature of that expression: Henry Digby certainly did. Was Nelson referring to what might have occurred after that embarrassing moment on deck, when he revealed Digby had exceeded his orders? That the commodore had been happy for him to do so had no bearing. Nelson had shipped young Conway to HMS *Agamemnon* and, after the ship's surgeon had seen to his arm, had dined the lad in his cabin, this while his coat was expertly mended. What had Nelson asked him about the Bay of Villafranca? What had Conway said?

His dignity as a captain had not allowed Henry Digby to enquire and if Pearce had done so, he was not saying anything – why would he? This left *Flirt's* captain in a state of some anxiety, for the way he had worded his despatch on the raid had skirted over his orders to Pearce, which had been verbal, while also being obscure as to what was the actual purpose, other than those going ashore should take what opportunities that presented themselves to discomfit the enemy.

Conway would not have been privy to the real instructions but he had certainly been there to witness the action. Had he praised Pearce and in doing so inadvertently diminished his captain, that was the worry, for he wished to impress this man. Nelson was close to getting his rear admiral's flag, while Sir John Jervis was coming out to take command of the fleet, so any residual resentments held by Sir William Hotham – and he had no idea if there were any – no longer applied.

Such an exploit, attached to the Digby name, something he had set out to ensure would be read as such, must elevate him in the eyes of these superiors, and who knew where that could lead? He suddenly realised the commodore was still talking and cursed himself for letting his mind wander.

'I won't have it, Digby. The time has come to take a stand.'

'I agree, sir,' came the reply, even although he was unsure of what Nelson was talking about.

'I am off to Genoa, and I intend once I get there to put my ship right outside the harbour mouth. Nothing will get in or get out until the slippery sods in the *Signoria* and that damned Doge of theirs stick to their word. If they try to get anything past me, be assured, I will sink it.'

CHAPTER TEN

Cornelius Gherson spent many days in the privateer's sector of Leghorn, walking the quays and examining the various craft, all sleek vessels and well armed, though his interest in those was limited. More often he frequented the taverns used by the crews, making no overt moves to be overfamiliar in surroundings he reckoned to be adverse to pushiness. This he knew from his own background, growing to manhood in the criminal warrens of London, places where a stranger stood out markedly and where suspicion of someone seeking to infiltrate any brotherhood of villainy was endemic.

He knew his presence had been noted by the people who patronised these drinking dens; the surreptitious glances aimed at him were frequent and often belligerent, but that he expected, given he was drinking in his surroundings, seeking to get a feel for the temper of various inns. In doing so it was impossible not to notice certain things, like who was enjoying a recent success, boasting never being a quiet affair, and sailors the world over prone to expending that which they had acquired in very short order.

There was rivalry, a factor he thought might be to his advantage. The various crews tended to form exclusive groups, suspicious of each other and inclined to hug to themselves information about prospective captures. As a natural observer and accomplished eavesdropper, Gherson hoped, even from minimal scraps of information overheard in passing, to build up a picture of how these letters of marque operated and where he might fit in to his advantage.

The captains mattered to him for they would be the employers. Some were the actual owners of the ships, others he knew from his own sea service were employed by wealthy men who saw funding such an enterprise as a worthwhile investment. From the comings and goings, as well as the whispered conversations that reeked of conspiracy, these men were in receipt of intelligence about possible captures.

He reasoned this would be gleaned from any number of sources and often it would be far from complete: scraps of news from a whole network of sources, which in its entirety allowed a picture to be built up of what trading ships could be profitable captures as well as in the offing. To merely go cruising and hope for success would be fruitless and costly; crews had to be fed and if they were not regularly provided with opportunity they would be tempted away by the more successful ships' masters.

On many occasions, and for several days, a whole crew would be missing, their vessel having slipped its mooring at dawn, going about their business. At other times, one out cruising would return either with a prize in tow, which meant a Frenchman, or with holds full of cargo to be sold, which implied a neutral had been captured. This lay outside the limits of what these brigands were permitted to do and led to speculation as to the fate of the captured crews, men who might bear witness to what was really piracy.

From the feeling that time mattered little, he became increasingly frustrated by the amount expended observing the number and designation of the various boats or, more often, being sat alone for hours on end nursing a goblet of wine. Nor could he ignore that which he lacked the means to enjoy: the young whores, comely and olive-skinned, who plied their trade in front of his eyes.

Limited funds could not be expended on carnal pleasure, which meant he was many nights, this being one, a disgruntled fellow making his way back to his lodgings, cursing Ralph Barclay for allowing himself to be killed in a battle he could have avoided, as well as the whole King's Navy for its inability to appreciate his qualities.

'Hold there, fellow.'

The voice, coming out of the darkness, in an unlit street not much wider than an alley, made Gherson's heart thump. He immediately dropped his head and made a move to increase his pace, only then to comprehend he had been addressed in English. Another voice spoke, also in his native tongue.

'If you look ahead, friend, you will observe there is nowhere for you to go.'

An injunction impossible not to comply with, Gherson saw his way blocked by the outline of two men, with one holding a lantern low down, which told him only, by the garb – baggy trews and striped stockings – they were tars.

With the same number of voices to his rear that spelt at least four and real danger, something he had experienced more than once in his life. Vivid imaginings along with memories raced through his mind – of being assaulted more than once or the ruffians once employed to throw him off London Bridge on behalf of a rich husband he had cuckolded. Leghorn was split by any number of canals, which might serve the same purpose as had been sought in the River Thames.

Proximity to the pair at the head of the alley forced him to stop, and that low-held lantern was lifted, this as a hand was laid on his back to push him roughly forwards and closer to the arc of light, the hat he was wearing lifted from his head.

'Him right enough: Barclay's factotum.'

'Fucktotem, more like,' came the sniggering response from his rear, 'him being so comely.'

'Who are you?'

'I think that is a question you might be obliged to answer first.'

The voice was different, more refined; it was the voice of the one who addressed him as 'fellow', which meant they lacked a name. Yet Barclay had been mentioned, so something about him was known. Slowly, Gherson turned round, aware of the feeling of dread in the pit of his belly, his knees trembling and knowing when he spoke his voice would likely betray his fears; by the light of another upheld lantern he registered there were five men in all.

'The name is Gherson.'

'Never knew the name,' came the response from one of the rougher voices, 'just the face.'

133

'Never one to spare a word for the likes of us, I recall, Cole. Looked more likely to spit on us than extend a common greeting.'

'But a fellow,' the man named as Cole replied, 'I have seen too often these last weeks, noseying around.'

'No,' Gherson replied quickly, wondering if the tremor in his voice was obvious. He felt he had good cause to be fearful; snoops in the London he knew only too well were generally fished out of the river of a morning.

'Well, this is no place to find out. Bring him along.'

With that the refined voice spun round, the swinging lantern giving a very brief glimpse of oiled and curled locks, with ribbon decoration on the ends, and a slight flash of what had to be gold decoration on the neck.

'Are you going to walk on or do I need the use of my boot?'

'Hold, Fred,' Cole jested. 'Can you not see it's terror that has him rooted?'

Gherson did move, aware of the sour taste of regurgitated wine in his throat, acid and searing, which did nothing to slow his teeming thoughts. How could these men know him, have recognised his face but not know his name, they being folk he had not acknowledged? It had to be sailors, must be aboard a King's ship and out here in the Mediterranean: that meant HMS *Semele*.

'Where are we going?'

'You?' Cole enquired. 'Might be perdition, less you have a good tale to tell.'

'I have done nothing untoward.'

134

'That we will find out,' the voice from the front growled.

They came to and entered a low wooden door, which opened on to a room that looked to be used for business. There was a high clerk's desk of the kind at which Gherson had too often toiled, seeking to find ways to cheat those employing him. There were shelves laden with ledgers and a round table with several chairs, one of which he was pressed down into, this while the candles in the sconces on the walls were lit to illuminate the whole.

There was no doubting the leader and he did not have to speak; the quality of his clothing and appearance was enough: good linen, a long waistcoat of fine leather as well as a certain cast of features allied to his expression, the whole slightly gaudy and every inch the buccaneer in a showy, old-fashioned way. He came to the table with a straw-covered flagon of the local Tuscan wine as well as a goblet, which he filled, Gherson noting it was not offered to the others present who were now lined up behind him. When he sat down, Cornelius Gherson found himself facing a handsome, sharp-featured creature with a thin moustache over full lips, wearing the kind of smile that could be taken very easily as a threat.

'Gherson?'

'Yes.'

'The name is Dutch.'

'Was. I am English born, as was my sire.' Gherson was vaguely sure he had seen this fellow and more than once, racking his brain to recall where and when without being able to pin it.

135

'Occupation, captain's clerk.'

'King's Navy, that says to me.' Gherson nodded. 'And what would a fellow of that occupation be doing hanging around in this part of Leghorn?'

'Looking for employment.' A raised dark eyebrow. 'My ship was taken by the French, the captain killed–'

'Barclay's dead?' Cole demanded.

'He is.'

'There is a God,' was the opinion of Fred.

A sip of wine was taken. 'My companions think you are a spy.'

'Soon as I spotted him, Mr Senyard, as I told you.'

'For the love of Christ, hold your tongue, Dan,' snapped Cole.

Senyard's eyes lifted to look over Gherson's shoulder and they were angry, which could only be at the use of the name. This was a man who wished to remain anonymous if he could and that could mean many things, not least that the easiest way to deal with this snooping captain's clerk would be to dispose of him. Did identification increase the risk?

'I am without employment,' Gherson croaked, all the saliva having gone from his mouth and throat. 'With my employer gone and no one in the fleet seeking my services, I came looking for a berth that would suit my skills.'

'Yet you did not think to identify yourself and ask?' Senyard growled. 'Instead you sat around with your ears pricked, or walked the quays looking at the boats and to what purpose.' It was not a question. 'What was it? Deserters? Information on the movements of the privateer vessels? Telling tales of what they brought in and from which captured vessels?'

'None of those things,' Gherson protested. 'I did not ask because I reckoned strangers to be unwelcome.'

'They are that,' a new voice growled.

Cole again. 'Right enough there, Cephas, as ever was.'

'Employment, perhaps with figures, in which I have skill.'

'Which passed on to the King's Navy would be of some use.'

'A service I hate,' was the desperate reply.

'A service in which you were employed and under no duress,' Senyard insisted.

'I rose to it from being pressed.' Both eyebrows arched then, which had Gherson gabbling on about how he had got from that estate to serving as clerk to Ralph Barclay. 'The captain needed someone to manage his logs and accounts. I was that man, and once he saw I could serve him proper–'

'What does that mean?' Senyard interrupted.

'He required a clerk who could write up the lists in such a way that it was accounted for on paper.'

'But?'

'Not in truth. There was always a bit more. I did the same with his investments, but to my own advantage as well as his.'

The last part was said in slight desperation; these men existed on the very edge of legality. He needed to convince them of his own credentials in

137

that area and it seemed to have some effect, for Senyard sat back and thought for several seconds, even taking a gulp of wine before responding.

'So you are a thief?'

'I look to my needs. That is why I came to seek employment in this part of the port, where I reckoned my skills would be most sought. I would not be so foolish as to behave in such a way with men of your stripe.'

The smile now was wolfish. 'You admit to stealing from your past employer as a recommendation for looking to do likewise here?'

'No!' Gherson protested, realising the impression he had created was wrong. 'I need paid employment so I can acquire the means to return home to England, which I presently lack.'

'And the quickest way to get that is by theft.'

'I would serve anyone who engaged me honestly.'

'Then,' Senyard snapped, 'sell us out to the first bag of silver waved under your nose, perhaps by a King's officer.'

'No.'

'I am wondering what to do with you, Gherson.' Senyard lifted his gaze to look over his shoulder again at the quartet behind. 'I cannot help but reckon my companions here, the ones who spotted you, have an easy solution.'

The 'Right there, your honour' was like a chorus.

'Please,' Gherson begged; he felt the warm wetness in his groin as he began to piss himself. 'I have learnt nothing and will not seek to.'

'It is lucky you are not dealing with one of the

138

privateer captains, Gherson, for they would take you out to sea and lash you to a cannonball before dropping you overboard. I cannot doubt that you gleaned some knowledge of what goes on in our commonwealth, only I hope it is of no account.'

'I know nothing.'

Senyard stood up. 'There is not a man born who knows nothing, Gherson, and just so you should know that you are unwelcome in this part of Leghorn, as well as the fact that your services are not required–'

'I was a sailor once and can be again. If my skills are rusty they will soon return.'

'Your desperation is even less convincing than your previous denials. So, I hand you over to my companions, though I do not permit them to do as they would no doubt wish. It is, however, necessary that you go from whence you came with some feeling that to return would be unwise and perhaps it will be a message too, if some fool sent you. Peabody, Danvers, Brewer and Holder will want to let you know that treating them as if they do not exist can be painful.'

Why had he named them?

'See, Gherson, now you know who they are as well as I. But I would abjure you to forget every name you have heard tonight, for if you are to be granted life, it is a gift only once in the giving. Do I make myself clear?' The reply was an affirmative sob. 'Gentleman, get this turd out of my presence.'

The hands that grabbed him were strong and they found it easy to drag a man too weak in fear to offer resistance. He was hauled out of the low door and back into the streets, their curses ringing in his ears. Pushed along until they found the spot they favoured, where there was moonlight by which to see, the first clout took him round the ear, this accompanied by a spat curse on the head of Ralph Barclay. A belt from a fist dropped Gherson to his knees. The blows and curses that followed literally rained down on him until he was on the ground, his hands over his hatless head, which turned fists to boots, a few of which got past his fingers.

'Enough,' Cole gasped.

A hand on his collar raised Gherson up to a half crouch, showing thickened lips, the upper one split and seeping blood. 'He's near whole, be nice to make a change to that pretty, sneering face of his.'

'Let it rest, Dan.' Cole said, crouching down. 'Now get yourself out of this part of the port an' don't think to come back, for if you do it will be knives you'll be facing, not fists and boots.'

The hand let go and Gherson fell to lie flat on the ground, aware of the pains he was suffering, as well as the sound of receding footsteps and jolly laughter. It was some time before he could raise himself up onto his knees, even longer to get to his feet. Staggering, he wandered for some time before he recognised the canal quay on which he had espied Emily Barclay, and that took him slowly, achingly, back to the room he had rented, a street away from the Naval Commissariat.

At this time of night few people were abroad, and none who made any attempt to look and see

140

if he required help. Such creatures, in a port frequented by the Navy of His Britannic Majesty King George, were no strangers to drunken and bruised folk making their way with difficulty through the streets and alleys of their port city.

He was required to rap on the door of his lodgings, which brought the owner to the door and he at least, once he saw the state of his lodger, had compassion enough to heat some water on the fire and fetch it so Gherson could begin to clean away the blood that had now begun to dry and cake his wounds.

In his sea chest he had a small looking glass and that told him, albeit by candlelight, of the depth of the beating he had received, the whole made ten times more apparent in daylight when he woke after a troubled sleep: black eyes, swollen lips and lower jaw, as well as bruised hands lucky not to have broken fingers.

Gherson reckoned he required the services of a physician in order to ensure the wounds he had suffered were superficial, and that led to a question of affordability. It was only then, when he reached into his discarded coat, he realised that one of his assailants had filched his purse. He was penniless, without even the means to satisfy the bill for his accommodation.

The welling feeling of despair made him weep, which led to a quick and painful attempt to hide the wetness as well as the redness of his eyes when his kindly landlord brought him a breakfast of fresh bread, fruit and coffee, his enquiries as to the cause in a language not even Italian but a local dialect, waved away.

The food and coffee had an effect, it being enough to remind Gherson of the many times in his life, since he had been evicted from the family home in childhood, he had been bereft of the means to eat and lacking anywhere safe to lay his head. He had survived, often even prospered by the use of his wits and those he would need now more than ever.

He was in a foreign port and country with nothing. Somehow he must find a way back to England where the people who had prospered from his clever manipulations of Ralph Barclay's investments would be duty-bound to care for him. The thought of how he had fooled Barclay in a way the old dolt had been unable to see cheered him up somewhat, though not enough to move without pain.

But it did, as he sat recalling his depredations, create the germ of a notion as to how he might get out of the bind he was now in.

CHAPTER ELEVEN

Emily Barclay was entertaining, her guests the leading female lights of the small community of fellow Britons in Leghorn. Mrs Udeny, the wife of the consul, Mrs Pollard and her daughter, related to a leading Levant merchant, and most tellingly, Mrs Teale, spouse and helpmeet to the Anglican vicar – the person who seemed to hold the conscience of the expatriate community in

142

her fat and reddened hands.

A lady of full proportions, those hands rested in her lap beneath a tellingly oversized bosom, one that seemed to have wandered downwards and far from its original location, while the jowly face and plump cheeks hinted at an inability to contain her appetites when it came to the local food. As of this moment, she was demolishing a substantial Italian pastry with some gusto.

This was in stark contrast to the others present, ladies who nibbled rather than ate, just as they sipped rather than drank the tea Emily had prepared, a rare treat in these climes. Mrs Udeny had a withered countenance to go with her innate mildness, as though the climate had drained from her any form of vital spirit. The Pollards had an air of beauty, the mother's countenance some-what faded, Caroline Pollard's still in the process of formation, for she was as yet only sixteen.

Enquiries, discreet but well intentioned, had been made to the state of Emily's health – in truth that meant the child – with various allusions to the questionable habits of the Irish doctor who lived hereabouts, known to consort with less than virtuous local women and be perhaps too fond of the wine flagon, a common slur now repeated by Mrs Teale in her carrying way.

'But you have little choice, my dear Mrs Barclay, but to throw yourself into the hands of Monsieur Flaherty. The notion of an Italian attending to you in childbirth is too horrid to contemplate.'

The use of the French designation was a calculated insult from the woman who saw herself as the doyenne of the English community: the man was Irish to his fingertips.

'I daresay, Mrs Teale, judging by the number of urchins running through the streets, that the locals have safe and well-tried methods of delivery.'

Miss Pollard blushed; such allusions were embarrassing. The other ladies were caught between the truth of what Emily was saying and the obvious fact that she had contradicted the vicar's wife, something few dared to do in fear of being the butt of her barbs. Emily had spoken without giving such a matter thought and was required to hastily qualify her words. At all costs she must be seen as respectable by this group.

'But of course, Mrs Teale, I bow to your superior wisdom.'

Murmurs of agreement followed that and the substantial bosom, magnified to deliver a rebuke, seemed to shrink as the lady's eminence was acknowledged. She glanced out of the window and seemed to take on its view of the harbour as if seeking a like countenance on the figureheads of the warships at anchor, to which she was, though not to her face, often compared.

'I may not be the one to have been here in residence the lengthiest, Mrs Barclay, but I judge myself to have a superior discernment of what is what.'

Mrs Pollard stiffened slightly; she had been here for two decades, fifteen years longer than Letitia Teale, spoke the local dialect fluently and had friends in Tuscan society. It had been she who had been seen as the person to pay attention to, long before the Reverend Mr Teale had landed on this

144

shore to take over the English parish church of St George, a building not of the highest quality. That the usurpation of social superiority rankled was only rarely apparent, but that did not disguise the fact that it was prevalent.

Emily was metaphorically biting her tongue, trying to recall how she would have behaved in the past, for instance at the home of her parents. It would not have involved even dreaming of checking the words of an elder woman as well as the wife of a divine. She was also thinking the events of the last two and a half years had altered her and not necessarily, in the article of polite conversation, for the better. How much of that was down to her late husband, how much to John Pearce and his iconoclastic way, was moot.

'It is such a pity that Sir William has departed for Naples,' Mrs Udeny ventured. 'He was such graceful company.'

'Manners of a real gentleman,' Mrs Pollard agreed, 'though my husband has said on more than one occasion that his officers were prone to question his judgement.'

'I always found him most pleasant to me,' Caroline said, in a meek tone, suited to her years. 'Like an uncle.'

The biting of tongue was necessary then. Emily knew more of Admiral Sir William Hotham than anyone else present, of his devious bordering on villainous nature, as well as what a certain officer thought of him, words that she could barely contemplate for the blasphemy, never mind mention in this company.

'His officers would do well to mind their manners,' Mrs Teale snorted. 'I do not say that the Good Lord put Sir William in command, an act carried out by human hand, but it is surely the task of his inferiors to recall they are just that, in the eyes of the Admiralty and the Almighty.'

A meaningful glance was thrown at the teapot, one quickly picked up by Emily. The stipend received by the Teales for their ministry was not large, quite the opposite: it was not a living that could be said to be adequate and probably reflected Mr Teale's standing in the church hierarchy. Tea, being expensive in England and even more so in Italy, was a luxury to which the divine and his wife could rarely rise.

She was hinting at a refill so the obligatory noises came from Emily, a bell was rung to order a fresh supply of means to infuse the leaves and the key produced to unlock the sideboard door that gave access to the tea caddy. If the hot water when it came was welcome, the note that came with it was not.

'Not distressing news, Mrs Barclay, I hope,' Mrs Teale enquired, her antenna as sharp as ever when it came to observing her fellow humans. 'You have gone quite pale.'

Emily waved the note and half turned to hide her dismay, aware she would have to say something while searching for the words, until the lack of time to concoct a tale obliged her to stick to the truth.

'My late husband's clerk wishes to call upon me.'

'Am I to judge that is a prospect you do not relish?'

Damn the woman, Emily thought, before castigating herself for the profanity; she was showing
too much of her emotions. 'He was not a man I
esteemed, Mrs Teale. I never quite got over the
feeling he did not always deal honestly with
Captain Barclay's affairs.'

'So you will not be inviting him to join us in the
very welcome tea?'

The thought of Gherson in this milieu filled
Emily with dread. He knew everything about her,
her husband, as well as John Pearce, and would
no doubt take great pleasure in exposure of her
sins in that department. If she hated him, and it
shamed her that she did, then it was fully reciprocated. The oily swine had many times hinted at
dalliance, an impudence she had rejected with
alacrity.

'I think it best I see him alone.'

'Alone!' was Mrs Teale's exclamation. 'Is that
seemly?'

'Am I to assume the meeting might be hostile?'
asked Mrs Udeny.

Emily was grateful for the question from a
woman who spoke little, which was surprising
given, as the consul's wife, she was by far the
superior in social rank, a fact which irritated
Letitia Teale and turned her into a bully, so determined was she to maintain her grip.

'That is a distinct possibility. I cannot help but
speculate that he wants something from me.'

'A sinner, then?'

'I think so, Mrs Teale.'

'What is this fellow's name?'

Emily had to produce a false laugh then, one

that sounded unconvincing to her ears. 'That is of no account, Mrs Teale. He would not be known to someone of your eminence and virtue.'

The flattery was essential; if this woman had the name, she might seek him out. When she used the word 'sinner' it was in a search for souls her husband might save. But she also had to be reassured; in her world women, not even widows, received men in their private quarters without another of their sex in attendance.

'When I say alone, I will ensure that the wife of the owner of this *pensione* is present.' She moved to the bureau on which lay her writing materials. 'Now forgive me, I must reply and ask him to call at a later time.'

'Would I be permitted access to the caddy while you compose?'

'Mrs Teale, how could I refuse?'

To say that the prospect of meeting Cornelius Gherson came to dominate her thinking for the next hour was an understatement, not least what he might be after. She would have sent back a refusal had she been alone, but that was impossible in the company of a group of people with too much time on their hands and a strong desire to indulge in gossip.

That none of them knew about John Pearce was a blessing; they could not or they would never have called upon her once, never mind several times. How that had remained hidden she did not know and could only assume a limited form of engagement between her present guests, their husbands, and the constant stream of visiting naval officers.

On reflection, that was absurd; they mixed all the time and there had to be suspicion if not knowledge of her adultery, and that drove her to the only conclusion that made sense: they kept such information to themselves to protect the reputation of one of their own and that was not her lover. The failure of a post captain, close to the top of the list and soon to be an admiral, to hang onto his wife, was no concern of civilians and death did little to alter that.

The rest of the time spent with the ladies became a sore trial, aware as she was of the glances being thrown at her by Mrs Teale when the old battleaxe thought she was not looking. The lady was suspicious by nature, God-fearing in a way that bordered on hypocrisy and so determined to hold on to her position that it would mortify her if anyone came into possession of idle chatter before her. With what Gherson knew she would be closer to heaven than sacrilege allowed, while Emily Barclay would be ostracised.

'You must come to me, my dear, if the journey does not tire you.' A meaningful glance was thrown at the hidden bulge in Emily's belly. 'Do not do so if it risks the welfare of the child – and yours, of course. I cannot tell you how much my dear husband the vicar is looking forward to performing a proper Christian baptism of an English child, a rare event in his parish.'

That the Catholics have them by the bucketload was a sentiment that had to be suppressed; when Letitia Teale said Christian, she meant Anglican.

'And you must tell me how you dealt with the

clerk fellow.' The fat, ruddy cheeks were swung to encompass the others. 'I'm sure I am not the only one dying to know. Now, I think it must be time we left you to your rest.'

Murmurs of agreement had the rest gathering what possessions they had brought with them, parasols and the like, which left Emily wondering how to play Letitia Teale, now drinking the last of her tea.

'Dear me,' she spouted, in a sudden flash of inspiration, 'I have a small gift for you, Mrs Teale.'

'A gift?'

That was aimed at Emily's back; she was at the sideboard fetching out a brown paper packet, with a handwritten designation telling all that it had been packed by the emporium of Fortnum and Mason in St James's Market.

'One of my late husband's colleagues brought me two packets of tea to comfort me for my loss.' Mrs Teale's eyes opened at such generosity, too much so to spot what was a blatant lie. 'I will never finish them both, so I wondered if you would accept the spare one. It would be a terrible pity if time rendered it less tasteful.'

The expression that engendered was composed of a whole gamut of emotions: greed for the tea, certainly, but also wonder at the notion of someone parting with such a quantity of such a scarce commodity. Then there was a moment when she thought to refuse, the reasons obvious, for this was an indication of the actuality of her status and lack of prosperity. Luckily, the first sentiment triumphed but would it have the effect for which Emily hoped and act to deflect her curiosity?

150

'Your kindness overwhelms me.'

'Stuff and nonsense, Mrs Teale. Where would we all be without your guiding hand?'

The response was a quite girlish refusal to accept that such a thing came close to being a fact.

It was the wife of the proprietor who showed Cornelius Gherson into the sitting room, the first obvious thing to register was the state of his face and the marks of what must have been quite a serious beating. It was telling to Emily that she had no feeling at all of sympathy, as she would have had with almost any other creature on earth.

'La prego di rimanere, Signora.'

That got not more than a knowing look, as Emily waved to ask the woman to sit down, which she did, a look of deep suspicion aimed at this much-bruised visitor.

'I need to see you alone.'

'That will never happen, Gherson, but you may speak freely, for the lady has no English.'

'Your condition suits you, madam. You were never short on comeliness, but being with child has given you an extra bloom.'

'I have no notion of why you have chosen to call on me, Gherson, but I would be obliged if your visit was as brief as possible. I do not find your company palatable.'

'The tongue has not altered.'

'Your reason?'

'I wondered if you found in your husband's papers his last will and testament.'

'How could I when he did not write one?'

That got a smile, though one that looked odd

151

with the swellings on the lip. 'And if I said to you I wrote it, he signed it, what then? It should be in the chest with the remainder of his correspondence, much of it relating to you and your shortcomings as a spouse.'

'Those I have declined to read.'

'So you are wise enough to care for your blushes.'

'You appear to be unwise enough to look to your well-being, judging by your condition.'

'The will,' Gherson spat.

'Does not exist, which you well know.'

'And if I say it does, then what?'

'I will ask you to leave, and I can assure you,' Emily said, with a gesture to the signora, 'this lady's husband has the means to find men who will remove you and no doubt add to your discomfort in the process.'

'Captain Barclay's prize agents are Ommaney and Druce.'

'I fail to see the point of you telling me something of which I am fully aware.'

'They are men of business, very successful and people who trusted me to handle your husband's affairs.'

'Then that seems to me grounds to dismiss them from a hand in mine. Anyone who trusts you must be a fool.'

'Including your husband?'

'Especially my husband, who only, I suspect, retained your services because you could be relied upon not to be fussy about breaking the law. Given he was cut from the same mould, you made a charming pair.'

Gherson made to sit down, which got him a sharp rejoinder that he was not welcome to do so, his response a shrug. 'I fear it will be my duty to write to Ommaney and Druce and tell them I have knowledge of the existence of a will, and one that leaves you with nothing. The estate of Captain Barclay was specifically attested to go to his sisters.'

'Liar.'

'They, being diligent, will no doubt refuse to allow you access to anything until my contention is proven or seen to be false. They would be remiss to do otherwise; indeed, they would be required to instruct lawyers with a brief look into the matter. That could take up a great deal of time, while the expenses incurred, as well as yours to defend it, would be much diminished by fees.'

'What do you want, Gherson?'

'You are so sure there is something?'

'I am not a fool. I don't trust you but I know you and, I will also add, merely having to talk to you makes me feel sick.'

That got a glance from Gherson towards the signora. 'Ten minutes alone and I would make you eat those words.'

'Then should it ever occur, and it will not if I have my way, I will have in my hand a knife, and I will use it.'

'There is a way to deflect this.' Emily arched her eyebrows in enquiry. 'The loss of my position has rendered my situation unpleasant. It is my desire to return to England, and I lack the means to do so.'

'And you wish me to provide them?'

'As a payment for my services to your husband.'

Emily wanted to scream and tell him to get out, but at the forefront of her mind was an image of Mrs Teale. As long as this slug was in Leghorn there existed a possibility they would meet, and for her and her carefully crafted carapace of respectability that would be disastrous. Gherson knew everything and would take great pleasure in disclosure.

She was determined to save the name of her child as much as her own; at all costs he must be born and raised without the taint of bastardy, while she had the means in her late husband's chest to make this problem disappear. The notion of compliance to what was nothing but blackmail rendered it no less unpleasant as a prospect.

'The ladies I saw departing the *pensione* were, I assume, acquaintances of yours?'

'I will advance you fifty guineas, Gherson, on certain conditions. The first is that I book and pay for the carriage fare to Vienna, which will ensure you depart Livorno. Then, that you write and sign a document supporting the lack of a will, which will earn you the balance. The third, once those are carried out to my satisfaction, is that I never set eyes on you again.'

She should have taken more cognisance of the look on the man's face and added that to her knowledge of his character. He was a good actor and did humility and gratitude well. But the fact that he fooled her was more to do with her needs than his.

For himself, Gherson was thinking, if you pay once, you will pay again and surely you too will

154

return to England and a comfortable life. Suddenly his prospects, even in the long term, did not look so bleak.

CHAPTER TWELVE

John Pearce was not a patient man, this he knew and accepted as one of his less attractive traits. But the pace of progression at the Naval Commissariat would have tested that quality in a saint. He could not help but wonder if there was a personal element in the way he was being treated, given the time it was taking to say if HMS *Flirt's* requirements could be met; what was available at all, added to when they could be on the quayside ready to be taken aboard, seemed destined to stretch to infinity.

He had crossed swords with the man in charge of supplying stores once before, an irascible Scottish captain by the name of Urquhart. He had more or less named him a disgrace to the service over a duel he had fought and what that individual saw as the deplorable manner of his victory. That took no account of the question of his merely being a proper naval officer in the first place.

He was desperate to use some of his time ashore with Emily Barclay, aware the need for discretion would cut into what was available. He could not just shirk his shipboard duties and stay ashore as long as he wished; to do so would expose him to rebuke, but there could be no barging into her presence and surprising her. His visit had, for appearances, to be a formal one, with his name sent in and her agreeing to receive him. Given the way she had sought to mix socially, it might be public, which made what was hard – seeking to persuade her of her folly – near to impossible.

With time to kill, he wondered at Digby sending him ashore in the first place. If he had given way in the face of the threat made to depose him, that had done little to ease their strained relationship. His captain knew Emily was in Leghorn and he could not suppose Pearce would pass up an opportunity to contact her, yet he seemed to be facilitating that which he abhorred.

The clock on the office wall told him time was ticking away so he sent a message to Urquhart by way of one of his minions, asking that he attend to him personally. That came back as a distinct negative, this delivered by a one-legged ex-sailor who, when Pearce indicated he had other business to attend to and that he would call back later, produced a slow shake of his head.

'Not wise, your honour. What's to say you won't be left short if another ship's officer comes in a'begging. It be dog eat dog round here, an' no error.'

'You don't mean first come first served?'

The head canted to one side and the eyes eschewed contact. 'If I were to say that Captain Urquhart has his favourites–'

'Of which I am unlikely to be one,' Pearce interrupted.

That got a crooked grin, exposing few teeth. 'Which is my way of saying, your honour, best

156

keep an eye out for another blue coat heading this way lest you be left sucking the hind tit.'

It was pointless to reflect that what was happening was unfair. His time ashore had to be limited and that which was available was disappearing at a rate of knots.

'Well, I have other business to attend to and I must take the risk.'

He made his way by the quayside to ask Lambert, in charge of the men who had rowed him ashore, to take his place at the commissariat, with added directions as to where he would be if and when he was needed. That got a sly knowing look from a one-time member of the crew of HMS *Larcher*, swiftly suppressed. There was little doubt in his mind as to what Pearce was about.

On the way and walking at pace he sought to rehearse the words he wished to use, his aim to get Emily out of Leghorn. If a voyage to England at this time of year was felt to be too hazardous, one to Naples was less so. A vessel hugging the coast would pass any number of safe havens into which they could retire to avoid inclement weather. In Naples she would come back onto the orbit of Lady Hamilton, who might well, as she had in the past, accommodate Emily.

She would certainly help with the necessary medical requirements to ensure, as far as it was possible, a safe delivery. Pearce also hoped that the ambassador's wife, given her own chequered past and what she had done to aid them already, would help him to persuade his paramour that his view should prevail.

He tried, out of courtesy, to ask for Emily in his

157

limited Italian, which earned him a blank look from the proprietor, who Pearce reckoned was being obtuse. His rising temper had to be contained, with the request to see the Signora Barclay repeated at the pace of a dim-witted child. He then had to wait again for what seemed an age to be shown up the stairs by one of the man's daughters, which meant, given the totality of the morning, he was in a far from benign mood on entry to her apartments.

'Lieutenant Pearce, how good of you to call.'

That was for show, with Emily nodding to the girl that it was safe to shut the door and depart. That she did not fly into his arms on that happening further affected his already fractured mood, so when he spoke it was with none of the supplication and gentility he had intended to employ when he set off from HMS *Flirt*.

'Should I be grateful merely to be received?'

'Would it not be best to form habits that will later be required?'

'Not for me, Emily.'

'John, I–'

There was only a few paces between them, covered quickly enough to shut off any more words and if she resisted his intention to kiss her, it was with feeble determination. This held until he extended the arms with which he had embraced her, to look directly into her lovely grey-green eyes.

'That is the greeting I expected from you, Emily, I did not think I would be required to force it myself.'

She detached herself and turned away, as if it

158

was all too embarrassing. 'What of my receiving you alone in my rooms? Do you not care what will be said if that becomes common knowledge?'

'You are well aware I don't give a damn.'

He observed the shrinking of the shoulders; Emily had always deplored his cavalier use of language. 'I should have asked the girl who showed you up here to stay.'

'For the sake of your reputation.'

'What else? I have made friends here in Leghorn, ladies who would be mortified at my receiving you in this manner.'

'And you care for their opinion?'

'I have made it my business to, as an upright widow.'

His response emerged as a near shout. 'We cannot go on like this. At least, I cannot. It is nought but hypocrisy.'

'You know my reasons.'

'And I don't accept them, Emily. I doubt there's a soul in the fleet who does not harbour some inkling of our association. You prate on–'

That spun her back to look at him, her eyes flashing with indignation, the word 'prate' repeated with venom.

'Yes, Emily,' Pearce insisted, his tone more discreet, though the level of stress was undiminished. 'You go on about respectability as though it is some kind of holy grail, when it is nought but a method of social conformity that suits the charlatan. How long do you think it will be before the rumours circulating here are repeated in your hometown?'

'Rumours are one thing, established fact

another. It is that which I seek to prevent.'

'So you would keep me, the father of your child, at arm's length in order to protect the reputation of your husband.'

'That is not the purpose and you know it,' she snapped.

'It is concomitant. Ralph Barclay will suffer no loss of standing for being a near-criminal martinet who maltreated you, and my child will bear his name.'

'Only until the proprieties allow us to be together.'

'And in the meantime I am supposed to exist on the crumbs from the great man's table and be grateful for my good fortune, is that it?'

'John,' she pleaded, 'my Christian soul does not allow me to thank providence for that which it has brought us.'

'Brought you, Emily. I want no part of it.'

Delivered in a cold tone it carried more truth than any of his previous clamour. A position never previously stated, but one he had determined on very soon after Emily had outlined the future she envisaged for them both, it was one on which Pearce knew her to be unshakable.

'Just so I make myself plain, I will not accept so much as a biscuit on Ralph Barclay's account. As to your proposition that I turn into some provincial nonentity, and pay happy lip service to a mode of existence I despise, that will not happen either. I came here today to ask that you leave Leghorn for Naples, where we can enlist the good offices of Lady Hamilton.'

'I am to go to Naples, not you?'

'Our good friend Michael talked to me of the way being with child changes a woman. What he saw as less obvious was how it also affects a putative father. If I am to be that, and regardless of it being a boy or a girl, I would want the child to be proud of me. That cannot be achieved as little more than a kept man and, as of this moment, I am at a loss to know what else I could do to realise a good opinion. But, for all its apparent drawbacks, I am a naval officer in the midst of a war and I already know that such an estate brings with it opportunity for gain.'

'You hate the navy,' she replied quietly.

'I would hate idleness more. I would hate to be locked into a society where I suspect my being would be screaming with boredom. You know me enough, I hope, to be certain I would not be able to hold my tongue if I were faced with opinions I both detest and know to be wrong. Could you not tell of my reservations when, having rescued you from captivity, I volunteered to serve aboard *Spark?*'

'Perhaps I was foolish enough to assume you went to sea in order to mitigate any chance of embarrassing me.'

'I required time to think, to seek to formulate an argument that might persuade you that I am right and you are wrong. I want to be with you more than anything I can think of. I want that I should be acknowledged as the father of my child and I don't give a damn who thinks it untoward. But I am not prepared to become that which you wish me to be to achieve it.'

'You would have it christened in your name and

161

proclaim to the world that it was illegitimately conceived?'

'Emily, I would not have it christened at all, except to please you, and I can assure you the first person to make comment of the child that was not praiseworthy would find themselves facing me and risking that their loose tongue might cost them their life.'

'You are as much a barbarian as my husband, then.'

'That is not true and you know it.'

'Do I? You come here in high dudgeon to tell me how I must live my life to please you–'

'That is untrue and you know it. I come here with what I think is best for us both, as well as what will be added to that. We can be happy, but not with me as some foppish dependant. Surely you have come to know me better than that. Do you think you will be content as the mistress of some dwelling in a provincial town?'

'I enjoyed a happy childhood in that provincial milieu you so despise.'

'But you're not the same person that departed as a bride. You have seen more of life in the last three years than the whole of the previous seventeen in total. You have seen the world, or part of it, broken vows it was unwise to have made, observed that when it comes to man dealing with their fellow human beings, unkindness is the norm not charity. Go to Naples and I, as soon as I can, will join you there.'

The rap on the door was unfortunate, for Pearce felt his arguments were beginning to carry weight. One of the traits he loved in Emily was

162

her courage, a mettle that had seen her defy Ralph Barclay even when he threatened her with disgrace. He would never be able to browbeat her into acquiescence; only a degree of logic plus a lack of an alternative to his notion of happiness might suffice. It was, of course, Lambert, come to tell him his presence was needed at the commissariat, where nothing could be released from the stores without him signing for it.

'I have to go, Emily, but I want you to know that I love you with all my heart.'

'Yet you'd have me be a naval widow, sat somewhere – and God only knows where that might be – while you are away at sea; alone with a new child you profess makes you proud, yet one you are quite willing to grow up as a stranger to you, while I could never be sure if you were alive or dead. At least my husband did not have such a fate in store for me.'

'Please, do not ascribe to him anything but base motives. He took you to sea with him to save on his expenses. It was brought on by parsimony not affection.'

'Tell me, John, what is the difference between your being at sea and not part of my life and being on land in the same estate? You seem to imply it is my silly upbringing that will cause a rift between us.'

'I do not seek a rift, Emily.'

'Is it not your pride that lies at the root of this? You would shame your child to protect it.'

'That is not fair.'

'Is it not? You wish to move me to Naples, where no doubt you would enlist Emma Hamilton to your cause.' Pearce blushed slightly, exposing the truth of that. 'What then? Our child is born. Do I remain in Naples hidden away from approbation while you sail the seven seas?'

'I would find a solution in time, one that would be suitable to us both.'

'No, John. I do not want for my child the peripatetic life you endured with your father, wandering the country with never a certainty as to where you would be laying your head.'

'It was not endured!'

'But it was not always comfortable, either. I know that, for you have told me.'

'I would not have changed it.'

'I know it has made you the man you are, a fellow in endless dispute, even, it seems, with the woman you purport to love.'

'If you doubt that, I am at a loss as to what I might say.'

'Love, John, brings with it often the need for sacrifice. I did that for you when we became lovers, abandoning everything I had been raised to believe in on the altar of how I felt for you.'

Another rap at the door brought a message, and even if it was delivered in Italian, a language in which even the most mundane act was imbued with drama, it was clearly one that called upon Pearce to hurry. The only thing it did not achieve was to throw Emily off her point.

'So when I ask that you do the same for me, I meet blank refusal. I have no desire and never have had to be a wandering itinerant. Even at our most desperate I envisaged a future where we would be settled with a home and a normal way of life, which even you must admit we have never had. So before you come to me with your ultimatum–'

Pearce cut right across her and in anger. 'It is not an ultimatum, Emily.'

She was unnaturally calm in her response, which made it more telling than it would have been in passion. 'I cannot see what else it can be. Do as I demand or our relationship must end.'

'I have never even hinted that.'

'How deep is a love that offers nothing but sorrow?' she asked, the tone rhetorical. 'Perhaps mine is supposed to be while yours is more shallow, more that of your gender than mine.'

Pearce knew he had to depart, just as he knew that to do so on such a note would not serve. As soon as the stores were loaded, HMS *Flirt* had orders to get back to sea and the disguised blockade of Genoa. Even if he felt he was being traduced by wayward feminine logic, he knew not to slam any doors.

'Emily, I can argue with admirals and bend them to my thinking. I have no fear to meet an enemy in battle and risk all to prevail. What I cannot do, it seems, is to even discuss with you what I consider best for us. I have made a proposal, which I hope you will consider in a calm manner, just as I hope you will see the sense of it. Now I ask that you favour me with a fitting farewell for I have to go back to my duties.'

It was heartbreaking, once he had come close, to have to use a hand to bend her head round so that he could kiss her, even more so that her lips were so cold.

CHAPTER THIRTEEN

The arrival of Sir John Jervis, brought out to the Mediterranean in the frigate HMS *Lively*, sparked immediate change. Sir William Hotham had been a gentlemanly sort of fellow, who saw a certain degree of languor as befitting the role of a leader of men. Jervis was the polar opposite. Indeed, if anyone had told him he lacked the finer qualities required of a gentleman, he would have taken that as praise; his language was as salty as his demeanour, which came from serving near a decade as a youngster rated as an able seaman.

His first command was that loitering in Leghorn was forbidden; Hotham had never minded a bit of laggardly behaviour, in which his officers, as well as those men trusted not to desert, had enjoyed a couple of extra days in port, able to sample the fleshpots and brothels if they were so inclined. For the more refined, they would partake of the opera and theatrical entertainments laid on by the locals.

Jervis was a strict disciplinarian and would have none of it. If you were not at sea or under his personal gaze and ready to depart at the bang of a signal gun, you were failing in your duty and deserved to be beached. His attitude was no less severe with the lower deck and it was made plain to his captains that the best way to maintain good order was with frequent recourse to flogging.

Nelson had sailed to San Fiorenzo Bay on notice of his arrival to have what he told everyone was a very testy interview with the C-in-C. He was soon back on his old beat but bad weather had brought all his vessels into Vado Bay. Being the man he was, despite it being a far from perfect place in which to shelter, the commodore had invited all the commanders and their premiers to dinner, a request that Pearce knew sat heavily on the mind of Henry Digby.

Unbeknown to him, Digby had sent back a note to say he felt it unwise to leave HMS *Flirt* with only a midshipman in command and one yet to recover from a wound at that. The curt reply, also unmentioned, pointed out the brig was at anchor and hardly required a first lieutenant to look to its needs; so both men found themselves sharing a boat, wrapped in heavy cloaks to ward off both the cold and the sea spray, sitting in close proximity and total silence, as it was rowed towards HMS *Agamemnon*.

Well aware of hierarchy and despite the disturbed sea, Digby stood off until all the post captains had gone through the entry port to be greeted with due ceremony. Only when the last, Taberly from HMS *Brilliant*, had hooked onto the gangway did he order the crew of the cutter to haul away, to then lean over and whisper in Pearce's ear.

'I would be most grateful, Mr Pearce, if you behaved with the modesty due to your rank and that you say or do nothing to embarrass the ship.'

'A task I think I can safely leave to you, sir,' was the equally quiet reply.

'Damn me, I am minded to get rid of you.'

'Then today presents an excellent opportunity. I am sure Commodore Nelson will oblige you, but not, I suspect, without asking some quite searching questions as to your reasons.'

The name of the ship identified the man in command and Tilley, Digby's coxswain, yelled it out in a voice loud enough to be heard on the mainmast cap, this as the cutter swung round to touch softly on the gangway base. Pearce was out first, convention having it that the superior officer should be the last to board, making his way to the entry port and the gloom of the interior, to watch as Digby was afforded all the respect due to a full captain: stamping marines and lifted hats from *Agamemnon's* officers. That complete, he was taken to the great cabin.

'Welcome, John.'

'Dick, it is good to see you.'

There were not many years difference between John Pearce and Richard Farmiloe, a couple at most, but on first acquaintance that had provided a noticeable gap. Not now, they looked what they were: contemporaries of a similar age.

'The wardroom is hosting the lesser beings, John, while Nelson sees to the captains.'

'Lead on.'

Never spacious for the men it was required to hold, the wardroom was now crowded and it was telling, the different reactions to the entry of John Pearce, who was left alone as Farmiloe collared a steward and two goblets of wine. Welcoming smiles came from the ship's own officers, men who had come to know him well and whose opinion had been mediated by Richard Farmiloe. This was set against a general stiffening and reserve from the other guests. The coldest glare came from Glaister, his counterpart in HMS *Brilliant,* a ship on which Pearce could class many men as kindred spirits. This fellow Scotsman was not one of them.

'Mr Glaister,' Pearce cried, taking savage delight in the way the skeleton-like face reacted as he moved towards him. The already unnaturally tight skin of his face contracted even more, as the new arrival, coming close, asked, 'And how are you enjoying serving under Captain Taberly? A pleasure, I'm sure.'

Glaister knew he was being guyed and the way he reacted was quicksilver in its effect. 'So sorry to hear about Captain Barclay, Mr Pearce. My sympathy, of course, goes to his wife but, I am sure, you are equally as mortified as the good lady to lose such a dear colleague.'

'A sentiment that has rippled through the entire fleet,' Pearce responded, with false empathy. 'But I wonder if, as naval officers, we should not be more concerned with the loss of HMS *Semele.*'

'A true naval officer might be.'

This was said in a voice loud enough to carry and turn heads. It had Dick Farmiloe hurrying over with those two goblets of wine, to quietly admonish both men.

'Gentlemen, stick to what you have in common please, not to what you see as dispute.'

'I will not be provoked,' Glaister insisted.

'Then do not glare, sir, for on such a countenance it is ghoulish.'

'Come with me, John.' The pressure needed to

get him away was slight, given he was a willing accomplice, with Farmiloe whispering, 'You have to have some sympathy for him, John, he does feel he has been unfairly passed over.'

'That is bad enough, I agree, but to have Taberly as his captain must be close to hellish. If he had shown the slightest willingness to accommodate my presence I would have commiserated with him.'

'Would you be angry with me if I said Glaister was not alone? There are too many here who do not know you as well as us Agamemnons.'

'I promise not to ruffle any more feathers, Dick.'

He was as good as his word, confining his conversations to those who served aboard the ship, most notably and safely with John Roxburgh, the surgeon, the subject being the slow nature of the healing of Conway's wound.

'If his vital spirit holds he will be cured, Mr Pearce, take my word.'

'And how is the commodore's health?'

'He is afflicted as ever, with colds and aches, none of which will diminish until he sees a tricolour he can attack.'

'And that brings about alleviation?'

'It is immediate, Mr Pearce, as if it was divinely inspired.'

Not wishing to question the assertion, it having been made with much conviction, that such a celestial intervention was possible, Roxburgh and he fell to talking about their homeland, a place that produced an inordinate amount of folk who pursued the profession of medicine.

'Your father would have pointed to education,

for which we can only thank the Kirk.'

Much as he queried divinity – his father Adam had derided such a thing in its entirety as superstition – neither of the Pearces could deny that the Elders of the Kirk of Scotland had indeed created a comprehensive system of schooling for their flock. It was the means by which such men as Roxburgh could rise from humble beginnings to pursue their chosen path.

The normally bigoted divines had insisted that every parish must have a school, and every pastor be qualified to teach Latin, Greek and mathematics. The result was a large number of educated Scots as well as a great deal of resentment from Englishmen who saw them occupy too many positions of merit, and more importantly, those of profit. To be termed a 'Sawney Jock' was not one of approbation.

Roxburgh had studied at the Surgeons' Hall in Edinburgh, where the tenets of his craft had moved on many years previously from the lowly pursuit still extant further south, where a sawbones was little better than a barber. And he had mixed with those attending the university, peopled with a strange mixture of students, from radical thinkers to obscurantist divines. One of the former had been Pearce's father.

'I did hear the Ranter speak more than once,' Roxburgh said, before qualifying it with an apology. 'I hope you take no offence at the soubriquet?'

'On the contrary, sir, my father took a perverse pride in being so called.'

'He had a silver tongue, right enough.'

Which got him nowhere in the end, Pearce thought but did not say. All Adam Pearce achieved was to be hounded by the government and finally, having annoyed them to the point of reaction, to be faced with a writ for seditious libel, a false allegation for sure but one that could end on the gallows. The irony that it was another polity that silenced him was not one he was prepared to ever allude to.

'He's gone now, Mr Roxburgh.'

'Leaving you to tend the radical flame?'

Pearce smiled and jerked his head towards the coast. 'I think I will leave that to the French.'

'Heathens to a man, God damn them.'

About to say that condemnation of an entire nation was to stretch the truth, Pearce was cut off by a loud voice calling from the wardroom doorway. 'Gentlemen, the commodore requests that you take your place at dinner.'

They trooped up the gangway, visitors as well as the ships' lieutenants, and made for the great cabin. On entry, each guest was received by Nelson, who had a slight pink glow already from that which he had imbibed. Seated, as the first course of soup was being dispensed, Pearce remarked to a neighbour, an Agamemnon, on the absence of Frank Lepeé, not with any great wish that the drunkard servant should be present.

'Gone, sir. The commodore finally got shot of him, which should have happened years ago. Not that his replacement is too much of an improvement; a Norfolk dolt called Tom Allen.'

'He's a tartar, Collingwood, and that is to the good. There will be no rest with Jervis at the helm

172

I can assure you, no sitting in San Fiorenzo Bay. Admiral Jervis is a close blockader by nature. He intends to keep his fleet cruising off Toulon and if the French do come out, to destroy them utterly.'

Even more flushed now, Nelson had banged his goblet on the polished mahogany of the table, while speaking loudly and emphatically, thus attracting every eye and every ear to his outburst. Pearce reckoned the arrival of Jervis would be good news to most of the officers present, frigate captains at best, while it might be less welcome to the commanders of the line-of-battle ships, happy to be at anchor in San Fiorenzo Bay. The captains there were split between those who had cleaved to Lord Hood and those who had supported Hotham, both sets now adrift as client officers.

The surprise was that Jervis had come out in a frigate and not a capital ship. Indeed, he should have been leading at least a dozen seventy-fours to replace those worn out by service, captained by men who owed any hope of advancement to him. Nelson supplied the answer: he had intended to come out in HMS *Boyne,* his flagship in the West Indies, but she had caught fire and blown up in Portsmouth harbour, taking down with her nearly all the admiral's possessions.

It had never ceased to amaze John Pearce the speed with which information spread throughout a dispersed fleet, the carriers being the men who hardly saw a day when some of their time was not spent on a ship's boat, carrying letters, moving officers as well as a dozen other purposes. The new dispensation in terms of discipline had been no exception. Everyone knew Jervis to be a flogger by reputation, anyway; that he would brook no indolence was only to be expected. Had someone alluded to the thought Pearce had just harboured regarding reinforcements? It was possible, as Nelson, flushed with more than wine, entered a strong opinion.

'The government does not understand the needs of the Mediterranean, sir, which is what comes of having a civilian as First Lord, something on which Sir John and I are in full concord. Chatham may have been a laggard in office but at least he was a soldier, albeit one slow to rise from his bed of a morning.'

Heads dipped at these remarks. Nelson had managed in one sentence to insult two very important people: the Earl of Chatham, William Pitt's elder brother, as well as Earl Spencer, who had been shifted into the position of First Lord when the Portland Whigs joined Pitt's government. It was drink that loosened his tongue, of course, and, even if he was held in high regard, there would be folk at this table who would report back in their letters home what had been said.

'Hear him!' Pearce cried, he too thumping the table with the flat of his hand, a purely mischievous act designed to increase the discomfort of those who worried at Nelson's outburst. Digby, sat next to the ship's parson, looked daggers at him, which had the target suppress the childish desire to stick out his tongue.

Dick Farmiloe was shaking his head, albeit with a quiet smile, indicating he knew what Pearce was about. Judging by the reaction of both Taberly and Glaister they were in complete agreement for once, which would be that he was a menace and that revived a previous reflection.

It was a sadness these two had command of HMS *Brilliant,* which barred him from going aboard to reacquaint himself with some of the men with whom he had first set sail from Sheerness. Oddly, he numbered as companions people who had helped Ralph Barclay to press him into the navy. But there was one other person he would have dearly liked to have come face-to-face with and that was the slug, Toby Burns, who, for reasons unknown, was not present.

'However,' Nelson added empathically, no doubt having sensed the mood, dragging Pearce away from his less than pleasant thoughts regarding Burns, 'we must acknowledge that such politicos have concerns of which we are unaware.'

The reaction to that was overplayed, with excessive noisy agreement; these men did not want to be associated with what had been said previously. Thankfully, the 'Roast Beef of Old England' was played, the platter brought in and if the beast that provided the huge joint was Ligurian, it had been well hung and properly cooked. Added to which, the decanters were doing the rounds to render jolly even the most miserable soul.

Not Digby. While most were flushed and red in the face from proximity to the stoves and too much Tuscan wine, he was in deep conversation with the black-clothed divine who served as chaplain aboard *Agamemnon,* known to the fleet as 'Eggs and Bacon'. It seemed what the man was hearing was making him uncomfortable. In tightly packed seating, he had edged his body as far away as possible from Digby, while his face, even if he was nodding, carried a hint of disquiet.

After ample cheese and copious amounts of port wine, Pearce sought his boat cloak and the deck for a blast of fresh air, away too from the fug of numerous pipes. He was soon joined in his pacing by Dick Farmiloe, the talk naturally turning to shared memories, not least for both, their service under Barclay.

'I am curious, John, how far would you have taken your case against him?'

'All the way to the Old Bailey,' Pearce replied. 'It would not have troubled me to see him hang.'

This was said even though he was unsure if it was true. As in everything with her husband, Emily caused complications. His actions had many times been as much to protect her as to bring down her husband, and even if he wanted vengeance, he was not sure an execution was included.

'It would have required you to testify; you were there.'

'That sounds very much like a question, John.' Pearce shrugged. 'To answer it, all I can say is that I would not have lied under oath.'

It had always had an interesting slant, talking to Farmiloe about that night in the Pelican Tavern, for he had been in Barclays press gang, not, being a midshipman, a very important part, but an accomplice nonetheless.

'Troubled, John? How could I be? I had never heard of the Liberties of the Savoy and had no idea where we were pressing was illegal. It was a duty I had never previously undertaken and I say to you now, I hope never to have to do so again.'

'I have a mind to stay in the navy, Dick. What do you say to that?'

Such an abrupt change of subject took time to elicit a response. 'Given what you have always led me to believe, I would say I'm surprised.'

'Is that avoiding the real question?'

'Which is?'

Pearce grinned and slapped him on the back; he was in the company of one of the few fellows with whom he could be reasonably open. 'You know very well. My prospects should I choose to do so?' The sucking in of breath was not reassuring. 'Be honest, Dick.'

'Truly, you will struggle to get round the stigma of your promotion to lieutenant. You experienced today the way it marks you.'

'I have another reputation to counter that, though modesty forbids me from listing it.'

The laugh that got was hollow. 'John, you are brave and you have proved it more than once. How do I tell you that the resentment you already engender is rendered doubly damning because of your perceived good fortune? There is hardly a man in the fleet who does not think they too could shine as you have, if given the chances you have been afforded. Such a feeling does not provoke admiration, it causes jealousy.'

That induced a period of silence and reflection, until Farmiloe posed the obvious question as to why he had suffered a change of heart. Pearce was not going to be open about that, even with him. How could he allude to impending fatherhood without invoking the name of the mother?

Come to think of it, did Dick Farmiloe know the name anyway? He could not enquire.

'I accept I have been lucky, Dick, but I must add that it has occurred in ways I have never sought, but in situations forced upon me by circumstances and more often by others. Yet as I stand here now and think of what else I can do with my life, the vista is a far from encouraging one.'

'You are not a dunce, John.'

'A sentiment you may find disputed in certain areas.'

The smile accompanying that was wiped away by Tilley, come to tell him that Digby was in the cutter and wondering where he was.

CHAPTER FOURTEEN

'I could have sworn you were in Digby's cabin; I heard your name called out more than once.'

Digby had taken to talking to himself and loudly enough for it to be obvious through the bulkheads; the surprise was the marine had only just heard it.

'Edward, I am amazed you have not noted it before.'

'There was a degree of cursing too.'

'He seeks to bring down on me divine disfavour.'

Though he had not witnessed the fact himself, this peculiarity had first been brought to him by Michael O'Hagan. In his capacity as servant, he knew everything that was going on aboard the ship and not just with the officers, for the hands talked to him as one of their own. His source had been one of the marines who took turns guarding Digby's door and could not help but be aware of what was happening on the other side. It was telling that if they were prepared to gossip to O'Hagan, none of them had even hinted at the fact to their own officer.

'How long has it been going on?'

'It started the day we dined on *Agamemnon*. When I heard of it, I assumed drink had played a part, though in truth I cannot say Digby imbibed excessively. What I do recall is him being in deep conversation with Nelson's parson.' That brought on a wolfish grin. 'Perhaps he was asking about exorcisms and how to cast out devils.'

'Or the weather has been the cause.'

'There may be truth in that. It makes me gloomy, Edward, and you will struggle to raise a smile 'tween decks too.'

The sky was slate grey, as was the sea, so that they merged to remove any hint of a horizon, melding into one and leaving everyone feeling as if they were in a cloying and disagreeable cocoon. At least the swell was within reason and not what they had suffered this last week: heavy rolling seas driven down from the north, accompanied by biting winds often full of snow that blew into and piled up in the bulwarks. From there it had to be shovelled overboard; given its weight, if left it altered too much the trim of the ship.

The stoves provided some relief from the cold if you could get close enough, which was not always

easy for the crew, given they had to jostle a shipmate aside to do so, with many seeking relief from
the cook's boiling coppers. Even in such conditions, beating to and fro off Cape Noli, the
course had to be reversed several times a day,
which sent the topmen aloft to work on freezing,
ice-stiff canvas, while below their confrères were
required to haul off rime-coated falls, with
chapped hands. It was worse in darkness.

'Will Digby have a Sunday service?' Grey asked.

The same thought had troubled Pearce; tradition – and the navy ran on that – said he would.
But common sense told him that to line the crew
up on deck to castigate them for sins numerous
as well as transgressions possible, when they
would be shivering, was unwise. His relationship
with Digby was affecting them and their feeling
towards him; such an act would only feed that
discontent.

'You could point out it would be cruel.'

That got a derisive snort from Pearce. 'For me to
counsel against it will only assure it takes place.'

A well-muffled Michael O'Hagan appeared,
bearing in his cupped hands a steaming cup of
spiced wine, which he surrendered reluctantly
given it was warming him through his mittens.
Pearce took it gratefully and looked meaningfully
at Grey, his servant getting the hint.

'Would Mr Grey be after caring for the same?'

'I certainly would.'

'Then I will tell your own man to fetch it up.'

That got Pearce a look saying 'Don't you damn
well dare ask me to provide'.

'Just pass on the message, Michael.'

'I think, if you don't mind, John, I will take my brew below,' Grey said.

The sky was darkening by the time the last bell of the eight was rung, bringing up the first dogwatch and Ivor Conway, not that he would have been easy to recognise, so well wrapped was he with everything he could find to ward off the cold. At least his arm had begun to mend, in the way of these things quickly once the process had begun, though he still favoured it by using his left hand where possible.

Pearce was glad to get off the deck, chilled as he was to the marrow. O'Hagan had made sure his personal stove was pulsating, which allowed him to strip off his own layers and allow the warmth it produced to near scorch his hams. His question to Michael was the obvious one and had to be asked: was Digby still at it? He could scarcely go eavesdropping close to the cabin door himself.

'Sure, the Lobster on duty this forenoon watch says the captain has taken to shouting even more.'

'It would do him good to get some air. He would brood less if he had the deck.'

'There's a worry that a fiend has got into the man.'

'What has got into the man,' Pearce responded impatiently, as the ship heeled, coming round as it was on a reverse course, 'is his own deceit and conscience. A devil forsooth!'

'It is all very well for you not to believe, John-boy, but there are others, and not just I, who know that the spirits are real and more likely to be of evil intent than good.'

'Stuff and nonsense.'

Pearce was not as vehement either way as some people; indeed, indifference was his usual position. Challenged he did not deny, unlike his father and any number of astute minds in post-Revolutionary Paris, that some form of divinity might exist, though his own view could not countenance an all-seeing and all-forgiving deity. He inclined to the case made by the philosopher David Hume that if there was a God, he was probably an inept one judging by what he allowed to happen. These much-rehearsed opinions were once more aimed at his friend, to get a familiar response.

'Jesus, it will take some prayer to save your soul.'

'What you're saying is that the crew are getting the quivers.'

The way tars behaved was larded with superstition. They were convinced any breach of their traditional habits was bound to bring on disaster, which inevitably meant drowning and falling into the clutches of Lucifer. If such nostrums never ceased to amaze him, there was another trait he could not fathom: so few of them could swim. It was as if they accepted such a death as a fate for which they were fitted.

'If I was to say,' Michael responded gravely, 'that the talk around the stoves would not make for happy overhearing, then I reckon it has to be attended to.'

'And how?'

That got him crossing himself as he replied. 'Captain's got to stop his ravings, and it be double silence needed in invoking the Devil.'

Warm now, Pearce could manage a smile. 'I was

given to understand it was me he was invoking, or should I say chastising, or so you told me. It's my name he is shouting out not Satan's.'

'He is calling the curse of Lucifer down on your head, I am told.'

'Then let it be known that I have a top hamper fit to bear it, Michael.'

A voice came through the canvas screen. 'Mr Conway's compliments, your honour, he asks can you come on deck?'

'In the name of God, why?'

'Summat's been spotted in the offing and the captain said you should attend to it.'

'You asked the captain first?'

'Aye, sir, I did, interrupting his mutterings when I knocked.'

Things were getting worse to the point where Digby was neglecting his duty. If it had been reported to Digby that something had been spotted, the ship's captain was required to respond, for in his hands lay the safety of both ship and crew. To pass it on to Pearce was close to dereliction. Should he remonstrate with him? Would doing so achieve anything but a direct order?

'Tell Mr Conway I shall be up presently, just as soon as I have enough clothing back on.'

It was with no enthusiasm whatever that Pearce began to dress in articles that, thrown on his cot, had barely been affected by the stove. Already wearing a flannel vest and two shirts, he added a kerseymere jersey, then a leather waistcoat and covered that with his thick boat cloak. Finally, a muffler was wrapped round both his head and neck, one thick enough to make it impossible to wear his hat.

'Once more into the breach,' he murmured as he pulled the canvas screen aside.

Michael was shaking his head. 'Don't help having you talking to yourself an' all.'

If John Pearce was feeling put upon, that had to be tempered by the fact that he was relatively well-off. The lookout, sat on the mainmast cap, who had seemingly spotted what he thought had to be the glint of a light, had it much worse, so Pearce's first act was to ask that he be relieved, ordering him below for enough time to ease his chill.

Something being spotted and the direction established, there was no choice but to call up the hands and set the ship on a new course to close, which also brought the master on deck. Dorling, having plotted the new course, shared with Pearce as he marked the slate it was to the north and thus they would be closing with the shore.

'Too far off, surely, to be a light on land?'

'Be a whole watch before you could sight one of those, Mr Pearce. That is, if you could see owt at all.'

'It could be imaginings.'

'Lookout was sharp-eyed, sir,' Conway interjected, 'and I think I saw the flash of it with my own eyes.'

'Very well. Cover the binnacle and douse our lanterns, Mr Conway. Canvas over the hatches too and no bells. We will go by my watch.'

'Clear for action, sir?'

Pearce thought about that for a bit. In these temperatures that would have the gun crews on deck for as long as it took to establish whether they

184

were needed at all and that could be hours. The hands on HMS *Flirt* were men of long experience; they could clear quickly and so it was best to wait. The second flash, two bells later, meant such a posture had to be revisited, though his conclusion was the same, albeit Conway was despatched to Digby to alert him, not that the captain appeared.

'Please go back to the cabin and say that I ask permission to clear for action.'

The reply that came back was negative; to clear would remove the bulkheads that formed the walls of his cabin and he was not prepared to countenance such disturbance on a mere rumour.

'It's more than a damned rumour,' Pearce hissed.

'What can it be, sir?' Conway asked.

Pearce wondered if the lad shared some of the crew's superstitions, so obvious was the quiver in his voice, then reasoned he was just cold.

'In the worst case it's a ship of war, covering its lights as are we. I think that unlikely, for if you are correct regarding the first sighting, whoever is out there is on a northerly course. Sense, if they saw our lights, would have them close if they were powerful or run if they are not.'

Aware that he was indulging in pure guesswork, Pearce had to reason there was no alternative to what they now had. Only Digby could order that they clear and it had been denied, which left the possibility he was indulging in wishful thinking, fitting the conclusion to his needs. If it was a warship and it was closing in this Stygian darkness, then the brig would not stand a chance.

'Mr Pearce,' said Dorling, after two hours of

185

the chase. 'My calculations put us close enough to the shore, enough to advise caution.'

'Very well, prepare to heave to and while the men are on deck, get the guns cast off, loaded and run out.' There was a moment then when Dorling thought on that; Pearce was acting in contravention of Digby's orders. 'My decision, my responsibility. One man to stay with the cannon, the rest to keep warm below, with a relief every bell.'

HMS *Flirt* came to a halt very slowly, allowed to drift until she lost all way, by which time he and Conway had been joined by Edward Grey, asking to be brought up to date. A glance under the binnacle cover told Pearce which way lay north and thus the shore, while Dorling, efficient as he was, could only give him and the marine an approximate position on the part of the Ligurian littoral off which they lay.

'Best guess, Mr Dorling?'

Another pause was long enough to indicate he did not want to be precise but eventually he elected to name Voltri, on the road west from Genoa, which the charts examined off the deck indicated sat in a long shallow bay backed by mountains, indeed a typical location on this shore, albeit with a stone beach split by a narrow Alpine river.

'There away, over the larboard bow.'

Pearce was fortunate to be back on the quarterdeck to see it, the same brief flash and a certain amount of satisfaction was to be had. The light was, in relation to the brig, very much where he had expected it to be. That was rendered mysterious when two other pinpoints became evident, stringing southwards, though not visible for any longer than what had been previously observed. This left Pearce in a quandary. Did they come from a single deck, for if they did, given the distance from front light to rear, he could be facing a capital ship of seventy-four guns or more?

'No sound, from anyone. No movement that is not necessary.'

'Let's hope the captain obliges,' whispered Grey.

The passage of time was a constant source of frustration at sea and one to which some became inured. Not Pearce; his impatience did not moderate, even if such a mood achieved nothing. What would happen would do so in its own good time and his under-the-breath cursing would gain nothing. His exasperation was finally mollified when half a dozen lights appeared, strung out along what he had to assume was a beach. He thought to ask Digby for permission but was unwilling to give him the chance to deny him the right to act on his instincts.

'Mr Conway, get the men equipped for shore duty, including muskets. Mr Grey, your duty is plain.' There was no need to say more: if the tars were going ashore so was he. 'Mr Dorling, get the boats alongside. You and Mr Conway will have charge of the ship while we are gone.'

'The captain?'

Dorling asked this, his voice anxious, for not only was he being landed with a responsibility he would rather not shoulder, Pearce was taking upon himself another duty he should have cleared with Digby.

'Is not on deck, Mr Dorling, and I am. The fact

he has not appeared, even after we have heaved to, tells me he has little interest or concern for what we have witnessed.'

'Begging your indulgence, I am not sure what that is.'

'And neither am I, but when what I can now assume to be more than one boat steals ashore in darkness, having sought to hide their presence on the way, I feel it is safe to assume they are up to no good. Even by your limited ability to give me a true position, they are landing on a shore occupied by our Austrian allies.'

'So the lantern flashes were–?'

'Checking their course, Mr Dorling,' Pearce interrupted, 'which is, I am sure, the same conclusion as you have reached.'

Michael was beside him with his sword, a pair of pistols with the belt that would hold them, that having a small cartouche for shot and another pouch for powder. He also had Pearce's hat.

'Reckon you'd want this on your head, your honour, lest they take you for a passing tinker.'

Strapping on his weapons and looking towards the hidden shore, he observed the string of lanterns heading inland, which had him chivvy everyone to get into the boats. He intended to take the cutter, Grey being in command of the jolly boat.

'Mr Dorling, if you judge there is any point in it, you have my permission to fire off the cannon, singly or a broadside, as you see fit.'

'How will I be sure there is a point, sir?'

'You will have to guess, as I am now, but you have shown yourself resourceful before. All I ask is that you do so again.'

He went over the side and called the oarsmen to haul away. Initially, Pearce had them do so strongly in what he might have called a fine calculation – in truth, it was more guesswork – to ease off once he considered the proximity to the shore demanded it. Men arriving in boats could not take them along and nor would they leave them unguarded.

There was no sign of the actual beach but there were a few pinpoints of lantern light from what he assumed were dwellings, both spread out and numerous enough, elevated in a few cases, to indicate a place of a greater size than a mere hamlet. A town probably, so Dorling's guess at Voltri seemed accurate.

'Ahead, sir,' Conway whispered, which had Pearce drop his gaze to see what looked like an odd-shaped outline, very faint but becoming steadily more obvious. There was a shore party alright and they had rigged a bit of canvas to shelter from the cold wind as well as hide them on the seaward side; sensible for their comfort but not if they had failed to set a lookout.

The hissing of the water was a sure indication of the shoreline, which, according to the charts, shelved hardly at all, a series of dipped oars employed to test the depth. Sure it was safe, men went overboard to push the boats in, the only sound the gasps of their being up to their thighs in cold water. No reaction came from up ahead, which led Pearce to believe he was about to achieve complete surprise.

The level of the water ankle-deep, Pearce ordered everyone out, but to stay still so he could get in a position to lead. He wanted Grey's marines at his heels. There being little chance of subterfuge once they were on the stony beach, it was a whisper and a rush that had Pearce slashing with his cutlass, cutting into that canvas screen to reveal two men huddled round a piddling little fire.

Their cries of alarm told him right away they were French.

CHAPTER FIFTEEN

Terror, coupled with shock and surprise, makes interrogation easy. So these two sentinels, already roughly handled, were only too willing to answer Pearce's questions, his sword at the throat of one being an extra inducement. They were from the French frigate *La Brune,* seen by himself and Nelson in Genoa harbour. The shore party, under their captain, had indeed headed inland, though to what purpose these crewmen had no idea.

Given they were well armed, and he and Grey having counted three cutter-sized boats, Pearce assumed it to be a raid designed to destroy the Austrians' defences of the same kind he had mounted on Monte Boroni. He left two men to tie them up and act as guards, and using their fire to light his own lanterns, all but one shaded, he led his party up the gently sloping beach.

Grey and his marines were close behind, but Michael O'Hagan was at his shoulder; he would not surrender the protection of his friend's back to anyone. Soon they passed from easy to traverse gravel to encounter increasingly large stones and eventually boulders of a size that necessitated that they use all the available lantern light to find their way.

Up ahead they could hear the furious barking of disturbed dogs, one no doubt having set off the others, with no canine being willing to miss out on the chorus. If they were guard dogs it did not bring out their owners from their beds or parlours, this proved as they found the way off the beach, using the edge of a thin watercourse. This led them into the narrow alleys that dissected the shoreside dwellings, seen to be shacks when a light was used to check their dimensions.

It was the French who had set off the dogs, which meant the party from *Flirt* could move with relative ease: the enemy would not know their continued barking was due to the presence of an enemy. Progress brought them to cobble-paved roads but not a sign of habitation; the locals were not venturing out to see what it was that was exciting their hounds, even those who had lamps lit inside and so could be assumed to be awake.

'Where to now?' Grey asked.

Pearce could provide no answer. He had been following his instincts in keeping to a straight line of progress, hoping to get sight of the French by their lanterns, not now possible because they would be hidden, cut off by high buildings, while his own indicated they were entering some kind of large plaza. This brought them to a set of steps leading to what he thought to be a church – a

191

cathedral, judging by the massive marble columns and a set of heavily carved but firmly closed doors showing in relief the passions of Christ.

'I have to own it, Edward, I am at a loss as to how to proceed.'

'If this is the way the French came, it is also the route by which they will return to their boats, which, whatever they are about, they must do and in no great time, if they want to get clear before first light. We must assume, surely, that they know our ship to be patrolling these waters.'

'An ambuscade?'

'It is that or a wander about and put our luck to the test. God forbid we should just bump into the enemy when they have the advantage.'

'I have just realised something I forgot to ask our pair of captures.' Grey did not seek to provide an answer, waiting until Pearce did so himself, this accompanied by a sigh at his own folly. 'Numbers, Edward. How many men do we face?'

'Three boats, John, so we should not be too heavily outnumbered.'

'Three cutters, I counted, which if they were full would bear more than twice as many fighters as we can muster.'

The crack of a shot had all heads turning, with cries of 'Where away?' It seemed to be everywhere as it echoed off stone walls, until Pearce silenced the whole party, calling on them to listen. The sound of shouting was faint but obvious, which meant whatever was happening it was close enough to be audible. To men who fought with enthusiasm when called upon to do so – and did so ashore on their own behalf if they felt the need

– there was no doubt it was such taking place, this underlined when several more shots rang out.

'March to the sound of the guns, John.'

Pearce did not respond to Grey immediately; he was too busy castigating himself for his laxity. As willing to fight as any man he led, he was less eager to lead them into a situation in which too many factors were utterly unknown. He had no idea what the French were up to and even less about what they faced in the way of opposition. Yet he had to assume that if the enemy were attacking something, they had to have some prior idea of what it was. Had those boats been crammed or half empty? If the former, it would mean trouble.

'I refer to numbers again, Edward, which means your suggestion preceding that shot is the best one. Let us make our way back towards the beach and seek a spot where we can catch our prey unawares.'

'It has gone quiet, dogs apart,' Grey said. 'Either our Johnnie Crapauds have failed or–'

'They have succeeded and are on the way back. Let us move.'

There was another error Pearce was then obliged to face: his own failure to keep his men together. In the spacious plaza some of them had wandered away in a situation in which it seemed unwise to shout that they should regather. He was in the process of making that happen when O'Hagan, still hard by him, grabbed his arm and spun him round.

'Look there.'

It was faint but evident, the end of one of the streets that led off the plaza showing a faint but

193

increasingly golden glow, which meant that the enemy was on the way back to their boats. To get ahead of them and have the time to set up an ambuscade was gone and even worse, Pearce reckoned, he had lost the time to get to the beach before they did with any degree of security. If they beat him, he could kiss goodbye to *Flirt's* boats and two of his men, which had to be set against the greatest good for the greatest number. How many would he lose in an open contest? It was a risk he had to take.

'Find cover and stay out of sight!' he shouted, there being a reasonable hope the still-barking dogs would mask his voice.

He ran for those marble pillars, each one large enough to easily conceal not just him but O'Hagan too, hauling out his pistols and cocking them ready to fire. Grey and his marines were spread out behind the other columns, the sailors he led nowhere to be seen, this as a line of lanterns carried by a body of men entered the plaza.

'Just in time,' he whispered to Michael.

Pearce had previously harboured reservations about sailors and muskets. It was not a weapon they were used to and, as for accuracy when firing, that was even less likely in the weapons they carried. A Sea Service Brown Bess was shorter in its barrel than the infantry musket by six inches, making it possible to employ it when surrounded by ropes and rigging.

It mattered not who had handled it badly, who had, in the act of cocking their weapon simultaneously pressured the trigger. What counted was that it went off, producing a bright flash from the far side of the plaza, followed by the familiar bang then a double crack, Pearce assuming this to be the fired ball ricocheting off stone.

The effect on the French was immediate: hastily, they retreated back into the street they had been about to exit, but not before Pearce got a handle on their strength. This produced a feeling of trepidation, given he reckoned – albeit the calculation was a rough one – they were outnumbered by over two to one.

'They must come back out, John,' Grey called, 'and when they do we shall pepper them a trifle.'

That display of confidence did not last, nor the hope for Pearce that with his inferior numbers he could use cover to even up the contest and the odds. The lights in that street began to fade until they were no more and that condition was maintained, which left only one conclusion: the sods knew of a different route back to the beach.

'To me,' he yelled, coming out from behind his pillar and heading swiftly for the roadway that would take him to the same destination. 'Michael, raise and wave that lantern so they can see the need for haste.'

The air was soon filled with the sound of running men, the boots of the marines louder than the sailors' shoes, none moving faster than the fellow in command. Lights mattered not at all now; he either had to get his party to the beach in time to set up a defence or, if that could not be achieved, to hole the French boats and get his men away and back to *Flirt*.

What hampered quick progress was those boulders, swept down from the Alps on a river that must suffer an annual spring spate, to pile up and oblige him and the men he led to pick a way through, the arrival of their enemies further along the beach as obvious to him as British lanterns must be in reverse. As a race it was too close for comfort; indeed, he came to reckon, that with their short head start, it was one he might well lose.

The shouting had two aims: to encourage those he led and also to alert the two sailors he had left to guard their captures, his hope being they would realise safety lay in heading towards his party, not that, at such a distance, he had anything other than a common language and indistinct yelling to tell them.

Grey acted without any orders from Pearce; he called for his quartet of panting marines to stop, take up a standing pose, then aim and fire, the four streaks emitted from the muzzles the first indication of the act. If four balls were somewhat less than that which was required, the result was quick to arrive, as the muzzle flashes rippled out ahead of them.

There was a temptation, as musket balls began to ricochet off the boulders, to ask Grey what in the name of damnation he was about. Against that it might be his action was the correct one, while the same applied to what was happening now, visible by the light of the lantern the marine officer was holding head-high to provide enough illumination for his Lobsters to reload, which they were busily engaged in carrying out, with all the skill and speed provided by constant practice. Soon they were up and firing another salvo.

'Mr Grey, as soon as you are reloaded once more we must close up.'

'Sir,' came the cheerful reply.

Pearce, as well as most of the sailors, had got through the boulders and onto the part of the beach where tide and time had worn away the bulk of the stones, making more rapid progress possible. It also allowed them to stand and fire off a ragged volley, with the marines joining them as swiftly as they could. That done, it still left the man who commanded them in a quandary.

If he rushed for the boats, they might well get to them and aboard before they could be stopped. But they would never get clear without bloodshed. Muskets might not be accurate at much over fifty yards. Poorly maintained and with worn barrels, which was common, they were not even accurate over ten yards. Yet proximity would ensure that men barely off the beach and trying to row, able to retaliate with no more than one salvo, would pay a high price. Reloading even a pistol in a rocking cutter or jolly boat was difficult and such a danger applied doubly to him and Grey; their red-and-blue coats would mark them out.

Yet the same was true of the French. It was clear whoever was in command realised he had the same dilemma for, having come some distance, they too had halted. The Flirts had reloaded, the marines doing so by rote so Pearce knew he could engage, if he wished, in an exchange of musketry, but that too had limitations. How much in the way of powder and balls had the French brought, what had they already expended and did it match or overbear that which his party carried?

The lack of firing made it possible to assume, and it could be no more than yet another guess, that his opposite number was as bereft of the means to engage in a long fight as he was. What was happening out at sea? Dorling must have seen the flashes of the muskets; what was he likely to do about it? Had Digby come out of his cabin to take charge? Lots of questions, no answers; he could not even see the outline of the brig or its lights, which he was sure he would have done if it had come closer to shore.

'Michael?'

'John-boy?'

'Time to test your notions. If it does not cause you to blaspheme against your religion, pray for a round of grapeshot from *Flirt*.'

'Already done, John-boy.'

'And no response.'

'It is not what the Holy Trinity is for. If we are in a stew, sure, it's of our own making.'

'Mine, not yours.'

Pearce was mentally listing the alternatives he could have pursued. Having found those boats on the beach, should he have gone back aboard HMS *Flirt* with the aim of closing off the enemy escape with her superior firepower? That took no account of his initial ignorance as to what he might face, the assumption of their being French heading for land included.

'Mr Pearce,' Grey said with stiff formality – he could be overheard by all. 'I sense we are at a stand.'

'We are, indeed. If it comes to a fight they have superior numbers, but how many will our opponents be willing to sacrifice in order to defeat us?'

The marine had come close enough to whisper. 'John, I hesitate to suggest we let them get to their boats and depart.'

'For which I am glad, for if the case was reversed I would take their men prisoner and smash the bottom of their boats.'

'Forgive me, I had not thought it through.'

'Something I think I have failed in since we set off.'

The advantage Pearce had was time; if the French did know there was a British warship off-shore, they would not want to be around at dawn or indeed anywhere within sight from the tops. That said, he could not fathom why *Flirt* had not responded to the flashes of gunfire, even to the point of sending up blue lights to find out what was happening. Surely if a good proportion of the crew was onshore and might be in difficulty, it was the least they could do.

It might have been the sight of the two French prisoners waving and pleading that broke the deadlock, not that the men Pearce had left were any better off if the enemy achieved control of the beach. In the grouped lanterns ahead, there was some kind of talk going on, for they had come together enough to provide a pool of illumination.

'A volley now might be to advantage,' Grey posited.

'There are more men outside that light than close to it and they too have muskets.'

That was said just for deflection; Pearce was thinking that a fight of any kind could be point-less. Whatever the men from *La Brune* had come

199

to do, they must surely have achieved. Any act of his would be too late to put a check on their aims while he risked losing many of his crew to wounds or death, and the end result could be capture, unless help came from somewhere.

He had a vision of a bloody contest and not only with musket fire. It would come to knives, clubs and Michael O'Hagan's axe, and his party was unlikely to triumph. Those who survived would be taken away in *Flirt's* own boats as prisoners and no amount of suffering on the part of the French would make that a good outcome. He was just about to hand his weapons to Michael, intending to then move forward and seek a parley, when those bunched lanterns parted; more than that, one of them was coming his way.

'Nobody moves and if anything happens to me, Edward, try to get off the beach with as many men as you can save. I advise they then disperse using the streets of the town to survive. The French cannot chase for ever, they must get away.'

'I will come with you,' Michael whispered.

'No, friend.' Pearce replied, handing over his weapons. 'If something untoward happens to me now, you will be the one who has to tell Emily. I would not want such news coming from a messenger who is a stranger to her.'

The lantern and the man holding it had stopped up the beach, parallel to the point where lay the combined boats, so it was to there that Pearce made his way, both men making sure their faces were illuminated, though there was enough spill for Pearce to see his opponent was still armed.

'*Bonjour, monsieur.*'

The voice was deep and rasping, though not in a threatening way, while his coat and gilt-edged hat marked him out as the captain. As to his face, well, the lamplight threw half his features into shadow and his hat masked much of the rest.

'*Parlez-vous français?*'

Having answered in the affirmative, Pearce then went on in French to outline the difficulties for both of them, an explanation that was met with evident surprise at his fluency, as well as nods to acknowledge he had summed the matter up well.

'*Mais j'ai advantage d'hommes.*'

'*Beaucoup d'entre eux vont mourir, non?*'

That mention of death for many gave the French captain pause, which implied that for all his advantage in numbers, he did not relish losing men any more than John Pearce. If he knew what he wanted, the Frenchman was not prepared to give it to him without making it seem like an act of goodwill, inviting him to quit the beach with a promise his boats would not be touched and neither would the men he had left on guard.

He was annoyed, and overly loud with it, at the implication that this *rosbif* lieutenant did not trust him to keep his word. However, the protests had an overdramatic quality, as if they were being advanced for show, which left Pearce wondering if the French captain felt the need to persuade those he led of the wisdom of compromise and was in fear of Revolutionary justice.

When the hand went to Pearce's coat the Frenchman stiffened, only to relax again when all that was produced was a watch. There was no need then for words; that in itself was eloquent enough – we can argue as long as you like, but time favours me – and that sped up the process.

'*Nous partons ensemble, oui?*'

'*Parfait.*'

It could have been comedic if it was not so potentially deadly. The two groups were deeply suspicious of each other and it would only have taken one misplaced word or movement to set off a bloodbath at such close quarters. But the French were as true to the agreement as the men Pearce led, getting into their boats – and if they grumbled at the red-coated marines remaining standing, with their weapons a split second away from being ready, only Pearce understood it.

As the boats were simultaneously pushed into the water, it was French oars that bit deep, to have them soon disappear into the darkness, with not a lantern visible. Pearce did not push his men to haul hard; he had no idea where HMS *Flirt* was. Why row with effort when they might as well wait for the sun to rise?

CHAPTER SIXTEEN

It seemed to take an age, from the first hint of grey light in the east, until it spread enough along the still lowering clouds to show their ship. HMS *Flirt* was hove to with, from what Pearce could see from his low elevation, the normal activities of the day taking place, as though a goodly proportion of the crew was not absent. The guns

202

were run out, everyone was at their stations and still, with Henry Digby on deck, a telescope to his eye as he swept the horizon for threats.

'Of which,' Pearce opined in a mordant tone, 'he will find none.'

The call from the lookout was faint evidence that they had been spotted, dark dots on a sea that matched the sky, and had those on *Flirt* possessed supernatural vision they would have found themselves surveying a most miserable scene. Their shipmates had been rendered listless by half the night spent in the boats, with the oars still in the water. The only real rowing had been done in order to get blood flowing and ward off the cold. Doubly galling to Pearce, Digby, who could not have failed to spot them, was acting as if they did not exist.

'Do you think we should wait till they house the cannon,' he shouted to Grey. 'Mr Digby may wish to test them?'

If it was a jest to lift the spirits, it signally failed to do so; what he got were grim looks that hinted he might have the right of it. Pearce immediately regretted the remark for it would only make worse a situation already bad enough and a sharp order to close was quickly obeyed. He saw his men aboard before he made the deck himself, to find Digby gone, Conway with his hat raised and his expression grim.

'You are to attend upon the captain immediately, sir.'

'Now there's a surprise.' He then turned to O'Hagan. 'Get yourself some breakfast and then me also. I doubt I shall be long.'

'He also ordered that the men you took ashore should resume their duties immediately.'

'Most of them have not rested for twelve hours.'

'His instructions were specific and he said not to be questioned.'

Which was exactly what Pearce wanted to do, but where would that leave Conway? The lad was just starting out on his naval career and if he did not get his head knocked off by a cannonball it might be a fine one. Digby had given the youngster a direct and unequivocal order. To countermand it would not do much good for anyone, so his voice was loud as he responded.

'Mr Conway, if you hear grumbling – and you will – stamp on it using my authority.'

He expected the cabin door to be opened for him as usual as he approached; it was not and given the eyes of the marine sentinel would not meet his, it was as good as saying you need to knock, which he did, to be met with a shout telling him to wait. The discourtesy was, of course, deliberate as was the time it took, several minutes, for permission to enter. That was followed by another bit of theatre as Digby sat, quill in hand, writing in the ship's log, which ensured his eyes never met those of his premier.

'Captain.'

'It is interesting to hear you use that appellation, since you seem commonly to show it little heed.'

'I–'

'You may speak when you are spoken to, Mr Pearce, and not before. I have matters to attend to that are more important than anything you have to say.'

Pearce felt his anger rise and fought to check it; it was bad enough to be so rudely interrupted, but to be treated like a nonentity was even worse. It took several deep breaths before he could answer in a voice that hid his true feelings.

'Given you are so occupied, I will call upon you at a more convenient time.'

'You will not. You will wait until I am ready to attend upon you.'

About to walk out, Pearce stopped, halted by the realisation that these very words had probably been rehearsed, which meant he was playing to the captain's vision of how matters would pan out. When talking to himself, he would be indulging in imaginary arguments in which personal success was assured, common enough to all, but rarely articulated out loud.

'I wonder if I can wait for what follows, Henry. What would your imaginings have me say next?'

He did look up then, quill poised and eyes cold. 'I do not have any inkling of what you mean.'

'The problem is that I compose my own responses, so if it does not suit what you have outlined, I can only apologise.'

The shout of 'Come back at once!' was half muffled by the cabin door being slammed shut, while for Pearce, the temptation to look back and wonder at what the marine guard thought had to be resisted so as he was not seen as seeking complicity. It did matter: what had happened would be all over the ship as soon as the Lobster's duty ended.

Michael had done as he was bid, so Pearce was able to eat his fill to the sound of the decks being

205

sanded and flogged dry. There would have to be another encounter, he knew that, just as he knew it would not be one-sided, for there were questions for Digby to answer. The arrival of Conway, who was reduced to stuttering when delivering his message, did not aid matters.

'Captain's orders, Mr Pearce, you are to be confined to your quarters until we return to Vado Bay. He has ordered Mr Grey to place a marine outside your berth to ensure his instructions are complied with.'

'A prisoner again, Michael,' Pearce hooted, as much to cover his anger as to make light of it. 'And you, Mr Conway, stepping into my shoes, a premier at such a young age. For all my good fortune you have surpassed me with many years in hand. Surely there is a flag awaiting you before you make your majority.'

For a youth who had expected to be roundly cursed, the response came as a surprise, so much so he was at a loss to respond, to which Pearce could only be sympathetic.

'Go about your duties, Ivor, and let me have concerns for my well-being.'

Pearce waited several seconds, enough to allay any chance Conway might overhear, saying softly to Michael, 'Get the word out to the crew, who may be tempted to act against this and make their displeasure known. They are to do nothing that will give Digby an excuse to claim them mutinous.'

'Are you sure you have the right of it, John-boy,' came the grinning response. 'Half the lads would see you keelhauled in the time it takes to spit.'

206

'Perhaps I could ask for it and fit in a refreshing swim.'

That made the Irishman shudder; if he indulged his friend in that habit, he neither understood the desire nor wished to share the experience. O'Hagan had many times termed John Pearce mad, having no more sense than the fish he swam with. But Pearce knew Michael would carry out his wish and his first ears to whisper in would be those who had been ashore with him last night, men who had come back aboard fully expecting a warm welcome and a tot of rum, to be ignored and put to deck swabbing.

His next caller was Grey, who, with one of his men right outside the canvas screen, had to be very circumspect indeed. 'A temporary measure I am sure, Mr Pearce, but one I am, of course, obliged to see implemented.'

'Have you found out if the flash of musket fire was observed from the deck last night?'

Grey winked. 'A dark, cold and damp night, happen even a trace of mist, which would have rendered mysterious anything seen.'

That was to be the excuse and such words could only have come from Digby. Grey, with his wink, was telling him he had heard from other sources and it had been plainly visible.

'Not something a captain would risk a ship for?'

'Not if he wished to keep his command,' Grey added with mock gravity. 'Which the captain made sure all knew.'

How had that played with those who had re-mained aboard, men whose friends were obviously in some danger? It was not just the shore party Digby would have to worry about in terms of maintaining discipline. Every man jack aboard would be cursing him, which left his inferior with a real dilemma. The man was plainly ill, without Pearce in any way being able to see how it had come about.

Certainly his behaviour in the action in the Gulf of Ambracia had bordered on madness, but whatever prompted his actions then had not seemed to carry through to his recovery. Had that been the trigger for his current behaviour, for Pearce could not, or would not, accept that his criticisms alone could be the cause of such a change.

'I will leave you now,' Grey said, which reminded a contemplative Pearce he was still there. 'You may call upon me for anything you need. Just tell your guard.'

The small folded note was dropped on his cot as the marine turned to leave and it remained there until he was long gone. Finally picked up and opened, the words inside came as little surprise and the information contained must have come from someone like Matthew Dorling. Digby had been alerted to the exchange of fire onshore, the sight of it barely registered as had the sound, and had come on deck to observe its continuance.

There had been no doubt in anyone's mind what it portended, their shipmates were in bother, only to have their fears dismissed as fanciful and not something to react to, which flew in the face of the palpable evidence. Digby had issued orders to hold to their position, with an aside that if there was anything to be concerned about, it was due to a certain officer who had clearly exceeded his position.

Grey's note finished with the words, 'Who, with you gone, was left to question him, John? Look to me for support and you will have it.'

Vado Bay was no more than a day's sailing distant but it was clear even before they opened the anchorage that there were only three frigates there, while HMS *Agamemnon* was absent. Digby hailed the senior captain to be told that Commodore Nelson had gone once more to Genoa to remonstrate with the Doge. From there it was his intention to make for San Fiorenzo Bay to confer with Sir John Jervis. Those by the binnacle heard Digby say, with some satisfaction, one word: 'Perfect'. Next came the order to shape a course for the main fleet anchorage.

News of this came quickly through Michael O'Hagan, added to the information that he had delegated Charlie Taverner and Rufus Dommet to keep him abreast of anything said 'tween decks that might spell trouble.

'Sure as there is a God in heaven, nothing will bypass Charlie. He has the ears of a thief, does he not?'

That was not said with any rancour, even if in the past that was exactly the life Charlie had lived. If Michael and he had the occasional falling out, usually from Charlie's too waspish tongue, they were nevertheless more than just shipmates. The Pelican bond was stronger than that.

For a man who appreciated the benefits of fresh

209

air as well as his occasional dips in the sea, the confinement was galling. Yet what he had said in the presence of Conway, that he was a prisoner again, was naught but the literal truth. One of Adam Pearce's more pointed pamphlets, questioning the rights of the monarchy and much else besides, had landed him and his son in the Fleet Prison. His incarceration now, set against that, was luxury.

San Fiorenzo Bay required no more than another day's sailing, unless the wind was foul. Reflecting on the word Digby had used as reported to him, Pearce saw this as portending an increased risk for him. Nelson was generally held to be soft in terms of discipline; Sir John Jervis by reputation as well as his actions already taken was anything but.

It almost made him laugh to think what was coming might accidentally bring about that which Emily desired. Having resolved to stay in the service to avoid living off Ralph Barclay's prize money, he might now find himself dismissed, if not from the navy, certainly sent home from the Mediterranean, and he could not envisage many senior officers rushing to employ him in home waters. He had in some way mitigated the feelings against him out here by his actions; that would not apply in the Channel.

Being surrounded by his canvas, with really only Michael to talk to and then in whispers, he was just as prey to fantasies, if quietly so, as Henry Digby. He saw himself on the fringe of the parochial society in which Emily would mix, catching an odd glimpse of her and certainly enjoying no intimacy, while also being allowed an occasional peek at his growing child.

In none of these imaginings could he see himself bearing it. He was, and had been all his days, too free a spirit for such a life and if he was not to take what he saw as tainted coin, how and on what was he to live? Perhaps he would take to emulating his father, traversing the country and seeking to stir the apathy of a too supine population, in which the rich cared nothing for the poor, outside, that is, the exploitation of their labour.

To be in even distant proximity to Emily without any physical contact would drive him mad, and he was man enough to know that to hold for a three-year period to chastity, out of love for her, was unlikely to work out in practice. Red blood coursed through his veins and while he was not vain, he knew that women were attracted to him, and he to them.

'What news on our hero, Michael?'

'Sure he is still talking to himself, John-boy, but he takes the deck and looks to be content.'

'Digby means to dish me.'

'Then you must stand up to it and tell the truth of what occurred.'

'The navy has a habit of taking the side of captains against lieutenants and truth is rarely a saviour.'

'You've only been cooped up a couple of days and already you are digging your own grave.'

It was necessary to make light of that. 'Happen I should have you do it for me, Michael, you being a dab hand with a shovel.'

Prior to being pressed, that was how Michael

had made his money: good wages for a fast-dig-ging navvy, on canals, turning farmland into formal gardens and hoicking out earth for the foundation of long rows of London houses. He was inclined to claim he had dug a trench from the west coast of England all the way to the Great Wen.

'I confess not to know as much of these things as you, John-boy, but if he calls for a court, then you can ask the likes of Dorling and little Con-way to swear to what they saw. And Mr Grey was ashore with you and will stand as witness to your actions.'

'At what risk to themselves?'

That saw the Irishman ball his great fists, knuckles standing out and proud. 'Sure I think a hint that they might meet Davy Jones for tongue holding will serve to have them talk.'

'That, Michael, would see you hanged, which thinking on it, is making me even gloomier.'

'Sure if Mrs Barclay produces a boy he will struggle to be proud of you.'

Did Michael know how the use of that name – he had never addressed Emily by any other – was even more depressing than the thought of letting down an unborn child? His friend was glowering, and no doubt in his imaginings, thumping several people for their transgressions.

'Mr Pearce, may I enter?'

'Of course, Mr Conway.'

The canvas was swept aside. 'We have raised San Fiorenzo Bay, sir, and the good news is that Commodore Nelson is there. The captain re-quests, once he has reported to the commodore, you prepare yourself to go aboard HMS *Victory*, which the admiral has taken as his flagship.'

'With him having got there before me?'

'Mr Pearce, I am not without sympathy, but–'

The interruption was brusque. 'You are too young for even the thought of coming to my aid, but please know I am appreciative of the sentiment.'

The hat was raised, then the boy was gone.

'Best bib and tucker, John-boy.'

'Nothing less will do.' That was followed by a glare at the unseen guard. 'And as soon as Digby has gone, I am going on deck, even if a file of marines tries to stop me.'

Which he did, wondering if his blue coat, no longer the deep colour it had been thanks to the Mediterranean sun, rendered him as elegant as he would like, only to then reason that vanity was misplaced. Given Tilley was with Henry Digby and the normal coxswain's crew with him, Charlie and Rufus had collared places in the jolly boat, which turned out to be a wasted effort. Digby was taking no chances, he had sent his coxswain back to fetch him.

Pearce felt all it needed was a slow drum roll, as he went over the side to sit in the thwarts and noticed that not a single oarsman would catch his eye or nod. When they hauled away, Tilley set no fast pace, possibly out of sympathy, but that did not suit his passenger, who wanted the whole thing over. He ordered the men to put their backs into it.

No ceremony attended his arrival on the flagship and he found himself, having made his presence

213

known to Jervis's clerk, on the main deck of a hundred-gun vessel he felt he had been obliged to visit too many times and in too varied circumstances when Hood held the command, while Hotham had flown his flag in HMS *Britannia*. Where was he now, that slippery knave?

Naples, they said, which caused Pearce to recall that Hotham was an old friend of the British Ambassador, Sir William Hamilton, and that took his thoughts to Emma Hamilton, her questionable background and present eminence, at least in Italy. The lady had been more than kind to Emily and helpful to him and she deserved his gratitude.

Did she deserve to have Sir William Hotham as a guest? He doubted they would get on.

'Lieutenant Pearce.' He turned to see Admiral Parker.

'Sir.'

'Sir John is waiting for you.'

'And Captain Digby, no doubt.'

'He also, yes.'

Making their way aft, the great cabin door was opened and he entered to see Jervis, a small, compact man with a grizzled countenance, standing, hands behind his back, in the middle of the room. Digby, hat in hand, was off to one side. It was not until he was right through the door he saw Nelson was also there and if his face was anything to go by, John Pearce was in for a rough time.

CHAPTER SEVENTEEN

'Admiral Parker has told me something about you, Pearce, and I have to say that I do not find it inspiring. If you address me in the manner he tells me you have chosen to use with my predecessors, I will send you home in the bilge of a cattle transport.'

How to play this; that was the vital question. Jervis came with the reputation of something of a martinet, never afraid to flog and had even been known to hang transgressors. He was not Sam Hood, who for all his irascible nature, after their first encounter, had revealed a core of fair-mindedness and, if it was well hidden, an appreciation of anyone who stood their ground. Added to that he usually required a service, which precluded the keelhauling he was constantly threatening.

Hotham's weaknesses extended beyond an inability to push home a fleet action and he had ruined his chances of overawing him by a chicanery that left him exposed. Hanging an officer was out of the question, and that was the only way for Hotham to ensure Pearce's silence. Neither of these traits applied to the admiral now glaring at him as if awaiting some form of barbed insolence. That failing to arrive, he growled out the complaint.

'I have a verbal report that you quite blatantly disobeyed your orders.'

The word verbal was important; Digby was, it appeared, not willing to put anything in writing that might come back to bite.

'Which if I understand it, sir, obliges you to call a court martial?'

'I am not, sir, obliged to do anything and you would do well to remember it.'

Pearce had been looking at Digby as Jervis responded, and if the man tried to disguise the tightening of his jaw, he failed to do so. What was his game? Was it that he did not relish a court martial now any more than he had previously because he would have to face witnesses who might not back up his contentions? If not that, then it was about laying the ground for something unknown, setting Jervis against him for some future act, which would see John Pearce taken out of his orbit.

With no time to think it through, Pearce was obliged to go on instinct, hoping the words he used would make Digby uncomfortable. 'Forgive me, sir, I merely referred to what I supposed to be custom and practice. I must, however, ask when I am supposed to have carried out this act of disobedience.'

'You know very well,' Digby barked.

'Your superior officer did not give you permission to set out with a raiding party, yet you chose to do so, putting the lives of the men for whom he is responsible in danger.'

'I acted only because the captain was indisposed.' That got more than a tight jaw; Digby's eyebrows near hit his hairline, with Pearce speaking quickly before he could verbally be refuted. 'Since he had not been on deck for many a watch and declined my request that he do so, I could only assume some malady rendered him unable to truly assess the situation.'

'And you could?' Jervis demanded, as if such a thing was scarce possible.

'I was called on deck by a messenger from the cabin. When what seemed strange became clear, I saw a chance to take action against what I was sure were our nation's enemies, which is surely the purpose of our cruise.'

'I gave an order not to act, Pearce; you did not heed it.'

'As I have just said, sir, you were in no position to make the kind of judgement I know you to be capable of because you had no visual evidence of what was happening.'

'If I may be allowed, Sir John?'

Jervis had not stopped glaring at Pearce and, as he swung to look at Nelson, the expression did not moderate in the slightest, which seemed to give the commodore pause.

'Very well,' the admiral growled.

'I do not infer by my question that you have acted properly, Mr Pearce, but I am curious to know what occurred in and around Voltri.'

Now there was an interesting question; surely Digby would have implied that nothing had happened. Pearce took Nelson back to the sighting of the lanterns, the fact that he had advised Digby of same, but sought not to make too heavy a point of his refusal to clear for action. He was in the act of saving himself, not ditching his captain, much as the temptation to do so existed.

It might come to that but it was better to stick

to his own story. Nelson sat forward as the tale unfolded, his bright blue eyes alight, making it seem as if he was imagining himself involved, this while Jervis indicated a degree of boredom by going to stand and look out of the casement windows.

'Given the captain seemed to me to be indisposed, I took it upon myself to act.'

'You say you had an exchange of musketry with these villains?' Nelson asked, after hearing what had happened in the plaza and the scurrying back to the beach.

'I did, sir.'

'That was neither visible from HMS *Flirt*, nor could we hear anything.'

Those words from Digby made Pearce's eyebrows move. What had happened to the fellow so wedded to honesty that he could stand before these three superior officers and tell such a blatant lie?

'But they got away.' Pearce nodded and referred to their superior numbers, which precluded prevention.

'And you brought your party back to your ship safe and sound.'

'Every man, sir.'

'Which seems to tell me,' Jervis said, without turning round, 'that you failed to follow through on your intentions. You went ashore, without orders, to catch and destroy what you assumed to be a French raiding party. At the very least, you should have inflicted casualties, even at the cost of some of your own.'

'Sir, I was obliged to come to an arrangement

218

with the man I assumed to be the captain of *La Brune*.'

'What kind of arrangement?'

Digby was smiling now, which told Pearce he knew. It also told him that if he personally enjoyed a degree of regard from the crew of HMS *Flirt*, it was not universal. Someone had blabbed.

'That he should depart unmolested, as long we were afforded the same courtesy.'

'I dislike what you call a "courtesy".'

'I had hoped the exchange of fire had been either heard or seen from the deck of HMS *Flirt*, sir, and that she would have come into view with her guns run out. Even the firing of blue lights would have forced the French to either surrender to me or flee. That lacking, I sought to hold them on the beach till dawn, which would have been fatal to their enterprise.'

'They showed great enterprise, Mr Pearce.' He looked at Nelson, still sat forward but eyes cast down, with him speaking in a voice that matched his pose. 'The object of their action was to find and remove from a party of Austrian officers a large sum of money – the equivalent of ten thousand pounds – intended to pay the troops holding the forward defences.'

'And you let them and it go,' Jervis barked.

He spun round, his ire no doubt stoked by the loss of what could have been prize money, that is, as long as the Austrians were not alerted to the recovery. So much for coalition allies.

'With respect, sir, how could I have known?'

'The fellow with whom you struck your bargain,' Nelson interjected, 'who is as you know skulking in Genoa because he is short-handed, is now using that sum of money to recruit sailors to man his frigate. On the next dark night he could well put to sea and we may lack the means to prevent him.'

'So much for enterprise,' sighed Jervis.

Given he was still looking irritated, Pearce had to assume that was his common expression.

'By your action, you have facilitated the needs of our enemies. However, and only God knows why, your superior forgives you for being over-keen to impress, because I am damned if I would, especially in light of the way you came about your rank, which I will have you know I am not alone in deploring.'

Jervis addressed Digby and asked, in spite of what he had heard, if he still held to his previous opinion, one obviously advanced before Pearce entered the great cabin.

'Magnanimity, indeed. Captain Digby has not asked that you be put before a court but he has agreed with me that you should be subject to a reprimand, in writing, which will, of course, be passed back to the Admiralty and reflect on any future...' There was a pause, before Jervis added, 'I was about to say "placement" or "advancement", but by God I hope you are never in receipt of either.'

Should he protest and demand a court? To accept was to hand the game to Digby, yet Pearce knew the law to be an unreliable beast – doubly so in the military sense – as had been proved in the trial of Ralph Barclay. It all depended on who sat in judgement; Jervis would decide that and he had just made his feelings plain.

The least he could expect was what he was being given now, but Jervis had alluded to the manner of his promotion from midshipman to lieutenant. It might have been at the hand of King George but that did not preclude a panel of naval officers, bitterly resenting what had occurred and presented with a chance to reverse it, from taking the opportunity to dismiss him from the service. Not only Digby would win, so would Emily.

She was receiving again, but this time a family that had moved overnight into a set of apartments in the *pensione* d'Agastino. It had not been a quiet occupation, as the contents of several carriages were decanted into the various rooms. There was a main parlour and bedroom for Mr and Mrs Wynne, as well as another suite for their two pretty daughters, girls younger than Emily, one of whom seemed to be in a permanent state of fluttering fright.

It was incumbent upon Leghorn to welcome them, for they had been displaced from a comfortable existence in Venice, they said, from fear of the French, an outcome much deplored given Mr Wynne, with his weak chest and seemingly even weaker resolve, had realised all his substantial assets at home to move to the warmer climes of Italy, only to find it unsafe.

In his wife, he had a reasonably practical woman who saw to her charges with no more than a modicum of fuss, though she was grateful indeed to Mrs Barclay, who had attended upon them come morning to see if they required any help to settle in, and who knew enough Italian to ensure the right trunks ended up in the right rooms.

'My dear lady, to trouble you in your condition is unconscionable.'

A platitude. Emily replied in the only manner she could, 'It is not so. I carry it easily.'

Mrs Wynne's eyes went to the swollen belly, which not even loose garments could now hide, a glance spotted by her girls and one that brought blushes to their cheeks; childbirth, the pains and most of all the causation, was as yet mysterious to the young ladies. Mr Wynne wheezed a trifle before mumbling his own thanks but did not stir from the chair he had occupied with an air of exhaustion.

Tout les anglais descended on the *pensione*, not that such amounted to a great deal in numbers, but the arrival of an English family coming overland was rare and a cause for much curiosity. The Udenys came as a couple, the consul husband exceedingly solicitous of the family's plight, his wife surreptitiously eyeing their possessions and very likely seeking to calculate their value.

Emily wondered if Consul Udeny was being somewhat over-elaborate in his commiserations, indeed, whether they were really required at all. The Wynnes were obviously wealthy, while they gave the impression of easy panic. No enemy blade had come within one hundred and fifty miles to threaten their flesh, and it was possible to wonder if their 'flight' had been necessary, or just the result of a wicked rumour and a degree of cowardice.

That did give Emily cause to wonder and reflect, for she had been raised in very much the same kind of society, albeit few of her parents' acquaintances were affluent enough not to fear and guard against a drop into poverty. When she observed Miss Eugenia Wynne all a'flutter, she could recall that she had once behaved in a like fashion, reacting to anything untoward or strange with excessive emotion. The sister, Elizabeth, who answered to the diminutive Betsey, might be physically very like Eugenia, but there was a glint in her eye that her sibling lacked, one that marked her out as a steadier creature.

Letitia Teale was not far behind the Udenys, hurrying to the *pensione* to establish her superior position and to immediately cow the girls and Mr Wynne, if not his wife. She too spotted money; of course, her husband would be saying special prayers for their safety and they must attend on Sunday, which with some sophistry managed to get round to the need for repairs to a building barely fit to serve as an Anglican church. When the Pollards arrived and all were crowded into Emily's parlour, the men were required to remain standing for want of chairs, this as the family told their sorry tale.

Why was she less sympathetic than the others, always assuming they were sincere? Here was a family with the means to go where they wished, a situation that had existed before the Revolution had sundered the peace of Europe. Though the word 'ravished' was never used, Eugenia seemed to think the entire series of events rippling out from Paris had been staged to bring down on her and her sister such a fate.

Emily had left that life behind. She was no

longer the provincial ingénue but a widow with a lover. She had spent time aboard a ship of war and seen much that had dented the delicacy of her upbringing. In addition, she had thrown herself into nursing men wounded in battle and had seen men die, while the Wynnes had had nothing more to worry about than their trivial concerns. No wonder she lacked empathy.

The banging of cannon did not unduly disturb the gathering, it being too common in Leghorn harbour, until Letitia Teale, ever alert to social opportunity, pointed out the number of firings, which indicated the arrival of an admiral and it could only be Sir John Jervis in HMS *Victory*. This was confirmed by crowding at the window – indeed, he was leading in half his fleet. The Wynnes seemed miffed that such an event overrode their tale-telling, even more so when Mrs Teale left in a hurry, in order, as she said, 'to properly arrange things.'

'What things?' was the weak question from Mr Wynne.

'Why, there's sure to be a ball for the admiral,' Mrs Pollard replied. 'Especially since it is his first visit to Livorno since taking over the command.'

This got a squeal of delight from the Wynne girls, who were now grouped with Caroline Pollard and, in their enthusiasm, making that shy creature seem even more withdrawn than usual. All talk of flight was abandoned in favour of trying to recall which trunk held the ballgowns, followed by enquiries as to the possibility of a local seamstress being engaged to make alterations.

'We simply must be seen in the latest fashion,'

224

Eugenia trilled. 'It would be too, too dreadful if our garments were dated.'

'Will we be introduced to the admiral?' Betsey asked, with a more calculating approach.

'Most assuredly,' was the response of Mr Pollard, the glint in his eye hinting that he would be being most attentive to their wishes. 'As an important supplier to the service, he will make acquaintance with me and I shall ensure you, young ladies, will not be ignored.'

'Mrs Barclay, will you attend?'

'I think my condition precludes it, does it not?'

Pollard was quick to pronounce on that too. 'Nonsense. Why, the bloom it gives you will light up the assembly.'

There was clearly too much enthusiasm in the praise, judging by the look he got from his wife, already sparked by his playfulness with the Wynne girls, which he did not miss and had him hastily add, 'Clearly, I would not suggest you indulge in too much dancing.'

'I meant my bereavement, Mr Pollard. Is it seemly?'

'Forgive my overlooking it, Mrs Barclay. I find it hard in face of your kind and cheerful nature to put the two in the same thought.'

That got Pollard a full wifely glare, quickly switched to a full and insincere smile, as the spouse turned upon their hostess. 'Surely no one will object, for it would be a curmudgeon indeed that would see you sitting all alone while the entire English community took its pleasure.'

This gave Mrs Udeny, with Letitia Teale gone, a chance to act the doyenne. 'I think I am entrusted to speak for society hereabouts, Mrs Barclay, when I say your presence, or should I say lack of it, would be sorely missed.'

'I wonder, Mrs Barclay,' asked Mrs Pollard, 'if you would stay close to Caroline? She is too shy to be left to tend to her own dance card and a woman of experience, which I am sure you are, can mark it for her so she is not embarrassed by the attentions of the Italians.'

The girl was embarrassed now, head low and looking into her lap, while Emily was thinking that to go to a ball would be a pleasant thing, for she had spent too much time in these rooms of late. When it came to chaperoning, there was little choice but to accede. That said, she did discern a reason why the request had been made and it had nothing to do with overzealous Latins. With Caroline in constant attendance, Mr Pollard would be obliged to contain his fancies.

But first a seamstress, because if anyone was going to need her gown altered, it was Emily Barclay.

CHAPTER EIGHTEEN

There was some pleasure to be had sailing in company with the squadron, given the power of decision lay in the hands of the commodore, though where they were headed and to what purpose was a mystery. Digby had again declined to share with Pearce the details of what was clearly an operation of some kind. Having been aboard HMS *Agamemnon* for a lengthy briefing, he had, as usual, made straight for his cabin on his return, the order to weigh on the commodore's order passed to his premier by a third party.

They were off along the coast again, heading west, passing the same sights as they had observed previously, some of which were now assuming an air of familiarity. The whole was visible because the sun was shining, the sky was clear with the air crisp and refreshing, while on the distant mountain snow sparkled.

As they approached the Albenga headland, that being the fishing village that gave the promontory its name, flags appeared at the masthead of the flagship, an order to two frigates, *Inconstant* and *Brilliant* to crack on. This they did, passing *Agamemnon* to windward, in order to get themselves some sea room. That was followed by a general command to clear for action, which Pearce executed.

The reason became obvious as they opened Alassio Bay. It was crowded with shipping: cargo vessels of various sizes, and as well as a French corvette, two galleys and a small gunboat acting as escorts. Given not all the cargo carriers could get alongside the not very extensive jetty, the bay was full of boats carrying cargo from vessels anchored in the roads, all of it, Pearce assumed, supplies for the Army of Italy. As soon as Nelson's ships hove into view, they immediately began to make for the nearest part of the shore.

Looking out to sea, Pearce observed the pair of head-reaching frigates swinging inshore to close

227

off escape to the west, while the first discharge of one of Nelson's lower deck twenty-four-pounders brought Henry Digby onto the deck, to stand for a moment in order to take in the scene, not least the great plumes of water being thrown up by the British cannonball. The shot was designed not to sink or damage anything, but to send a message to say it would be wise to surrender.

It failed in several cases: the corvette immediately cut her cable, seeking to get underway – the purpose to flee not to fight – to try to get clear before her exit was blocked by the frigates, and that showed wisdom. To engage a sixty-four-gun ship-of-the-line would render her matchwood. The galleys had also cut their cables but they moved with more speed; oars in the water took less time than setting sails and they could move rapidly in very short order.

All eyes aboard HMS *Flirt* were on the flag as the signal broke out, a series of numbers telling some vessels to engage in a general chase to the west, this to capture the galleys, while other frigates were given orders to close – with what? Flag signalling was, even with the most talented signaller, far from comprehensive.

Pearce was confused but if he required enlightenment, there was no way it was going to come from Digby, which left him to assume that prior instructions had been issued as to how to act. He was not alone in his desire to know what was planned: all along the deck men were crouched by their guns, with only the captains on their lanyards able to see anything, and they, despite the strictures against talking, were relaying what was happening to the rest of the squadron.

'Mr Pearce, we are to close with the cargo vessels and take possession of them one by one. The guns will remain run out but they will be employed only, should it be necessary, to warn the ships' captains not do anything foolish. Please detail parties of men to take to our boats, sufficient to act as prize crews.'

'Sir.'

'You will remain on the quarterdeck, however. Let Mr Conway and Lieutenant Grey enjoy some activity without your interference.'

That being yet another calculated insult, there was temptation to say he could forgo the glory of taking a few cargo vessels given what he had already achieved. Yet Pearce held his tongue; it was too public a place to exchange barbs with Digby, but there was another reason: the midshipman's chest had positively swelled at the prospect of leading men into action, even if it was a rather soft duty. HMS *Flirt* was not going to fight anything even remotely equal and probably it was not going to fight at all, but Conway did not care.

The French gunboat was near the shore and closing, those aboard obviously intending to beach their vessel, which meant they could be ignored. Pearce got his parties sorted out as ordered, this while the brig closed with the cargo vessel furthest out in the roads, and he had the boats away, sure there would be no trouble.

A boat appeared from behind the bow, with those aboard rowing furiously to get away, which led to the supposition there might not even be a crew for Conway to capture. Grey was heading for another ship, to which Pearce despatched a ball aimed to wet their deck. There was no need for more: this was not war.

That situation did not apply on HMS *Brilliant*. As a spectator, Pearce had already observed her begin to close in on the corvette, the enemy yet to get a full set of sails drawing. The two lightly-armed galleys, having been anchored further west, were in the wake of their consort and catching up, as always better equipped for lighting when the wind failed to favour a square-rigger. Their great advantage, especially inshore and in shallow waters, lay in their manoeuvrability. As such, if they would never overwhelm a well-handled frigate, they could do serious damage if not checked.

HMS *Inconstant's* commander, being the senior, Thomas Freemantle, took the corvette – there was more honour in such a capture – leaving *Brilliant* to ensure the galleys could not close to form a combined defence. As Pearce watched his old ship alter course, he could not help but pray for two things, given they were clearly going to fight: that his old shipmates suffered no harm, while two people he had good cause to hate might get their just deserts from French gunfire.

Toby Burns, one such person, observed from the quarterdeck, looked to be praying but he was creating a false impression. In command of a quartet of eighteen-pounders, his gaze was fixed on the nettings above his head, in his mind imagining half the top hamper being shot to pieces and then slicing through the nets to crown his skull.

Pearce's other bête noire, Captain Richard

Taberly, was cursing quietly on the quarterdeck, seeing the orders he had been given as demeaning. With the firepower he could bring to bear, a galley, by its very nature lightly constructed, was not much of a match. Being two did not do a great deal to alter his feeling of being patronised, given there were brigs in the squadron just as fitted to take on those adversaries.

Given her deeper draught – Alassio Bay was quite shallow – Nelson had stood off to let his smaller ships operate in waters more suited to their depth of hull. Yet there was no doubting the menace or the ability the commodore had to give chase to any vessel that broke out of the screen he had set up. Nor was he willing to leave every cargo vessel to his brigs; *Agamemnon's* boats were in the water and racing for the cargo ships, which obliged Digby to become somewhat animated, this at the thought they might beat his crew to the captures.

'More shots across those bows are required,' he yelled.

Pearce hid a knowing grin: gunfire would make cautious any boat parties approaching an enemy vessel, *Agamemnon's* included. Given it made no real difference who got aboard first, John Pearce took a savage delight in carrying out that order with a degree of sluggishness. Any money from prizes would be shared throughout the squadron, regardless of who did what. Orders obeyed, he went back to watching *Brilliant*.

Toby Burns would have given his eye teeth to be anywhere other than where he was at this

231

moment. His imagination was far too vivid for his own good and he could see dangers and risks that flew outside the bounds of what was humanly possible. Having complied with the order to lever his guns round and forward did not result in any employment of muscle by him, if you excluded a tongue to pass it on. He went back to his bloody visualisations of his broken self until a new set of instructions were issued.

'Mr Burns,' called Glaister, his well-modulated Highland tone of voice carrying clearly, 'we need to take the lead galley on the prow and halt them choosing when they can close. Fire immediately your cannon bear on the target.'

There were many things in which Toby Burns was deficient; for instance, he had no idea, while he was expected to know without being told, that the ability of a galley to swing on a penny represented their greatest advantage, that being something his superiors intended should be denied to them. Damage to the forward scantlings might be enough to hold them and have those oarsmen see water enter their deck, which would have them thinking that to abandon ship would be better than continuing to row.

He was about to demonstrate another one. The act of firing cannon from a moving vessel, at another warship, was not a problem yardarm to yardarm. Such simplicity did not extend to deflection, aiming off true at a moving target while in motion yourself. This required a certain knowledge of range finding, trigonometry and ballistics. Toby Burns lacked these, yet knew his orders to be explicit. Glaister had told him to fire as soon as he

232

was sure his shot would strike the target and that too he would be required to pass on.

There were guns banging out all around the bay yet, bathed in sunlight, it looked so tranquil, if you ignored the clouds of black discharged powder billowing out from the fighting ships. If it appeared so to him, it was less so to the gun crews he commanded. Their sole vision was through the gap the cannon muzzles left in the ports, so the first sight of the enemy would come with the tip of a bowsprit. That was why when Burns gave the order to fire, not in a shout but with a loud croak, he was startled when one of his gun captains shouted 'Belay!'

Toby, realising the demand had been obeyed, swung his head to exchange glares with the man who had produced it. Martin Dent was, to his mind, a cheeky sod, a skylarker first encountered as a drummer boy, who had grown into a damned show-off as a nimble topman and that had rankled too. Dent moved through the rigging and yards as though he was a monkey, this while the now acting lieutenant could recall many times when he had struggled to look competent.

Dent, now a gun captain, spoke over his shoulder; he was peering along the muzzle and out through the gun port. 'You was a mite too early. Give the command now and make it loud enough to be heard by the binnacle.'

Seconds passed before the command was given, evidence of even more confusion in Burns' mind. He had to leap clear as the recoil brought one of the eighteen-pounders jumping back towards his legs, restrained by its lashings too close for comfort. Behind that came the billowing and acrid black smoke, through which he could see the men he commanded swabbing and reloading without reference to his presence.

'What you aiding him for?' demanded Blubber Booth, his voice gasping through exertion and carrying too much flesh. He was another hand who knew Burns of old and had no time for the bugger.

'Don't want to look shoddy, do we?' Dent called. 'If he gets it wrong, it will be we that gets the backwash.'

'Shoddy, mate. Won't look none other with that turd givin' us orders.'

The voice of Glaister came through a speaking trumpet, ordering Burns to fire again, to then give the command to the rest of the larboard cannon to do likewise as soon as they had a target. Toby Burns, once his second salvo was discharged, looked over the hammock nettings, wanting to see the effect. It having struck home, he was quick to take inordinate and undeserved pride in the damage inflicted.

The lead galley's figurehead had gone, as well as half its larboard bulwarks. An enemy that should have swung to get broadside on was doing the very opposite: she was turning away, this while her consort was using his oars to come up on *Brilliant* to starboard, which left him confused, until he realised he must cross the deck to the cannon and crews who could engage her.

Taberly had the helm put down to come broadside on to this threat and whoever commanded the galley, knowing what was coming, was disinclined to face it. The tricolour, on its single amidships mast, came fluttering down like a fowl peppered with shot, evidence that the halyard had been hastily cut. That was followed, albeit with more composure, by his damaged companion. Their flag was properly lowered.

'Mr Burns, to me and bring with you those you wish to form a boarding party. You are to take command of that damaged galley and prepare to get it back to Leghorn by whatever means you find appropriate.'

Astern, the boats, let loose to avoid their being damaged, manned by a couple of oarsmen each and full of livestock, were called in. On deck, the cannon had to be housed before those who would take possession of the prizes could arm themselves with their chosen weapon: a cutlass, knife or a club. Pulling towards the damaged galley, Toby Burns could not believe he was engaged in anything remotely close to reality.

He had dreamt of this sort of adventure as he made his way from his home in Somerset to Sheerness in Kent, there to join his ship, as well as his Uncle Ralph and Aunt Emily. He had been sure then of his glittering destiny; nothing since had remotely lived up to expectations.

Yet here he was now, in command of a boarding party and about to take possession of an enemy vessel. For once the pistol he held was in a hand that did not shake, nor did it bother him that there was a battle taking place behind his back. Broadside after broadside was being fired as HMS *Inconstant* battered the French corvette into submission.

Toby Burns was lost in his own world, mentally composing the letter home to his parents, one that would be passed to his relatives and the family acquaintances, and he sought to conjure up an image of how it would be received. For once it could consist of exploits real and welcome, not lies in which he had described with brio events in which he had been near rigid with terror.

The oars on the galley having been shipped, he found himself close to curious faces examining the approaching boat and the folk in it, fellows with an emaciated appearance.

'Looks like we will have to care for a great number of prisoners, lads.'

'Don't he know they is prisoners already,' Blubber Booth spat. 'Lord alive, we's freeing them.'

'Belay the talking', was Burns' response, this as the fellow on the tiller hooked onto, below the open gangway, another boathook used to keep them clamped to the hull. There was a moment of confusion then, as Toby realised that with a pistol in his hand he would struggle to climb up the man ropes, his solution being to stuff it in his pocket, which got a joshing reprimand from Martin Dent.

'Might be a notion to uncock that, your honour. If it goes off close to and aimed at your gonads, who's to say what it will remove.'

He should have told Dent to be quiet. With his new-found confidence, it would have come out properly as a strongly-voiced command and not his customary croak. But the image of what he might suffer if he knocked the hammer and fired the pistol accidentally was enough to ensure he saw to that first. Then he grabbed the man ropes and got his feet on the slimy battens, slipping with one foot only to find sailors ready to save him a dipping by pushing his backside upwards.

He arrived on deck to find a scruffy-looking individual, in a less than impressive uniform, holding out his sword, flat on both hands, the crew gathered by the bulwark behind him. The convention, from one gentleman treating with another, was to refuse to accept but Toby was never going to pass up on such a trophy and he took it eagerly, even if he noted it did not appear to be a blade or hilt of any distinction.

He did know to give his name as well as that of his ship. But anything else seemed pointless given the enemy captain did not understand a word of English. Behind him the men he had led were clambering aboard, half their number quick to gather and drive below the enemy crew without either ceremony or instruction. The rest stayed close to Burns, who was taking no action, just staring at the captain.

'Might be a notion to take him to his cabin, Mr Burns. There will be things there, paper and coin, that Captain Taberly will expect you to hand over.'

'For a common seaman, Dent, you are both overfamiliar and too talkative.'

Dent had a lively countenance, a cocky manner as well as eyes that seemed to be able to dance. He did so now as he touched his forelock. 'I best mind my P's, your honour, with you being such a hero.'

How many times had he had that word thrown at him? Even if it was not said out loud, the accusation was in the looks he got from the crew of the frigate. He had stolen the glory gained by John Pearce and none would let him forget it. Normally crushed by that, he did not feel anything like the same now. Did he not have command of a captured vessel? Did he not have in his hand a surrendered sword? For him that wiped the slate.

He indicated to the Frenchman that he should lead the way to his cabin, following in his wake, while recalling his duty and ordering Dent to inspect the damage and report. That, added to the 'Aye aye sir', made him feel really good. He did not see, because it was behind his back, the ringed fingers and the waving wrist that told all what Dent thought of him.

Even if he had seen it, the effect would have faded as he entered the cabin, a goodly part of the whole of the ship and comfortably furnished, for this, and it might last for several days, would be his. It was with new confidence that he went back on deck to issue his order.

'Take the captain to HMS *Agamemnon*. The commodore will wish to question him.'

When the fellow was led away, Toby Burns re-entered his quarters, to savour for the first time the joy of having a space he could call his own, one he did not have to share with anyone.

Moving the galley presented no problem; as had been pointed out, the rowers were not free men. A couple of them were captured British sailors, the rest criminals or those who had fallen foul of the Revolution. The promise of freedom was enough to have them row willingly to wherever the Royal Navy wanted to take them as long as it was not back to the rule of their previous slave-drivers, men who now took turns to ply the weighty oars themselves and suffer the blows for poor performance they had meted out to others.

Added to that, Toby Burns did not have much to do in the way of navigation, he was sailing in convoy with the second captured galley and the corvette, the only blow to his contentment the fact that the two brigs, HMS *Flirt* and HMS *Troubadour*, had been detached from the squadron as escorts.

That would mean when he reached Leghorn, John Pearce would be there too. It was necessary to ensure he avoided a meeting at all costs.

CHAPTER NINETEEN

Emily Barclay would have scoffed had anyone intimated she was excited at the prospect of the forthcoming entertainment, now definitely planned for Friday, denying the fact that she did feel a thrill to be going for the first time in her life to what could be called a Grand Ball. The only shortcoming was her condition, which, with the conclusion of her term approaching, meant she would be unable to take full pleasure from the event.

Previous experience of dances and routs did not compare; the Assembly Rooms in Frome could not stand as significant against the grandeur of an Italian Archbishop's Palace and its receiving-room-cum-ballroom. Already visited as an individual, she recalled its glittering chandeliers, fabulous statuary, as well as walls and a ceiling decorated with elaborate religious paintings by famous artists.

In addition, the main guest was Vice Admiral Sir John Jervis, which, with over half his fleet arriving in his wake, would mean a whole clutch of senior officers attending. The closest she had come to such a level of sophistication had been at a ball in Sheerness, where she had danced with several naval officers, one or two quite senior, though the real fun had come from the gaiety and dexterity of the younger attendees.

In doing so she had incurred the wrath of her husband – absent and pressing seamen – being exposed for the first time to the distaff side of his nature, hitherto solicitous if somewhat reserved. His new young wife had been berated for shaming him by her exuberance as reported to him and Emily had still not forgiven Horatio Nelson for being the source. It was he who had told Ralph Barclay how much she had enjoyed herself. Despite the view expressed by John Pearce that he was really a decent fellow, to her he was a sneak.

Her husband at that time had another cause to be angry: Emily had been drawn by other naval wives into an excess of spending at the ship's chandlers as well as other tradesmen emporiums, women who had insisted her newly appointed captain would require the means to entertain both his officer and his peers, let alone his superiors. A strapped Ralph Barclay, seeing the cost and quantity of what she had purchased, had demanded the whole lot be returned.

Having spent several happy days in preparation,

in the company of the Wynne girls and the Italian lady employed, through gestures, sign language and drawings, to do the more elaborate embroidery, the feeling of anticipation had grown to make her feel content, an emotion that had lately been in short supply. Emily was even able to abide Eugenia Wynne's occasional vapours at the prospect of meeting some handsome naval officer, though equally likely to appear to near faint at the dread of being caught alone by some predatory Tuscan lothario.

'If they are as ardent as the Venetians,' she lamented, 'who are ever in search of an alcove, I shall be shamed for eternity.'

'You tested eternity quite often, I recall,' Betsey remarked, which got her a stuck out sisterly tongue from her older sibling. 'If you flutter your eyelashes at every man you see, you cannot be surprised that they sense encouragement and seek privacy.'

'I have never encouraged an advance in my life,' was stated by Eugenia, quite forcefully.

'And never sought a compliment.'

That reply was larded with sarcasm and Emily, having watched them these last few days, had observed they competed with each other quite heartily and, very likely, for the same attention.

The sewing, stitching and company, really the supervision of much of the work, took Emily back to a less disturbed life, to the years before she was married and all the complications of that disastrous union. The activities happening in these rooms did not differ so very much from what had taken place at home prior to some important local event: parties, weddings, the ball after the county fair.

She and her friends commonly gathered in each other's houses to make or mend, seeking to follow the latest fashions from London and Paris as sent down by the newspapers, while endlessly speculating on what they might encounter, for marriage was in all their minds, as it was in that of their calculating parents.

The last occasion had been before her nuptials. Recalling those days, Emily could now see what she did not really pick up then: the undertone of reserve her lifelong companions harboured regarding the prospect of her forthcoming marriage. Those friends had seemed enthusiastic, yet she now saw that differently, how they had disguised the undercurrents of reserve they felt, which unknown to them, mirrored some of her own.

The reasons were starkly apparent in recollection. Previous communal speculations had always centred round some handsome and surprising suitor, a youth hitherto ridiculed come to comely maturity or some thrilling visitor calling upon a neighbour. Captain Ralph Barclay was no Prince Charming; indeed, at twice Emily's age, and with a rather spartan manner, he was a questionable catch.

The real push came from her parents, added to the feeling, general to her gender and the mores of her society, that to refuse a proposal carried with it real risk, for it rarely remained a secret. One man rebuffed made others cautious. To be seen as difficult and hard to please would never do; the longer a girl remained unattached, the greater the fear of eventual spinsterhood, a fate held to be worse than death in the fledgling female imagination.

Now, Emily, so close in age to be more like an elder sister than an aunt, had the Wynne girls asking her about the build-up to the occasion and the joy she must have felt. This brought back all the suppressed feelings she had experienced on that crisp winter day, for she had been no June bride, while the gap between the proposal and the event had been measured in weeks, not months. Ralph Barclay was in a hurry, war was looming and he had been told by the Admiralty he was on course to be given a frigate.

Nor was the ceremony the stuff of legend, for it seemed brief and hurried. If she was, and her mother and father were wont to stress this, marrying a man who had an entail on the house in which she had grown up, he was not in a position to splash out on any extravagant service. Five years on half pay had obliged Ralph Barclay to use all the wiles he had learnt at sea, to weave and bob, in order to stave off a raft of creditors, trades folk, shopkeepers and merchants who had been obliged to wait too long to have their bills settled.

'I doubt I shall sleep tonight,' Eugenia exclaimed, as usual throwing up her hands as if the prospect was life-threatening and putting a momentary check on Emily's memories. 'My heart is beating hard now, but in a near dream state I think it may burst.'

'How fine you will look, sister,' Betsey remarked, 'with puffy eyes and drawn cheeks. Quite the belle of the ball.'

Now Eugenia was manufacturing alarm, which

Emily, needle in hand, was determined to stave off, in order to avoid her collapsing once more into a chair, to demand that someone fetch the salts.

'You will sleep and you will dream, Eugenia, and in those you will imagine great happiness and a blissful and sunny wedding to the most handsome man in the fleet.'

'Do you think so, Emily?

'I know so,' she lied; she already had the heart of that individual.

'Because it happened to you?'

'Of course,' came another lie, accompanied by a smile denoting bliss.

She had not dreamt of happiness on the night before her wedding, nor had she enjoyed what followed and such thoughts took her back not to a church in winter, or the house Ralph Barclay shared with his sisters, but to Lymington in the New Forest and the night she and John Pearce had first become lovers. How sweet that had been, how pleasurable, how different from the rough and painful coupling when Ralph Barclay had taken his due as her new husband. That forced her to say to herself 'Enough!' There were matters at hand to be dealt with and they were not gifted with an excessive amount of time.

'Now, I say, you must ply your needles, or we will not be worrying about puffy eyes, but loose threads.'

John Pearce could not avoid getting sight of Toby Burns, really quite close by, though communication was impossible besides being undesirable. Both were on their respective quarterdecks, he still and observant, Burns pacing about in the manner of a *poseur,* the French word applicable given that which appeared obvious, the showing away he was indulging in. He was forever strutting to some point by the bulwarks to raise his telescope, pull it out to its full extent and gaze at an empty seascape, as if there might be some threat in the offing and he was just the fellow to meet and deal with it.

'Sure he's Admiral Toby in his thinking, John-boy.'

This was Michael O'Hagan's view, related as he stood over Pearce, razor in hand, scraping away the lather on his chin.

'I hope I didn't act like that on my first time in command.'

'Jesus, you were given to causing grief by lording it,' came the reply, the smile taking the sting out of the waved razor. That was before Michael cocked an ear and bent to his task again. 'Can you hear it?'

'How can I not?' Pearce replied, as a series of muffled shouts came through the bulkheads.

'I swear he gets louder by the day.'

'Does shouting to God aid salvation, Michael?'

'There are those who say so, but in Ireland we tend towards the quiet, lest the heathen English hear us and put a price on our prayers.'

'So Digby is a heathen?'

'He is, and a troubled one, but not for sure alone in that. Do you have a plan, John-boy, for when we raise Leghorn?'

'Several, and one of them is to find "Admiral" Toby Burns and box his ears.'

'The devil take you, you know that's not what I meant.'

'I shall call on Emily as an old acquaintance and a once junior officer of her late husband.'

'With certain parties in port also? You might as well fly a set of flags.'

'I can't not call, can I?'

'Even if it might be wise to avoid it for her sake? Why not send a message, to meet somewhere where you will not be seen?'

'The messenger?'

'You have three fellows willing if Digby will let them ashore.'

The shaving finished, his chin washed and towelled, Pearce stood up. Michael lifted the bowl of hot water, preparing to take and dispose of it overboard while his 'master' pulled back the screen so he could exit without spilling, to find Ivor Conway on the other side, his hat immediately coming off his head.

'Mr Dorling's compliments and we have raised sight of the Leghorn lighthouse.'

'You look worried. Why?'

'Lookouts tell us the harbour is full of tall masts – warships, they reckon. Mr Dorling is sure it must be Sir John in *Victory*. Wants to know if there is to be extra prettying, for he will have a spyglass on us, for sure.'

'Even if he does, he will be a happy man to see that we and our consorts have captures and thus will not be too fussy in his inspections. By the time we anchor he will have calculated his eighth share to the penny. I know Mr Dorling thinks he might find fault with us, for he has that reputation, but

246

the French corvette will take his attention first. Have you informed the captain?'

'Not yet, sir.'

Conway should have gone there first. Why he had not required no great intuition, given the man had taken to what his marine guards called 'occasional raving'. If he had done that in the presence of authority he would have risked removal, but Pearce had seen him in such a situation in Nelson's dining cabin and, if Digby had not seemed to take much pleasure from the event, he had done nothing to shame himself and nor had his behaviour manifested itself on deck. He was obviously capable of restraint in public.

'Then I suggest you do so now. Captain Taberly will certainly be called upon to report to the flag and perhaps his junior commanders also. Mr Digby will want to ensure he is in his best bib and tucker for the occasion.'

'They say Sir John is fond of the cat, sir.'

'He may be, and a fool for it to my mind, but that is not a punishment extended by admirals to midshipmen.' The kindly tone was replaced with one false but gruff. 'That however does not apply to first lieutenants who find such creatures hanging about and not attending to their duties. Especially not those seeking to shift such duties to another.'

Ivor Conway blushed, for Pearce had smoked his purpose: to get him to take the news of the likely presence of the fleet to Digby.

'Don't be afraid, Mr Conway, and even if you are, keep it hidden. Whatever the captain is going through it does not extend to taking lumps of flesh out of his fellows, however young, tender and tasty they might appear.'

'Will we be going ashore, sir?'

Slightly thrown by the question, it was the voice, now somewhat deeper than the croak of a few weeks ago, which alerted Pearce to the drift of Conway's question. He was coming to manhood; indeed, he might have already made his way through that stage of his growth and begun to contemplate those things he might gain from it.

If he had, the fleshpots of an Italian port would seem like a looming paradise, which had his superior wondering whom he could detail, not to keep the lad away from temptation – there was not a human born who could achieve that with passionate youth – but someone who could ensure he avoided the obvious dangers of both disease as well as the one quite common in young and fresh dippers: the forming of a misplaced *amour*.

'Damn me, Michael,' he opined, when Conway had gone and O'Hagan had returned, to be told of the lad's progression. 'I am becoming like a pompous parent.'

'Without, sure it be, recalling your own first temptations.'

'Michael, you would scarce credit, even if I told you, how many of those Paris afforded me in the year '91.'

'By the way you're grinning, I can guess. But our mid's question raises another: will we be getting a run ashore?'

'Not if I request it. Speak to Mr Grey, who can ask on behalf of his Lobsters. Not even Digby would grant them liberty and deny it to the crew.'

248

'Is it not that you should speak to Mr Grey?'
The response was a reluctant nod.

If Pearce had seemed relaxed about coming under the scrutiny of the flagship, that did not apply to others. Toby Burns saw the sudden burst of activity on the deck of HMS *Brilliant* and wondered what it portended, for his lookout had yet to inform him of the cause. When it was eventually reported, he had a genuine cause to be angry.

Could he bring it off? This question assailed him. If he was entitled to respect and got it in a showy way, Toby Burns knew only too well how he was perceived by the men he had fetched aboard this galley. Yet the need to display authority in such a setting promised less behind-the-hand ridicule than that he would have faced aboard the frigate, a fact he pointed out to his leading hand, Martin Dent.

'His name will be taken and his tardiness – or was it his blindness? – will be reported to Captain Taberly.'

Dent knuckled his forehead, which if it was prescribed as proper still left Burns wondering at what motives lay behind the bland expression on his face. 'Which will see him at the grating for certain, your honour, with you being asked to plead his case, Porky Ditton being from your division.'

That drained the blood from Burns' cheeks; he disliked witnessing flogging, which was awkward given Richard Taberly was a strong proponent of the punishment. Even worse, and he had experienced this, were his feeble pleas for mitigation,

249

which never served to gain amelioration. Then his duty obliged him to watch the blood and scarring with a pretence at indifference.

'I would add, your honour, that the mainmast cap on this barky is a mite lower than those of *Brilliant,* so happen Porky didn't see it as clear as others.'

The word 'bollocks' sprang to mind, which had Burns castigating himself for blaspheming, only to then realise that Dent, who was smart as well as cheeky, was offering him a way out, which meant the crew were well aware of his squeamishness. How to play it? It would never do to just give way.

'I hear what you say, Dent, will bear it in mind and make a decision prior to our dropping anchor.'

The knuckle was at the forehead again, the dancing eyes steady. 'Very good of you, your honour, an' sharp thinkin', if I may be so bold.'

Damn the man, he is not fooled one bit. Change the subject, Burns.

'Meanwhile, we have done a great deal to turn this filthy French barky into something the King's Navy could serve in, but if it is true that Sir John Jervis is in the offing, I think we best do more.'

Dent was not fooled by that either. They had scrubbed out the galley, which, typically for a French warship, could not even begin to match the standards of cleanliness that were common in a British man-o'-war. Vinegar had been sent over from their mother ship and the whole vessel now smelt of it, this while the slave rowers had been shaved and obliged to wash weeks if not months of grime from their scabby bodies.

The decks had been tidied as well, fraying falls trimmed and useless articles struck below. If more was to be done, it was not for increased order or cleanliness; it was to appease Taberly, who would, without doubt, have a discreet eye on his acting lieutenant's behaviour. Given the young man's unpopularity, Taberly would not be alone.

It was not long before the rituals began, with endless banging guns, Digby on deck to be seen to be carrying out his duties, boats in the water as the three captains were called to attend on the flag. This, after a short interval, was followed by the sight of the admiral's barge, with its carefully clothed crew, pulling away from HMS *Victory*. In the place of honour was the stern countenance and steady presence of Sir John Jervis, heading first for the captured corvette, manned by men from *Inconstant*. Then, his inspection complete, he came on to the first galley.

Burns had to hang on hard to his sphincter as the admiral was piped aboard, while nothing in the look aimed along the deck did much to mitigate his concerns. He had to pray that naught was amiss as Jervis carried out an inspection, being especially attentive to the released British captives who had been galley slaves, while nodding to the rest when they expressed their gratitude for their freedom. Odd they would gain that; the British tars would renew their service with the fleet on HMS *Brilliant*.

'I daresay she is not as you found her, Mr Burns?'

'No, sir.'

'French dogs live in filth and are content to do so,' Jervis growled, before adding. 'Your first experience as commander of a prize, Captain Taberly tells me.'

Toby could not help but glance past Jervis's shoulder – the admiral was not that much taller than he – which was immediately picked up and commented upon.

'He's in the cabin of the captain of the fleet, sipping wine and making his report. I was going to enquire if you enjoyed what you have experienced, but that is superfluous. If you have not, you're no good to the navy.' The hard voice softened. 'I recall mine and the misery of returning to my normal duties, but it serves to feed ambition, which is valuable to an officer. Well, it is time to say thank you, Mr Burns, and proceed to the other galley.'

'I am very glad to have made your acquaintance, sir.'

'Daresay, lad, but you'll get another chance, even if it is a slim one. There's a ball in the Archbishop's Palace tonight in my honour. Too damn insultin' to turn them down, which I would like to do.'

'It can only be deserved, sir, surely?'

'Maybe so, maybe so. Any road, all officers to attend, no exceptions. Begins at seven.'

With that, Sir John Jervis was piped back into his barge.

CHAPTER TWENTY

'I have no desire to go to a damn ball, Michael, and there's an end of it.'

'Do I not have a recollection of you sayin' you might stay in the navy, John-boy?' That got an irritated nod. 'Then I don't see it as serving to go and ignore a direct order from an admiral.'

'While I would remind you how often I have done that before.'

'Holy Mary, that was fine when you didn't give a shite, an' from what I am being told by some of the older hands, this one is a right bastard.'

'Not a soubriquet from which I would except any of them.'

'It would aid what we's discussing if you talked English.'

'They're all bastards to my mind.' Pearce stopped to raise his head in a contemplative pose and look at the overhead deck beams. 'Mind, Michael, if everyone is at the ball–'

'Sure there'll be few prying eyes to see you call on Mrs Barclay?'

'Could I ask you to stop calling her that?'

'You can ask, but habit forces me not to oblige. Besides, what else in the name of Christ risen would I call her?'

'Miss Raynesford, which is her maiden name and the one we used when...' The voice trailed off; there was no need to elucidate.

'And I would look a right eejit callin' her that and her carryin' a child.'

'I could go to the ball and slip away. Who's going to notice I'm missing?'

'Would it be that I am hearing some sense?'

'You are, brother, so get the iron on the stove, a tub of fresh water, and we will see to my uniform.'

'I best do Mr Conway's as well, for he will be so eager to find a trollop and fire away he's likely to singe his coat.'

Such endeavours were taking place all over the harbour, for Sir John had decreed that on this night there would be no shore leave for anyone other than officers and midshipmen, who had also been commanded to attend, each ship standing no more than an anchor watch. The hours after dinner were spent in preening, with some discussion, yet even more private thoughts, on the lax morals of Italian women, which were ruminated upon more in hope than reality.

Naturally, Digby declined to share a boat with John Pearce, which had he and Grey in one and Conway with the pariah in another. As they waited in a queue to get ashore, Pearce found himself playing the part of an older sibling and advising Conway not to pay too many visits to the punch bowl.

'For it will be a heady brew.'

'How do you know this, sir?'

'I have been to one of these affairs previously, Mr Conway.'

'And was it pleasurable, sir?'

Pearce had to turn away to hide a smile, or was

254

it a blush, as the memories of that occasion surfaced. 'In many ways it was very pleasurable.'

The long trail of officers, clad in the best they could manage and with their swords at their side, made their way to the Archbishop's Palace, on a route lined by hundreds of lanterns and curious locals, to be finally brought face-to-face with the kind of magnificent edifice that always irritated Pearce, a building of soaring towers and elaborate construction.

How many times had he sought to persuade Michael O'Hagan of the folly of his papist religion? Not that others were different. Such creeds were no more than a conspiracy to fleece the poor, so lazy clerics, who probably had no real faith in God to speak of, could live in luxury, no doubt with as much female companionship as they desired. Why did an archbishop of any denomination need a palace when the man they worshipped lived so humbly? Every Italian city would have one, and in England, the Archbishop of Canterbury had two, as well as a stipend of twenty-five thousand pounds a year.

If the local *ton* had to produce invitations, such a requirement did not apply to the Royal Navy; their uniforms were their calling card and very soon Pearce found himself within the candlelit great chamber, a cup of punch in his hand, surveying the scene with his usual jaundiced but amused eye, while seeking to ensure Conway, now with a bunch of fellow midshipmen nudging each other, did not get up to anything untoward. Young Hoste was with them, his leg in plaster from having tumbled down a scuttle in Alassio Bay.

There was always danger in such occasions; the ball would be attended by local youths who matched in age and assertiveness their naval counterparts and they too would partake of the punch bowls. Given the presence of young women, who would be seen as objects of desire, competition was inevitable. Some would be sisters or cousins and the Italians were noticeably touchy about the honour of their female relatives. Too forward an approach or any ribald sally was a recipe for trouble, not aided by the fact that the midshipmen were wearing their dirks.

He saw the group drift into one of the many side rooms that abutted the great chamber – the location of the punch bowls – casting a casual eye on the band setting out their music stands and instruments, wondering how long he would have to remain there before he could slip away unobserved. The thought made him smile; who cared enough to keep an eye on him?

'Lieutenant Pearce, is it not?'

He knew who had spoken before he turned to face her, just by the low timbre of the voice and the Tuscan-accented French. Thus the movement was slow, the smile of greeting a trifle forced.

'Contessa.'

Her hovering hand, not demanding, merely habit, obliged him to take and kiss it. When his gaze lifted, he was reminded of her beauty, which had proved such a previous attraction. High cheekbones, flawless skin not masked by powder and well-defined eyebrows that had seemed in conversation to have a life of their own, this added to a ready smile and an animated personality.

256

'As I saw you I wondered if you deserved to be snubbed. Did you not treat me somewhat badly the last time we were in company? Running off, my honour besmirched and never a word to follow.'

The besmirching was a jest, while the occasion referred to had seen John Pearce fleeing her bedchamber, a hurried exit carrying only his breeches, obliged to abandon his coat and hat. They had been laying in post-coital bliss when the hallway below began to resound with loud threats, made in Italian but unmistakable, coming from another fellow who claimed he had the rights to her affections.

She had named the irate person as a young and too ardent buck called Paolo, who mistook the depths of her feelings. She had also translated, and was somewhat amused in doing so, the nature of the menace. The suitor was not alone, he had men enough with clubs in hand to subdue this *inglese* swine, that followed by a promise to castrate him.

As he fled, leaping from a first-floor window, her pealing laughter had been in his ears, while the tale of him making his way through the streets of Livorno clad in only his flapping shirt had sped round the fleet. If it was wont to amuse some, it had done nothing to enhance an already questionable reputation.

'The English have an expression, Contessa, that discretion is the better part of valour. Given the fate you outlined for me, it seemed fitting to adopt that course and depart.'

She laughed again and that was charming, as was the inviting twinkle in those lovely black eyes. This brought on a certain uncomfortable girding, which he knew he must resist. He was in a vulnerable state as a man who had lately been denied intimacy, not only because he had to stay away from Emily, but also it being debarred by her condition.

'Do I still have to fear retribution?'

'No. Paolo has moved onto other women and is, the poor romantic creature, as passionate and silly about them as he was for a while about me.'

'To be replaced by?'

That, in reality quite impertinent, was out of Pearce's mouth before he realised the consequences. He was asking her if she had another lover and the nub of the enquiry could only be deciphered as renewed interest on his part.

'The men hereabout are too eager. Paolo was not alone in such a fault and they tire me with their demands.'

The way it was said, fan waving, the low voice, the slightly conspiratorial gaze added to a very minor twitch of the lips, was designed to tell John Pearce she was not only available, but she found him attractive enough to be willing to renew their relationship. If anyone had asked him how he could be so sure, he would have boastfully been obliged to reply that he possessed prior experience. In Paris, when he had been as young and ardent as her Paolo, he had met women like the *Contessa*, free spirits who knew how to subtly convey desire.

Pearce was aware of several things, not least that the room was filling up. There were too many eyes for comfort, which given his previous adventures had caused so much comment, left him on dangerous ground. Most disturbing was his own reaction to what was a clear invitation to not only pay attention to her but also to revisit her bedchamber, this from the same fellow who had so recently been advising Conway to keep his breeches buttoned.

'I am sure you must circulate, as must I, for obvious reasons.' He was saying that discretion was necessary for both and her nod was confirmation that she got the point. She was, after all, a married woman, which mattered even if her husband never interfered with her liaisons. 'Perhaps we can talk further later?'

That smile again. 'Most certainly, Lieutenant *Jean*.' The lack of a surname spoke volumes.

As he moved away, naturally glancing around the room, his eye was drawn to a group consisting of three young ladies, as well as a more elderly couple, who looked to be parents. The women were well dressed in fine embroidered garments, each wearing a turban of a different design, one cooling herself with a furiously flapping fan in a chamber becoming increasingly warm. It was not until she decided to also examine the room and turned side on to do so that Pearce saw first her shape and then her face, to realise it was Emily.

It was only a second before her gaze alighted on him, to be, and this was disturbing, immediately switched away. Angry, Pearce made straight for her and she could not avoid seeing his approach out of the corner of her eye, and then spun to face him full on, this accompanied by what he thought was a rather forced smile.

259

'Why, Lieutenant Pearce, how good it is to see you.'

To call her Mrs Barclay stuck in his craw, but he had no choice and he responded in the appropriate manner, albeit he struggled with the tone.

'I hope I find you well, madam.'

'Tolerable, Lieutenant, which in my condition is all I can ask for.' She must have interpreted his direct look as portending a breach of their arrangement, for the wave of her encompassing hand was immediate and a perfect ploy to stall. 'You must allow me to introduce you to the Wynnes, father, mother and their two lovely daughters, Eugenia and Betsey.'

'Delighted to make your acquaintance, sir,' said Mr Wynne, a fellow of bushy whiskers and sad eyes, which went with his frown. 'I came tonight, keen to meet some serving officers and to find out what the chances are of the Revolutionary beasts overrunning Italy.'

Pearce had to clutch hard on his sword hilt to keep his voice steady. 'There is an army in place to stop them, sir.'

'Oh, Papa,' Eugenia squealed, with a flutter of her eyebrows at John Pearce, 'can we not put aside this dreadful war for just one night?'

'For myself,' Betsey responded, 'it could go away for ever.'

If she was less outré in her exclamation, there was no doubting the look in her eye, and to Emily, who observed it, there would be sound reasons for she had been through them herself. The man just introduced was tall, handsome and with strong features. Even his rather severe countenance, not a natural cast, seemed to fit the occasion.

'I am sure Mr Pearce can lay your concerns to rest, Mr Wynne. He was, after all, one of my late husband's most trusted and reliable officers. A steady fellow, Captain Barclay used to say.'

That was aimed at him, and if it was a complete denial of the truth, it was a warning to stick to the conventions as well as their masquerade. The temptation to blow the gaff (how odd he thought of such a nautical expression) was overwhelming but had to be contained. Public humiliation would not serve, but a private exchange must happen, though right now he must play the game.

'Mr Wynne, there is also a hard-working fleet of His Majesty's ships of war, well able to aid the armies of the coalition and humbug our enemies. Had you looked in the harbour today you would have seen a trio of recent captures, and I think your daughters have the right of it. There is certainly no danger present tonight.'

He had looked to Emily on that last pronouncement, well able, as was she, to relay coded messages. Just then the band struck up, playing a rather off-key rendition of 'Rule Britannia', this as Sir John Jervis entered in the company of the Austrian governor, both glittering with stars on sashes and breast, to stand until the tune was brought to a conclusion and Jervis could proceed to introductions.

Behind Jervis came Hyde Parker, Nelson and a clutch of his senior captains: Hallowell, Collingwood and Troubridge. The entrance of the dignitaries had taken the eyes of the Wynnes,

261

which allowed Emily and Pearce to exchange an unobserved look, one full of worry and pain for her, clear frustration for him, for he could not speak without it being overheard, which meant his request had to be formal.

'I do hope I get a chance to talk further with you this evening, Mrs Barclay. We have so many memories to share.'

The way her cheeks reddened, highlighting her freckles, brought forth a feeling of sympathy. That had to be overborne by his need to be able to talk to her alone and he was not going to be deterred by her very obvious hand rubbing over her belly, the oft repeated plea to consider their child.

'I respect that you will be busy, much in demand with your late husband's friends, but I have high hopes you will find a small amount of time for me.'

Some young girls in search of a spouse have highly developed antennae, mainly brought on to see off potential rivals. Pearce could not fail to notice Betsey Wynne fell into that category. If her eyes showed nothing, she seemed too practised for that, her narrowed nostrils indicated a deep and unwelcome curiosity. It was time to move on.

'Until later, then.'

Emily was looking past him, Pearce thought to avoid eye contact. 'Perhaps, Mr Pearce, but I need to find time for my relative, Toby Burns. I believe you will recall my nephew with as much warmth as you remember my husband?'

He turned to see Burns standing by the entrance to a side room in company with Glaister and

262

Taberly, all three sipping from the small punch cups, and if his hand had occasionally tightened recently on his sword hilt, it was near to painful in its grip now. He had no real gripe apart from a personal dislike of Glaister, but the other two stood very high on his list of animosities.

This was not the place to do anything about it; Jervis was circulating the room and getting very close to the Wynne party, which had Pearce start to move away, the movement alerting Burns to his presence. The toad was gone in a flash, darting into a side room, and it seemed beneath dignity to rush after him so he took a few paces back and addressed Emily again.

'I am sure he will seek you out as soon as he is given leave by his commanding officer.'

That too was false: Emily had as good as disowned him, having witnessed his blatant lying under oath, which had saved her husband from real censure at his court martial. The time taken by that allowed Jervis to close and Pearce was afforded a cold look from the admiral, which he was damned if he was going to put up with.

'Sir, I have just made the acquaintance of these delightful people, whom I'm sure would be honoured to be introduced to you.'

That did not improve a look that was on its way to a glare, quickly altered when he saw what he was being offered, which showed if he was a tartar, he had a soft spot for young ladies. His face cleared and his eyes positively danced.

'May I present to you, Mr and Mrs Wynne and their truly delightful daughters, Eugenia and Betsey.'

The latter was the most forward, quick to close and curtsy, smiling puckishly as Jervis took her hand and raised her up, one she in turn held on to for longer than was necessary, this to delay the introduction of her sister, which made inelegant Eugenia's method of forcing her way in, though she was treated with like courtesy.

'And finally, sir, Mrs Barclay, the wife of a late and gallant officer sadly killed when his ship, HMS *Semele*, was forced to strike to the French.'

If Jervis even got a sniff of the underlying sarcasm, it did not show, for he was as keen to meet a pretty woman of twenty as one of eighteen, though there was no smile on his face now but a look of deep condolence, quickly expressed after Emily's hand was kissed.

'A loss to the service, Mrs Barclay; I read the report of the loss of HMS *Semele* and if it does not elevate a man to lose a ship to our enemies, the manner in which he does so may enhance his reputation. Your husband fought well and it is to be hoped you are soon to be blessed with a son who will follow in his father's footsteps.'

There was no response to that but agreement, with Pearce having to hide his amusement, and it got worse. 'I seem to recall from Sir William Hotham's account of things, you were the officer in charge of the exchange, Pearce?'

'I was, sir, and happy to be so.'

'Mrs Barclay, I rate this officer as a scoundrel, for reasons with which I will not bore you, but I cannot help but feel your heart lifted to see he had come to fetch you from captivity?'

'They did indeed, sir, I'm sure,' was Pearce's

mischievous interjection, necessary to cover for Emily's very evident confusion. She literally did not know how to respond and was no doubt looking for hidden meaning in Jervis's words. To buy her time to compose herself, he added, 'As were the crew, particularly Mr Conway, who now serves as a midshipman on HMS *Flirt*.'

'This Conway was at the battle, was he not?'

'He was, and so was I a witness.'

'I want to hear and not just read of it. Fetch this Conway aboard and the pair of you can tell me the tale.' He turned to Emily. 'I daresay I can stand an hour of the rascal's company and tale-telling. I will, however, not ask you.'

'It would be wasted, sir, for I saw nothing. I spent the whole encounter helping the surgeon with the wounded on the cockpit.'

Jervis shook his head slowly. 'I have been known to opine that I am not in favour of marriage for a naval officer, seeing him as lost to service once he is wed. Yet if he has the sagacity to marry one such as you, Mrs Barclay, I fear my stricture would not hold.'

'Most kind,' came with a bob, a half curtsy.

'You, madam, are welcome to visit me at any time of your choosing, for the service owes you a debt.'

The sombre look lifted as he turned to the Wynne girls, the look impish. 'And I would be delighted to welcome you too, such charming creatures. Mr and Mrs Wynne, you, of course, must escort them to HMS *Victory*, given we admirals can be rogues and I would not swear my officers would hold back from seeking to appeal to them.'

That sent Eugenia into a flutter of ecstasy; Betsey merely produced a wide smile, while Emily looked uncertain before saying it would be near to impossible, naming her impending confinement as the reason.

'I will send my surgeon ashore forthwith to see you are properly cared for.'

'Most kind,' she repeated.

'Must move on,' Jervis said, 'and do my duty to our hosts.'

CHAPTER TWENTY-ONE

Thoughts on Toby Burns now occupied John Pearce, though getting hold of him was hard. He was obviously watching out and determined to avoid a confrontation. Pearce was delayed in his search by having to drag away from the punch bowl a loud-mouthed disgrace to the service called Garforth, the information regarding his name and his ship provided by another midshipman, not entirely sober himself.

This specimen, serving in HMS *Brilliant* and far from the first flush of youth, was one of those coves determined to take as much as his body could contain of what was going for free, the effect on his manners being deplorable. He was determined, also, to taunt the local youths. The only thing that did not see him skewered, for they too would be carrying weapons, were the slurred insults, indecipherable anyway but incomprehensible in English.

Pearce took him outside by the scruff of his collar, dragging him to one of the archbishop's fountains to duck his head a dozen times until he promised to behave. 'If I see you at the trough again, I'll throw you in whole. Just thank your lucky stars Sir John did not see you or he would disrate you to a common seaman.'

Renewing his search, the seemingly fruitless situation was resolved by Dick Farmiloe, who had cornered Burns and held him in conversation long enough for Pearce to catch up. The fact that the little toad was worried became evident before he got close enough to ensure he could not once more flee, for he was in deep conversation and only saw the approach at the last moment. His panicked look alerted Farmiloe, who stepped away to get between the pair.

'Hold, John, for the love of God.'

'That is the last person you should be appealing to when talking to me.'

A firm hand was placed on his chest, with Burns moving swiftly to get right behind his saviour. It was only out of respect for a fellow he considered a friend that Pearce allowed himself to be halted.

'I fear you have misjudged your man.'

'He's not a man, he is a bug, only fit to be crushed by my shoe.'

'Will you hear me out?'

'So you can plead his case?'

'Me first, then Toby, for he has a case.'

'For ensuring I was pressed twice into the navy. That will be some excuse.'

'I was ordered to do it by my uncle, Mr Pearce,' was the plaintive cry. 'He insisted if we met another King's ship you should be handed over to them.'

'You did not have to obey.'

'John, he was a new midshipman; Barclay was his uncle and the man who would advance his career.'

'Heaven help the navy if it is to depend on him,' Pearce snapped in a fine display of hypocrisy; having denied God, he was now calling on the heavens. 'You did not see what he was like when we were trapped ashore in Brittany in order to try and satisfy Barclay's greed. I have never seen such a snivelling and useless wretch.'

'Keep your voice down. Eyes are turning this way.'

'They can be damned.'

The look on Farmiloe's face, worried but determined, got him the result he wanted; time to speak, which he did with a quiet but insistent voice.

'Toby is as much a victim of Ralph Barclay as are you, John. He has been browbeaten, threatened, exposed to more danger than even you and all because he was coerced into telling lies. He thus became for you a witness when you showed determination to pursue the case. That made him a threat to Barclay.'

'I doubt he required much coercion, Dick.'

'Remember you said the letter Toby sent to London was not one you were sure came from his hand?' A sharp nod and a glare at Burns. 'Well, this is the first time since then I have had a chance to talk to him and he has just told me what he wrote.'

'And?'

'It was totally at odds. The letter sent to your lawyer was not composed by him; indeed, even if Toby went out of his way to plead mitigation for his actions, it more or less refuted the evidence he gave at Barclay's court martial. Someone else wrote the letter of which you spoke.'

'I knew it.'

'Do you have any idea who?'

Pearce was just about to name Hotham's slippery Irish clerk, Toomey, when a voice boomed out. 'You sir, Pearce, what the devil are you about?'

He turned to see Taberly flanked by Glaister and Henry Digby, which was singular in itself given they were far from friends; indeed, Pearce was of the opinion, based on past experience, that they heartily disliked each other.

'I hear you have laid hands on one of my midshipmen and here I find you in what I can only suppose is a case of threatening Lieutenant Burns.'

'If you mean Garforth, he was stupid drunk and close to getting a knife in his vitals from the locals.'

'He is a member of my crew, sir.'

'And a fine representative one. The man is a lout.'

'And what is it you are doing with Mr Burns?'

'It is none of your damn business and relates to his past activities.'

'I am his captain, which makes it my business.'

'Please, Mr Pearce,' came the weak plea. 'I

269

would not want it known.'

'What, Burns?' was the softly expressed reply, too low to be heard by Taberly. 'That you are no hero but a weakling, or that you lied under oath to a court martial.'

'John,' Farmiloe pleaded, but with more force.

'Mr Burns, to me,' Taberly insisted. 'Come away from Pearce.'

'An order I second,' said Digby.

'What is it to you, Henry?'

'That you besmirch the name of me and my command by your behaviour.'

'Something you will no doubt be yelling at the bulkheads for days to come.' Taberly looked confused; he had no idea what Pearce was talking about. 'Digby won't tell you, Taberly, but he has taken to cursing at his walls and calling his maker down upon my head. Everyone on the ship reckons him mad.'

'Gentlemen, what is going on? Your raised voices are disturbing the other guests.' Nelson had a punch cup in his hand and even at a distance Pearce could see his eyes were slightly glazed, a fact that must be obvious to Taberly et al., they being so much closer. 'If you are in dispute, I urge you to leave it aside.'

'I will not have one of my midshipmen ducked in the fountain like a common villain.'

Nelson looked confused but not for long, given it was explained to him by Taberly, with him adding the behaviour now seemed to extend to Toby Burns, a lad the commodore knew well from the sieges of Bastia and Calvi.

'It would not please me,' he said, 'to have to

270

order you to desist in whatever is going on, and I would be even more reluctant to bring it to the attention of our commander-in-chief.'

Pearce knew he would get no more out of Burns with this lot present and in some senses he had, without the detail, confirmation of that which he had already suspected. But that element he wanted, for if he had been required to give up his pursuit of Barclay by his demise, and of Hotham to get free Emily, the underhandedness of the latter still rankled. If Burns would cooperate then the sod could still be brought to book, the fact that he was no longer C-in-C of the Mediterranean being neither here nor there.

'Dick, get from Burns a promise to meet with me and I guarantee my temper will be kept in check. I want only the information he has passed to you, vouchsafed to me.'

He wanted more, a written account of the whole rotten affair, but this was no time to say so. Another commotion outside in the garden took everyone's attention until a midshipman rushed into the side room crying that one of his number had been stabbed. Nelson might be slightly drunk, but that did not prevent him acting with purpose and he commanded the officers present to join with him.

The party exited through the floor-to-ceiling windows to find the whole body of fleet midshipmen, dirks out and drawn up for a fight; Hoste, balancing on one leg with them. Opposite stood a line of young men with various weapons and angry faces, certainly with knives of greater length than the standard issue for midshipmen.

271

When they moved back as ordered, Pearce saw Ivor Conway, seeking to look ferocious, the movement back also revealing the body lying on the ground. It was Garforth, not dead because groans were audible and he was twitching, while his identity was easily pinned by his near-bleached and shabby garments and the visible holes in his shoes. Seeing retreat, the local lads moved forward until the officers' swords came out, not to threaten or employ, but to ensure no further fighting took place.

'One of you, find a surgeon,' Nelson said, moving between the two conflicted lines. 'And somebody else, locate for me anyone who can speak both English and Italian.'

'We could order our mids away, sir,' Taberly said.

'Think of their pride, Mr Taberly, for this will not be their only visit to Leghorn. And we have the honour of the fleet to maintain. We must first find out the cause and who bears responsibility.'

Roxburgh appeared and ran to kneel over Garforth, only to pronounce, after a quick examination, that he was suffering more from drink consumed than a debilitating wound.

'He has been pierced but nowhere vital.'

Next came Pollard, the merchant who, having lived in Livorno for many a year, knew the language fluently. What emerged was a sorry tale: a drunken Garforth seeking to grab the bosom of a local girl – their dresses were mirroring the latest French fashion, which allowed for a tempting show of décolletage – had been in receipt of a slap for his effrontery. Threatening to retaliate in kind, one of the Italian boys – a neighbour of the victim,

272

it transpired – had stepped forward and knifed him.

'Please tell them that the navy will discipline the miscreant and put up their weapons.' That did not go down well and was only acceded to when a sharp order had the mids sheathe their dirks, with Nelson addressing them. 'We must, gentlemen, have harmony here, for we cannot stay at sea without a base of supply. Now I suggest if you are not minded to behave yourselves, you return to your ships.'

The officers were now faced with two sets of disgruntled youth, with the odd fellow on either side needing to be dragged away by his companions. Finally, the whole broke up and began to drift back into the ballroom, Hoste with his crutches once more, Pearce noting the incongruity. As he sheathed his sword, the mellifluous dance music soared, in contrast with the exterior mood and this reminded him he needed to go back inside and seek to detach Emily from her party so they could talk. Drifting indoors in the wake of the midshipmen, he noted that Toby Burns had disappeared.

'Remember my request, Dick,' he said to Farmiloe. 'Don't let Burns duck it.'

'He will come if he believes you will not harm him. Judging by your tone of voice when you growled your demand, I'm not sure I would.'

'All this talking has left dry my gullet. Let's have some of that punch.'

'It's a strong brew, John, Italian in its contents. I doubt it would serve in England.'

'It will serve here and now, my friend.'

'From what I heard, you could use a few more

of those. I had you and Digby down as–'

'Not friends, Dick.'

'But the clear animosity he just displayed?'

He tried to explain it, but in truth it was impossible to find the key that unlocked the nature of what Pearce insisted was a malady. Events in the Gulf of Ambracia were related, as well as Digby's reneging on his clear undertaking to help get redress for what could have so easily been a deadly fiasco. It was clear Dick Farmiloe was struggling to believe what he was being told and Pearce, sick of explanation, was not in the mood to press the truth of his case.

'Is that Mrs Barclay, I see?'

Pearce spun round to look into the main chamber, to see Emily dancing, a slow waltz, not very energetically, with Admiral Hyde Parker. He acknowledged Farmiloe was correct, then examined him to see if it produced any hint of their association. It did not, and if Dick Farmiloe would not allude to it, he had to assume it was because he was in ignorance. That, however, did not apply to Digby, in a position to glare at him as he, she having returned from her dancing, approached her.

Emily was now part of a much larger crowd, which included Pollard, the fellow who had helped with his Italian. But there were many more: a cleric judging by his garb and several middle-aged women, one with a substantial bosom and enough hip to ever be steady on her feet. His crashing of their company was blatant and if some seemed surprised and bothered, that did not apply to the Wynne girls, they too fresh from the dance floor

274

and perspiring slightly, given their more energetic displays. From them he got a smile of welcome.

'Please, John,' Emily whispered when he came close enough, her fan employed to hide her moving lips. 'Do not disgrace me here, of all places.'

'Mrs Barclay,' he said out loud, for she looked a trifle drawn, 'you must be tired. If you wish to depart early and require an escort to see you to your accommodation, I would be happy to oblige, given it would scarce be safe that you should do so alone. After all, I owe so much to your husband. I would not be a King's officer without his efforts.'

'Mr Pearce, allow me to introduce you to Mrs Teale, the wife of the vicar.'

The lady had moved up behind him as he was speaking and if she was not a person of surpassing comeliness to begin with, a deep frown rendered her even less attractive. Pearce could not know for certain, but he guessed her to be a busybody. It was in the cast of her eye, denoting a woman with a nose for gossip and a desire to spread it.

'You knew the late Captain Barclay, sir?' she demanded, before Emily even had a chance to make an introduction.

'With the exception of this dear lady, possibly better than anyone. He was never shy of showing me his character in a very open fashion.'

'I did not know the captain myself,' she sniffed, as though that was the fault of Barclay.

'Then you missed a rare opportunity to meet with a singular fellow.' Unable to resist a dig, he added. 'I am sure you would have got on famously.'

He was enjoying the exchange, but Emily was

not, for if anyone could smoke out that something untoward was going on it was Letitia Teale; she had the senses of a feral cat.

'Perhaps if I can introduce you to the others in our party, Lieutenant Pearce.'

'Delighted if I have yet to meet them already,' was the reply; he was in this company and determined to remain so.

More introductions followed and he noticed, as he moved around, the two Wynne girls were rarely out of his eyeline. That held until a pair of officers, one Captain Freemantle, came to ask for a dance now the girls' cards had run through. Emily had been watching him like a hawk but she was not wholly attentive; she saw Henry Digby approaching and the look on his face, which promised trouble and demanded she interrupt the pleasantries and quite sharply.

'Is that not your commanding officer, Mr Pearce? He seems rather put out.'

That had him spin away and move to intercept Digby, the hand that took his arm to pull him in another direction far from gentle, the command to unhand him ignored.

'I don't know what you have in mind, Henry, but if you upset Emily, I swear I will make your life hell.'

'You don't have the power.'

'I wonder how you would handle a mutiny and what that would do for your precious career.'

The point struck home; Pearce enjoyed the confidence of a crew he had commanded in HMS *Larcher.* Could Digby match that? The notion he might not was in the feeble response.

'The truth should come out.'

'You will not break my heart by doing so, but you will hers. Is that what your Christian duty tells you to do? You think you knew Ralph Barclay, but you did not and I seem to recall you had little time for the man when you served under him.'

'He did not deserve that which you brought down on him.'

'He did and more. Perhaps one day his wife will tell you all. There's no point in my trying because you won't believe me, but the man was a beast as well as a liar and a coward.'

'You're right, I do not believe you and it pains me to have you on my ship.'

'Ask that I be removed.' That got a stony face. 'You can't and I am not going to relinquish my post, so you and I will just have to rub along as best we can.'

'Lieutenant Pearce,' the Contessa cut in. 'I know we agreed to circulate but I fear that game has been played for too long.'

Digby did not smoke her French, but the way the words were said and the look that accompanied them were obvious enough for him to deduce what this beautiful and elegant woman was seeking to communicate. As he began to move away, he spluttered in his indignation.

'You're worse than I imagined, Pearce; you're a damned satyr.'

The reply came in an Irish accent, that of Michael O'Hagan, who Pearce knew well enough to mimic, even if in his mockery he was talking to Digby's back. 'Jesus, it'll be four Hail Marys for that one, Henry.'

He began to turn to the *Contessa* di Montenero, composing himself to refuse her offer while simultaneously searching for words that would not offend a person he knew he liked beyond mere carnality. Before he could open his mouth, a noisy commotion broke out behind, which had him jerk back to see a crowd gathering round Emily, who was standing looking down at her feet, to where, on the marble floor, lay a very obvious pool of fluid.

The hurried 'forgive me' as he rushed away lacked any *politesse* for, if most of his gender had no idea what had occurred, he did: Emily's waters had broken. His knowledge was entirely due to the peripatetic life he had led in the company of his father who, being a constant visitor to the workhouses they passed on their travels, knew all about the various stages of childbirth, having witnessed every one.

Supposedly a blessing, it had often seemed to be a curse to the poor, another manifestation to Adam of the way the world was set to favour the rich. A workhouse did not extend to the provision of a doctor or even a midwife, and if there were no willing fellow inmates to assist in the event, a miserable birth was certain. In truth, death was too common a fate for both mother and child.

On one occasion, son John had witnessed his father as he aided a poor wretch of an unwed girl, cast out for her disgrace by her family, to give birth by the roadside. A boy was the result, to be immediately and noisily washed in a nearby stream. John held the baby, swaddled in his cloak, all the way to the local church, while Adam carried the mother. If the child was lucky, there would be some local worthy whose wife could not conceive and a good future could be assured. If not, then a hard life lay in store.

Emily's plight beckoned her lover, who did not care what impression he created by rushing to her side, only beaten by Roxburgh, who ordered that a carriage be brought to the front doors immediately. The amount of curiosity engendered by the way Pearce, in a very solicitous manner, helped her to make her way through the now static throng he ignored, only nodding to Sir John Jervis, who abjured Emily to take care and give the navy a sturdy son.

'Do not be alarmed, Emily. You will go into labour but that can take hours, if not days, plenty of time to get around you those able to ensure a safe birth.'

'John, I'm frightened.'

'So am I, my sweet, so am I.'

That got a surprised reaction from Roxburgh, but no comment except to say that he was a surgeon and her condition was not one he was accustomed to dealing with. A doctor should be called.

CHAPTER TWENTY-TWO

He might have been able to accompany Emily out of the Archbishop's Palace and, indeed, share the carriage with her, this taking them swiftly back to the *pensione* d'Agastino, but once she was in her chambers he was shooed out in short order by the stern lady of the establishment. If she gabbled in Italian and was incomprehensible because of it, the message was plain; with the arrival of a child impending this was no place for a man.

He was thus downstairs, pacing back and forth in the prescribed manner while seeking to imagine how he would deal with fatherhood, when the local females to whom he had introduced himself at the ball appeared. They demanded to be allowed to see Mrs Barclay or at the very least be given a report on her progress. While they were talking to Pearce, the first yells of pain echoed though the building, which had those ladies who had gone through the experience nodding in recognition.

Mrs Teale was acting as the leader of the tribe and, as others made their enquiries, she spent more time in a narrow-eyed examination of John Pearce. There could be no subterfuge now; his attentions had focused too much of her gaze on his actions. This did not fit with the image of an officer who merely knew her husband, quite the opposite. Letitia Teale being the wife of the local

Anglican divine meant in this instance, where there might be a scandal to uncover, her social supremacy was unchallengeable.

'I think, sir, we require an explanation. Your solicitations towards Mrs Barclay were singular in the extreme.'

Pearce was determined to be polite but firm. 'Require, madam? By what right do you require?'

'The right of a person who holds dear, and it is thanks to God that I do, the good reputation of the English community.'

It was fortuitous that the doctor arrived just then, in time to overhear the last part of the exchange and his Irish brogue did much to puncture the pretentions of Mrs Teale.

'Well now, would that be the reputation for near to spitting on the locals and callin' them apostates for their way of worship?'

The substantial bosom swelled in indignation. 'It is not required of you, Doctor Flaherty, that you give an opinion, merely that you attend to your patient.'

The man, with the slack smile of a drinker, shot back. He was obviously in no fear of this person who perceived herself as a paragon of virtue. 'Happen, one day I will be called upon to attend to you, Mrs Teale, and then I'll hear your confession, me being sure you have sins aplenty to seek forgiveness for.'

'I may confess to the sin of despising a fellow human being, sir, and that would be you.'

'Now there's no need to be trying to cheer me, is there?'

He slid through the offended group of women

281

and took the stairs two at a time, which had Mrs Teale opine that at least he appeared to be sober for once. That declared, she turned back to John Pearce.

'Are we to assume, sir, that you have some interest in the forthcoming birth?'

He had been given time to think by Flaherty. The last thing Emily needed at this time was that her carapace of respectability should be shattered and he reckoned this woman was of the kind to make sure she found out all she needed to know even before the child was born.

'I acted out of habit, madam, and indeed from a genuine friendship with the late Captain Barclay. I was friend to his wife as well as him. It is safe to say they were both kind to me, and as a fellow with seven sisters, all younger than I am, there can be no mystery to the act of procreation and all its manifestations.'

That brought blushes to the female cheeks.

'In short, Mrs Teale, what happened to Mrs Barclay is not something to cause me wonder. And how could a good friend stand by when everyone else, apart from Mr Roxburgh, seemed rooted and inactive in what could have been a delicate situation?'

'Inactive, sir?' Letitia Teale demanded, as the dropping heads of her companions testified to the truth of the assertion.

Pearce made an effort to sound emollient. 'How could it be otherwise, madam? I do not doubt that you were stunned but, as a serving naval officer, I am accustomed to act as quickly to avoid social embarrassment for Mrs Barclay, as I would be if I was in battle with our enemies.'

'Yet we find you still present,' ventured Mrs Udeny.

'I admit to a proprietary interest.' That got raised eyebrows. 'When Captain Barclay knew his wife was with child, he asked me, as a friend, to see to her needs if he should suffer...' He paused then, fingers pinching the corners of his eyes and his head hunched, sending a plain message of distress. 'It is almost as if he foresaw his own passing, for he knows there is no more dangerous place to be than the quarterdeck of a man-o'-war in battle.'

It was from under dipped eyelashes that Pearce examined the effect of what he had said, pleased to see most of the women were brought near to tears by what seemed tragic, possibly by a genuine feeling, just as likely by the conventions by which they lived, which demanded that the loss of life be treated as a tearful calamity. Not, however, the paragon.

'Then I think it would be safe to say, sir, that you have discharged that obligation. We are here now to offer whatever comfort Mrs Barclay requires while you, I am sure, have your duties to perform.'

There was no choice but to agree. 'I would take it as a kindness to be kept informed of what happens and when.'

'Then listen for the bells of the Anglican Church, Mr Pearce. The birth of a healthy English child will be pealed to the heavens so that all of right mind and faith can rejoice.'

There were two things Pearce wanted to say and could not: first the child had a Scottish-born father and secondly that if the birth happened on a Sunday morning, now not much more than twenty-four hours hence, it would be hard to hear the small bells Mrs Teale spoke of, when every church in Livorno would be summoning their Catholic faithful to Mass.

He did not hear Mrs Teale say, sotto voce as he left, 'Seven sisters, forsooth. I wonder if he is Irish too.'

He had little choice but to return to the ball, still in full swing, because the boats needed to take the officers and midshipmen back to their ships were not due to come to the quay before two bells in the middle watch. He was, however, in a brown study and far from in the mood for either dalliance or jollity, which severely dented what interest the Misses Wynne had in him as a prospective spouse.

They were still the object of much attention, called on by a steady stream of suitors, both naval and local, to grant them the honour of a dance, while Sir John Jervis, loudly claiming *droit de seigneur*, was a frequent partner of both. With their original party gone, the girls, young and flirtatious, had attached themselves to those surrounding the vice admiral and he seemed to revel in their company. Given their pealing laughter, they reciprocated his feelings, his rank and station, as well as his salty jests.

There was no chance of Pearce cogitating on anything other than Emily and her situation, not least to wonder how he could contrive to visit frequently without arousing suspicion. That old battleaxe Teale would soon persuade the others, if she was so minded to, that there was an odour of something untoward in his attentions. He had stalled her but that might prove temporary.

'John, you look miserable. Come join me in a cup or two?' Edward Grey was tipsy, but amiably so, with a silly grin accompanying his words. And then I suggest we must pay some attention to the ladies, especially the Italians, for who knows what opportunities might present themselves, eh?'

'Are you sure with what you have consumed you will be stallion enough?'

'Never fear for Ed Grey, John,' came with a hearty slap on the back. 'I am as able as the proverbial bull.'

'Any sign of our esteemed commanding officer?'

'Gone. Dragged off young Ivor Conway, who could scarce walk.'

'He's in for a long wait on the quay.'

'No. He ordered his boat in for the eleventh hour. Said I should return with you and reminded me that I was on duty as usual at dawn.'

'We are on anchor watch,' Pearce protested, to a look from Grey that said he was wasting his breath.

No other ship in the harbour would act as if they were at sea, but Digby would, just to spite his officers, him especially. It was then the purpose dawned. Digby knew he would want time with Emily and had set out to deny him any real opportunity. If he disobeyed, either by commission or a lack of knowledge, he could be reprimanded again which, if it was not fatal, would act as another mark against his name for future deployment.

'He must spend his entire time with me on his mind.'

It transpired he was not the only one to return to the ball, after all Mrs Wynne had deserted her daughters and would want to ensure they did not do anything too outré. And with her were Mrs Pollard and Mrs Udeny. Most important of all, and with her beady eye on him, was Mrs Teale.

'Now there's a rare beauty,' Grey exclaimed, albeit he slurred. 'Now, for such a creature I would defy Digby.'

Fan waving, the *Contessa* di Montenero was coming towards them both. Pearce thought for a moment that, even if he doubted Grey could perform as he should and his pretentions to bovine abilities notwithstanding, an introduction to her might make his night. It was the eyes of Mrs Teale that changed his thinking. What better way to deflect her suspicions could there be than...

'*Chère Contessa, je suis désolé. Pardonnez-moi, je ne vous ai pas fait attention.*'

'I say, John, you do have a way with the old Crapaud lingo.'

Ignoring Grey and still speaking in French, he insisted it was time they danced together, and with a degree of determination that surprised even her, he took her hand and led her out onto the floor, Grey's voice in his ear but humorously so.

'Damn you, Pearce, I had my eye on that filly.'

The waltz being all the rage, he soon had his arm around her waist, to begin to swing her through the dance, every time he faced the battleaxe producing a big smile, a lean forward and a definite hint he was imparting something intimate.

'What is it that you are up to?'

'I have to admit a smokescreen.'

'The lady to whose side you rushed is special to you, I think.'

He was facing Teale, so he produced an unprovoked, false laugh, his word in the ear ploy used once more. 'The child is mine.'

That got him an amused look, which once more stirred uncomfortable thoughts, not aided by her quite heady perfume. 'Were you careless?'

'If I was, I have no regrets,' he said firmly, before explaining to her, through several dances, the whole affair, though not the ramifications of the consequences but, and this was the hard part, the difference between what passed as acceptable in England as against what was the modus vivendi in Italy.

'There's a lady over your shoulder who, when I spin you, will be looking at us with some concentration.' The turn was swift and smooth. 'Do you see her?'

'Who could fail to? Though I have seen cliff faces of a more becoming nature. And do not assume what you call normal in Italy is the case outside the class to which I belong. It is not unknown for Tuscan fathers to kill their own daughters if they disgrace the family name.'

'Barbarous.'

'So you are seeking to deflect her curiosity?' A nod, then another of those disconcerting smiles, her words larded with mischief. 'I am bound to ask how far you are willing to take that.'

'I have no idea,' he replied truthfully.

That got a pealing laugh, one loud enough to carry to the Teale ear. 'Which means you have no idea if you are English?'

'I know I am not,' he replied, not bothering to name his patrimony.

'Then it is possibly time I called for my carriage. It can only aid your screen of smoke if we are seen to depart together.'

The response was a sigh; his mind might tell him one thing, his body was telling him another.

There was no racing through the streets in his shirt this time, but Pearce did have to hurry, as well as engage a local bumboat to get him out to HMS *Flirt*. The feelings of guilt only really assailed him in that boat. He had been too pressed for time to consider how he had betrayed Emily and at such a delicate moment, while telling himself it had been justified hardly cut the mustard. But then, to his mind and morals, there was nothing untoward in once more sharing the Contessa's bed, and given his lack of recent congress, he had been a hearty and more than one-time lover.

It was also a very new expedience to a fellow who had never previously had to worry about fidelity. In all his escapades, he had consorted with women who never pressed for such a promise and might have been, in fact, deterred from receiving him if they thought him too serious. And that brought to him that all his previous lovers had been married and experienced. Emily might have been the former, but she was certainly not the latter.

If he acceded to her desire to wait three years before he could even begin to court her, what had just taken place would not be a one-off event. He was a man, and if he was out of Emily's orbit, which he would have to be to remain even partially sane, temptation was bound to arise and it would not need the basilisk eye of a Mrs Teale to ensure he succumbed.

Such reflections had to be put aside as the bumboat, rather untidily, bumped into the side of the brig, which got him a glare from the ship's carpenter, Brad Kempshall, on deck and carrying out repairs.

'Damned Italians,' Pearce called in a jolly voice, knowing they would not understand and that Kempshall, with the British tar's disdain for foreigners of any hue, would be pleased by it. 'Can't ply an oar to save themselves.'

'If they bump this barky again it'll be their damn saints they'll need, for I shall skin them.'

He leapt aboard, not only sated, but ready to dash down a quick cup of coffee and avoid answering any questions from Michael O'Hagan regarding where he had been, only informing him of Emily's condition and that the baby was due, which had the Irishman crossing himself again.

'May the Holy Mother of God see over her.'

'You will be pleased to know the fellow whose care she is in is one of your fellow countrymen, name of Flaherty.'

Michael grinned as six bells rang, which meant Pearce had to be on deck well before the first hint of daylight. 'Then half the work is done.'

Apart from Digby, Pearce was the only officer who took his place without a hangover, to look his captain in the eye and dare him to say anything. Both Conway and Grey were bleary-eyed and suffering badly, that rendered even more uncomfortable when Digby gave orders to get

289

ready for sea. Tempted to ask when these orders had been received, that died in his throat as did every question to his captain.

He had no choice but to put into practice what was required, noting that HMS *Troubadour* was also preparing to pluck her anchor, which meant the instruction had come from the commodore before the ball had even begun. There was no point in being irritated, certainly no possibility he would give Digby the satisfaction of showing it, and he then wondered if his captain had departed the Archbishop's Palace knowing what had occurred with Emily. Surely yes, but was he au fait enough with the travails of childbirth to smoke what came next.

It was a wistful John Pearce who looked over the side as they were hauled over their anchor, the stomp and go on the capstan sounding steady as it came up from 'tween decks, the fiddler's scraping bow less cheering. The topmen were aloft, darting about in their usual cavalier fashion, to loose the canvas that sheeted home began to draw, this as the man on the wheel spun the rudder to aim the prow for the harbour entrance.

The sky was grey again with dark clouds over the distant hills dense enough to obscure them completely, which reflected his mood. However, no amount of staring could get his gaze through the walls of the *pensione* where, at that moment, attended by Flaherty and the wife and daughter of the proprietor, Emily, screaming in pain and being urged to push in both English and Italian, gave birth to a baby boy.

The cord was cut, the sole of the feet slapped to

bring forth the first yelling complaint of the next generation of Pearce's family, and had he been present – not in the room, for that would have been frowned upon and considered odd – he would have been furious when the doctor said to Emily, 'Mrs Barclay, you have a son, and one I take leave to suggest your late husband would have been proud of.'

When the child was washed, and Emily's needs taken care of, it was swaddled and handed over for his mother to cradle in her arms. Then and only then, through her exhaustion and continuing pain, could Emily whisper in one tiny ear.

'Welcome to the world, Adam John Pearce.'

CHAPTER TWENTY-THREE

It was back to the slog of endless patrolling off the Ligurian coast, the tedious business of interdicting shipping to ensure their cargoes were as the manifest said and not supplies destined for the French. They were still in their defensive lines and no doubt suffering, but not as much as their opponents. The situation in the lower Alps was much worse for the coalition forces.

They had to guard the passes the French could use to march into Italy. Away from the coast the temperature dropped alarmingly, while the weather was ten times worse the higher the elevation. It was reported soldiers were dying at their posts from the cold, or falling asleep during blizzards to be buried in drifts.

The weather was not pleasant at sea either. If the sun shone it meant a biting north-east wind. When absent, those same leaden skies that so depressed the spirits were prevalent and that was without the permafrost of gloom brought on by the relationship between Digby and John Pearce, though the captain's oddities no longer excited much comment; everyone was, by now, accustomed to them.

Pearce had the added distraction of Emily. She must have given birth by now and he was concerned for how she had fared. This was mixed, of course, with short bouts of self-justification or remorse for his betrayal. In more melancholic moments, he imagined her dead from the shock of childbirth, an all-too-common fate in his recollection, added to which babies too often struggled to survive the event as well as the attendant sickness to which they were very prone.

To that was added the feeling of isolation, so the sight of HMS *Agamemnon* on the horizon was welcome indeed. She closed, then let fly her sheets, to request both Digby and Babbage, the master and commander of HMS *Troubadour*, to repair on board. This gave Pearce an opportunity to seek news, so he sailed *Flirt* as close to the sixty-four as was prudent, then hove to so that he could exchange shouts with her quarterdeck.

Nelson's premier, Martin Hinton, was on deck and he got a greeting. With him stood William Hoste, still hobbling on his sticks yet doing his duty, for it would be weeks before his leg healed. Pearce addressed his enquiries to the youngster and if it sounded like extended commiseration, it soon turned into a request for news of events in Leghorn.

'Sir John Jervis has taken the Wynne family on board *Victory*.'

'Whatever for?'

The look on Hoste's face did not match his words. 'Kindness, I imagine.'

The implication seemed obvious; the old rogue had been anxious for the company of the girls at the ball, which was odd given his reputation for being crusty and a confirmed bachelor. Clearly, Jervis had enjoyed it so much he wished to continue, but that was of no account in the pursuit of what Pearce really required, which was a long time in coming.

'Oh, and Sir John stood as godfather to Mrs Barclay's boy.'

'It has to be said on a decent barky that would call for an extra tot of rum.'

This pronouncement came from Michael O'Hagan, listening to the exchange, as was the entire crew who were scarce in ignorance of what Pearce sought. He also took the liberty, in full view of his shipmates, of slapping his friend on the back, before turning to the fellow who called for three cheers to tell him to hold his tongue. What was known on the brig could not be shared with the crew of Nelson's ship or any other.

'Did you get a name?' Pearce asked, with some trepidation. 'I know Mrs Barclay quite well.'

'Adam John, I think, sir. Baptised in the font of St George's with a real crowd present, every officer who could attend and all the English community of Leghorn.'

It was hard for Pearce to hear that and hold his tone of mere curiosity, given his heart was swelling, feeling too the prick of tears in the corners of his eyes. He was the father of a son, yet Emily had agreed to a swift baptism. Did that portend a weakness in the child? He could not ask

'Well, I daresay the whole fleet is pleased for her.'

'Lusty little brat, by all accounts, Mr Pearce. He yelled fit to shake the rafters when they wetted his head.'

'Healthy, then?

'Full of vim.'

Digby and Babbage appeared by the gangway, wrapped in heavy oilskin cloaks, which brought the exchange to an end. The sea was running too strong for use of the entry port so they were obliged to descend to their waiting boats, which put off on the heavy swell to row the short distance to their respective ships, not without difficulty. By the time a spume-splattered Digby was back aboard, *Agamemnon* had reset her course and was pulling away, Hinton with his hat raised.

'Mr Pearce, you will oblige me by containing yourself. It was embarrassing to be in the company of Commodore Nelson and have you yelling away like a fishwife and I will not refer openly to the purpose.'

'Even you cannot help being pleased for Mrs Barclay.'

This was accompanied by a wide grin. If Digby had cared to look, and he sought to avoid it, there were men grinning all over the deck. Even not seen, it was sensed.

'I think it our duty to be back about our task.'

Still scowling, he left the deck and the brig was put back on course with a very happy premier on the quarterdeck. How he would have liked to have obliged Michael's notion of an extra tot, but that kind of distribution was not within his gift. He was determined to celebrate in private and ordered that a bottle of good Tuscan wine be opened and allowed to breathe.

Just coming off duty at this time of year was a pleasure, to be out of the wind and exposed to an immediate feeling of warmth. As usual, the stove was hot, and with only one chair and no space he gave that to Michael and sat on his cot as they both drank to mother and child, naturally speculating on what had happened since they departed Leghorn.

'Mr Pearce, sir, captain requires you on deck.'

'I will join him shortly, Mr Conway.'

'The order was at once, sir.'

It would have been easy to shout at the youngster, but what was the point? He had delivered the message he had been given and there had also been a bit of a wobble in his voice on the second part, which told Pearce he had been a reluctant mouthpiece for what was an unnecessary command. He drained the wine in his glass, O'Hagan immediately doing likewise.

'I'll stop the bottle for later.'

'No, Michael,' Pearce replied, beginning to wrap himself in layers of clothing, 'finish it if you wish.'

'Sure you're always at me for my drinking, are you not? Now here you're telling me to.'

'I know your capacity and there's scarce enough

295

left for me to worry. And we are celebrating, are we not?'

He was through the canvas, holding on to the memory of the times he had seen his friend drunk and they were far from pleasant. Seriously in his cups, O'Hagan commonly wanted to fight the world and no one was safe within the orbit of his fists. That left a frown on his face as he came on deck to exchange looks with Digby, who obviously took the expression as being aimed at him, which brought forth a blast.

'When I say at once, Mr Pearce, it does not mean at your convenience.' The object did not deign to reply; he could not be bothered. 'If you care to look over the starboard quarter, you will see we have work to do.'

He was right, a fact which sank Pearce's heart. There to the south-east were the topsails of what appeared to be three large merchant vessels and he knew he would be obliged to take the cutter and inspect them, which meant a soaking in this sea.

'Signal from *Troubadour*, sir,' Conway called, his eyes on their consort and the signal book in his hand. 'We are to close and clear for action.'

'Nonsense,' Digby responded. 'They are traders, not warships.'

This emerged before he realised he had spoken out loud, not that he would be heard beyond the quarterdeck for it was not any kind of bellow, more the normal level of a fellow talking to himself. No one nearby reacted, yet it was noted by John Pearce, given how contained Digby normally was in public.

Babbage, being the senior, was obliged to give an order he clearly disagreed with and on this occasion his premier was inclined to agree. Merchant vessels were never a threat and if they showed reluctance to heave to, a single ball and a rising plume of white water was generally enough to make them comply. It could only be their size that had brought on the order, for they were deep-hulled vessels near to the size of an East Indiaman and they would thus have several cannon.

Still in a reverie of drinking to the fact of fatherhood, it was some time before Pearce saw what must have stirred Babbage to clear both brigs as a precaution. The merchant vessels, clearly on course for Genoa, were flying no flags and that made them suspect. Having heard Pearce give the instruction to clear, Digby had his watch in his hand to time how long it took, a stern look on his face, one which was utterly wasted.

He commanded men who knew well their duty and went about it efficiently, hampered if at all, only by the heavy swell, which rendered easy movement difficult. As soon as the task was complete, Pearce was ordered to haul in the cutter and take a boarding party to the nearest vessel. *Troubadour* would do likewise and the first completed would take the third.

There would be no race for it was a tiresome duty with its own habits. First an argument about the right to board a neutral vessel; that was never conceded without dispute, made doubly difficult by rarely having a shared language. Matters did not improve on the deck, with both crew and master usually being obstructive, as papers were examined to establish the cargo and then the holds checked to ensure a match.

Pearce began to clamber down into the cutter, already full of rowers as well as marines with their muskets to threaten, if that was required. There came the boom of a cannon, which he assumed came from *Troubadour,* to be disabused when a plume of water landed beyond *Flirt* and at a short distance, having sailed through her rigging without doing damage.

He was back on deck in a flash, shouting that the cutter should be cleared and cast off astern once more, back on deck in time to see the flags – red crescents – break out at the merchant mastheads, immediately followed by a blast from four cannon on each one. Combined, that more than matched a broadside from a single brig.

'Turkomen, Mr Pearce,' Digby yelled, his face alight, his eyes gleaming. 'And carrying contraband for certain. Attend to your station.'

Having cleared, both the brigs were down to topsails, having clewed up the courses, given they were vulnerable to enemy shot and posed a danger, especially if the canvas caught fire. That meant progress was slow, added to which the Turks, who had the wind and were still under full sail, swung beam on. *Flirt* had her prow aimed amidships on the one Pearce had been set to board, which put her at a real disadvantage.

The only cannon that could be immediately brought to bear were the two bow chasers and to them Pearce went to take command, sending the first balls away quickly, then using a glass to try and see what was happening on the higher decks, for if they were to board now it would be opposed. Trading vessels did not normally carry large crews, economy being the watchword of their owners, but in this case he could see the deck was full of men, which indicated they had been determined to fight from the outset. It also underlined that whatever they were carrying, they did not want it inspected.

Two of the vessels, one in the van and the fellow bringing up the rear, held their course while the third dropped away slightly, which allowed his consorts to close up and provide something of a protective screen. On a normal ship this would have been the subject of speculation – it probably was on *Troubadour* – but not on this deck. There was no point in Pearce conferring with Digby to search for a reason: the man would not respond.

Babbage, being closest to land, had made his own decision and reset his course. That was to crack on as much as he could to get across the bow of the lead vessel where both that and the one being shielded would be exposed to his guns. He was clearly seeking to make them either fight or heave to, this as both brigs were subjected to heavy and fairly accurate fire, which came with a weight of shot and frequency Pearce found troubling. Whoever was manning those cannon were not behaving like cack-handed merchant seamen, but more like the crew of a ship of war, and soon the rigging began to shred as the Turks peppered it with chain shot.

Digby yawed in response and that allowed Pearce to employ his starboard battery in a rolling broadside that took chunks out of the target's bulwarks. But that was never going to stop ships of a heavier draught than *Flirt,* so he had the guns elevated to take out that full top hamper, a suit of sails which indicated this trio was in a hurry.

The next Turkish salvo ignored *Flirt* to concentrate all their round shot on *Troubadour,* obviously seen as posing the greatest threat. One lucky ball hit her halfway up her mainmast, doing massive damage. The broken timber, as well as a mass of rigging, began to topple, thankfully looking to be going over the larboard quarter. This was bad enough in itself, but the effect was to swing her off her course while the need to clear away wreckage took her temporarily out of the battle. It also meant Babbage's aim was thwarted and the lead two ships had a far better possibility of getting away, given his chances of resuming the pursuit speed were utterly diminished.

Having let Pearce have a crack at disabling one enemy, Digby came back onto a closing course, which meant only the bow chasers could bear again, this as the Turks did something unusual once more, the way coming off the rear vessel, it immediately losing speed. This sent a clear indication that whatever was in the holds of the other merchantmen was of such importance this one was prepared to be a sacrificial lamb to ensure his consort got clear.

He wanted to shout at Digby, stood like a rock on the quarterdeck, to tell him they would be best to ignore the offer of a possible capture and pursue what was the prime target, even if it meant putting on more sail to overhaul her and suffering what damage would be inflicted.

'Mr Pearce, that fellow before us requires to be boarded. Mr Conway, takeover the main-deck cannon.'

Responding to the shout, Pearce lost his temper; it was precisely the wrong thing to do. 'We must ignore that, sir, and take up the task Captain Babbage has been obliged to abandon.'

'Do as I say, get your boarders ready.'

Pearce strode up to the quarterdeck to remonstrate, outlining his conclusion to a man now puce of face. 'Damn me, sir, I reckon you shy.'

'What kind of fool says that? Perhaps the type whose life was near forfeit through his own folly. We should pursue the two running away.'

'Obey me or I will have you drummed out of the service, which will be a blessing.'

The gleam in Digby's eye alerted Pearce to an obvious fact. To disobey such an order in the middle of a fight, and one in which it was very likely that Captain Babbage had lost hands to that falling rigging, was all he would ever need to ensure John Pearce never got to air his own grievances. The navy hated a coward and that was how he would appear.

'I wish the log to show that I disagree with you on your analysis of what must be done.'

'Enough have heard you, Pearce, now move or I will have a marine shoot you.'

He would get away with that; indeed, be applauded by his peers for acting toughly. Michael O'Hagan was by his side proffering weapons and providing whispered advice. 'You can't fight the sod, John-boy.'

Spinning round, Pearce saw that Conway was

301

doing a reasonable job, getting off a salvo as the brig yawed once more and he found himself yelling orders for boarders even if in his heart he knew it to be foolish. A captain was a monarch in his own deck and Digby was that man. What followed were routines practised often: the distribution of weapons was swift, the boats hauled in to be manned by marines and as many of the crew as they could accommodate. All the while, the exchange of cannon fire continued and it was a miracle, given the chain shot being aimed at them, that nothing serious had carried away.

The boarders naturally went over the protected side into craft bobbing up and down through ten feet and then Digby altered course to give his boats a clear run, using his cannon to occupy the Turks, who surely did not have enough men to both ply them and protect their deck from being overrun. In this Digby was doing exactly what was required, if you excluded the utter folly of not seeing the battle as a whole.

Captain Babbage, no doubt aware that his chances of interdicting the remaining pair of Turks was close to zero, had launched his boats too, though Pearce noticed his jolly boat was being employed to fish members of his crew out of the water. That broken mast and tumbling rigging, which included the boarding nets, must have swept a good number overboard, and given their determination not to learn to swim, some must drown.

The Turks, having tried one salvo with depressed cannon – it had gone over the approaching boarders' heads – had ceased to ply them, which

302

allowed Digby, before Pearce and his men got close, to sweep the merchantman's deck with grape in order to keep them away from the side. That had to cease as they got too close. Pearce ordered the boats to split up, one under Edward Grey going towards the stern, the other two heading for the bows, over which one would aim to board.

Pearce's boat carried on to get round the other side and use the hull as protection. Then Digby could not only sweep the deck with grape once more but with the need for defence taking the men away from the Turkish cannon, he could come alongside with near impunity. Soon the boarders were joined by two Troubadours who knew the drill equally well.

'No boarding nets, John-boy,' Michael yelled, waving his favoured weapon, an axe. 'The heathens have opened us their door.'

'They trust their God as much as you trust yours.'

The Irishman's face was close to glowing; he loved a fight and in this instance no drink was required, the anticipation mirrored in the faces of the others. Before them was a prize ship and that meant money. When folk back home talked of their Wooden Walls and the men who sailed them – praised in wartime, a pest in peace – did they know it was not love of country that animated them in such a situation? From captain to waister the King's Navy was, in the main, driven by a lust for profit.

CHAPTER TWENTY-FOUR

Ahead of the boarders from both brigs and lining the bulwarks lay a sea of dark faces, many turbaned, some with muskets, one with a strange metal helmet. Thankfully, these weapons, compared to those plied by the marines, were doubly inaccurate in the hands of those unused to them. The Lobsters would employ theirs to keep anyone with a knife, axe or sword away from the grappling irons that were about to be thrown to hook onto the hammock nettings.

Both sides were yelling insults, seeking by noise to break the resolve of their opponents, more important to the navy men who had the harder task, as they struggled to get their boats pressed to the merchantman's tumblehome.

Help would come from Digby and his cannon, for that could not be defended against if a resistance also had to be mounted against boarders, unless the Turks had manned their vessel with a crew to outmatch a man-o'-war. Pearce and his opposite number from *Troubadour* waited for the blast of grape that would kill some of their opponents. It should certainly lower the heads of the rest as they sought cover, which would create the opening needed to clamber up the scantlings, already being slammed with axes to create footholds.

They could hear the sound of cannon fire and almost feel the thud as round shot hit the hull. If

Pearce wondered what Digby was about, damaging a ship about to be taken as prize instead of using grape, there was no time to ponder, for to do so was to invite heavy losses. He yelled, ordering his men to throw the grappling irons prior to an attempt to get up the side, hoping at both prow and stern others would be doing likewise. They should find it easier to get to the deck, he and his party having pinned the defence. If the Turks departed to secure those points of access, it would in turn facilitate his task.

The navy men in total, if you included those still on *Flirt*, should outnumber the Turks by a decent margin. The defenders could not be everywhere, and in part, the task of those attacking amidships was to threaten and create a circumstance that gave just as much of a chance for others to succeed. With Digby also coming alongside on the other beam, their enemies would be in a real quandary. They could not ignore Pearce and his men, but the brig hooking on could deliver the most telling assault. Boarding from deck to deck, varying heights notwithstanding, was simple and it would have to be countered immediately.

Seeing a sudden diminution of the numbers lining the side, and being aware that men were in very real danger of suffering wounds, Pearce prepared to move. He did so as the cutter rose on the swell, one that for a brief moment diminished the distance needed to be covered. It was far from easy but this again was something the crew trained for, aware that it took a strong stomach for any man, not by nature a fighter, to stand fast in the face of a slashing cutlass blade.

305

He discharged the two pistols Michael had given him, more for disruption, then grabbed a part of the rigging, a rope shot away and hanging conveniently, to haul himself upwards, feet on the planking. As he came abreast of the nettings he had to clap on with one hand and haul out his cutlass with the other, to then swing at an exposed head, the fellow aimed at ducking away and allowing him to make a few more feet.

Behind him and despite the swell, the marines he had with him reloaded with calm certainty. Two of them sent their balls either side of Pearce to drive back those determined to stop him, allowing him to get his feet on the hammock nettings, from where, once upright, he could fight on equal terms.

That he achieved and he was not alone, yelling and waving his blade when he felt the rush of air and the crack of passing shot, this as his captain, wholly inappropriately, fired the round of grape he should have discharged sooner. If the Turks suffered, so did the Flirts. Pearce saw Rufus Dommet fall backwards, in the act of doing so taking down with him two others clambering up the side. Another of his party fell and, missing the boat, plunged screaming into the sea, the man in command having no idea if he had fallen from fright or a wound.

Whatever the stupidity of Digby, it was deadly to the Turks as well, which created gaps in the defence that could be exploited. Several of his men got onto the deck and began to contest it, the clanging of swords and the thud of clubs and axes now the dominant sound, and that included his own. His blue coat marked him out as a leader and thus attracted an assault by a pair with hooked swords.

Luckily for Pearce they were swingers and hackers, driven by passion rather than skill, while wasting the breath they needed to fight in useless shouting. He was silent and concentrating, first defending the arced blows before getting under the guard of one to slice open his gut, which had him stop still in amazement. There was no attempt to finish the man off; that would take his blade out of play.

But it was necessary for him to retreat a few paces in a classic fencing style, to avoid a hack from the wounded man's confrère. This put his back up against the nettings, the feel of the obstacle causing a temporary distraction. Sensing opportunity, the Turk facing him, a gleam of triumph in his eye, lunged with his blade at full stretch, his forward leg bent, aiming a blow with the point that Pearce parried with an underhand sweep.

The gleam faded as his opponent realised he was now exposed, this as Pearce's cutlass continued the movement, swinging upwards to take him under the chin and cut open his jaw. Now it was time to stab, as shocked, the man stood unprotected. He tried to bring his weapon up to prevent what was coming but it was too late. The full thrust was through his coloured waistband in a blink, leaving him to look with surprise at the hilt. He held Pearce's cold, indifferent eyes for a second, before sinking to his knees, by which time the cutlass was free to deliver the killing blow.

There were three contests going on now, one towards the prow, another on the poop with Grey's red coat very obvious, as well as the one in which Pearce was engaged. That could not last, yet there was no hint of surrender; the Turks kept fighting, even when it must have been obvious to them their cause was hopeless, so much so that John Pearce could pause from the conflict to take in his surroundings.

The first observation was the clear gap between the deck on which he stood and that of HMS *Flirt*. He was amazed to see she was still standing off from the prize, not as she should be, hooking on with grappling irons and hauling herself alongside. For whatever reason, Digby had not acted as expected and that could only be to do with the other two Turkoman vessels. Yet looking east, he saw the bait had done its job. Such was their rate of sailing there was a good chance they would make Genoa harbour, even if Digby set off in immediate pursuit.

The Turks still fighting on the bait ship were now bunched in a tight circle, being clubbed and stabbed, or skewered by Grey's sword, one having a defending arm near removed by Michael O'Hagan's axe. Given they were selling their lives dearly and to no purpose, Pearce went to the mainmast and swiped at the halyard. The red crescent came tumbling down but still the Turks kept struggling, stopping abruptly only when a booming cannon fired in the distance.

Pearce turned to see a billow of black smoke coming from one of the fleeing pair, and when he looked back the effect was remarkable. Every one of those still fighting immediately dropped their weapons and fell to the deck, arms outstretched. It had obviously been the signal for which they had waited, which meant the man who had ordered them to sacrifice themselves was saying the need no longer existed.

'Round them up and get them off the deck, if you please, Mr Grey,' he called, before ordering others – sailors – below to check for damage, for he could not trust the marine with such a task. 'Let us ensure she can float. Casualties, Michael?'

The Irishman was back beside him in minutes. 'One dead for certain, he took a ball in the head and Rufus has one in his shoulder, they tell me. A couple of broken bones from falling into the boat, cuts and bruises aplenty and one fellow still shiverin' for being ducked.'

'Make arrangements to get those who need attention back to *Flirt*.'

Those orders being carried out allowed him time to thank the Troubadours for their efforts and to enquire of their previous casualties. Not much daylight was thrown on that by the midshipman in command, whom he now recognised as one of the fellows he had stopped fighting in Leghorn, outside that the losses were heavy and the damage serious. It included their premier, who had been crushed under a falling spar, Captain Babbage escaping a similar fate by a whisker.

'The capture is yours, Mr Pearce, so with your permission I will take my men back to *Troubadour* where I daresay we will be needed.'

When the reports came back, there was nothing gone below the waterline but a great deal of

309

damage on the main deck; he went to the side to hail Digby and report.

'May I suggest, sir, that the prize should immediately set sail for Leghorn? If you send over our carpenter, he can undertake any necessary repairs on the way.'

'A job for a midshipman, Mr Pearce. I will send Mr Conway to take command presently.'

That was malicious. The man taking a prize was generally granted the task of taking it into port, where he would also receive praise from more than the navy. It was not a statute but it was custom and practice, and Digby was flaunting it to get at him. As it was, Captain Babbage arrived before Conway, having spent on the way a short time with Digby. He came aboard with an odd look on his face; he was smiling but did not look happy. How could he, Pearce thought, he had lost his first lieutenant and they were good friends.

'Mr Pearce, you have done well.'

'Thank you, sir,' came the reply, alongside the feeling that Babbage wanted to add something else but was hesitant, a gap that lasted too long and one Pearce filled. 'Your own men did much to contribute, as did my friend, Lieutenant Grey.'

Grey, standing beside Pearce, got a nod. Then Babbage asked the marine to excuse them, which meant he wanted privacy.

'I suggest I check on the cargo.'

'Most useful, Edward,' Pearce replied, even more curious now.

'I have also come to request a favour. You will have observed that my ship has suffered serious damage?'

You had to only look over the water to see the truth of that. The broken mast was now cut away and floating free, though there was a boat with a line on it, while on deck Pearce saw a hive of activity as the crew busied themselves in rigging a jury mast and carried out repairs to the quarterdeck.

'I cannot order you to this, but I would ask that you allow me to take this prize into Leghorn.'

Given he was not going there anyway, that was a request he was only too willing to grant and he said so, adding, 'As long as Captain Digby has no objection.'

Babbage was a controlled sort of fellow, so the venom of the response was a surprise. 'Captain Digby will do as I bid and I will brook no refusal from him. It, sir, falls entirely into the orbit of your good nature.'

He paused then, with a flicker of a glance at the deck, which showed clear embarrassment. 'Mr Pearce, I have been one of the many who questioned your right to your rank, for which I now apologise. I have seen how gallant you were today and I assure you that right will never be questioned by me again. And please be certain I shall make known to everyone, including Sir John, that this capture is yours, not mine.'

'We took it jointly, sir, your men and mine.'

'Under your command, and that I will emphasise even if I praise my own.'

'Thank you, sir.'

'No, sir, I thank you, and when my ship is whole again, I hope you will do me the honour of dining with me as my special guest.'

'Nothing would give me greater pleasure,' he

lied. The offer was genuine but dining with tars was apt to require the kind of tale-telling that he found tedious. 'And may I say how sorry I am for your losses, especially...'

There was no need to finish; Babbage knew what he meant. 'Aye, we have lost this day a gallant officer.'

'Sir, since you will be holding burial services, if you would see to my one dead casualty I would be grateful. It would also serve, I think, to take the wounded back to Leghorn.'

'Certainly. Please return with your men to HMS *Flirt* at your own convenience. I will send over a crew to take charge. Meanwhile, Captain Digby will have to maintain the duty we have alone. Let us hope he does it with more wisdom than he demonstrated to us today.' Another hesitation, another dropping of the eyes, and the voice when Babbage spoke had a weary quality. 'The pity is, Mr Pearce, with my mainmast gone, I was unable to signal that he should follow a different course of action.'

Pearce was unable to respond to that, not that he could for Babbage was heading for the side. He was not speechless but he was surprised, having just been told Digby had acted imprudently.

'Silks, John, bales of the stuff in every colour it is possible to imagine.' It took time for Pearce to realise that Grey was talking about the cargo. 'There will be new gowns aplenty for the ladies of Leghorn, your Contessa included.'

That got Pearce a look of wonder when he blushed.

There was something even odder about Digby, obvious when he returned to the brig, a tightness to his jaw even more pronounced than hitherto, added to a hundred-mile stare. Babbage had broken a convention when he commented negatively on the actions of his fellow captain. This had Pearce wondering what had passed between them in the short time the senior man had been aboard. It must have been a blast for taking the bait of a prize instead of chasing the others; as always, he could speculate but he would never know.

It was back to the tedium again, beating to and fro, taking to the boats to argue with the captains of merchant ships. The Americans, even if the language was easy, were the most vehement about not allowing him to board, spouting much about liberty. He agreed with their stance on republican virtue, just as he knew what they were afraid of. The merchant marine of the United States was full of deserters from the Royal Navy, but he could never convince them he had no interest in the crews, only the cargo.

The combined carpenters of the fleet, aided by the Italians, got HMS *Troubadour* back to sea in record time, and when she rejoined, it was in the company of Nelson as well as *Brilliant* and *Inconstant*. If Pearce was not privy right away to what was imparted to Digby, the sister ships of the squadron were full of gossip and in Liguria it was the main topic of conversation. One of the Turkish vessels, no doubt carrying the fellow who had fired that cannon ordering surrender, had contained in its hold gold specie to the value of six million pounds, repayment of loans from Constantinople to the Genoese bankers.

'Old Nellie is hopping mad,' was the addendum, which was hardly surprising.

He was not alone, as every man in the ship could calculate what, even adding the Troubadours, each of them would have gained in coin.

'Rumour doin' the rounds, John-boy,' said Michael, as usual in possession of more information than Pearce, 'is that our captain has got a bad smell to his name.'

'So he should.'

Having had time to think on it only reinforced Pearce's opinion that Digby had acted foolishly and Babbage must have told him so, but the upshot was much worse. Due to his inability to see the wood for the trees, he had let slip six million pounds. Surely it was a tale that would get back to England and what would that do for his precious reputation? Had he acted like that because the suggestion had come from Pearce? Did malice extend to blinding a hitherto competent officer to his duty? Whatever, Pearce could summon up no sympathy.

There was another conundrum: ever since that encounter, Conway seemed to have undergone a change of attitude. While not in any way insubordinate, he was far from the attentive soul his premier had come to expect. In addition, Pearce noticed the crew, hitherto indulgent of the youngster, had begun to make jokes about him and not pleasant ones.

With his own continuing concerns, he had little time or inclination to worry about such a state of affairs, seeing it as, perhaps, one of those moods young fellows get into, in which they seem to see everything as a chore and become uncommunicative to an alarming degree, this generally due to the alteration from childhood to manhood. It took longer to sense that Michael O'Hagan was hiding something, which for him was more than unusual. Gone was the endemic castigation in joke form by which he reminded his supposed master of their true relationship. He seemed to be a bit on edge and it came to a point when Pearce demanded to be told what he had done to cause upset.

'Holy Mary, why would you be thinking I'm upset?'

If there had been any doubt, the look of false innocence was very obvious to a man who knew O'Hagan too well to be fooled.

'Are you hiding something?'

'Never.'

'For the love of the Christ in whom you place so much faith, be honest. What have I done? It's not just you, it's Conway as well. He's gone from dogging my footsteps to avoiding me, and as for talking, well, he seems to have lost the art entirely.'

'Would I be keeping things from you, now?'

'You have in the past: the drubbing you gave those Bullocks in Leghorn for one, which was laid at my door.'

'Jesus, I was no part of that, it was Charlie. I was too drunk to know what was goin' on.'

'Well, something is going on now and I want to be told.'

'And what if I'm keeping it from you for your own sake?'

'Emily,' Pearce exclaimed, his stomach contract-

315

ing sharply, only to get a shake of the head from O'Hagan. 'The child?'

'No.'

'Well?'

'I have other things to be about than standin' here blathering.'

That said, O'Hagan was through the canvas, leaving John Pearce none the wiser.

CHAPTER TWENTY-FIVE

It was possible to speculate that the arrival of such a large sum of gold and silver in Genoa had an effect on the commanders of the French Army of Italy. Perhaps, because the news of the failure to impede the delivery spread like wildfire, it may even have reached Paris. What would be obvious to all was that specie to the value of six million pounds could not be all the Ligurian bankers had in their vaults; there would be much more. This in turn served to bring into sharp focus that the Po Valley was the richest region of Europe and had been for three hundred years.

To General Kellermann, in command at Nice, the seizure of the northern regions of Italy would be seen as a military goal, an area in which to contest with the forces of the coalition and defeat them. Yet it was one that would have to wait until the conditions under which the army laboured – lack of supplies being one and the weather another – could be addressed.

For the recently formed Directory, which had replaced Robespierre's Committee of Public Safety, there would be another priority and that was the pressing need for money. For a nation in turmoil seeking to survive revolts as far apart as Brittany and the Rhone Valley, with a near worthless currency, the much derided paper assignats, the news of such a delivery could appear to be a lifeline and one that would secure the Revolutionary state they now ruled.

'Gentlemen, the French have acted. They have driven in the Austrian outpost at Loano and we must stir ourselves to ensure they do not have the ability to press home such an assault.'

With so many officers aboard, ships' captains, premiers and marines, Nelson had chosen to address the assembly on the main deck of HMS *Agamemnon*, his cabin lacking the space for such numbers.

'It is unfortunate that the Baron de Vins has chosen at this time to temporarily hand over the command of his forces due to ill health, but his chosen successor, Count Wallis, has assured me he will support any effort we undertake to help check our common enemy.'

John Pearce, near to the rear of the assembly but tall enough to see the commodore, wondered at the pause then, as well as the look on the Nelson's face; it implied his thinking did not encompass that de Vins, the most senior general of the coalition armies, should countenance relinquishing his responsibilities at such a critical time.

'Swift action is required and that we can supply. I have determined to use such forces as I have at

317

my disposal to clap a stopper on Monsieur Kellermann's intentions, by effecting landing in force
behind the enemy advance, which I have been
assured our allies will actively support. We have the
men to do this without in any way diminishing our
abilities as a fighting squadron.'

Ever the active commander, Nelson was involved in a touch of sophistry there and it had to
be deliberate. Sailing a man-o'-war was one thing;
to have sufficient men to carry that out while
simultaneously fighting an equally powerful
enemy was quite another and as for Austrian support, that could be wishful thinking. He was taking
a risk and making light of it, but as Dick Farmiloe
had pointed out more than once to Pearce, that
was the nature of the man.

In some sense Pearce was only half listening;
what would happen was outside his control, men
senior to him would make the decisions and his
task would be part of the execution. He was still
pondering on that which he had learnt from Toby
Burns, who had agreed to talk to him as long as
Farmiloe was there as a mediator. He had heard
the truth of Ralph Barclay's court martial, keeping hidden the fact that he knew it all already
from a fair copy of the transcript.

As Burns related subsequent events, ones in
which his midshipmen peers had seen him as
being much favoured in the way of opportunity by
Sir William Hotham, it looked to be the opposite
to his interrogator. It seemed to John Pearce that
the youngster had been endlessly put in harm's
way as a matter of policy and it was not hard to
discern why. He knew too much and was also a

weak fellow, one it would be foolish to rely on to remain silent.

Pearce knew now how the correspondence between London and Toby Burns had been corrupted. His attention had naturally wandered from what Nelson was proposing as he thought on Hotham's dastardly behaviour, as well as that of his clerk. This led naturally to a reflection of what he could do about it, which was interrupted as a murmur ran through the assembly and brought his mind back to the present and what was happening before him.

'Sorry, Dick, what did he say?'

That got him an odd look from Farmiloe, but also enlightenment. 'We're going to cut and seek to hold the road to Loano just beyond Albenga, the object to starve the forward French soldiers of sustenance, which will allow this Count Wallis to counter-attack. The aim is to make them withdraw from Loano and that achieved, we can re-embark.'

Having been on this coast for three months, Pearce did not need a map to tell him what that entailed. Just east of Albenga the road from Nice to Genoa ran right along the shore. Ships could bombard it and also act as support to men on the ground, ensuring that anyone seeking to dislodge the landing party, from either east or west, would face deadly naval gunfire.

'It seems a splendid plan, John.'

'If it's so fine a plan, Dick,' Pearce responded, his voice kept low, for Dick was standing right beside him, 'why are we not landing soldiers instead of sailors and marines?'

It was not often Richard Farmiloe looked to

openly disagree with Pearce; his expression now indicated that was clearly the case. At its root lay a fault, one to which many engaged in warfare were prone, even someone seemingly sensible like Farmiloe. The attractions of activity often overrode clear thinking. It was happening now and his friend was not alone. A ripple of excitement was animating nearly everyone present but there were exceptions; he was not the only one to display doubt.

What Nelson was proposing smacked of a degree of desperation, brought on by an inability to get the men who should be doing the fighting to move. Even as a lowly lieutenant, far from the places where tactics were discussed and decisions were made, he could see how tardy the coalition armies were when it came to movement. Their lethargy was a common complaint whenever two naval or marine officers got to together to converse. Nelson was proposing to use what force he could muster to do their job for them. The fleet did not lack the means to transport the Austrians and plant them behind the French advance and, if necessary, more shipping could be found.

'We are short-handed throughout the fleet, Dick. Can we afford the losses this might entail?'

'I would say our commodore is asking us if we can afford to lose Genoa as well as the Alpine passes.'

Pearce had to admit there was truth in that. Sometimes adventure was the only option based on another factor. When the campaigning season arrived, the aim of the Austrians should be to drive back their enemies and destroy them and that was claimed as the intention. If there was a man in the fleet that believed it, Pearce had yet to meet him. To the coalition armies, holding the enemy in place until their morale cracked seemed their true objective.

'I will now convene with my senior officers in my cabin, gentlemen, and put bones on what I have outlined here.'

'Most of which I seem to have missed,' Pearce whispered.

Henry Digby had not lost the habit of talking to himself in private, if anything it had got worse. The only change since the meeting on *Agamemnon* was his regular presence on the quarterdeck, where outside issuing orders, he tended to brood quietly and alone, standing, chin on chest. If it appeared he was gnawing on some major problem, John Pearce, and probably the entire crew, felt sure it related to his premier.

When he did spare anyone a glance – Pearce got many when his back was turned, though he was not alone – there was a look in his eye that was unsettling, a sort of unblinking stare that implied the person so singled out had better look to their conduct. It did nothing for the atmosphere and generally relief came when he returned to his cabin.

The other fellow now acting differently was Digby's servant: short-handed, the ship could only muster one per officer. He had never been one to say too much to anyone and since the perceived sickness had manifested itself, he had behaved as though nothing was amiss, smiling but remaining silent at what became regular ribbing by the cook's coppers. Now he had begun to skulk about in a manner not too distant from that of his master, refusing to engage with his shipmates and certainly not, as he had been from the outset, willing to discuss his master and his malady.

The journey of the squadron to its destination would be a short one and Digby, in an uncommon burst of openness, made it known that he personally would command the landing and subsequent action of his crew. His premier would be going with him and so would Conway, along with a third of the crew, with Pearce reckoning he saw it as a chance to show his mettle to his seniors and perhaps do something to burnish his tarnished reputation. He was also doubtful about his own inclusion.

'I half expected him to leave me behind, Michael.'

'For fear you might steal his thunder?'

'He can have as much of that as he chooses and the lightning as well.'

'At least you know what you're about, John-boy, and that makes a change.'

Information about the proposed landing and its objectives had come from Captain Babbage, now with his broken mast repaired and his ship once more in service. He had returned to the squadron and brought back with him Rufus Dommet. He had been lucky: the bullet he took had touched nothing vital, which led to much ribbing from his fellow Pelicans about swinging the lead.

The invitation to dine with Babbage came as promised and had to be accepted, to the clear irritation of Digby, which made the prospect somewhat more attractive. As usual, even before the port was in circulation, he was required to describe his previous exploits. It then took time and some subtlety to move on and get Babbage to tell him what Nelson had outlined.

'It is to be hoped we are going ashore in numbers more for show than fighting. What information we have states that French morale is not of the highest. The hope is they might crumble faced with a counter-attack from the Austrians when they also know their supply lines are cut.'

'Which means, surely, they will try to retreat by the road west?'

'As a rabble, is the hope, in which case it is our task to pose a check and allow enough time for the Austrians to pursue and destroy them.'

The available marines, many of them actually soldiers sent to sea service to cover for an endemic shortage of proper Lobsters, would set up a defence to the east centred on a bridge over the River Centa. To the west they would take up station at a point where the mountains came right down to the sea and left only a narrow space for the coastal road.

'A proper Thermopylae, the fellow designated to occupy it insists. He says, as long as he's supported, he can hold it with half the numbers led by Leonidas.'

'I would point out, sir, the Spartans were ready to die,' was the morbid response.

'I am sure our marines will not let us down.'

'Mr Grey is of the opinion, given the distances involved and the possible need for a quick re-embarkation, which of necessity might be messy, it would be better to take up a position away from the River Centa bridge, if one can be found.'

'Does he now?' Babbage asked, with a look that implied a mere lieutenant, and a young officer to boot, should do as he was bid.

'Sir, I described to you his behaviour at the Gulf of Ambracia.'

'So you did, Mr Pearce, and if it sounds exemplary, I also recall you telling me he somewhat exceeded his orders.'

'In which case I described it badly.' That was followed by a sly grin. 'Grey is the kind of fellow who seizes any opportunity that comes his way – rather like our commodore, in fact.'

Babbage had to ponder on that; a man who had got his command rather later than most of his contemporaries, he was not one to let pass what sounded very like a condemnation of a senior officer, that of course being tempered by the fact he was the host.

'I think both you and I must defer to Commodore Nelson when it comes to the deployment of those he commands, your Mr Grey included.'

Standing with the marine on the quarterdeck, as they passed the point at which the River Centa flowed into the Mediterranean, it was impossible not to remark on the very obvious sandbar which, covering the estuary and leaving only a small gap, made it, even at this time of year, impossible for any vessel with a deep hull to get upstream. Small trading vessels of the coastal kind could be accommodated but little else, which meant the bridge it was proposed to hold would lack close support from the fleet, a fact made much of by Grey. The notion of taking ashore barrels of powder and blowing it up fell on the very clear need that it would be required for any subsequent allied advance.

'The fellow to command that part of the operation, and under whom I have been delegated to serve, is called McArdle, out of *Brilliant*. Not a marine but a Bullock by trade of the 65th Regiment of Foot. Bought his commission, of course.'

'By your tone I sense you don't rate him highly.'

Grey smiled. 'If he fights as well as he boasts we will drive all the way to Paris.'

That brought a smile to Pearce's lips. 'Would it be remiss of me to point out you'll be facing in the wrong direction?'

Grey's response was mordant, not humorous. 'Highly suitable for an officer, I reckon, not to know his arse from his elbow.'

Being the only vessel inshore, HMS *Flirt* was not going to cause alarm in the French; such a sight was commonplace along this coast. The enemy might not have been quite so sanguine, if they could have seen further out to sea, where the whole squadron was under sail, awaiting a signal from Digby to say that the landing was feasible, one which was sent within two bells of that sandbar.

On receipt, Nelson closed with the shore and began to bombard the road, the sound of which alone would stop the flow of traffic from Nice: supplies and possibly fresh companies coming forward. Every boat was put to getting the marines ashore first, soon to be followed by a third of the men under Nelson's command and such was the ferocity of the gunfire, for a time, there was no opposition at all.

The situation did not last; when it came to the service that had best survived the Revolution, it had to be the French artillery, numerous in the level of its ordnance and plied by well-trained gunners. Obviously, some field guns had been on the road and they were now deployed to engage in a duel with Nelson's frigates, so the latter part of the landing was carried out to the sound of cannon fire, soon brought to a halt when the ships' gunners turned to grapeshot, which forced the field guns to withdraw.

Grey having already departed, Pearce and Conway came ashore behind the boat bearing Henry Digby, with his inferior marking the fact that in the presence of seniority there was no attempt at hiding away at all, quite the reverse. Digby was standing in the prow of the cutter, one foot on the forepeak like some Viking warlord, which, to the mind of the person watching him, rendered him absurd.

Ahead was a small bay and a strand of narrow sandy beach that, given the numbers, looked as if it would be seriously cramped once everyone was ashore. On the eastern arm there was a sort of breakwater made of boulders, one that had probably been there and regularly replenished since ancient times, designed to stop storm waters from washing away fishing boats hauled up above the tidal limit, and he marked that as a place to set up camp. In addition, there was the usual straggle of

326

peasant huts, few in number and no doubt full of vermin, the occupants now long gone with their meagre possessions, alarmed at the sight of what was coming ashore.

'Mr Pearce, I leave you to see our men settled until I find out where they are to be deployed.'

These orders issued as he landed, Digby strode off to join Captain Benjamin Hallowell, who had been designated as the commander of the enterprise. He stood with a group of other blue coats at the rear of the beach, not that such a garment showed. They were all well wrapped up to ward off the winter chill, this while a party of tars worked to set up for them a main tent. Chairs and a stove stood nearby, ready to be put inside so that these elevated officers could confer both seated, in warmth and free from fleas.

'Stack the muskets and then firewood, lads, or we will feel it come darkness.'

'Can feel it bitter now, your honour,' came the reply from Lambert.

The men, Conway with them, went off in groups to the nearby foothills, to collect the means to make a fire, which left Pearce standing looking out to sea with nothing but idle thoughts, soon interrupted.

'Savin' your presence, sir?' He spun round to look into the cheerful face of Martin Dent, his own lighting up. 'Saw you land and had to come and give a greeting.'

'Martin, you look well.'

'Same compliment to you, Mr Pearce.'

'Does it gall you to call me that instead of John, adding a curse at my black nature, of course?'

327

'Never in life. You have prospered an' no doubt deserved to have it.'

'There are few with a blue coat who would say amen to that. If you wait, Michael, Charlie and Rufus will be back presently.'

'Daren't. I reckon Mr Glaister will miss me and if he don't, Captain Taberly will, not that he's hereabouts.'

'A lovely pair, Martin.'

'None sweeter,' came the reply, larded with deep irony. 'They make Barclay, God rest his soul, look saintly. Best be off about my duties. It was good to see an old shipmate, if I may make so bold.'

'For me too.'

The boats were now coming in with food and small, empty barrels, knocked up by the ship's coopers, which those on land could fill with water. Digby appeared once more, to announce in a rather sententious manner that Captain Hallowell had decided, the beach being too overcrowded and getting worse, the men needed to be spread. Given the hills backing the beach were a mite steep for encampments, that meant moving east along the coastal strip to where it opened out to provide space.

'So let us make a virtue out of necessity, Mr Pearce.'

If he used the name, it did not extend to eye contact: Digby was talking to the whole compliment, not his premier, and he did so with an unblinking stare and a look on his face, as well as an air that was, even for him, unusual enough to be remarked upon. He looked like one of those characters in a religious painting gazing on some unseen divinity, though his commands were crisp enough.

'Some of these water barrels being fetched ashore need to be taken to the River Centa bridge and it is in that direction we must shift, so I have assured Captain Hallowell that is the task to which we will see. Choose a spot to set up camp on the way and, Mr Conway, come back to me at the command tent so I know where to send up food and biscuit.'

If he had set out to annoy his crew, Digby could not have done better and the glares aimed at his back when he departed said so. The Flirts had just got a fire going and elbowed themselves enough space, hard by that boulder breakwater, for a degree of comfort, while beside the blaze lay a heap enough of wood to get them through the night. Now they were being told to abandon both the comfort and their pile of kindling, which would be quickly appropriated by others, to carry instead empty barrels.

There was no choice but to obey and they began to gather up their possessions and move, their spot being taken over by others before they were even out of sight, though for Pearce it had a positive, given he could see how Edward Grey was faring. It was no great distance they had to cover, not much above a mile, a spot to camp found about halfway to the bridge on the edge of the wooded hills. Conway, with a small party, was delegated to make it comfortable with an added injunction to the midshipman to inform the captain at his own convenience.

'And find out how in detail we are to be fed, Mr Conway. I don't wish to suffer grumbling stomachs as well as whispered cursing.'

The approach to the bridge was over flat open ground and Pearce found a comrade far from happy. If one reason was his doubt about the position being held, the other was the man in command, pointed out to him as Captain McArdle from HMS *Brilliant*. Pearce was just as put out to find Taberly there as well, tempted to challenge the black look he received, only to rate it as unnecessary and more likely to please the sod than trouble him.

The Flirt marines were fully occupied building defences, one of the drystone ramparts set back from the bridge and along the riverbank from behind which they would fire their muskets in some safety from retaliation.

'I'll have my lads fill the barrels, Edward,' Pearce called, an order to do so given with O'Hagan in charge, which took them away to the source pointed out by Grey, a nearby well.

'My captain tells me it is a duty for which your premier is well suited, sir.'

This loud response emerged when Grey reported to his superior it was in hand. In the mouth of McArdle, the accent of Ulster was strong and ugly, a factor which doubly annoyed Pearce. It was one he had heard many times before and he knew it could be musical in its charming lilt. He turned to face McArdle and there behind him was a grinning Taberly, who had no doubt put him up to it. It was necessary this time to respond.

'While you, sir, look to me as well-suited to employment as a night-soil man.'

The ruddy countenance went an even deeper red. 'Damn you, sir—'

McArdle got no further as Pearce cut right across him. 'I should leave cowards to fight their own battles, sir, and not let yourself be a foil for their concerns. If you insult me, I will insult you in return, though I do not know you and care not a farthing for the lack of my knowledge. But this I do need to point out to you: if you persist with your effrontery, then you must take the consequences.'

'Happen when I have dealt with these papist dogs,' he barked, nodding towards the east, 'I will be obliged send someone to call upon you.'

'At your pleasure, sir,' Pearce responded, glad that Michael O'Hagan, away filling those barrels with the others, was out of earshot; the jibe against Catholics might have got McArdle a clout. 'But perhaps you'll find your papist dogs more than a match, given they have trounced everyone sent to contain them, including the Duke of York, the royal dolt who considers people like you suitable material for the army he commands.'

'Come away, John,' was the request of Grey, with a tug on his arm, an appeal he was happy to obey.

'I reckon to have won in the denigration stakes, Edward,' Pearce said, with a sly grin. 'What do you think?'

All he got in reply was a sigh to indicate that life would not be improved by his sallies.

CHAPTER TWENTY-SIX

Nelson and HMS *Agamemnon* had gone off to chivvy the Austrians into acting as they had promised. In the area controlled by the now more dispersed navy, there was, besides gentle muttering, near silence. The French field guns having withdrawn in the face of the ship-board gunfire, it was assumed the enemy would be looking for a way round the obstacle set up by the marines on their so-called Thermopylae.

The flotilla had finished landing everyone and everything required, including barrels of salted beef, sacks of peas and a number of cannon as well as the necessities that went with them. So, on a beach still crowded but not excessively so, as night fell, it was to the east that minds turned for there, beyond the River Centa, lay a French army that, if all went to plan, should soon be in desperate straits.

Closer to the bridge than others, the Flirts had made the best of their discomfort. Having fetched ashore double hammocks, these were stuffed with brushwood on which to sleep, though Pearce, using skills he had learnt in the company of his father, rigged up cut timbers into a frame that allowed his to swing clear of the ground.

Cooking pots had also been landed and were fetched up from the beach with which to boil beef and duff, though food had to be consumed seated on the ground and not at a mess table, washed down with water rather than local wine. Nevertheless, an air of contentment prevailed, John Pearce quite taken, and not for the first time, with the adaptability of those he led.

Aware of his own endemic discontents, he was somewhat shamed by the stoic nature of the sailors he led, men who seemed to expect little and to accept their lot whatever it was; these were fellows who took what life threw their way. Once fed, they had set about making themselves as comfortable as possible in places where they could rest and talk, as well as lay their heads for the night, watches employed to act as sentinels. This was not a precaution taken against the French but rather the locals plus their own. It was fully expected that tars from other ships would be looking to pilfer if they could, which had Pearce issue a stern warning to his own to stay close to their campfires.

On a cloudy night a sky that should have been filled with the flashes of discharged ordnance, this as the Austrians bombarded the French lines, stayed resolutely blank. There came no distant boom and reverberation of cannon fire, which must echo at the very least to the men holding the bridge. Indeed, had it not been for the anticipation, it would have seemed as if the world was at peace.

McArdle had set flaring beacons on the far bank to put light to any approach, which if extinguished also served to alert the marines. This Pearce observed, having come forward in twilight as much out of boredom as interest. Mentioning the lack of noise had Grey advancing a strong opinion: it was only partially the case that the Austrians must attack.

'There is no food out there at this time of the year, John, so living off the countryside, if you take out what folk have stored to get them through to the next harvest, will not sustain an army. Monsieur Kellermann, as long as he is held on his front, must eventually retreat or see his forces fall apart, and that will secure for our allies the repossession of Loano.'

'So we need not concern ourselves at all,' was Pearce's sardonic response, the tone missed by a deeply serious marine.

'If I have a worry, it is that stuck out here we lack the means to stop him should he retreat in good order.'

'Which I have been assured will not happen,' Pearce joked. 'Captain Babbage claims they are a rabble going forward, never mind back.'

The jesting tone was missed. 'Which sounds to me like a dangerous notion, in which Babbage underestimates our enemy. He may be right, but if he is not, we are too few to stop them, even with every sailor we can muster. All we can do is put a check on their retreat, which does mean if the aim is destruction, our allies have to be part of the action. Only they have the numbers to fully pursue and engage.'

The soldiers/marines had made a reasonably comfortable encampment, probably more accustomed to the need than sailors. Those drystone ramparts, not much more in height than that required to protect a man kneeling to fire his musket, provided a degree of shelter from the wind coming down off the mountains, as well as reflecting the heat from their fires.

Before the light faded, Grey had been sent to reconnoitre the river upstream, another officer following it to the shore, both able to pronounce that the Centa, though not in the spate that would come with the spring thaw, was, thanks to recent rains, running fairly strongly. It was enough to make a crossing without boats very difficult, that being an article the enemy would struggle to assemble. Nevertheless, two-man patrols were going out regularly to sweep the riverbank and ensure there was no threat.

Having lingered too long and aware that he must look to his own, Pearce, using a pitch-dipped torch, made his way back to the Flirts' encampment. He came with the knowledge that, in Grey's opinion, if anything was coming their way, it would not arrive until first light. Ahead of him lay the endless fires of the various contingents, all to the west of where he had set up camp, including the most numerous: the party from the commodore's departed sixty-four.

The whole, to anyone observing it from out at sea, and it was safe to say there would be French gunboats out there, must look formidable, as if an imposing force had now cut off the forward elements of the Army of Italy; in darkness the enemy could not know it consisted only of men from Nelson's squadron. They were well aware that the Royal Navy could land where they wished and transport their allies to such locations as well, which must induce caution when they reacted.

He came into the arc of his own fires to find his men sitting round chatting and smoking their pipes, wondering what plans were being formulated to counter their presence, with only the one mystery: where was their captain? Pearce was told he had not shown his face, with an air that they were grateful for the fact.

'Gone back to the ship most like, John-boy,' was Michael O'Hagan's quiet opinion. 'To yell at his bulkheads and sleep by his lit stove, dreaming of salvation.'

It had been a far from warm day and naturally the night was cold and getting more so, it being one, even sat around a fire, in which an extra covering was needed to warm the back. Yet it was not the weather that froze a seated John Pearce, to make him spin round, this while the men rose to their feet. It was the unmistakable sound of ragged gunfire, and if the flashes were faint and distant, he was certain they were from the area around the bridge.

'Muskets, lads,' was the command. 'Get them primed and loaded but keep away from the fire as you do so. Mr Conway, check that every man has the required cartouche of ammunition as well as the weapon.'

The weapons, stacked in interlocking piles, were grabbed and loaded, Pearce was seeing to his pistols, this as Michael voiced a bit of a complaint. 'Seems we're a mite out ahead of the main here. Sure it was better on that beach.'

'Do we move to help the Lobsters?' Conway asked, which saved Pearce from answering his friend, who was looking to have his swear at Digby.

'Not in darkness and if we were to carry torches, it might be we would make ourselves targets. We have no idea of who and what we might face so no, we wait here to see what develops.'

The frigates out at sea tried to provide illumination, firing blue lights and aiming them to burst over above the land. This was only partially successful, certainly not strong enough to show what was happening in the area where fighting was taking place, located by muzzle flashes. But those rockets did cast the shoreline in an ethereal glow, enough that it might allow men to move forward. There was one party that did not disdain to employ torches: a gaggle of officers led by Hallowell and when he got close enough, he immediately asked Pearce, in his American twang, for an appreciation of the situation as he could see it.

'I think that falls to me, sir,' came from Henry Digby, stepping into the arc of torchlight, his eyes wide with suppressed indignation. 'I command these men.'

'Mr Digby, you were surely not present prior to your joining with me?'

There was an implied question in that: if they are encamped here, why not you? Another rattle of musketry came floating across the flat landscape to leave that query in the air, with Pearce butting in, despite Digby's claim to seniority.

'There's not much to see, Captain Hallowell. You would have to get much closer to know what is happening.'

'Which I suggest you do, Mr Pearce,' was Digby's bitter rejoinder. 'Indeed, I find it hard to understand why you are still here.'

337

'I'm looking to the needs of our crew, sir, and happy to go forward when there is clear reason to do so.'

McArdle might be a boaster in Grey's estimation but he knew that anything breaking the peace of the night was going to cause alarm. He sent a messenger back and it was fortuitous for the fellow, a corporal, that Hallowell, the man he needed to so inform, had come halfway to meet him. He had been required to move along the old Roman road in a mixture of darkness and the intermittent glow from the blue lights.

'A small party of the enemy sought to cross the bridge, sir,' the marine reported. 'Captain wants me to report they will be held, though he lacks the means or the desire to drive them off, which would only cost us dear. We're safer behind our defences than out in the open.'

'Does he require support?

'No, sir.'

Digby piped up. 'If I may suggest, Captain Hallowell, my men are close to what is happening. It would do no harm that I should lead them forward so we are near to the centre of activity, just in case this fellow's officer is mistaken.'

'There goes our night's rest,' hissed Charlie Taverner, even before Digby had finished his offer.

'You're sure your men are up to it and willing?'

The reply was angry. 'They will do as I command, sir, or face the consequences.'

Hallowell addressed the marine corporal. 'Very well, you lead them forward and ask Captain Mc-Ardle to deploy them as he sees fit.' Then he turned to address Digby. 'It goes without saying,

338

Mr Digby, that in this situation McArdle has the seniority.'

It was a tight-lipped Digby that replied, 'Sir.'

'Are the men ready to move immediately?'

Answered in the affirmative, Digby then took a torch from one of Hallowell's attendant tars and set off with McArdle's messenger, the Flirts on his heels with their muskets slung. There was much muttering behind him; not averse to a fight, this was not the natural element to men bred to the sea and if they were minded to raid ashore in boats, this smacked of being too much like proper soldiering for them to be at ease. Added to that, they were, for the second time that day and on the impulse of Digby, abandoning a camp they had made near to comfortable in order, it seemed, to spend a cold night away from any hope of warmth.

If their commander was aware of it, he paid no heed and neither could John Pearce. Right at Digby's heels, his nose assailed with the odour of burning pitch, he was deep in conjecture. Was Digby, with his offer, genuine in his desire to aid the marines or just showing away to impress? If he declined to share a rough bed with his men, he certainly seemed to be overeager to be seen as heroic, nothing showing this more than the pose he had adopted when he came ashore.

He was under a cloud for what had occurred with those Turks so he would need to pull off some stroke to counteract it and bolster his reputation as an enterprising officer. This had Pearce hoping it would not be something rash and including him, only to feel he was being selfish and to extend that wish to the rest of the crew. As they made their way, the sky, hitherto cloudy, began to clear, not yet enough to see easily but with a hint of night sky overhead and stars appearing through a sort of haze.

Up ahead there was still musket fire but it had come down to discharges by sporadic individuals, these appearing to emanate from a small number of French weapons. From what could be observed, it was being ignored by those defending the western exit of the bridge, no doubt unwilling to waste powder and balls on what appeared to be pinpricks.

'Sir, I reckon we are getting too close to be waving a torch, and the cloud cover is breaking enough to see without it.'

The marine corporal had certainly thought so; he had run on ahead as soon as he was sure of his route.

'Fearful, are we, Mr Pearce?'

'Only of folly, sir.'

If that response had any effect, it did not show. Digby strode on, seemingly impervious to the fact that he was bound, when he got within anything like range, to make himself a target. Proximity to his person would endanger the members of his crew; the torch would invite a ball, and given musket inaccuracy – and it made no difference if the weapon was French or British – it was just as likely to hit someone to Digby's rear. Pearce got right behind him and what he thought was the likely line of shot and it was obvious he was not the only person to discern the risk: everyone was shuffling to get behind their captain, all except one.

'Mr Conway, might I suggest you walk behind me.'

'Not much point in bein' behind that one,' came a voice from the rear, 'too much the titch.'

The defenders had been obliged to douse their fires – the glow made them targets – which made Digby's torch even more obvious and that applied to his attire: blue coat and scraper and so clearly an officer. He was bound to attract attention and, sure enough, a series of distant flashes had everyone ducking, this added to a shout from ahead in that accent of Ulster to cease to be an idiot and chuck away the flame.

All Digby did was drop it forward so it lit the ground ahead of his feet, which was a partial victory for common sense, if not the full requirement. When a hunched McArdle appeared within its glow, it was to remonstrate with Digby for his folly. He took it with some force out of his hand, then threw it behind the wall constructed earlier. That was followed by a command that everyone who had come forward should do likewise, this obeyed with alacrity.

'And you too,' was McArdle's final command, to a still erect Digby, or so he assumed.

'I cannot see it serves to look shy before an enemy.'

'To whom am I speaking?'

'Henry Digby, master and commander of HMS *Flirt*.'

'Well, in my opinion, it makes less sense to be carried off a field of battle on a plank of wood,' the Ulsterman spat. 'So far I have lost no one even to a wound, so do as I say and get behind cover.'

Just then one of the balls fired from across the bridge, ricocheted off the stones under which the Flirts were sheltering, scattering sharp pebbles. It was enough to make Digby obey.

'I did not ask to be sent more men.'

'Captain Hallowell thought it necessary,' Digby lied, which tempted Pearce to contradict him, only to suspect it would be useless.

'It would serve you better to go back from whence you came. You are not marines, so having you here only adds to my woes. If you elect to stay, remain silent and remain still.'

'Where is Mr Grey?' Pearce asked.

He half suspected that McArdle, if he recognised the voice, would very likely refuse to tell him. It seemed he did not; if his response was of the same gruff nature he had employed with Digby, the answer was quick in coming.

'Where his duty demands, behind the next defensive position closer to the sea.'

'Then,' Pearce asked, 'may I suggest we are too crowded here and some of us should move to another position, which has the virtue, if anything does happen, of rendering us more useful.'

'Declined,' Digby replied sharply, only to have it countermanded by McArdle.

'Which would matter, sir, if you were in command here, but you are not. The proposal is a sound one but I suggest it will be necessary to move quickly, lest our ships send up any more flares. If they do, even although the light is a glim, you will be caught in the open.'

'Sir, I object,' Digby shouted, in what was an inappropriate manner. 'These are my men and I command them.'

'To which I pay no heed. Whoever you are making the request, carry on.'

Before Digby could object once more, Pearce reeled off the necessary names, which naturally included his Pelicans. In total, it amounted to half the twenty men brought ashore. Conway was left with Digby. A shout from McArdle required Grey to show a light though the sky was still clearing. Unshaded several times it allowed Pearce to lead his men to where his comrade was sitting, back against the stones, and chewing on an apple.

'What in the name of creation are you doing here?'

'Not my idea.'

'I daresay I can guess who then. I saw him with that damn torch, John. He's trying to get himself killed again.'

'That or lay a ghost. To be more accurate, six million ghosts. Flirts, take turns to sleep.'

'On what, your honour?' came a querulous enquiry.

With no fires to huddle round, the whole lot, Flirts and marines, spent an increasingly cold night as the sky above filled with starlight and a new moon, one not relieved by movement of any kind. Throughout, the enemy on the far bank kept up a steady if fragmented fire to keep them from sleep.

CHAPTER TWENTY-SEVEN

The combination of a clear night sky, cold ground and even colder stones made sleep fitful at best, or shivering wakefulness at worst, not aided by Grey needing to change the men on patrol. Those so roused were not wedded to silence and their complaints tended to wake their forced companions, and being shipmates made no odds. This often ended up in dispute to which Pearce had to put a stop. He had some sympathy, not least because he was chilled to the marrow himself, dropping in and out of short dozes, one of which he was in when a shout of alarm rent the air.

The two men out doing the duty were not going to stand and dispute. They fired off their muskets and ran for cover, this as the rolling murmuring sound of mass movement came from the direction of the shoreline. If there had been one point at which it was thought unlikely an assault would come, it was from that direction. With so many warships offshore, it was seen to be probably suicidal.

It was Edward Grey who nailed the possible route by which they had got round the river barrier: that bar of sand that, in silting up the estuary, provided a possible crossing at low tide. How it had come about mattered less than that it was happening and there was no time for rumination. Behind their position, they could hear

344

McArdle shouting to get his units into a defensive posture as, once more, rockets split the night sky. They burst open to show an outline of what they faced, an attack in some strength, added to which, the direction from which they were coming rendered the stone rampart defences close to useless.

'Look to your weapons, 65th,' McArdle shouted.

Grey was not about to stand on ceremony and demand recognition or rights. He had his lads up and made sure the tars from *Flirt* complied also. The captain of the nearest warship, HMS *Inconstant*, clearly had some sight of the problem from his blue lights. He fired off his cannon, which must have been at full elevation and the effect was telling: screams of death and destruction came from the enemy lines but more importantly was the fact that the French advance halted.

'Form a line and present,' Grey commanded, having been gifted the time to do so.

McArdle retained only enough muskets to keep secure the bridge. He sent most of his men to join Grey, the numbers swiftly formed into three lines, sailors kneeling to the fore, so a steady fire could be maintained – two ranks loading while one fired a salvo. It had an effect, yet it was minimal compared to that of Freemantle's cannon.

McArdle shouted again. 'Mr Grey, we must withdraw, but sting them as we go. Tell your tars they will need to load on the move.'

'Hold there!' The voice of Henry Digby was unmistakable, as was the obvious fact he was leading the other half of the Flirt contingent, including Conway. 'We do not run from these trouserless scum. Look! They have stopped; they are beaten.'

'Sir,' Grey protested, 'we are being asked to engage in a phased withdrawal, which we can only achieve as one and we cannot contest the numbers.'

'The men I command do not run.'

'You, sir, damn you, sir, what are you about?' McArdle yelled. 'I have given clear orders.'

'Which we will ignore. Lads, what do you say?'

'Sir!' Grey protested; he was ignored.

'Follow me,' Digby cried, his physical posture like that of some actor in a heroic play, arm out, head up as if he was appealing as much to heaven as humanity. 'We will write our names in the annals of the service. A single charge will put this rabble to flight.'

Pearce wanted to say, 'You are out of your mind.' He did say, 'We are obliged to follow Mr McArdle, sir, as Captain Hallowell outlined.'

Digby was looking for enthusiastic heroism but it was in short supply; not a man jack had responded to his passionate cry, in fact, it set up a murmur of complaint, this as the look of utter confidence slowly died, a reaction no doubt triggered by the voice of his premier. It was replaced by a stony glare as those eyes, unnaturally open and forcing up the brows, swung round on Pearce. A pistol was raised as well.

'Go forward, you coward, or die where you stand.'

'Tryin' to do for 'im again, are you, with your bumboy Conway and your damn grapeshot?'

'Stow it, Lambert,' O'Hagan growled.

'I had to obey the order,' Conway squealed, sounding very young once more.

'Hell as like,' Lambert spat.

'They're regrouping, we must go now,' Grey insisted, getting between Digby and Pearce to put a hand on the pistol barrel and press it down.

'What are you talking about, Lambert?' Pearce demanded without looking: he knew the voice. His attention was taken by a fellow in a black coat, high headgear and a tricolour sash to match the one round his hat. He too was waving his sword, exhorting his men to advance and enjoying as much success as Digby.

'Ask the bumboy,' Lambert growled, 'who fired grape when you was on those Turkomen's bulwarks? Killed one of our own, I reckon.'

McArdle came bursting forward, his red coat visible now in a sky beginning to turn a light shade of silver, his rasping command larded with fury. 'What are you about, Grey?'

'Mr Grey, to you,' Digby screamed, spit flying.

'He'll be meat for carrion if he does not move and that, sir, applies to you.'

The French began moving forward again, albeit slowly, which drew another salvo from *Inconstant.* The frigate must have lookouts in the tops, ranging their fire, for the first fell in between Grey's useless rampart and the enemy so another salvo followed quickly, dropped shorter, to cut great swathes of carnage as round shot sliced though soft flesh to halt the advance, this as the defenders saw another set of masts behind *Inconstant* and moving, a second frigate coming up to join in the bombardment; the situation of the enemy was deteriorating.

'Sir,' Grey insisted, addressing Digby. 'Look

before you and what do you see? Men in their hundreds.'

'Pitiful creatures.'

'Who must come on because they cannot go back.'

Pearce was slow to realise what Grey was driving at, something entirely missed by Digby. Withdrawal for the French would take them into an arc of close-range naval gunfire from two frigates, which few, if any of them, would survive.

Their now deranged captain hauled out his sword, waving it in the same manner as the French leader and he began calling out exhortations probably in a similar vein, seemingly oblivious to the fact that no one was responding, but it left Pearce at a loss, not something that lasted. He swung hard and felled Digby, Michael stepping forward as he went down to relieve him of his sword.

'Mr Conway,' Pearce said, waving a now sore set of knuckles, 'take the captain's pistol.'

'Sir, I–'

'That is an order. Captain McArdle, lead on.'

'Should have left you with your idiot,' the Ulsterman growled, he having finally recognised Pearce, 'save me the bother of killing you. Now for the love of Christ form up for a retreat, and pray to God we can manage it.'

'Will Hallowell not send reinforcements?'

That got a look of scorn from McArdle, replicated in his tone of voice. 'Are all tars stupid or do I just imagine it? There's no point, which should be obvious to even your Bedlam inmate. Do you see an Austrian anywhere?'

'No,' Pearce admitted, which was as good as

saying they were not coming.

'We can't hold this bridge and once they can cross it we will not be able to hold the beach either, so if Captain Hallowell has an ounce of sense he will already be re-embarking his men. Now we have been graced with time I never thought we would have. Your delaying should have cost us dear but it has not. It would be foolish to push that luck too far.'

Digby was on his hands and knees, shaking his head and laughing in a maniacal way, his words coming out slowly through his mirth. 'I have you at last, you swine. Striking a superior officer will see you paid back for the slights you have aimed at me behind my back. Now obey my order and prepare to attack.'

Digby was lifted, still laughing, and Pearce put a man either side of him to make him move and to prevent him staggering about as well, for he seemed to have lost some control over his limbs. They withdrew, stopping frequently to form a line and threaten a pursuit that became too close. Behind them the French were now pouring across the River Centa bridge to fan out and spread across what was a flat, featureless flood plain, while ahead Pearce could just see the beach, now full of an activity that equated to being ant-like; small figures in constant movement doing that which McArdle had described, getting off the shore everything so recently landed.

Eventually, they came to a line where the ships' cannon, four in number, had been set up which had a giggling Digby seeking to embrace one, still laughing but now making noises of endearment utterly out of place. The lieutenant in command was looking at Pearce with a strange expression on his face, as if he was somehow to blame.

'Do you wish us to remain here?' McArdle enquired, to which he got a negative reply.

'You are to head straight for the beach, sir, and wait to embark. Your own boats will be plying to and fro.'

'And these cannon?'

The lieutenant jerked his head back to the cart by which they had got them here, and the triangular frame made of cut logs and fitted with triple-block pulleys by which they were to be hauled aloft for loading.

'We will try to get them off but if we have to, we have the means to burst the barrels.'

'The cart, where did you acquire it?' Pearce asked.

'It was in the holds of *Agamemnon*. Happen the commodore will lose that too. Bit of powder should make of it a decent bonfire.' He looked into the distance, hand shading his eyes for the sun was now up over the distant hills, low and glaring. 'Now, I suggest you move, gentlemen. The French are coming on in strength.'

'You'll give them a blast, I hope,' McArdle asked, his reddish face now illuminated by that sunlight.

'They're loaded with grape right enough, sir. A bit of Crapaud blood will make my day.'

'It tempts me to stay for the sight of it.'

'If you can run fast and be sure of a boat, I have no objection.'

Digby, an object of deep curiosity, as well as fear of contagion from someone clearly mad, was lifted from kissing an eighteen-pounder and led away by two of his crew, with Pearce, Grey and the rest following, including McArdle's men but not their commander. They were well out of earshot before Pearce spoke.

'What was that jibe about grapeshot and the Turks, Michael?'

It was a time before he got an answer, the Irishman slow to respond and he had a good look at a now gibbering Digby before he did answer.

'When you came up onto them bulwarks with your sword waving, Digby ordered the guns to fire.'

'Loaded with grape?' Pearce asked, a sick feeling in his stomach.

'Conway obeyed, even if he knew it was wrong. Those who stayed aboard said it was in his face. He could have refused, but didn't.'

'You think Digby deliberately tried to kill me?'

'Looks that way, with Conway calling the order to fire, even if he could see you plain.'

There was no avoiding the wounded tone in what followed. 'Why didn't you tell me before, Michael?'

Michael indicated Digby, ahead and now nearly being dragged to the beach. 'Sure, I reckoned you to kill him.'

'What makes you think I won't now?'

'Holy Christ, will you look at the state of the man? He is possessed by devils, is he not?'

'He's possessed by something but not fiends. Mr Conway, to me.'

'He's only just above a nipper, John-boy.'

That got a nod as the midshipman approached,

351

the look in his eye an awareness of what might be coming, one that reminded Pearce of Toby Burns. This boy was different, or was he? His excuse mirrored that of Burns. The stuttered explanation of his need to obey an order got them to the shore, where Coxswain Tilley was busy plying back and forth with *Flirt's* cutter. The look on his face as he saw the condition of his captain was one of wonder mixed with horror.

'Get him in the boat and keep a tight hand on him, Tilley. He's likely to jump in the sea and I am not sure I would want to go in and save him. Get him aboard and into his cabin, with the marine sentry inside the door not out.'

The 'Aye aye, sir' was not hearty.

'Am I to go aboard too, sir?' asked Conway, his voice tremulous.

Pearce was weary – they all were from a disturbed night and the anxieties of the morning – so his response lacked passion. 'Where else would you go? Do you wish to wait for the French?'

'It's just...' He could not finish the sentence.

'You obeyed an order, Ivor. Perhaps in your naval career it might be an idea to learn how to disobey some. Take a bit of advice, find another berth. The crew of our ship will never forgive you, even if I do.'

'I am grateful, Mr Pearce.'

'And I am alive, which is all I can ask for.'

Digby was resisting those trying get him into the cutter, yelling about the need to stop the French and issuing stupid orders that bore no relation to reality. Pearce now had his explanation as to why he had been so hated and reviled. He could see now it was an affliction of the mind, one which had grown progressively worse until this very day had tipped Digby into palpable madness.

He heard the cannon he had passed go off, which was a signal to hurry. All the boats from the brig were now full and taking his men back to their berths. In the end, he was left alone with Michael, on the beach, neither talking, Pearce thinking of everything and gloomily so: Emily, his baby son, HMS *Flirt*, now without a captain, the navy in general, his father and how they had lived as well as how he had died.

'You need a boat, Michael, Mr Pearce?' It was a smiling Martin Dent. 'Seems your lot ain't lookin' to hurry you two back aboard.'

'Sure, I'll be thinkin' of joining the Revolution, Martin,' Michael joked, 'but if you're offering?'

'Taberly will roast you, Martin. I'm the last person he would want you to rescue.'

The eyes were alight and the smile broad. 'I can live with it, John.'

'Live. That we must all do.'

With that, Pearce clambered into the cutter of HMS *Brilliant,* and once sat a thought occurred. 'Martin, this could be the very boat that Michael and I were thrown into when we were hauled out of the Pelicans.'

'Likely true, Mr Pearce, very likely true.'

With the last of the men back on their ships, Hallowell gave the order to weigh and led them back to Vado Bay, for Pearce, a period of inactivity. Digby, still gibbering, was shipped to Leghorn, where it was expected he would eventually be

353

transported back to England. After two winter weeks at anchor, a message came from HMS *Agamemnon,* ordering him to quit the brig and find his way to San Fiorenzo Bay, the fact that Nelson had not seen fit to see him first an indication that it boded ill.

No provision was included in how he was to get there and that being easier said than done, and in the absence of any orders to the contrary, he packed his sea chest and took the pinnace, with the Pelicans as crew, with their dunnage, and sailed it there himself. Not for the first time, he was kept endlessly waiting by an admiral. Jervis was not about to put himself out for a mere lieutenant and in the end he never got to see the man. It was to Hyde Parker's cabin he was directed, to find a stony-faced senior officer and to receive news he could not decide about, good or bad.

'The fellow taking over HMS *Flirt* is adamant he does not want you on board.'

'Am I allowed to enquire who that is, sir?'

'Name of Glaister, moving from *Brilliant.*'

'Then I can only be grateful for his malice,' was the smooth response, which was not well taken: junior officers were supposed to plead.

'As he is moving, there is a berth on HMS *Brilliant* serving under Captain Taberly. Not premier but second lieutenant.' Parker looked a might perplexed. 'He seems quite keen to have you, which I have to say is singular on this station.'

'I would be minded to decline.'

That got an angry outburst. 'Would you, by damn!'

'I know Captain Taberly, Admiral Parker, and

354

he is not an officer many men would rush to serve under.'

'That, first of all, is a calumny of a fine officer. Second, you do know the consequences of such a refusal?'

'I do.'

He was in a cleft stick; turn down a commission on the frigate and he would not be offered another even remotely suited. But to serve under Taberly was to have as a captain a man possibly worse than Digby. That was the way of the navy, you served where you were directed; there was no personal choice. Odd to think that Emily might get her victory after all, for as Parker had said, there was a dearth of captains willing to have him on board.

'I take it Captain Babbage has been given a re-placement for his late premier?'

'The answer is yes, not that it is any of your concern.'

Hyde Parker then went into study mode, fingertips on chin as he contemplated what to do with this man he no doubt reckoned a pest.

'I have one more offer to make and it is the last.' Pearce merely nodded. 'The transport vessel HMS *Tarvit* is to return to England with men sick, old or bearing wounds. She is a rented private vessel, presently without a commander, and that is a lieutenant's command.'

'Would I be allowed to see Admiral Jervis?'

'No. He has deputed me to deal with this.'

And get shot of me, Pearce thought. The offer of Taberly was a blind; Jervis had made plain his dislike and when it came down to it, he was no less cunning than Hotham. The prospects for him on this station as long as Jervis held the command were nil. Perhaps it was time to shift, and also, if he could find a place in some home posting, it might solve the problem of Emily. He would be able to see her, but not have to play the county squire. In reality, there was no choice.

'Is she here?'

'Leghorn and ready to sail within days.'

'Then I accept.' Pearce stood and looked down at Parker, forcing a smile, one that hinted at success not failure, added to the delivery of a barbed valediction.

'I cannot wait to see my good friends, Pitt and Dundas. I'm sure they will want to hear all about matters out in the Mediterranean from someone with no interest in personal advancement.'

If that was bluff, it was enjoyable, causing Hyde Parker to produce a deep and uncomfortable frown. And what I am not going to tell you is that I will take Glaister's pinnace and he can get it from Leghorn how he pleases. He will also find he is short of three hands, hopefully before he has time to do anything about it.

'I will proceed to Leghorn immediately, sir. I bid you good day.'

'It is that very thing, Pearce, a good day.'

CHAPTER TWENTY-EIGHT

'It's not desertion, Michael. I am pulling the old trick of taking my followers with me when changing ships on the excuse I was temporarily in command. You will be entered in the muster book of *Tarvit* and I will pen a note to Glaister. I'll wager we'll find *Tarvit* to be short-handed, there's no way Jervis is going to properly crew her going home, and if that is the case, moving you can be justified afterwards.'

The pinnace was scudding along, the weight of Michael O'Hagan on the larboard side welcome in keeping the boat stiff on what was a fine breeze. Pearce was amazed that no one, Parker included, had enquired how he was going to get from *Victory* to where he needed to be. He had not hung about to give them the chance, cribbing some stores, water and biscuit then setting off. Likewise, Parker had said *Tarvit* was ready to sail, which should mean she should be fully provisioned and that too was suitable for he could weigh swiftly. If he hung about, Michael, Charlie and Rufus might have to be returned to *Flirt*.

'Happen a different name in that muster book, John,' Charlie suggested. 'Done it afore an' it keeps the beaks at bay.'

'I'll think on it.'

'Miss old *Flirt*,' Rufus said. 'Good bunch of shipmates, they was, though abaft the mast

357

'weren't too settled.'

'Blame me,' Pearce joked.

'We did,' was a chorus, with Rufus adding, 'Drove poor Digby mad.'

'Command of you lot would do that without any aid from me.'

'Is a transport run like a man-o'-war?'

'Charlie, I couldn't tell you.'

'Sure that's to make us feel better,' O'Hagan opined.

'Michael, I hate to disabuse you, but I don't know everything.'

'Holy Mary, the truth at last.'

The pinnace was not spacious, especially with Pearce's sea chest and the dunnage of the others taking up space, and neither was their diet good or the journey comfortable. Yet to Pearce it was a joy to be in the company of his friends with no authority around to enforce hierarchy, with plenty of ribbing – quite like old times, really. They spent one night at sea and raised Leghorn around two bells into the forenoon watch, unloading their possessions in a harbour full of merchant vessels and not short of men-o'-war, one being HMS *Victory* in the company of several seventy-fours, to then abandon the pinnace at the quayside.

Tempted to go straight to the *pensione* d'Agastino and visit Emily, he knew that would have to come last; there was too much to do if he wanted to weigh quickly. He needed to tell her he was going home and that he would wait for her there. She could contact him through Alexander Davidson, his prize agent.

The first task was to visit the harbour master's

office, there to find out at which mooring his ship lay in what was a crowded anchorage. That done, and it took time, they hired a local wherry, not without difficulty and language misunderstandings, to get them to *Tarvit*, on the way passing those warships seen on arrival, as well as the many boats plying to and from the shore, many bearing King's officers and coming by in close proximity.

Their presence worried him, not for himself but for his companions, doing all they could to keep their faces hidden as they passed by the fighting vessels. Time in the navy made them, as far as dress was concerned, look like what they were and all they had as protection was his blue coat until eventually they found their destination.

Lieutenant John Pearce came aboard *Tarvit* to no welcome at all, no whistles or stamping marines, only curious faces and what seemed a degree of indifference. A chartered transport had few of the offices of a warship; no master-at-arms, purser or other Navy Board appointees. The necessary positions were filled with civilians granted temporary certificates by the Admiralty to protect them from such things as press gangs and over-officious functionaries, the most important to Pearce was a big-shouldered bear of a fellow called Michael Hawker, who was acting as first mate. He would do much of the sailing and crew management.

Those already aboard were employed by the private owners, were paid by them, so still owed them allegiance. They would acknowledge a blue coat, the navy insisting in a chartered vessel carrying Admiralty possessions or people that one

359

should be in titular command, but they would not bow to him in any respect other than that which they would show to the captain of a merchant vessel.

He checked his cabin, spacious and reasonably well furnished with sleeping quarters, a dining room as well as a separate bureau, Michael installing himself in the adjacent servant's quarters to find a larder bare of so much as a lump of mouldy cheese. By the time he had sorted out his dunnage and cleaned to his high standard, he found Pearce had gone on a tour of inspection, so he went to find the ship's cook. Charlie and Rufus, with the habit of previous practice, had found themselves berths with the rest of the crew, who, if they wondered at their status, did not yet care enough to enquire.

This inspection Pearce carried out in the company of Hawker and Tobias Fuller, the clerk-cum-representative of the shipping company, who sailed with the vessel and would combine with him to keep the necessary records: what provender went to men for whom the navy was responsible, what went to the crew and was charged against the vessel's owners. The list of ship's stores as well as the quantity of wood and water had to be matched to the goods themselves before Pearce could be satisfied he was not being dunned, and he signed the various ledgers before it was time to inspect the 'cargo'.

Tarvit had been rigged out as a hospital ship, the patients already loaded. Thus she carried a surgeon who would be responsible for the welfare of the sick and wounded, some suffering from serious injuries, more from bodily afflictions too numerous to count. The surgeon also had the necessary loblolly boys to provide the care the patients needed. Looking at some of the cases, he wondered if they would indeed see home: there would be burials at sea, for sure, not a cheering thought.

The rating patients were accommodated in hammocks on the open lower deck, but there was a screened-off portion with brand-new bulkheads for those of rank sufficient to justify a degree of isolation and/or privacy; in essence, two lieutenants to whom he declined to make himself known. In the forepeak were accommodated those seen as having a weakness of the mind and there, careful not to speak or be recognised, he found Henry Digby strapped to a swinging cot, talking to himself ten to the dozen; in addition, two other souls staring at the deck beams in mute silence.

'You say you know him?' asked the surgeon, who, with a strong West Country accent had been introduced as Stephen Byford.

'Very well; too well,' Pearce replied, going on to provide a filleted explanation. 'Is there a chance he may recover his wits?'

Byford shook his head, though he was quick to point out that little was known about afflictions of the character, never mind the causes. 'Did not King George himself suffer from a cranial malady, yet we are told he is now once more of sound mind?'

Tempted to say that was not an opinion many naval officers would agree with, Pearce held his tongue. He also declined to share his own doubts

361

about royal sanity. To do so would impress: how many people could say they had met King George? He could not decide if silence was driven by a desire not to show away or a feeling that denigrating the sovereign might not go down too well, given the enthusiasm in Byford's voice when he mentioned the King.

Michael found him outside the Bedlam berth – that name was given it by Byford – to ask for money to stock the bare larder. He needed to go ashore in the company of the ship's cook and lay in some private stores, and enumerated a list: wine, cheeses, smoked hams. When he got to eggs his friend lost patience.

'Enough, Michael, go and purchase what you need, enough to get us to Gibraltar.'

The key to the sea chest was handed over and the Irishman told to help himself to money. There was no shortage of funds: Pearce had the coinage paid to him in Brindisi from the action in the Gulf of Ambracia, very little of which he had been able to spend.

'You're a trusting soul, indeed, Lieutenant Pearce,' Byford exclaimed, when Michael had departed. 'I'm not sure I would be handing over such access to a servant of mine.'

'That is because you don't know him as I do.'

An inspection in the company of Hawker and the carpenter showed she was sound of hull, though some of the running rigging was in a poor state. Wear and tear to wood, canvas and cordage had to be recorded, the cost passed to the Navy Board for reimbursement and there was enough evidence of that to be just accepted. This, once

362

he and Hawker had compiled a list, had him going ashore with the clerk, Fuller, first to beard Captain Urquhart and see if he could acquire some of his precious and hoarded stores, next to visit Emily at the *pensione* d'Agastino.

'I have ships of war in want of even a nail,' Urquhart barked. 'What makes you think I will accede to your request? This commissariat is here to provide for the King's Navy. If you want anything for a chartered ship, you go to a ship's chandler.'

'It would save paperwork, Captain Urquhart. These are bills which fall to the navy to pay. It would be easier if the navy just provided, would it not?'

'For you, perhaps, Pearce, not for me. I have no mind to have the Admiralty clerks damning my accounts.'

'It would help to get rid of me,' Pearce replied gaily, sure he was flogging a dead horse. 'Fit me out and I will be on my way home, never to darken your door again.'

The notion obviously appealed, because on that unsmiling visage the lips moved a fraction, but nothing was forthcoming so off they went in search of another way to be supplied. To purchase from a ship's chandler, the money first had to be acquired from the company's agent and that could only be done by Fuller. Pearce, impatient and getting more so, found himself visiting the bureau of none other than Mr Pollock, to whom he had been introduced at the ball and this allowed some gentle enquiries about Emily.

'A woman of grace and beauty, sir,' Pollock responded, to then assume that air of conspiracy that passes for safe exchange between men discussing any subject deemed lubricious, dropping his voice to do so. 'I think you would not be surprised if I said that were I not a wedded husband, Mrs Barclay is a woman who would not want for my lack of attention.'

'And the child?' Pearce asked, annoyed.

'A small price to pay for such a reward,' Pollock stated, before again dropping his voice as if imparting a confidence. 'Why, sir, you know her, I recall, and I doubt any man who has clapped eyes on the lady would wonder at her in a situation of delicate congress.'

'I think we came to access some funds,' Pearce replied, his irritation showing. 'Mr Fuller, would you please deal with this and expeditiously? I will wait outside.'

'Prickly lot, these tars,' Pollock said to Fuller, when Pearce had vacated the room.

Buying cordage on Pollock's credit was the simple part; getting it delivered to the ship was not, the chandler insisting it would have to be fetched from his warehouse and that could not be done until morning. Pleas from Pearce that he was desperate fell on deaf Italian ears, as well as a raft of gestures and excuses, many of which did not add much to elucidation. He was tempted to take out his sword, only to reckon it would cause a rumpus and that he did not want. He wished to slip his mooring quietly, not with a noise.

'Mr Fuller, I bid you go back aboard. I have one more chore to perform of a private nature.'

The look that got from the man, small, ginger-haired, with rimmed spectacles and bad skin,

364

spoke volumes: he assumed the private nature to be carnal, which had Pearce wishing the fellow was correct, albeit not in visiting a bordello. It was dark by the time he got to the *pensione* and could announce himself to the owner, asking for Mrs Barclay.

'*Partito questo pomeriggio.*' That answer was accompanied by a wide gesture, with Pearce struggling to make sense of what he was being told, and that took several additional enquiries and much gesticulation to solve.

'Gone where?' led to more confusion.

'*A prendere la nave.*'

That Pearce understood, being close to French, but it did not get him very far, because the owner, having said she was going aboard a ship, had no idea which one she was travelling on. Out in the harbour there were a dozen flying Union flags. Whichever vessel, it was must be weighing in short order: Emily, with a newborn child, surely would not go aboard prematurely. The only people who would possess that information were in the harbour master's office. They required to be paid by ships anchoring in Livorno up to the time of departure. It would have been a solution except when he got there, he found it closed.

To return to *Tarvit* or stay ashore? The latter seemed sensible, even if he had to admit what he was after might have already weighed while he was trying to sort out stores for the vessel he now commanded. Recollection of coming ashore provided no enlightenment; he had not been paying attention to such things as ships plucking their anchor and this put him in a quandary. The chandler was supposed to be delivering his cordage and canvas first thing in the morning, but you did not have to be in Italy long to realise that time was, to the locals, a mutable concept. 'First thing' could mean sometime before dark unless the fellow was chivvied early.

The conclusion took him back to the *pensione* d'Agastino and a set of rooms for the night, oddly the very same chambers so recently occupied by Emily, though having been cleaned they retained scant evidence of her presence. A heightened imagination made it seem to him as if there was a miasma of her being there, her scent and that of a baby and he went to sleep feeling as though she was there, sharing the bed, the baby in a basket beside them, to sleep as well as his infant son. He woke in the same manner as Adam John, early and needing food.

Bill satisfied and having been fed, he was outside the harbour master's office, which serving sailors opened early, to find himself in a queue for attention as newly arrived captains haggled for a mooring fee, and others – and these he took note of regardless of nationality – settled accounts prior to departure.

His request being an unusual one, it took time to explain, longer to get a response. Why did he want to know? Was there some form of criminality in his enquiry? Finally, he found that the good ship *Nevern*, out of London, had plucked its anchor at mid afternoon the day before, taking advantage of an advantageous wind.

He also got the information that no other British vessels were due to depart for days and none, as far as they knew, were destined for home. If it was chastening, at least he knew which vessel she was likely to be on and *Tarvit* might overhaul her, especially if he could get away soon. Luckily, he was not required to settle an account; that was a bill that went to Urquhart's Navy Board.

It took half the morning to get the ship's chandler to fulfil his obligation and no fewer than a dozen hints he might resort to violence. Finally, the purchases were on the quayside, where the Italian purveyor began to haggle for a boat of a hull size sufficient to carry them. While the sod was engaged in bargaining, the usual cacophony of guns announced the arrival of another King's ship. Since he had seen much of her in recent actions, he knew it to be HMS *Inconstant*.

There had been, and still were, several cutters landing people, officers included. Gunfire had them stop, stare and congregate and it was not long before one of their number, satisfied with naming the newcomer, realised the reprobate John Pearce was along the same quay and pointed him out. Pearce had been in the Mediterranean a long time, had visited many ships and been visible from the quarterdeck of too many others, so his identity was no mystery and nor was the attitude of those blue coats now staring at him in an unfriendly way.

That did have him draw his sword – he had to get a move on – to put an end to the endless price negotiation, wringing of hands, emotional pleas and slapping of Italian foreheads. He assumed it would do nothing for his reputation: to be seen waving his sword at a civilian, who cowered in a manner that would not have disgraced a thespian.

367

The scene would be recounted throughout the fleet to further diminish what little standing he enjoyed.

It was a fiery and impatient John Pearce who got the supplies loaded and if he upset Hawker by his manner, his order to weigh immediately was so brusque he was required to apologise, using the excuse of an old acquaintance on *Nevern* who he wagered he would beat home. This did little to temper the looks he was getting from the crew, if you excepted Charlie and Rufus, who were full of smiles.

In supervising the weighing of the ship, he was joined on deck by O'Hagan, who got a more honest explanation.

'Holy Mary, all you need to do is beat her to Gib, John-boy.'

'I must try to catch her before she gets home, Michael. Once there and back amongst her own, I'll never persuade her to abandon her silly notions.'

'Sure, you'll struggle even then, if I know the lady.'

The anchor was plucked and Hawker gave orders to set more sail, a task carried out with none of the haste of the King's Navy. Pearce was obliged to raise his hat to the quarterdeck of *Victory*, which did not elicit a like response, no more than a slow hand to a scraper. He realised that apart from appearances he was superfluous, though he felt he should stay on deck till *Tarvit* cleared the harbour entrance.

'We have coffee, I take it, Michael?'

'Enough to get us to the Caribbean.'

'Then get the water boiling, my friend.' Pearce lifted his head to air redolent of fresh seawater; the stink of the port, of human waste and rotting food, was fading. 'And let us take pleasure in our freedom.'

'Minutes it will be, John-boy. Do you wish to take it on deck, your honour?'

The salutation got a grin. 'In my cabin, Michael, please. Mr Hawker, may I leave you the deck?'

'Aye, she will sail easy on this wind.'

'Call me if you require my presence.'

The look that got implied pigs might fly, so Pearce made his way to his cabin, to open the door and find a smiling Emily sitting in a captain's chair, in her lap their swaddled child, behind her, a grinning Michael O'Hagan. Pearce's jaw dropped; his Pelicans had known all along, hence the smiles on deck, which left him speechless.

'John, Admiral Jervis offered me free passage home, as the widow of a deserving officer. He did, however, warn me to have a care of you, for you are, he says, a scoundrel.'

'I will revise my opinion of the man.'

'I'll be after making that coffee, John-boy,' O'Hagan said, going straight off to his pantry and leaving them alone.

Emily stood as he moved to kiss her, only to be commanded to take from her his son. Cradled in his arms, he bent to kiss the child, noting the perfect features in miniature and feeling for the first time in many a day that the future was one of hope and happiness. There was a look in Emily's eye as she added, 'I hope you will not object that I chose to occupy a part of your cabin, Mr Pearce?'

'Damned effrontery,' he replied as he bent to kiss her cheek.

The publishers hope that this book has given you enjoyable reading. Large Print Books are especially designed to be as easy to see and hold as possible. If you wish a complete list of our books please ask at your local library or write directly to:

Magna Large Print Books
Magna House, Long Preston,
Skipton, North Yorkshire.
BD23 4ND

This Large Print Book for the partially sighted, who cannot read normal print, is published under the auspices of

THE ULVERSCROFT FOUNDATION